Claire Irvin is one of the UK's most successful magazine editors. She is currently editor of *SHE* magazine, and has previously been editor of *ELLEGirl* and *Sugar*, editor-at-large of *Grazia*, and acting editor of *Company*. She has also contributed to titles including *Harper's Bazaar*, *InStyle*, and the *Mail on Sunday*. Claire lives with her husband and daughter in Cambridgeshire.

D0876456

COUGARS

Claire Irvin

sphere

SPHERE

First published in Great Britain as a paperback original in 2011 by Sphere
Reprinted 2011

Copyright © Claire Irvin 2011

The moral right of the author has been asserted.

*All characters and events in this publication, other than those
clearly in the public domain, are fictitious and any resemblance
to real persons, living or dead, is purely coincidental.*

All rights reserved.
No part of this publication may be reproduced, stored in a
retrieval system, or transmitted, in any form or by any means, without
the prior permission in writing of the publisher, nor be otherwise circulated
in any form of binding or cover other than that in which it is published
and without a similar condition including this condition being
imposed on the subsequent purchaser.

A CIP catalogue record for this book
is available from the British Library.

ISBN 978-0-7515-4533-3

Typeset in Bembo by M Rules
Printed and bound in Great Britain by
Clays Ltd, St Ives plc

Sphere
An imprint of
Little, Brown Book Group
100 Victoria Embankment
London EC4Y 0DY

An Hachette UK Company
www.hachette.co.uk

www.littlebrown.co.uk

To the Snugglers: Stu and Amelie Rose

Acknowledgements

And now my chance to thank the people who helped make *Cougars* happen.

Sheila, the goddess of women's fiction, and the best agent a girl could wish for. My fantastic editor Rebecca, publicist Hannah, Manpreet and everyone else at Little, Brown who worked on the book and gave me such a warm welcome.

My gorgeous husband Stu and the cheekiest girl in the world, Amelie Rose, for all your love, support and inspiration. And for drowning out my typing with cheek. I love you more than anything.

To my amazing Mum and darling Dad, I'd love to give a true appreciation of your role in this and everything else – but I can't find the words. Which makes a change . . .

My baby sister Hev for, well, being Hev.

To Margaret, for, amongst many other things, taking care of the Rose (and my sanity), and to Tony, for letting her.

Huge thanks to Meribeth, Arnaud and Nanette for enabling me to live the dream (or should that be live the brand . . .): be Editor of *SHE*, the best magazine in the world *and* write a novel. And to the *SHE* team, especially Marie, for coping with all the madness so well.

To Carly, who actually makes me feel laid back.

To Jenny for all the long days and Suzy, Dave and Lily Pie – our extended family around the corner – for the bail-outs, but mostly for the fun.

Last but never least, my long-suffering friends (you know who you are). Oh, alright then: Karen, Jacqui, Carla, James, Laura, Sam, Jo, Rich, Damian, Adz, El, Ruth to mention just a few. You deserve a big shout out for not rolling your eyes every time I chose my laptop over a night out, understanding 'sorry, I'm on deadline' – and for still being there when I'm not.

COUGARS

Prologue

November

BUY ONE, GET ONE FREE

Caroline Walker straightened her vintage Gucci skirt and looked around furtively at the muddle of harried office workers, discombobulated tourists and street entertainers milling about in the cobbled road. Covent Garden at lunchtime. The same as usual. Except . . . Not the same.

She didn't look any different either. She had the same air of stylish, successful entrepreneur that had made her a favourite of glossy fashion magazines the world over – the creative genius behind one of the most glamorous global luxury goods brands, and retail's most lucrative legends in the making. She was the poster girl for a generation who believed they could have it all – beauty, babies and business acumen – and who, by and large, had achieved it.

But behind the familiar sleek facade, soignée Caroline Walker was finding her current circumstances a bit challenging. Caroline prided herself on coping with any situation work or play threw at her – but right now, she was feeling more than a little anxious. She looked up nervously at the Boots store in front of her. The fact that she had made a trip to the pharmacy at all was unusual: if she needed anything during the day, it was generally Trudi, her loyal PA, who popped out to pick it up. But today's 'anything' wasn't exactly standard. And it certainly wasn't the kind of thing she'd ask an assistant to pick up for her. Well, not at this stage in her life, at any rate.

A glamorous twenty-something, dressed head to toe in Topshop Unique, bashed Caroline's left shoulder and tutted as she barged past her. Caroline shook herself. She detested ditherers – the type who dallied uncertainly in shop doorways or in the middle of busy pavements – and yet dithering was precisely what she was doing right now. She ran a manicured hand through her glossy raven hair, and stepped decisively into the pharmacy.

Once inside, she narrowed her lively green eyes to make out the signs above the shelves of toiletries. Bath collections, shampoos, conditioners, feminine hygiene products. None of which she was looking for. Caroline felt mild hysteria well up inside her. The fluorescent store lights started to dance and the signs blur. Oh please! Not a panic attack, surely … She took a deep breath and gripped hold of a display stand of lipsticks for support. She felt completely out of her depth – something Caroline Walker had become totally unaccustomed to.

Looking around wildly, she caught the eye of a bored-looking store assistant standing behind the electronics desk chewing gum and suddenly began to feel more hopeful. Tentatively, she gravitated towards her. An unwieldy point-of-purchase stand prevented her getting too close to the counter, and

Caroline had to lean across to make herself heard. The girl sighed irritably and tried to avert her gaze.

Caroline cleared her throat. 'I'm looking for the pregnancy tests,' she half whispered. The word 'tests' caught as she spoke, coming out as a little choke. She smiled, but twitchily, and she was certain it looked more like a grimace.

She shouldn't be doing this at forty-two. She shouldn't be doing this at all.

The girl sighed again, this time in defeat, and leaned across the counter towards her. Caroline felt a wave of relief: the girl had obviously realised her embarrassment at her current predicament and was going to help her. Help her get out of this hellish situation.

'Kath, where are the pregnancy tests?' the assistant bellowed in a shrill monotone to a colleague several aisles away.

The woman turned around and raised her eyebrows as she took in Caroline's expensively blow-dried hair, chic designer outfit and red face.

'Over here, Mandy, next to the Durex,' she hollered back, pointing very obviously at the next aisle. She gave Caroline a kindly look – and then raised her voice even louder. 'You came on the right day – there's a buy one, get one free offer on!'

Caroline shrank into her Balenciaga biker jacket as every one of the shoppers in her section of the store turned to stare with interest at the posh forty-something who was looking for a pregnancy test.

Cheeks burning even more now, Caroline thanked the girl in a strangled voice and started her walk of shame down the aisle. Past the packets of folic acid, past the rows of condoms –

why would anyone ever want to browse so many different kinds of johnny? she thought absently – and along to the rack of pregnancy tests.

As she looked at the boxes stacked up in front of her, the brand names started to blur and merge together. How on earth did you choose one make over another? wondered Caroline. Was there an optimum brand? How many did you need – was there a call for a back-up option? And did they have different quirks? Caroline picked one up and studied the packaging. It seemed this one actually spelled out the word pregnancy for you: that seemed rather brutal. Conclusive, yes – but what if it wasn't the word you wanted to see . . .?

Spotting 'Kath' eyeing her with undisguised curiosity, Caroline shoved the box back on the shelf, and picked up one advertising a blue line on the front. She recognised the brand. That was the classic tried–and–tested version, wasn't it?

Caroline made her way back to the till. Mandy took the test from her and ran the bar code under the scanner.

'This one's buy one, get one free,' she said to Caroline, and pressed a buzzer under the till.

'Oh, that's fine, don't worry,' muttered Caroline, rummaging in her bag for her soft toffee-coloured leather Sapphires & Rubies purse. Why was everyone so set on giving away pregnancy tests?

But Mandy didn't hear her. 'Jules! Can you get me another pregnancy test?' she called. 'It's a . . .' she looked down at the box for confirmation. 'It's a Clearblue one. A three pack.'

Caroline looked at her in horror, and then dropped her gaze to the box in the assistant's hand. It was, indeed, a three pack. Mandy's colleague brought over the free product.

'That'll keep you busy,' she said with a wink.

Caroline felt another rush of heat to her cheeks. She pulled a ten-pound note out of her purse and handed it to the cashier. She had to get out of here!

The cashier looked back at her. 'That's £19.99, not £9.99.'

Caroline stared at her. Twenty pounds? How on earth could anyone *afford* to find out if they were pregnant or not? She dipped back into the bag and pulled out her purse again. She rarely carried much cash. There was a loud clatter as a pile of loose change fell from the coin section and scattered all over the floor.

Cursing her clumsiness, Caroline bent down to pick up the coins. Her face was bright scarlet now, and the blood was pulsing around her ears in shame. As she stood up, the cashier's mildly pitying look made her blush even more furiously.

'Thank you,' she said meekly, exchanging the cash for the plastic bag containing the tests. Caroline shoved them into her pale pink suede bag – her own design – and pulled the zip closed. Or at least attempted to. She pulled and pulled, but it wouldn't budge. The leather fringing was well and truly caught in the zipper. Design fault. *Her* fault. Hands trembling with shame and exertion, Caroline dipped her head and, Boots bag and belongings spilling out of her handbag, hurried out of the store.

She turned right and took a deep breath of cold November air. As the lunchtime crowds swallowed her up on her way back to the boutique on Floral Street, Caroline felt herself relax and she shook her head in disbelief at the state she'd got into. So she'd bought a pregnancy test. So what. So did thousands – millions – of women every day. What made her any different?

She blocked out the voices that immediately flooded her mind. *Because you're forty-two. Because you're meant to be done with all this. Because it's* you. Instead, she picked up speed along the cobbles to the smart black shop front with the Sapphires & Rubies logo etched in gold, and pushed open the door.

The boutique had the library calm of a very exclusive store. The grey-green panelled walls set off the cream armchairs dotted around to give the effect of the smartest Kensington drawing room – comfortable, welcoming, but oh-so-stylish – and subtle lighting picked out handbags, purses, stationery and shoes carefully spaced along the shelves. The smell of the finest leather permeated everything: subtle, chic, expensive.

But instead of finding the sanctuary she'd hoped for, Caroline realised that the boutique was the last place she should have come. Coming back here to do The Test was never going to be easy: to reach the staff bathroom upstairs, she would have to navigate her way past at least three well-heeled regular clients, and her two perky assistants. Caroline felt panic rising again as the urge to race through the store, to be on her own and lock the door, overwhelmed her. Fighting it, she tidied her overflowing bag, pasted on a practised, businesslike smile to disguise her racing pulse and strolled through her store as if she'd popped out for nothing more significant than a skinny latte.

'Hi there Tamara, how are things? Those peeptoes are so you! Mrs Fothergill – it's been a while since we had the pleasure. Have you seen our new range of ostrich-skin clutches? Jenny, could you show Mrs Fothergill ... thank you. Denise! How are the twins? Excuse me while I just—'

Still smiling, Caroline backed up behind the counter, through the door and up the tiny, winding, windowless staircase to the reception of her offices above.

It was aesthetically a million miles from the cosy, subtly lit chic of the boutique below. The focus of the bright, open plan reception was a long, cream low-slung coffee table and cream leather sofas. The gently curved reception desk – also cream – bore the weight of a huge vase of oversized lilies. Behind it, floor to ceiling glass gave on to open plan offices beyond, housing Caroline's small but perfectly formed team of design, marketing and financial talent. Plush camel carpet led to Caroline's own glass-fronted office in the corner of the room, but for once this wasn't her first port of call. Nodding at Trudi, her personal assistant, she veered off to the bathroom to the right of the reception desk and locked the door gratefully behind her.

From the depths of her bag, her phone rang. Dismayed, she rummaged around in it. Three rings. Four rings. Her voicemail would click in another ring . . . Just in time, she pulled out her BlackBerry. As she saw the caller ID, her heart sank. Babs. Her mother. How did she *know*?

Fortunately, the voicemail cut in before she had to reject the call. Caroline could just imagine Babs, tutting furiously at the phone before leaving a clipped message. She hated it when she couldn't get hold of her daughter. Which, let's face it, was often. Feeling shaken, Caroline sat down on the closed toilet lid and took a deep breath. She pulled the packet from her bag and stared at it. The instructions blurred as she read them, and she was surprised to find her hands shaking as she unwrapped the first test. Ridiculous really, to be doing this cloak-and-dagger routine for the first time at her age.

The test done, Caroline sat back on the toilet seat and waited. As the seconds passed and she gazed at the unmistakable blue line appearing on the stick, her heart sank.

Forty-two years old. A successful international entrepreneur. A divorced single mother. And pregnant. The question was: by whom?

Chapter 1

Nine months earlier

SO THAT WAS THAT, THEN

'You did great today, my darling. I'm so proud of you.'

Behind the wheel, Caroline Walker turned to her pretty seventeen-year-old daughter in the passenger seat and smiled indulgently. Rachel smiled back uncertainly from underneath her heavy dark fringe.

'Yeah? Do you really think so, Mum?'

Caroline felt her heart go out to her daughter who, for all her 2011 bluster, glossy-magazine grooming and feigned self-confidence, was so similar to herself at that age. Tall, slender Rachel had the same dark, shiny straight hair, emerald green eyes and fine-boned features – but the likeness didn't end with looks. Like her mother before her, Rachel was a straight-A student who was happiest with her head in a book. (When she wasn't obsessively texting, Facebooking or tweeting, of course.)

'Honestly, darling. I don't know anyone else who could have handled questions on whether a slug can think, or how

9

many aeroplanes are flying above Oxford RIGHT NOW, with such aplomb. Those entrance interviews have got even harder since I applied all those years ago. It sounds to me like you will have rocked their world.'

She turned briefly to her daughter again, and they shared a hopeful smile.

Then a shadow passed over Rachel's face and she returned to texting on her iPhone. 'Shame Dad didn't make it, though.'

'Oh, darling, I know. He was so disappointed. But don't be too hard on him – I can't think of another time he's let you down like that. You know he always puts you before every-thing else – whatever his business meeting was today, you can be sure it was very important indeed.' Caroline indicated to turn right, feeling unsettled at the mention of her husband. An unfamiliar knot appeared in her stomach, and she tried to shake off the feeling of dread which had suddenly overcome her. Les never missed anything that was important to his daughter, despite his position as CEO of TSBB, the most suc-cessful private banking division of any UK high street bank. Yet this morning he'd announced he'd be unable to accom-pany them to Rachel's interview for a coveted place at Oxford because of an urgent business meeting with a Scottish client in Edinburgh.

'Well, his loss,' said Rachel, still sulky. 'He missed out, big style.'

'I'm sure you'll have plenty of opportunity to show him Oxford, should you decide to go there,' said Caroline firmly. She was determined this wasn't going to be blown out of pro-portion, especially as earlier Rachel had seemed to shake off her disappointment pretty quickly with all the excitement of exploring her potential new university town. 'Anyhow, you know how fractious he gets shopping. It was probably a good thing he wasn't there.'

Rachel turned and grinned conspiratorially at Caroline: the restaurant lunch and shopping trip that accompanied a day out together was a long-held tradition and one they both treasured. 'He's been acting weird for ages, Mum – and you know what? I'm glad he wasn't there.'

Caroline breathed an inner sigh of relief as the cloud over Rachel lifted. The last thing she needed at the moment was an atmosphere at home.

As she turned into Adelaide Road, however, Caroline found herself unable to shake her feeling of unease at Les's absence. She'd tried to dismiss it as irrational, but now it seemed logical. Caroline thought back over the past few months, to their October half-term holiday in the Maldives, when they had rowed more than ever before, and when Les had seemed unaccountably irritable and restless. Since then, there had been frequent and unexplained absences at dinner-times. Les's breath was often tinged with alcohol as he crept into bed after yet another late business meeting or international conference call. When he was home, he seemed distant and preoccupied. God, even last weekend at their Cotswold home, rather than spend Sunday morning lounging around over papers and coffee, he'd disappeared off on a long walk on his own.

Caroline bit her lip. Never since she'd met Les, when she was a green Cambridge graduate applying for TSBB's trainee scheme and he was already a senior part of the bank's DNA, had she ever had to fight for his attention. Bewitched by her beauty and her brilliance, he had quickly swept unworldly twenty-two-year-old Caroline off her feet – with his power, his money and his charm, how could he have failed to? – and he'd become her first lover. Their courtship had been a romantic whirl of idyllic picnics, weekends away, and high society parties, until, six months later, Les had proposed in Greenwich Park. He'd taken her hand on the same bench she'd sat dreaming on season after season, year after year, as she grew up from a fairytale-focused little girl into an idealistic young woman.

The doomsayers, sore at the disappearance of one of London's most eligible bachelors from the society dating scene, had been quick to predict the relationship's end. How could it fail to fail? Even forgetting the twenty-year age gap, there was no chance a mere slip of a girl – however pretty – could hope to keep a man like Les happy for long after the honeymoon.

But, last they had. Something about Caroline had not only unearthed Les's inner romantic, but his domestic side, too, and he'd been keen to start a family as quickly as possible. Rachel had taken a couple of years to arrive, but once she did, Caroline had been happy to abandon her fledgling career in finance for a life as a devoted – and super-privileged – stay-at-home mum.

'It's on the right here, Mum. Mum?'

Caroline jumped as Rachel's voice brought her back to the present, and she realised she'd almost overshot the Washington pub, the scene of her daughter's party tonight and their current destination.

'Sorry, darling, I was miles away.' She pulled over, braked, then leaned across and kissed Rachel's freckled nose. Her daughter wrinkled it delicately and looked worriedly out of the car window at the group of girls gathered outside the north London nightspot. 'Mum! Honestly.'

Caroline laughed and put her hands back on the cream leather steering wheel of the BMW X5. 'Don't worry, darling, your street cred is still intact – none of your friends would have seen that! And anyway, you've got to humour me for the next few months. I won't be able to kiss you goodbye every time you go out when you're at university. *Or* provide you with on-tap taxis, come to that.' She and Les had been determined to keep Rachel's privileged upbringing as down to earth as possible, and whereas some of her private-school friends had chauffeur-driven cars to ferry them from party to party, Rachel had been brought up to value the time out that her parents took to make sure she got home safely. She'd learnt the importance of telling them where she was, and not outstaying her curfew. Caroline felt a pang as the prospect of Rachel leaving home became that little bit more real. Another rite of passage nearly completed: her baby really was growing up.

Rachel laughed and patted Caroline's knee. 'It's Dad who's going to miss out on all the taxiing around,' she reminded her mother. 'He's the one who normally does the late shifts after all!'

With that she clicked off her seat belt and clambered out of the car. 'I'll see you later!'

'Make sure you text me in good time when you want to come home,' called Caroline to Rachel's disappearing figure, and she got a wave in response. Rachel didn't even turn her

13

head. Caroline smiled to herself and pulled off, driving carefully through the spring evening streets on the short way back to her Primrose Hill town house.

Caroline turned into the gravel drive outside her smart stucco-fronted home, pulled on the handbrake and sat gazing unseeingly at the ornamental bamboo in front of her, lost in the Enid Blyton bubble of Rachel's early years. From there the bigger picture of family life drifted into view. Sometimes she struggled to reconcile her current ambitious, successful self with the twenty-five-year-old who'd been happy to give up all her prospects for a life of unwavering domesticity. But with her time spent between their homes in London, the Cotswolds and New York, life had hardly been run of the mill – and it had never been boring. Yes, of course Les could be a control freak and occasionally overbearing – but that was part and parcel of his enormous drive, after all. He might not be spiritual or particularly intellectual, but he was searchingly analytical and also fun, spontaneous and romantic – with the bank account to back up even the most extravagant gestures. And not only was he a loving, attentive daddy to Rachel, he was also, Caroline supposed, the father figure she herself had always craved, and as his cherished and mollycoddled wife, she had every material possession she could ever have wished for.

A bang on the back windscreen startled her and she jumped in her seat as a face peered in at the window.

'Evening, Caroline.' She let out a sigh of relief. It was Christian, a recently unemployed banker from across the road turned neighbour from hell. He'd ploughed all his newfound spare time into local activities, creating a new church coffee

14

morning, reviving a Neighbourhood Watch scheme and generating an unholy level of gossip. 'Are you taking up residence in there?'

Caroline shook her head and pointed at her BlackBerry, as if she'd been caught out on a call. It seemed to satisfy Christian, and he disappeared. She'd been parked up for several minutes now. Shaking herself out of her reverie, Caroline clambered out of the 4×4 and walked purposefully to the door. Motherhood was hardly the easy way out for anyone, she reminded herself, chiding her omnipresent inner critic for bringing up the spectre of her long-forgotten dreams of a career in finance. For despite her academic success, she'd been dead set on following in her absent father's footsteps as a City trader. Why, she still couldn't fathom – it wasn't as though she'd ever really known him – but deep within her burned an instinctive desire not just to follow in his footsteps, but to overtake them – to show him she was as good, if not better, than him. And to prove, once and for all, that he'd been a fool to walk out on her and her mother.

Instinct. Caroline kicked off her classic tan loafers and placed her keys and her handbag on the mahogany hall table, next to a large round vase of pink stargazer lilies. She breathed in their familiar scent. Pink for home, white for the office, she recited absent-mindedly. (White were her favourite, but Les said they reminded him of funerals, so what seemed like a hundred years ago they'd settled on pink.) Caroline pulled her mind back to what was really bothering her. Instinct. It had got her where she was today, she reminded herself. She'd relied on it throughout school and university, when all around her friends were having their heads turned by ponies, or fashion, or boys – faltered by drink and drugs – and she'd kept her head down, doggedly studying for the highest grades. She'd used it to get through the first taxing stages of the graduate interviews for TSBB. And most importantly, she'd used it to transform a fusty old leather goods brand into Sapphires & Rubies, a coveted luxury label producing shoes and bags owned by every It girl around the globe. Instinct. Something was wrong with Les, she knew it – but she just couldn't put her finger on what.

Hearing the pad-pad-pad of Pusspaws, the family tabby, crossing the polished walnut floor, Caroline turned and bent to stroke his furry ears, then strolled through into the state-of-the-art kitchen and pulled a sachet of cat food from the cupboard under the sink.

'Three guesses what you want, eh Pusspaws?' The sound of her voice echoed around the spacious kitchen and unsettled her: the house always felt eerily empty when both Les and Rachel were out, and Caroline was glad of the old cat's company, even if he did have an ulterior motive. She smiled as he purred loudly, winding himself around her ankles and through her legs in anticipation. She placed the bowl of food on the cat mat and, moving over to the silver Smeg fridge, pulled out a half-full bottle of Chablis. Pouring herself a glass, Caroline took a sip and half-heartedly checked out the contents of the fridge. Some limp celery, a mouldy block of Black Bomber cheese, and an ancient jar of chutney. Lucky she had little appetite, really.

As she closed the fridge door, Caroline heard the whir of the fax machine from the study across the hall and wandered across to it.

The compact bookshelf-lined study, with its tiny window overlooking the rose-covered side alley between theirs and the next house, smelt overwhelmingly of Les. It was where he dealt with their affairs, paid the bills, filed all their papers. Les had joked in the past, with an undercurrent of concern, that if anything should happen to him, Caroline, for all her business nous, would not have the first idea where to find even his will. Long ago, when she was setting up Sapphires & Rubies, Caroline had spent days at a time in here, but now she had the smart offices above her Covent Garden shop she hardly ever came in. She smiled nostalgically as she remembered the adrenalin-fuelled days and sleepless nights of trying to turn around a fossil of a business.

The fax machine finally spat out the paper, and Caroline turned it over: a memo from a faceless HMRC clerk about one of Les's business concerns. She placed it on the leather-bound desk for Les to look at the next day, and was about to leave the office when a half-opened drawer in the bureau caught her eye. She leaned over to push it closed, but it wouldn't budge. It was wedged full of bank statements. Placing her wine glass on the desk, Caroline pulled out the top few to try and free up the drawer.

As she uncrumpled the papers to replace them neatly, Caroline frowned at the unfamiliar logo. The statements were in the name of Les Walker, but they weren't for any of their normal family Coutts accounts. Instead, they were from a small independent high street bank – a former building society – that Caroline wasn't aware she and Les even banked with. Her heart started pounding uncomfortably. Loyalty to Les told her not to read on – to put the papers back where she'd found them and not to pry any further. But something else – that dratted instinct again – drew her eyes like a magnet back to the pages and the transactions recorded on them.

With mounting horror, Caroline read down the statement. It was a current account, with what looked like a healthy balance topped up by a generous monthly sum paid in from another account. The banking reference was 'entertainment', and the account number looked familiar, but even with blood rushing around her ears, Caroline refused to let loyalty overrule suspicion. Instead, she reluctantly – but compulsively – read on.

Several large and frequent payments were listed, to hotels and restaurants around the country. Nothing odd about that. Les loved hotels. He loved to dine out. In fact, she and Les spent a great deal of time – and money – indulging their love of fine wine and Michelin-starred food. The only odd thing about this list was that Caroline had never been to any of them.

Trying to focus logically on what this all meant, Caroline took a gulp of wine and scanned the dates again. Not one meant anything to her. She couldn't for the life of her place any of them, or work out what she, Rachel or Les might have been doing on those days. Perhaps it was simply some kind of business expense account: an 'entertainment' fund from which Les wined and dined his many senior clients.

Trying to ignore the doubting voices in her head, and the sick feeling deep in the pit of her stomach, Caroline carefully folded the papers over and went to open the drawer to put them away. There would be a reasonable explanation for this. She would put it to Les as soon as he arrived home tomorrow, and he would tell her what it was, and they would laugh together at her idiocy. Rather than being angry at her worries, Les would, she concluded, be touched that after twenty years together he could still make her feel like a gauche schoolgirl in the first flush of love with him.

As Caroline pulled at the drawer, she noticed another stray piece of paper lodged at the top. She tugged at it, ripping it slightly as she pulled it free. It was folded into three, but it was thicker than the statements; better quality paper, and cream rather than recycled white. As she unfolded it, a discreet logo appeared from underneath a PDQ receipt stapled to the top left corner.

Caroline let out a small cry and covered her mouth with her hand, knocking her wine glass on to the tiled floor, where it landed with a tinkle of broken glass. She fell back into the leather office chair and read the bill through again, a low moan emanating from deep inside her as she did. The words seemed strange, alien, as if written in a foreign language. But the meaning was crystal clear.

The receipt was for drinks, dinner and a hotel room. For two people. In a double room.

The date was Les's birthday the previous month. The very same birthday he'd claimed to be celebrating with a boys-only golf weekend.

Caroline's instinct, as always, had been spot on. Here was the irrefutable proof she'd subconsciously been seeking.

Les, like her father before him, had let her down. Abandoned her.

Les was having an affair.

Caroline folded the receipt carefully and tucked it into her jeans pocket. Too dazed to do anything but sit, too numb even to cry, Caroline stayed seated at the desk as darkness crept into the room around her. Paralysed by shock, she let a multitude of emotions wash over her – hurt, of course, an asphyxiating, disorientating hurt. But there was also white anger, at how Les could betray her; a gnawing fear, at what lay ahead; and strongest of all, a searing sense of loss.

Eventually, she lifted her head and stared blankly into the darkness outside.

So this was it, then.

This was divorce.

Chapter 2

Extreme Divorce

'I'm still not convinced, Maz . . . are you sure they're not too "mutton"?'

Caroline turned right and left, looking at her gold leather Balmain trousers worriedly. They were tighter, shinier and shamelessly sexier than anything she'd worn in the past decade. Undoubtedly, they fitted her beautifully, clinging to all the right places, and matched with a loose-fitting chiffon blouse with a keyhole neckline, a superfine gold necklace and black suede shoe boots, were perfect for a night at a Soho bar and club. Perfect for someone in their twenties, that is. Maryanne looked her up and down appraisingly, then threw her head back and laughed. In spite of her current dilemma, Caroline smiled at her best friend's infectious throaty cackle.

'Honey, if I looked half as good as you do in those, I'd still be ruling Hollywood.'

Caroline tutted and sent her a despairing look. Maryanne was lying back on the day bed in the dressing room of her luxury Mayfair apartment twirling a martini between thumb and forefinger, her thick red hair spread around her like a gor-geous Titian mane. Maryanne's big brown eyes, petite Pre-Raphaelite beauty and *Carry On* curves were the polar opposite of Caroline's tall, slender beauty, but there was no doubt she was still a head–turner – even if LA's casting direc-tors had long ago dismissed her unfashionable voluptuousness and relegated her to 'character actress'.

'If you hadn't thrown in the towel at the first hurdle, you mean.'

Maryanne sat up in mock outrage, picked up the nearest inanimate object – a French Sole ballet pump – and threw it at Caroline.

'Take that, you witch! How dare you insinuate that I have no gumption or staying power?'

Caroline whistled softly. 'Well, let's look at the evidence. At university, after nearly three years of study you sodded off weeks before your finals to chase the bright lights of Hollywood.'

Maryanne held up her hand in acknowledgement. 'Guilty as charged, m'lud,' she said cheerfully. 'And look at the splash I made over there! Million-dollar movies, a BAFTA, even an Oscar nomination ...'

'... and then you shipped out the minute your star was on the wane,' reminded Caroline.

Maryanne stood up and drew in breath theatrically. 'I was offered the role of an agoraphobic grandmother who was too fat to leave her bed!' she shrieked. 'I'm sorry, honey, but if ever there was a time to cash my chips in, that was it. Over twenty-five means over the hill in Hollywood, and I've never been one to outstay my welcome. What's that saying – quit while you're ahead?'

'You could have stuck it out for other character roles,' reminded Caroline. 'It hasn't hurt Meryl Streep or Emma Thompson.'

'Prosthetics and a fat suit don't call for much "character acting",' retorted Maryanne. 'And anyhow, Meryl and Emma didn't get swept off their feet by Anthony Richardson.'

Caroline smiled again at the memory of Maryanne's outrage on the day she'd called to tell her about the demoralising job offer – swiftly followed by girlish excitement the following day, when she'd called again to announce she'd accepted aristocrat Anthony Richardson's proposal of marriage and was about to return to the UK for ever – but this time, as an honorary Brit.

In true Maryanne style, she'd thrown herself into her new role as eccentric Mrs Richardson-Cook, the crazy, glamorous American wife of one of England's richest men, and divided her time between their Wiltshire pile and smart penthouse pied-à-terre in London. Caroline, with her own star in the ascendant as Sapphires & Rubies began to take off, was thrilled to have her friend closer to home, and they had picked up their friendship again as if the intervening years of glittering stardom (Maryanne) and domesticated bliss as a stay-at-home mum (Caroline) had been the merest blink of an eye.

'True enough,' agreed Caroline. 'But who ever said forever love and a career were mutually exclusive?'

'Watch it, Walker, I'm in charge of your night out, remember,' Maryanne warned. 'Anyhow, I've stuck it out with Anthony for over a decade – that's more staying power than most women in good marriages without a pre-nup would manage!' With the words barely out of her mouth, Maryanne realised her faux pas and held out her hand to Caroline as her face fell.

'Oh honey, I'm sorry – that was thoughtless of me.'

Caroline blinked back the tears that had unexpectedly sprung up, and refused Maryanne's offer of a hug. 'No, no, don't be nice to me, Maryanne. I'll lose it, and then I'll smudge my mascara,' she said, reaching for a tissue and folding it gently under her lower lashes. 'It's all right – I'll have to get used to it, won't I?'

There was a moment's silence as Caroline pulled herself together. Enough already. The past few weeks had been traumatic, to say the least, but tonight was meant to be a break from the revelations of Les's infidelity – an affair with a colleague lasting seven months (and counting, Caroline added to herself, sure despite his protestations that it was over). Tonight was meant to be a break from the endless recriminations, the seemingly infinite retrospective of their life together and the constant questioning over how, just how, they'd reached this point.

But reach this point they had, and with a depressing sense of inevitability – starting, she supposed, from the night she'd discovered Les's affair – they were now embroiled in increasingly bitter divorce proceedings.

Perhaps naively, Caroline had instructed a lawyer to oversee a 'quickie' divorce, one that would protect both their public images and those of their companies, enable them to move on and heal the wounds as speedily as possible, but most importantly shield Rachel from the unseemly sniping and infighting she and Les seemed unable to avoid.

However, she'd failed to factor in Les the Control Freak.

For only the second time in their married life, Les was faced with a situation in which he could not control his (soon-to-be-ex) wife. And unlike the first occasion, when she'd bought out Sapphires & Rubies without accepting his financial or commercial help, this situation couldn't be explained away as something that would eventually benefit both him and his family. It was exactly the opposite. This was divorce. Extreme Divorce.

In spite of her despair, Caroline now laughed at Maryanne's words. Maryanne nodded sympathetically in response to Caroline's resolve to move on and sprang to her Louboutin-shod feet before repeating her earlier advice for good measure.

'Well, honey, you never do anything by halves – and happily married power player to multimillionaire single working mom in just a few short weeks spells Extreme Divorce to me!' Maryanne raised her half-finished martini to Caroline and downed it. 'And my role now is to make you forget Les Cheatin' Walker ever existed. C'mon, let's hit the town!'

Half laughing, half sobbing, Caroline allowed herself to be pulled across to the door of the apartment, stopping only to pick up her clutch bag. No one knew better than Caroline that there were no half measures with Maryanne. There was also no one's shoulder she'd rather cry on. But Maryanne had her own methods of cheering people up. Unorthodox methods. Tonight, only one thing was for certain: expect the unexpected . . .

Caroline gazed at the Londoners strolling along the West End streets enjoying the early evening spring sunshine, and felt a pang of regret that she wasn't one of them: on her way back from work to a welcoming family home, casually dressed en route to the theatre or looking forward to a relaxed restaurant meal.

'You don't fancy taking in the new exhibition at the Royal Academy, do you?' asked Caroline hopefully as they drove slowly down Piccadilly.

'Dressed like this?' Maryanne indicated her black sequinned strapless Dolce&Gabbana minidress. 'Are you nuts? I can't tell you the number of strings I had to pull to get us in to Waikiki tonight. And anyhow, there's more fun waiting for us there than in some stuffy old art gallery.'

Caroline sighed. There was no point in arguing. They'd always been polar opposites – Maryanne, fearless, gregarious, tireless; Caroline, quieter, more reserved. It had been that way ever since they'd first met, thrown together as room-mates in the hotbed of undergraduate halls of residence. Caroline, then Caroline Tremathayne, was the perfect Oxbridge student – smart, pretty and dedicated. Secretly determined to prove herself to the father who had deserted her and her mother when she was six, she eschewed all social events in favour of her books. She had frustrated the hell out of party-loving Maryanne, whose dedication to good times had eclipsed even Caroline's devotion to reading, and who had spent as much time trying to get Caroline out of the library as Caroline had spent in it. But as it turned out, Caroline could be equally determined, and Maryanne had had about as much success changing her friend as she had had with her studies. Still, an unlikely bond had grown between the two, and although Caroline got a first and Maryanne didn't even graduate, the end of university had marked the beginning of a lifelong friendship. When Maryanne jetted straight off to the States, to an audition that led to her first starring role and a glittering Hollywood film career, their friendship had endured and they had become transatlantic correspondents, writing, phoning, and latterly emailing with all of life's major moments (and quite a lot of the minor ones too).

Some things really did never change, reflected Caroline ruefully. For Maryanne's luxury penthouse apartment in Mayfair, read their dusty halls of residence, and for the latest neon-lit sceney cocktail bar in Soho they would soon be entering, read their old Student Union bar, and you'd got yourself the same old Caroline/Maryanne tug of war. She stole a glance at Maryanne, buzzing at the prospect of a night out and looking two decades younger than her forty-two years, and grimaced at the thought of what lay ahead. The latest glamorous 'It' bar and club, currently providing the gossip columns with a stream of paparazzi pictures of girl-band members and TV presenters falling into taxis or on to the pavements. The irony was that when it came to work, Caroline found this kind of socialising a breeze. Much of her current career success was based on her ability to turn working a room into an intellectual art form; to spend just the right amount of time saying just the right thing to just the right people. To leave having created just the right kind of new contact, or client, or impression. Parties, for Caroline, were work. And yet this one was for play – and that made it a horrendous prospect. Couldn't they just have gone out for dinner instead?

Apparently not.

Don, Maryanne's regular driver, turned off down Conduit

Street, winding his way around Mayfair towards their destination. As he pulled up on a cobbled side street, Caroline felt her stomach turn 360 degrees.

'So, honey, you ready to rock?' grinned Maryanne, retouching her lipgloss excitedly.

'As ready as I'll ever be,' groaned Caroline.

'As usual, I'll await your call, ma'am,' Don said, in his gravelly sixty-a-day East End voice. You'd never guess from his reverent manner that he was a former boxer and reformed car thief.

'Okey-dokey, Donny baby,' trilled Maryanne, and Caroline suppressed a smile. When speaking to him Maryanne always felt obliged to be even cheekier and breezier than usual, almost to counteract his starchiness.

Inside, the bar and club was dark, and it took a few seconds for Caroline's eyes to adjust from the sunny evening. Caroline wobbled as her spindly Sapphires & Rubies stilettos caught in the pile of the soft plush carpet. As they descended the gently curving staircase Maryanne grabbed her arm excitedly and kissed her on the cheek.

'You look gorgeous, honey! Let's go party!'

'Are you sure a members' club isn't more "us"?' offered Caroline weakly, as Maryanne pulled her down the final few stairs, but her protests were swallowed up in the pounding music. As a bouncer opened the doors into the bar for them with a flourish, the music suddenly grew louder.

Beyond the entrance was an unfamiliar world of plastic palm trees, upturned barrels of rum doubling as tables, circular leather banquettes and buffed-up barmen wearing leis and grass skirts. It was shoulder to shoulder with beautiful twentysomethings, all wearing body con clothes, swaying to the R&B soundtrack and bathed in a peculiarly green/pink glow, courtesy of the lights at the base of each of the 'trees'.

Maryanne, still with a firm grip around Caroline's wrist, pulled her through the pulsing throng and up to the wave-shaped bar. 'Welcome to Waikiki London' flashed a neon tube hung above the optics.

Welcome to hell, thought Caroline.

'So honey, whaddya drinking?' shrieked Maryanne.

'What?'

Maryanne leaned in to Caroline's ear, and her piercing shout nearly ruptured her friend's eardrum. 'I said, whaddya drinking?'

Caroline stared at her, her mind rendered blank by the assault of noise, and panic. What *was* she drinking?

'Sancerre,' she said automatically. 'I'll have a glass of Sancerre.'

Maryanne stared back at her in disbelief. 'Honey, the closest thing you'll get to a fine wine in Waikiki is Lambrusco,' she deadpanned. She turned to the barman, who was winding his body to the music as he waited for the order. 'Two mojitos, honey,' she said confidently. 'And don't hold back on the rum!'

The barman winked as he turned to make the cocktail, wiggling pert buttocks at her flirtatiously through the fronds of his skirt.

Caroline was gobsmacked. She'd expected they'd feel like two old lushes out on the razz together, but not only did Maryanne look totally at ease in here, no one else seemed to be batting an eyelid at the pair of them.

Unless – was that a guy doing a *double take*?

29

In spite of herself, Caroline felt a delicious, long-forgotten shiver as she noticed a handsome guy further along the bar blatantly checking her out. OK, so this was never going to be her scene – but as a night out, it might not be quite as bad as she'd imagined.

Giving the guy a flirtatious look, she turned back to Maryanne.

'Cheers, Maz,' she said with a wink, and took a sip of her cocktail. Yep, that was nowhere near as bad as she'd expected either. In fact, she could almost get to like it.

'Cheers, honey,' said Maryanne with a wicked smile, clinking her tumbler noisily against Caroline's and taking a huge glug of her drink. She turned to survey the heaving mass of people around the bar. 'So, what say you we go find ourselves a perch near the dance floor?'

Caroline nodded tentatively, took a deep breath and followed her friend as she sashayed through the crowds. The mass of people thickened as they approached the dance floor, and just a few steps from it Maryanne stopped and placed her glass on a tiny chest-height table.

Caroline looked at her expectantly. No chairs. Not even a stool. Oh well. She placed her clutch carefully on the table, checking first that there was no drink spilled there.

Maryanne nudged Caroline in the ribs and spoke into her ear again. 'Check out the eye candy at two o'clock. I'd do him – whaddya reckon?'

Caroline followed her eyes to a tall black guy a few yards away, standing at least six feet tall and wearing tight black trousers and a shirt that showed off the rippling dancer's physique underneath.

Caroline giggled. Of course, he was gorgeous – if you were under thirty. And so, she noticed, was his equally tall, but less athletic-looking companion. 'His friend's more up my street,' she said, with a sarcasm that was lost on Maryanne.

The bass line had turned to more of a rumba, and next to her Maryanne was moving sensuously to the beat. Caroline found herself becoming lost in the music and, slowly, she let herself be moved by it too. She looked around as if in a trance. This really wasn't so bad after all – even if it was more Rachel's vibe than her own. She took a long sip of her drink through the straw and was dismayed to find she'd drained it.

'Same again?' she asked Maryanne, waving her glass at her.

'No need,' Maryanne replied, indicating behind her with her head, her eyes shining. 'I think the cavalry's just arrived.'

Caroline cast an incredulous glance over her friend's shoulder as the two guys they'd been eyeing up approached them, carrying drinks.

'Hi,' said the black guy, holding up a tumbler, eyes firmly on Maryanne. 'We noticed you're drinking mojitos. Mind if we join you?'

'Not at all,' replied Maryanne in a sultry tone Caroline had never heard before. 'I'm Maryanne, and this is my friend Caroline. And you are . . .?'

'Andre,' he replied, only taking his eyes off Maryanne to briefly acknowledge Caroline. 'And this is Richie.' He ran a finger delicately up Maryanne's arm. 'Nice dress.'

Maryanne shook her hair back from her eyes. 'That's my arm.'

'Nice arm,' he said, the corners of his mouth twitching with amusement.

31

Caroline laughed at the joke, then stopped abruptly. Maryanne was totally cracking on to someone a generation younger than she was!

To her left, Richie cleared his throat loudly. 'So you're Caroline?' he said hopefully. He had highlighted brown hair shaped into a quiff at the front, and was sharply dressed: skinny jeans, pointed shoes, a vintage rock tee and an over-sized blazer. He was definitely hot, thought Caroline. Exactly the kind of boy she'd expect Rachel to bring home.

'Yes, I'm Caroline,' she replied pleasantly, resisting the urge to add 'and what's your mummy called?'

'You come here often?' he asked, without the slightest hint of irony. Caroline shook her head and had to take a sip of her mojito to stop herself from laughing out loud.

'Not really. Do you?'

Richie shook his head and took a swig of his bottled beer.

The music changed to salsa, and Caroline's heart skipped a beat. She loved Latin American music. Instinctively, she started to sway again in time to the beat. To her right, Andre was standing behind Maryanne and running his hands down the sides of her body as she did some impromptu salsa steps. Seeing their natural ease together, Caroline felt stiff and awkward, like her mother dancing at a wedding, and she stopped abruptly.

Richie put his arm around her and brushed it across her buttocks, and she jumped as if she'd been shot. He didn't seem to notice. 'Do you fancy going out for a smoke?'

'I don't smoke,' she stammered.

He moved closer to whisper in her ear – so close that his lips tickled her earlobe. 'Neither do I.'

Caroline stared at him, flabbergasted. 'Oh,' she said, at a loss for anything else to say. He was hitting on her! 'I – I think I need the loo,' she managed, and, ducking out of his embrace, escaped in the vague direction of the bar.

The club had filled up since they'd entered, and Caroline had to push her way through the mass of revellers, lurid drinks and the sweet smell of musky aftershave to make headway. She looked around her desperately. She was chronically short-sighted, and without her glasses any signposting further than an arm's length away was unintelligible. Not for the first time, she wished she didn't have such a phobia of putting her fingers near her eyeballs – really, contact lenses would make life much easier. Here, there were neon signs everywhere, but they could have read 'loser' and 'sucker' for all she knew.

Finally, she found a toilet door and, grateful, pushed against it with all her weight. For a split second, she stared in confusion. It was a toilet all right, but something was wrong: the smell, the atmosphere, the layout ... the men! Horrified, Caroline took in the very masculine figures standing at the urinals and one guy doing up his zipper. Face burning, she backed out and stood to one side of the door. Next to her, a hard-faced girl with a Croydon facelift ponytail and a Bart Simpson tattoo on her shoulder was texting, and Caroline tapped her on the shoulder.

'Excuse me, where's the Ladies?' she asked politely.

'Over there,' replied the girl in a bored voice and pointed vaguely back towards the dance floor.

'Over where?' repeated Caroline, struggling to hear above the thumping bass and feeling the telltale prickle of a panicky sweat starting under her armpits.

'Over THERE,' insisted the girl, as if Caroline were stupid. Caroline, following the direction of her arm, saw a neon light and finally found the relative calm of the Ladies.

Ears ringing from the music, she rushed past the smiling toilet assistant and a boudoir-style dressing table groaning under the weight of complimentary hair products, perfume and lollipops, and locked herself in one of the plush cubicles.

Suddenly, she started to laugh. What an idiot. She was one of the most respected businesswomen in London – stylish, successful and, it so happened, now single – and yet she couldn't handle a night out in one of the hottest new night-clubs in the city? So it wasn't exactly her cup of tea – certainly not her kind of cocktail. So what? No one was forcing her to stay. She'd go back, grab Maz, and take them both on to another hot spot – somewhere a little more suited to *both* of them.

But when she squeezed her way back to the table, her friend was nowhere to be seen. She caught sight of Richie, chatting up a pretty blonde much closer to his age, and he acknowledged her with a sheepish smile. She grinned back. Bless him. She looked much more his type – Caroline could see she had done him a favour by rejecting his advances.

Searching the crowds on the dance floor, Caroline finally spotted Maryanne. She lifted her arm up to attract her attention, but stopped halfway in shock. Maryanne was in the middle of a fast, furious and frankly filthy salsa with Andre. Yes, she looked amazing – her tumbling red waves catching the light, her pale limbs almost translucent against his dark skin – but there was nothing platonic or innocently flirty about their gyrations. So close you could hardly even tell

34

them apart, they had worked up a visible sweat. Maryanne's already figure-hugging dress was clinging to her even more sexily, and Andre's black shirt was now stuck to his buff contours with perspiration.

Caroline watched, open-mouthed, as the track worked up to its climax. Maryanne and Andre stopped, collapsing into one another in joy – and then kissed passionately. Caroline frowned. The aim of the evening seemed to have totally changed. Maryanne was a married woman. This wasn't just harmless fun.

This was cheating.

Making her way over to her friend, Caroline grabbed Maryanne's arm and pulled her to the side of the dance floor. Andre, still panting, stood laughing and basking in the admiration of fellow dancers.

'Maz, what on earth do you think you're doing?' she hissed.

Maryanne was genuinely shocked. 'I'm having some fun. What does it look like I'm doing?'

Caroline gave a brittle laugh. 'But Maz, you're married! And anyway, he's young enough to be your son.'

Maryanne looked back at her, her eyes hard as flint, glittering like black diamonds. 'It's just as well I haven't got a son to upset then, isn't it?' Caroline flinched. Maryanne's lack of children was not a subject anyone dared broach often – if ever. 'Loosen up, Caroline. We're meant to be having a good time!'

As she turned away Caroline grabbed her arm again.

'But at what cost? What about Anthony? What would he think if he could see you now?'

'He'd probably think – Oh, so *that's* what she's been missing

35

all these years!' spat back Maryanne. Again, Caroline physically flinched. 'You don't get it, honey, do you? You don't even realise just how good you've had it.'

Caroline opened her mouth to protest, but Maryanne held up her hand to stop her speaking.

'Caroline, even your divorce has more passion in it than Anthony and I have ever had between us. Yes, of course I love him. More than I could say. And I know he loves me. But sex, physical intimacy, a good, hot, seeing-to on a Saturday night? Slow, lazy sex on a Sunday morning? Never mind a quickie before he leaves in the morning – we've rarely had so much as a passionate snog since our wedding night! We're sexorexic, me and Anthony. There's a whole lot of love but not one iota of lust there. And that's fine for Anthony. He wrote the rule book. He didn't want kids. OK, I gave him that one. But I still have needs, Caroline, the same as you. I may not have the offspring to prove it, but I'm the same as any other woman!'

Caroline stared speechlessly at her friend, the music pulsating intoxicatingly around her head as realisation dawned.

'And so . . .'

Maryanne tossed her head proudly, eyes shining with unshed tears.

'That's right. I've taken to having lovers. And not just any lovers. Young lovers – the younger the better – all energetic, in shape and up for it.'

Caroline grabbed hold of the table to steady herself. For some reason, she was shaking.

'My hairdresser, our estate agent, our gardener, even Don's teenage son – I've had them all, Caroline. I'm a cougar – I like young, fresh meat. The younger the better.' Maryanne looked over at Andre and gave him a reassuring smile. 'An older man might jeopardise what I've got with Anthony,' she continued hotly. 'Get too serious, want to come clean. I dunno. But these young guns – they're the safe option. The sexy option. I can't get enough of them, and they can't get enough of me.'

Maryanne looked around for her dancer. Seeing Andre standing uncertainly to one side, she stretched out her hand invitingly and nodded towards the dance floor. She turned back to Caroline unrepentantly.

'And you know what? Tonight, I'm going to have me some more.'

Caroline watched in astonishment as Maryanne, high on the heady mix of drink and desire, stepped back out on to the dance floor. She looked incredible. Who was Caroline to berate her for finding what small comforts were out there?

But one thing was certain. It was not comforting Caroline. Time she got the hell out of there and reacquainted herself with people of her own generation. There was no way she was cut out for affairs with men half her age.

No way at all.

Chapter 3

THANK GOODNESS FOR BOOTS

Caroline gave her soon-to-be-ex husband a curt nod through the car window, waved enthusiastically at Rachel as if she was still a little girl – still, she supposed, desperately trying to shield her daughter from some, any, of the hurt she was going through herself – then drove off with a heavy heart.

Knowing Rachel was loath to spend time with her errant father was bad enough, but seeing the oh so familiar sight of Les in early morning disarray – hair still shower-damp, cologne freshly applied, no doubt a crumb of toast in the corner of his mouth – had done nothing to lift her spirits after the disaster of the previous night. Who had Les woken up with that morning? Who had made him his coffee? Whoever it was, she wouldn't be there now, not with Rachel's arrival imminent, but Caroline felt the breathless twist of the knife as the reality of Les's infidelity again hit home. It compounded her innate sense of misery, the associated grubbiness she felt after a night in the cattle-market enclave of Waikiki and the shock she still felt from Maryanne's revelations. And although this morning's scene was reminiscent of that of dysfunctional families across the country, dropping her daughter off to spend time with her absent father at his new St John's Wood bachelor pad seemed to have deepened her despair at the situation she now found herself in.

Several minutes later she arrived at work. She smoothed down the lightweight brocade of her midnight blue Caroline Herrera shift dress and slipped off her pumps – a practical morning staple since the days of doing the school run before work – in favour of a spiky pair of courts. (Unlike other entrepreneurial female peers, she refused to 'butch up' for meetings with even the toughest client and she found that heels enabled her to look her business associates, especially male ones, in the eye, doing wonders for their acquiescence and respect, as though she was subconsciously meeting them on their terms.) She slung a three-ply cashmere cardigan over the back of her battered art deco leather chair (Caroline wondered how long it would take Trudi to subtly remove the cardi and hang it carefully on a padded hanger behind her office door) and pulled a pair of biker boots from a cavernous leather holdall ready for the Kings of Leon gig she was taking Rachel to that evening. From Audrey Hepburn to corporate ball breaker to MILF in three easy shoe changes, she thought with a sudden giggle. The power of accessories . . .

A frown clouded her face as she thought of Rachel and Les holed up together in his new flat working on Rachel's business studies assignment together. A no doubt guilt-ridden Les had taken the morning off to spend with his daughter during her study period to help her with the project. Ever since Rachel's interview day – the day his affair had been busted –

Les had been the model father again, present whenever required and making a real show of putting his daughter before work, despite her obvious disgust with him. Like today, for example. Just a few weeks ago, he and Rachel could have worked on this at home after dinner. Just what lengths would she and Les now have to go to, to ensure a fair distribution of their love for Rachel – while never encroaching on each other's territory?

Not that she'd been particularly covetous of her own time with Rachel last night, she thought with a shiver. Never again! The whole evening – Maryanne's revelations included – felt like a bad dream. Caroline sat down on her chair and switched on her Mac thoughtfully. What in earth was she going to do about Maryanne?

Impulsively, she picked up her iPhone and dialled her friend's number.

'Hi, it's Maryanne. At least it's not, because I'm not here. Leave me a message, honey!'

Caroline clicked off resignedly without saying anything and looked at her Cartier watch. It was still only 8.15 a.m. Maryanne was never an early riser. She was still probably in bed. In bed – with Andre?

'Coffee!' Caroline looked up with a start and smiled warmly as Trudi placed a steaming mug of black coffee down in front of her. However early she arrived at work, it seemed that Trudi was there before her, quietly but efficiently filing, fixing and phoning, ensuring Caroline's complex diary of meetings, conference calls and evening appointments ran like clockwork.

'Thanks, Trudi,' she said, smiling more brightly than she felt. Trudi frowned at her.

'Are you OK, Caroline? You look tired.' She searched Caroline's face penetratingly from under a heavy blonde fringe and spiky black eyelashes. She moved away as if satisfied she'd found the answer. 'How was last night?'

Caroline shrugged nonchalantly. 'Oh, you know.'

Thank God Trudi DIDN'T know, she added silently to herself. Heaven forbid that Maryanne's indiscretion should ever get out. Although she looked on her team as extended family, and knew every twist and turn of their personal soap operas, Caroline guarded her own privacy fiercely. She gave her assistant her trademark level gaze, her green eyes expressionless.

The divorce papers had been served a matter of days ago, and they were still at the formally polite stage of speaking only through solicitors. She had made it clear that for all of their sakes – but most of all Rachel's – they should make it as quick and as civil as possible. But Les, she knew, wanted her back. He was going to fight her at every stage – and there was no way that, if he didn't get his own way, things could ever stay civil. Sapphires & Rubies would be an easy way to get at her.

The irony was that Les had always partially viewed Sapphires & Rubies as a weakness of his, not hers. For when she'd first talked about setting up the business, Les had assumed it would be a joint venture, with him providing the funding. But Caroline didn't need any money. She'd already got it – thanks to a small but steadily growing trust fund her father had created for her when she was born. It had matured years earlier, but, full of bitterness at the way he treated her mother, Caroline had refused to cash it in. Now, however, she decided to set aside her emotions and look on the fund as the ideal way to finance her new business. There was no place for sentimentality in business, after all – and if she was going to succeed she had vowed to toughen up, and start as she meant to go on.

After weeks of wrangling and careful negotiations, Caroline had acquired Sapphires & Rubies for a song, and with her canny rebranding and eye for opportunity, it had become an immediate success. The fusty old leather goods brand produced shoes and bags that suddenly appeared on the arms and feet of every It girl around the globe, picking up on women's desire for beautifully crafted super-products – with the price tag to match. Caroline not only understood what women wanted, she understood their lives, and how they juggled work, home and play. And like every collection that followed, her initial launch had tapped right into the zeitgeist. For the next decade, Caroline's business flourished and her international profile with it.

It had been fun, and exciting, but it hadn't been easy. Yes, Caroline had had help – a wonderful nanny, and a housekeeper – but she didn't believe in simply handing her child over to someone else for five full days a week. Les was a fantastic father and had worked long hours – as he'd always done – but he hadn't got up at 5 a.m. every day to make up for leaving work at a baby-friendly hour later in the afternoon. And it hadn't been Les who, whatever crisis was emerging at work, had left at 4.30 p.m. in order to make their daughter her tea, bathe her, put her to bed, and latterly to help her with her homework.

Sapphires & Rubies was Caroline's. She hadn't built it up into a flourishing company – shrewdly inviting the right kind of investment at the right time, resisting takeover bids and generous offers for her majority shareholding over the years – for nothing: and no one, least of all Les, was going to take it from her now.

'So, shall I run through the rest of your day?' Trudi's voice, confident and businesslike again, brought Caroline back to reality with a start. 'Your mother called. She's apparently had no luck getting hold of you on your mobile, so I promised faithfully you'd call back . . .'

Caroline wrinkled her nose. She loved her mother dearly, and the moment she'd told Babs about Les's infidelity, Babs had decamped from her Hertfordshire home to stay with Caroline and Rachel. And during those first, long, bleak, heartbroken weeks, Caroline had never been so glad to have her close by. Babs had cooked, feeding Rachel and attempting to feed Caroline. She had cleaned – technically, there was no need as Caroline had a daily come in – but the sight of Babs pottering about with a duster had been as much of a comfort to Caroline as her soothing words whenever Caroline had broken down. Which was a lot.

But as Caroline started to come to terms with it all, the fact that her mother's support wasn't limited to home was beginning to grate. In fact, she couldn't seem to let even thirty minutes go by without a call from Babs, checking up on 'how she was'! Supportive had turned into stifling – but right now all Caroline had the energy for was to ignore it.

'. . . At 9 a.m. Ali is coming in to run through PM5 with you – she's given me a printout of the figures in case you want to give them the once-over first. Then at 10 a.m. there's the board meeting.' She paused and gave Caroline a meaningful look over the top of her notepad. 'I've already checked that the air conditioning is set to how Elaine likes it.'

Caroline allowed herself an amused smile. Elaine was a former backbench Tory politician who had lost her constituency in the Labour landslide of 1997. She now split her time between quangos and a variety of executive directorships. Like Caroline and Andrew Brockenwich, the retired CEO of a supermarket chain – who, in contrast to Elaine, normally attended AGMs in a battered tweed jacket and red cotton trousers – she held a 30 per cent share of Sapphires & Rubies. The remaining 10 per cent was held by Molly, Caroline's ebullient finance director.

'And Isabel wants to show you the revised designs for the spring/summer ranges, so I've squeezed her in just before lunch. She'll come to us, I've asked her to board them up so you don't have to mess around with lots of sheets of paper . . .'

Caroline looked at Trudi fondly as her PA dutifully recited the rest of the day's events. Trudi was the sartorial opposite of her own immaculate grooming and the epitome of dressed down Shoreditch cool in her Marc Jacobs military jacket, skinny Sass & Bide jeans, and Converse All Stars. Caroline was proud of the working environment she'd created at Sapphires & Rubies, from the shop floor to the design studio. She employed individuals and encouraged them to remain so, dressing – within reason – to reflect their personality, to work to flexible hours that suited their modus operandi, lifestyle or childcare arrangements. (Despite her privileged life, Caroline herself found the struggle to find the balance while juggling work, family and children dispiriting, and was keenly aware of how much more difficult it must be for single parents or those on a fraction of her salary.) Amongst her staff, Caroline was famous for her level-headed approach to business, her intrinsic glamour, her instinct for what consumers wanted before they even knew themselves what they wanted, and for never raising her voice. The result was a happy, loyal workforce and low staff turnover – which, she knew, played a major part in the continued success of her business.

'. . . And then at one you're due at the shoot, so I've left the rest of the day clear as you always end up getting tied up at them . . .'

Caroline chuckled, before mentally reprimanding herself for forgetting the shoot for her next advertising campaign. It would be one of the most important campaigns of her career – launching a fragrance. Last year's launch of a diffusion range of men's and women's accessories had made the Sapphires & Rubies brand just about attainable for the UK's young style elite, and the brand's first scent, Precious, was aimed at expanding the brand without compromising its exclusivity or its cachet. She couldn't even blame her marriage breakdown for today's mental block – not directly, anyhow – but last night when she'd returned home from Waikiki, she'd become lost in shocked reflection on Maryanne's revelations, instead of preparing for the next day.

She had to pull it back. The business needed her, just as Rachel was going to need her as the divorce progressed. Maryanne's crisis could wait. (Especially as Maryanne didn't seem to think it was a crisis at all . . .) Despite her wealth, Caroline's life was a delicate balance of priorities, all demanding more of her attention than she could devote to them, and with the pain of Les's betrayal already shaking their fragile status quo, she couldn't afford to let anything else threaten the delicate fabric of her life. And after the disaster that was last night, that included other men, too . . .

Thank goodness for boots, reflected Caroline, as she climbed the dusty whitewashed stairs to the second-floor studio in her bikers. There was no way she'd have attempted to navigate these stairs in her heels, and pumps just seemed so – well – insignificant for the executive director of an advertising campaign. Maybe Sapphires & Rubies should branch out into them. She'd often toyed with the idea of producing a collection of boots – if only to save herself a small fortune every year!

Pushing open the double doors into the studio, she was met with the familiar scene of a shoot in pre-production. To her left, a row of models sat on high stools in front of a long mirror surrounded by dressing-room-style lightbulbs, and a long table piled high with cosmetics, hair products and heated rollers. Each was attended by a hair or make-up artist working frantically to perfect their campaign 'look' – brushing, backcombing, and beautifying.

'Caroline, darling!' A tanned, muscular guy in rolled-up jeans and espadrilles sashayed over to her, arms outstretched in greeting.

'Hi, Giles,' said Caroline, hugging him warmly. 'How's it going so far?'

'Fabulous, darling!' said Giles excitedly. 'At least, Bob's looking pretty good!' He gestured over to his second assistant, who was standing in front of the white backdrop looking deadpan into the camera as the first assistant tested the lighting on him. 'Come and see!' He grabbed her hand and shimmied back to the camera to show Caroline the results on the digital screen. Giles had to be the gayest straight man in London, she thought wryly, following him obediently. If you didn't know him, you'd never guess he had notched up most of London's hottest female models on his bedpost, and was now living with a successful glossy magazine editor twice his age. Humph. So, that must make *her* a cougar, too, thought Caroline. She'd never thought of it like that before, but Maryanne seemed to have opened her eyes to it going on all over the place. How many more of them were there in action?

Caroline peered over Giles's shoulder in delight. No wonder he was so in demand. He was a genius with lighting as well as with photographic angles and concepts, transforming even Bob, his frankly hairy and aesthetically challenged assistant into something bordering on attractive. 'Good work, Bob – are you sure you don't want a part in the campaign?' she quipped, eyes dancing.

'Oh, you couldn't possibly afford me,' he shot back good-humouredly.

A light touch at her elbow alerted Caroline to Angie, the shoot stylist, standing patiently to her right.

'Hi, Caroline. I wondered if you wanted to take a look at the clothes? I've got Adam and Irenie styled up already, and you can tell me what you think before I dress the rest.'

Caroline nodded eagerly. She hated all the preparation for a shoot – the hours of standing around, creating the set, choosing angles and setting the lighting to the nth degree. But finessing the look, trying different set-ups and directing pose and expression until you got The One – well, that was right up her street. She followed Angie over to a long black screen, behind which was a makeshift dressing area lined with rails of clothes and a rack on which Angie had styled up several outfits. An assistant was pinning the back of a chiffon blouse on an Amazonian black model with a shimmering Afro, and a male model was rifling through some of the clothes on a far rail, his back to Caroline.

'Caroline, this is Anna, my assistant, and Zia – who I think you met at the casting?' Caroline nodded smilingly at the assistant, who nodded back, mouth full of pins, and shook Zia's hand, giving her an approving look.

Caroline sniffed the air appreciatively, giving Angie a knowing look. 'Is someone wearing Precious?'

Angie grinned. 'All the models are. I always try to get a scent that reflects the mood of the shoot – and with this one, I didn't have to look very far!'

Caroline took a deep breath of the vintage-style scent again, a powdery fragrance that evoked the smell of old-fashioned compacts, and which had made her suddenly nostalgic for her own girlhood.

'Hi – we haven't met. I was in New York for the casting. I just wanted to say thanks for the job. Love the creative.'

Caroline turned at the deep, husky voice behind her. It was attached to the most gorgeously chiselled jaw, wavy black hair and curiously grey-green eyes that she'd ever seen. Adam. No, they hadn't met. So why was he smiling at her as if they had . . .?

She looked sideways towards the full-length mirror in the corner of the dressing area and checked her appearance. In comparison to Zia and Adam's glowing youth, she felt like a ninety-five-year-old crone.

'Well, I'm glad,' she said, meeting his eyes again, pulling herself up and struggling to regain her gravitas. That was the one thing she had on them both! 'It's an important campaign for us.' She remembered him now, from his 'book'. Models always looked so different in the flesh to the pictures in their portfolio. Usually, they were a disappointment. Adam Geray most definitely was *not*.

And here, in person, he was every bit as perfect for the campaign as his book – such as it was, for the few jobs he'd done in what seemed like a very short career – had suggested. His role in the 1970s style campaign was as the sexy foil for each of the two main girls: Zia and Charlene, a cool blonde sophisticate who was also a Harvard grad and oozed upmarket cool. A pair of wide-legged palazzo pants and a tiny floaty vest top were hanging up waiting for Charlene to have the finishing touches put to her blown-out waves, and Zia was currently pulling a tiny mini up over her endless gangly legs. Adam's hair had been styled in a 2011 take on the *Saturday Night Fever* quiff and he was wearing a tight button-down T-shirt and sharply pressed vintage Farrars. It was perfect. *He* was perfect.

Abruptly, he leaned forward and lowered his voice. 'How did you find Waikiki?'

She jumped and, absurdly, felt a blush start to creep up her neck and over her face. How did he know she'd been there?

'Well, I—' she stopped and cleared her throat. Pull yourself together, Caroline, you're acting like a teenage loon. Or more accurately – and even worse – a *middle-aged* loon.

49

She shook her head, letting her hair back fall over her shoulders. 'To be honest with you, it's not really my scene. I was there with a friend,' she added defensively.

'Yes, I noticed,' he said easily. Then, by way of explanation: 'I was also there last night. Also with a friend. My idea of hell, to be honest.' He smiled, his eyes crinkling at the corners. 'I wish I'd had the guts to introduce myself now. At least then we could have kept each other company in purgatory.'

Caroline gave him a fixed smile back. This was not the kind of conversation she was used to having with a model on one of her shoots. This was not the type of conversation she was used to having at all. But somehow, she couldn't tear herself away . . .

'You don't strike me as the nervous type,' she said artfully as she gained control of the exchange. 'I'm sure that's not the real reason why you didn't introduce yourself.'

'No, you're right,' he said honestly. 'The truth is, I was nervous. But I also didn't think it looked that good – you know, being out clubbing the night before a big shoot. I don't know how you do it. All I've got to do is be available at midday, and then stand here and look pretty. I would imagine you've been working since the crack of dawn. Respect!'

He made a fist of his hand and extended his arm towards her in the act of mutual admiration she'd seen Rachel do so many times with her friends. Caroline laughed out loud and returned the gesture.

'Well, I guess there's a first time for everything!' she said. 'No one other than my daughter has ever attempted that move on me. And, I might add, that's the first time a man has ever noticed the lengths we working women go to in life.'

She glanced back at Adam, and stopped short when she saw the way he was looking at her. Understanding. Intense. But more than that . . .

'And that's the first time anyone I admire has called me a man,' he murmured, so quietly Caroline could barely hear. Uncertain how to react, she turned away.

'Adam, you're wanted!' One of the make-up artists shrieked. 'I need to do more work on those bags under your eyes. I know we're shooting in soft focus but they are taking the piss!'

Caroline hid a smile. The production team were seasoned experts – she was confident they'd had a lot worse to deal with than disguising the effects of a late night. But despite herself, she was amazed. Adam must be all of nineteen – only two years older than Rachel – yet he'd noticed *her* last night?

Of course he did, a voice inside her head reasoned. *You just gave him the biggest break of his career. Of course he noticed you in some two-bit nightclub THE EVENING BEFORE THE CAMPAIGN SHOOT.*

Not for the first time that day, a vision of Maryanne grinding her hips against Andre's flashed through Caroline's mind, and she felt uncomfortable. Bloody Maryanne. Couldn't she have kept her cradle-snatching ways to herself?

A loud, upbeat bass started thumping from the studio sound system – designed to keep everyone's mood high and a sure sign work was about to start in earnest. Catching sight of Adam and Charlene playfully pushing each other around in front of the backdrop, Caroline decided to push the whole encounter to the back of her mind. She was blowing everything out of proportion – again. Time to get a grip. She had a shoot to do.

★

'OK everyone – it's a wrap!'

There was a ripple of appreciative applause from the production team dotted around the studio, and Zia and Adam clambered down from the plinth they were precariously balanced on, grinning at the satisfaction of a long day over and a job well done.

Caroline, still clapping her hands above her head, wandered across to look over Giles's shoulder as he had a final flick through the takes from the last set-up of the day. One glance confirmed what they'd all known right from the start of the shoot: this one was a winner, with take after take of amazing images. The hardest job wasn't going to be finding one that would hold the campaign – it was going to be rejecting any of the other perfect compositions. It was all Caroline could do to stop whooping out loud.

'You're a genius, Giles!' she exclaimed, and hugged his shoulder in delight. 'I'd take you out for dinner to celebrate if I didn't have to be at this gig in like –' she consulted her Cartier Tank Française watch. 'Oops! In, like, twenty minutes. I'm meeting Rachel. Gotta dash. Thanks everyone!'

Caroline gave a general wave in the direction of the drinks fridge that the crew were currently crowding round in search of a cold beer, and turned to dash out of the door. As she spun around, she crashed into something and jumped back with a start. It was Adam, who grabbed her elbow to steady her as she rocked back on her heels in shock. With his other hand, he rubbed his cheekbone. A throbbing just above Caroline's temple made her realise it must have been her head that had struck him.

'Oh! I'm so sorry!' she exclaimed.

'I'm not,' he said, grinning at her cheekily. 'Are you in a rush?'

'Yes! I'm off to a concert, actually. That is, a gig. To see a band. To see Kings of Leon.' Silently, she kicked herself. So cool, Caro, so cool.

He dipped his eyes. 'Oh, right. A date.'

'No!' she almost squealed. 'I mean yes. With my daughter.' He looked up at her again. 'She's seventeen,' she added unnecessarily.

He gave a small laugh. 'She's only two years younger than me. We might have been at school together.'

Caroline felt confused. 'No, I don't think so,' she observed. 'She's at Cheltenham.'

Adam's eyes flashed. 'Oh, well, that's far too posh for me.' He turned to go.

Caroline grabbed his arm. 'Cheltenham *Ladies*' College.'

He gave her an embarrassed smile and scuffed his foot along the concrete studio floor. Caroline was suddenly aware that members of the crew were watching them with interest. Exactly why *was* she hanging around chatting to a nineteen-year-old?

Adam looked up at her, fixing those grey-green eyes on her, and once again she melted. His grin was more confident again, his tone teasing. 'So where do you hang out when you're not at Waikiki or a Kings of Leon gig?'

She shrugged and indicated her watch apologetically. 'Look, I really must be—'

'Only, I was wondering if I'm permitted to ask my boss out for a drink tomorrow?' he said quickly before she could finish. 'That is, if you still are technically my boss any more now the shoot's over?'

Caroline's jaw dropped, and she looked over her shoulder again.

He laughed shortly. 'It's OK, no one's listening. Well, how about it?' He was moving his weight shiftily from one foot to the other now, obviously feeling he'd overstepped the mark.

Caroline looked at him. Really, he was almost the same age as Rachel. It was a preposterous idea. Of course she wouldn't. Couldn't. *Shouldn't* . . .

'I'll take that as a yes,' said Adam, with a wink. 'I'll call your office.'

He wandered off, leaving Caroline free to dash off to her gig. As she hurried away, she didn't dare turn around to face the crew. She felt something welling up inside her, and she had an uncontrollable urge to giggle. Almost running now, she sped out of the studio and down the fire exit stairs, the urge getting greater and greater. As she reached the first floor, she stopped and leaned against the wall to gather herself and laughed out loud, the longest and hardest since she'd split from Les. She was going on a date. With a nineteen-year-old.

How the hell was she going to get out of this one?

Chapter 4

RIDICULOUS FORMALITIES

'I'm sorry, Caroline, I simply don't understand what you're trying to achieve with these ridiculous formalities. We're her parents, for God's sake – and she's nearly eighteen. The only custody we'll be worrying about in a few months is when she's been arrested for getting too drunk at her Freshers Week!'

Caroline shot Les a contemptuous glance as he got up from the sofa and went to fill his coffee cup from the pot on the table in front of him. The sight of him filled her with a surging sense of anger. His expensively cut greying hair, his permanently tanned skin, and cornflower eyes set deep into high cheekbones. He'd discarded the jacket from his navy Savile Row suit and she could make out his lean, tennis-honed contours under his crisply ironed shirt, cuffs caught at the wrist with the cobalt cufflinks she'd bought him for his fiftieth birthday. She felt her throat constrict. How did the familiar suddenly become so unfamiliar? How did someone's actions affect how you perceived everything about them? Les had been her everything – her rock. She knew him so well she used to look at him without really seeing him. Now, although his appearance was unchanged, he was like a stranger to her. A hard, aggressive, unwelcome stranger.

This is not your home any more, Les Walker, she thought, gritting her teeth. *You gave up the right to swan around this living room when you invited another woman into your bed.* Our *bed*. It was Caroline's home now – hers and Rachel's – and the sooner Les got used to it, the sooner they could all move on.

Caroline's lawyer, Adrian Green of the prestigious Green, Howe & Western partnership had suggested that she and Les try and sort out childcare arrangements amicably between themselves before sending them on to be set out formally by their legal representatives. Caroline had protested, but he'd insisted this was the correct first step in attempting a successful separation. What Adrian hadn't factored in was that Les was going to resist any progression of their split every step of the way. If Caroline wanted a divorce, then fair enough – but he sure as hell wasn't going to make it easy for her.

She took a deep breath and willed herself to stay calm. She studied an imaginary speck on her Nicole Farhi trouser suit, one frustrating heartbeat away from composure. She'd dressed carefully for this, their first 'summit meeting', the soft tailoring of the cream linen mix relaxed enough for her to feel comfortable but formal enough to say she meant business. The expensive coffee-coloured silk camisole under the jacket was no mistake either – the flash of tanned, toned skin a careful reminder of exactly what Les was missing. At the thought, Caroline's heart turned to stone, and she fixed her estranged husband with a level gaze. 'You know it makes sense, Les. With our combined schedules, if we don't have a fixed agreement we'll spend the whole time not knowing which way is up – and the person who's going to suffer most is Rachel. With pre-agreed parental rights, we can arrange our work and social schedules around it, rather than the other way round.'

Les took a sip of coffee and shook his head sadly. 'Caroline, you make it sound so clinical. Anyone would think we're getting divorced!'

The attempt at a joke fell flat, and Caroline bit her lip. There was no point in rising to the bait – Les was a wind-up merchant, and she knew his joviality was covering up his real feelings. Allowing herself to get annoyed by him would inevitably end up in a blazing and ultimately unproductive row, and what was the point of that? Not to mention, arguments indicated passion, and they were a little beyond that now.

Sensing his failure to make progress, Les changed tack. He smiled down at her and perched on the arm of the sofa she was sitting on.

'Caro, darling, this whole thing is crazy. The easiest thing would be for me to move back in.' He held up his hand to shush her as she opened her mouth to protest. His voice was softly persuasive, almost wheedling. 'Not back together, obviously. Not yet. But think about it. We're both using the same base, and we can make Rachel our priority together – just like we've always done. And under the same roof, we can work on our differences. It makes sense, baby.'

Caroline winced at the use of his pet names for her. Unable to bear his proximity, breathe the smell of him, even sense his body heat, she stood up and wandered over to the window to gaze out over their garden. The carefully tended lawn was the vivid green of early morning springtime, and the beds around it were full of plants and flowers on the verge of bursting into life. All those early springs spent together lovingly planting bulbs, those autumns collecting compost, those summers sat out lazing on the grass – with Rachel first in a pram, then toddling around, chasing bees and falling over, then playing with friends leaping in and out of paddling pools. And all the time, her and Les together. Didn't count for much, did it, when someone else could come along and blow everything out of the water?

She spoke without turning. 'None of this makes sense, Les. But it's happened. And we have to deal with what *is*, not what was. You've made your bed –' her voice caught in her throat at the word, 'and now you're going to have to lie on it.' She let the words hang on the air, accusatory in sense but melancholy in tone. There was silence as they absorbed the full weight of the meaning. Even Les managed to refrain from cracking a joke.

A bird flew out of a tree and startled Caroline out of her trance-like state. She turned from the window. The spell had obviously been long broken for Les, who was typing something into his BlackBerry.

'You know, I'd really rather we let our "people" set this up, Les,' she said, suddenly wanting to see the back of him. 'But in the short term, I think Rachel said she was coming to you this weekend – something about a charity match she couldn't get out of?' Rachel shared her father's love of tennis and they often played doubles together. Now she was going under duress – reluctant to spend time with her father, but too well brought up to let other people down.

Les looked up and frowned. 'No, it's not this weekend,' he

said, consulting his diary. 'I think it was the one afterwards. This week we're due at—'

He stopped short as he realised his mistake. Caroline stared at him, stunned, eyes blurring with tears. At the inadvertent mention of his mistress, she felt as if someone had knocked all the air out of her.

'We?' she repeated, stupidly. '*We?* Were you planning on "we" moving back in here too, Les, when you were planning our romantic reconciliation? Where did "we" fit into your plans for rekindling family life?'

'Caro,' he began helplessly. 'Caro, I didn't mean . . . it's not what you think.'

He stood up from the sofa and upset his coffee cup. Cold coffee sloshed over the side of the saucer and on to his suit. 'Fuckit,' he swore, pulling a handkerchief from his pocket and rubbing furiously at the stain.

'That's what got you into this mess in the first place,' Caroline spat, all attempts at retaining her dignity now gone in the searing pain of new hurt. He couldn't even make the effort to hide his new hussy from her. Well, if that was how it had to be . . . She picked up her handbag and slung it over her shoulder. 'I have to get to work. My "people" will be in touch with your "people", Les. I'm assuming you can show yourself out?'

She watched as he looked up at her miserably, hunched over in defeat, all the swagger gone out of him.

'And you can leave your key when you go, too,' she added, wanting to make him feel just every little bit as bad as he had made – was making – her feel. '"We" has spent enough time in this house – in my bed.' She took a rasping breath, desperate to escape from this nightmare. 'I wouldn't want any confusion to lead to a repeat performance.'

With that, she stalked out of the living room, slamming the door, and marched through the double height hall. She almost mowed down her mother, who had appeared from the kitchen at the noise and was standing quietly by the door.

'Sorry, Mother,' said Caroline as she rushed past.

Babs, a sprightly woman, shook her head sadly. Caroline had inherited her father's looks, and where she was tall and thin, her mother had always been more sturdy, with thick, wavy blonde hair and Labrador brown eyes. The hair, swept back into a loose bun, was now greying at the temples. Her skin was lightly tanned from all the time she spent outdoors, but curiously unlined and belied her sixty-eight years but the eyes were as bright and alert as ever – testament, she would say, to the fact she never touched a drop of alcohol. The only liqueur she ever kept in her pretty Hertfordshire cottage was an ancient bottle of brandy she had occasionally 'for medicinal purposes'. Right now, those eyes were boring a disapproving hole into her daughter.

Caroline stopped at the front door with her back still to her mother. She didn't need to turn to know that Babs was still giving her that reproachful look. 'What, Mother?' she said between gritted teeth, mentally counting to ten so she didn't bite her mother's head off.

She wasn't just hurt – she was angry. She wanted to prove to Les – and herself – that she could survive this. And in doing so, she was seeing things a lot more clearly. Seeing Les for what he was, for a start. Questioning her own part in all this. And spotting the holes in Babs's unconditional support. Like her unspoken disapproval because Caroline wasn't responding to Les's overtures. That, despite the ultimate betrayal, she wasn't doing everything she could to try and fix things. Because, however proud Babs was of her daughter's success, and however much she basked in the way Caroline had taken on her own work ethic and independence, part of her had still been aghast when Caroline had announced she was going into business all those years ago. Why on earth, reasoned Babs, would you work and risk the delicate fabric of your family life when you had no financial need to? It was bound to end in disaster. And disaster – however much it had or hadn't got to do with the fact that she was a successful working mother – pretty much summed up Caroline's life right now.

'Nothing, darling,' said Babs with pursed lips. 'Just don't be too hard on him.'

'Hard on *him*?' repeated Caroline in disbelief. She opened her mouth to say more – but shut it before she uttered something she would regret. She stomped across the hall and out of the heavy, wide front door. She ignored Christian, standing across the road watering his front garden with a hosepipe, as he unashamedly stared at her running from her own house. Hands shaking, she got into the car, turned on the ignition and squealed out of the drive.

Only when she was a couple of streets away did Caroline allow herself to pull over. Leaning over the steering wheel as if doubled up with pain, she broke down, huge, gulping sobs racking her thin frame.

She sat there for what seemed hours until her phone beeped with an incoming text.

Morning Mrs Walker. Got your number from your PA. Used

work as a cover! Just checking you're still on for tomorrow. I'll meet you at the Pembroke Castle at 7. Adam x

She stared at it as if it was written in a foreign language. Then, finally, through her tears, she started to laugh.

Meeting at the pub. How very twenty-something. She shook her head at the prospect. But a niggling thought refused to go away. It could be just what she needed. So why the hell not?

Caroline gave Trudi a pinched good morning smile. 'No calls for the time being,' she said abruptly and Trudi nodded efficiently. Caroline's jaw was set, emphasising its delicate contours, and her eyes were hard and cold. It wasn't often that her boss came into work under a cloud. But Trudi knew better than to try any small talk when she did. Caroline slung her bag on to the desk and closed the door carefully behind her. The window overlooking Floral Street had been opened earlier that morning, and she took a deep breath, filling her lungs with mid-morning spring and the lily-scented air conditioning. It was a heady mix, and as it both revived and calmed her, she felt some of the tightness in her body ebb away.

She sank into her chair and ran her fingers through her hair. Just how, exactly, had her perfect life disintegrated so thoroughly and slipped through her fingers so completely?

She bit her lip. She had hardly even considered whether leaving Les was the right decision. As much as it hurt, and as much as she knew the easiest way – for Rachel and Les, at least – would be denial, to sweep the whole thing under the carpet, to forgive him and take him back, it wouldn't be a way she could live with. Caroline felt a stab in her chest as she thought about Les – by his own admission – still seeing the woman he'd betrayed her for. A woman he'd claimed meant nothing to him. And whether she did or she didn't was of no comfort to Caroline. If she did, the thought that Les could be in love with anyone else was too painful to bear, and if she didn't, then what did that say about Les, the man Caroline had built the foundations of her adult life upon? That he was so weak he'd prefer the company of someone he didn't give two hoots about over trying to win back his family and reconstruct a life with?

Nope, the hurt, the recriminations, the lack of trust – she'd never get over any of them. After all, she'd lived with the repercussions of her father's affair long enough – how her mother had never got over him deserting her and Caroline for a younger woman, how Babs, despite the fierce independence with which she'd fought for her daughter's future, spurring Caroline on through university and into work – had never allowed herself to trust another man. And how, if Caroline's marriage and a granddaughter had not come along to distract her, Babs would have been eaten up by her own bitterness. One thing was for sure: Caroline had been raised never to forgive infidelity, and whatever reasons Les might now claim he had – and whatever her mother now said to try and excuse his behaviour – he had, in Babs's own words (if not at the time directed at him) crossed the line. And although Babs had been nothing but supportive, beneath the stoic smiles and the tight hugs, there was an unspoken 'I told you so'.

Keen to banish the thought of Les from her head, Caroline

picked up her message pad and skim-read it absently. The MD of one of her main suppliers. Confirmation of her regular weekly hair appointment at Daniel Galvin Jnr on Friday. Her mother, who seemed to have called here the moment Caroline had stalked out of the house. Maryanne.

Maryanne?

Caroline's heart leapt as the image of her warm, kind friend popped into her head. Maryanne! She would know how to handle Les. She would put a funny spin on it, take her shopping, make Caroline feel better.

But as she remembered their last encounter, and the harsh words they'd exchanged, Caroline's joy dissipated. A heart-to-heart with Maryanne was the last thing she needed right now. They had a lot of making up to do – and revisiting Maryanne's sexless marriage and her penchant for illicit encounters with practical strangers twenty years her junior was exactly the last thing Caroline felt like doing.

Caroline turned to the copy of the *FT* lying on her desk. Those familiar pink pages were reassuringly solid on this day of moving foundations, and Caroline felt herself relax a little as she picked up her Mont Blanc fountain pen and started her daily routine of navigating the mix of international business news, comment and analysis and marking the stories she wanted Trudi to copy and file for future reference. Her pen hovered over the lead story in the Companies section. MORTON EYES £5m KIDSTER BUYOUT. She chuckled comfortably. Now that was a hopeless cause. Kidster, an ailing luggage manufacturer, had suffered from a run of bad press of late. Allegations of sweatshops, price fixing – not to mention the financial director having been caught embezzling tens of thousands of pounds – the business had it all, and it would take a monumental amount of cash and cunning to turn it around. It wouldn't do Morton any good in the short term, and even with the canniest marketing plan in the world, long-term success was doubtful. Caroline allowed herself a gleeful smile. Still, if Morton wanted to put itself in that position, who was she to protest? Morton was her main competitor, and, until a couple of years ago, the UK's number one luxury goods firm. That is, until Sapphires & Rubies had taken over the top spot. Which had made Morton's CEO, Don MacCaskill, Caroline's biggest rival. There was certainly no love lost between them. As heir apparent to the Morton fortune, and with no major business threats on the horizon, until the early nineties he'd had an easy life, lording it in the previously closed shop of luxury goods. But once upstart Sapphires & Rubies had established itself, Morton had begun to feel the heat – and now MacCaskill was really having to work for the first time in his life, doing everything in his power to regain his lost crown. And, it turned out, discredit Caroline in the process. But Caroline wasn't worried. She was confident in where the business was headed, and just as importantly, her board were confident too – and if MacCaskill was so uncertain of his position that he was having to run after new acquisitions to boost the net worth of Morton, then she really didn't have any need to worry. She relaxed a little more. Business was always here for her. Maybe she needed to channel a little of the dogged self-belief that had got her this far in work into her personal life.

On impulse, she picked up the telephone and dialled Adrian Green's office.

'Adrian? Caroline. Caroline Walker.'

'Morning, Caroline. What can I do for you?'

The voice on the other end of the line was reservedly friendly – the careful measured tone used between business associates and sometime social acquaintances.

Caroline cleared her throat, suddenly feeling like a petty child.

'Well, it's Les,' she began haltingly. She stopped.

'Yes?' responded Adrian.

'Once Les realises he's not going to win me back, he won't be taking any prisoners,' she burst out, abruptly. 'It will be every man for himself.'

She took a deep breath and willed herself not to cry as she reduced her once idyllic life to a few lines of naked, bitter truth.

'That means Rachel, of course, but I think he'll stop short of involving her too much. She's too important to him.' She paused, praying that she was right.

'So what else is there, exactly, Caroline?' ventured Adrian softly.

'My company, Adrian.' Caroline didn't raise her voice, but it was laced with a venom and ferocity that surprised herself, and she imagined she heard Adrian draw in a sharp breath. 'Sapphires & Rubies. When this gets nasty, Les will do his best to take it from me, I know he will. And we have to make sure that doesn't happen. We have to.'

Half an hour later, Caroline rubbed her temples wearily. Work usually energised her, inspired her, but today's events were quite simply wearing her out.

The rest of the conversation with Adrian hadn't particularly helped her mood. It was as bad as she'd feared, if not worse. In the event of a 50/50 split of their assets, Les could argue that he was entitled to half of her share of the company. But with a 30/30/30/10 split between her and the other three major shareholders, that would reduce her shareholding to a minority share. It made her vulnerable. And, she was discovering in her personal life, vulnerable wasn't something she enjoyed being. Of course, the same could apply to Caroline's entitlement to half of all his business concerns, and in an amicable separation they would almost certainly work to ensure that these concerns were divided up logically and fairly.

But logical and fair, she knew, wasn't the way Les worked when his back was up against the wall. He would go for the jugular – and Sapphires & Rubies was definitely Caroline's weak spot.

In despair, she looked in the small desk mirror next to her computer screen. The fine lines beneath her eyes seemed deeper than they had earlier, a pair of frown lines had appeared in her forehead and she was sure there were pucker lines developing around her top lip. But what did she expect? She was a middle-aged, exhausted, crabby, working mother and soon-to-be-divorcee. It was no wonder she was starting to look like one . . .

And in thirty-three hours exactly, she was due to meet a nineteen-year-old wannabe model at a pub for a drink. He was twenty-three years her junior, and she had clearly gone completely mad. There was no way she was on for it. No way at all.

She'd call him and cancel. Caroline's stomach lurched. OK, so she'd get *Trudi* to call him and cancel. But she needed to cancel him. ASAP.

Chapter 5

THE THREE-GLASS CEILING

Caroline held the box of waxing strips closer to the light and squinted at it. Why the bloody hell did they always print the instructions for home beauty kits so small? Why the bloody hell hadn't she booked a salon wax instead? And why the bloody hell hadn't she cancelled this stupid date when she'd had the chance?

There was a knock at the door.

'Caroline, darling, I'm not sure what you're doing in there, but I've just put the kettle on for a cuppa. Would you like one?'

Caroline put the box down and bit back her instinctive four-letter reply. As if tonight's antics weren't already making her feel like she'd regressed twenty years, her mother's presence was increasingly taking her back to teenage thoughts – and teen behaviour. If it wasn't so tragic, it might even be funny.

She raised her head to call through the door. 'No thanks, Mother – I'm just about to have a bath.'

There was a pause, and she could picture Babs shifting from

one leg to the other, so as to put her 'good' ear to the door. 'I know, darling – that's what you said. It's just that I didn't hear the bath actually running, so . . .' She let the comment trail off, and Caroline mentally finished it for her. '. . . *so you thought you'd come and have a nose into what I'm actually doing.*'

She waited until she heard her mother's footsteps pad further down the hall, and then, tossing the instructions aside, emptied the box of wax on to the cool marble of her bathroom floor next to the fluffy towels she'd discarded after her shower. She picked up the nearest strip. Sitting here in her underwear in the familiar surrounds of her spa-like white bathroom, leaning against her ceramic roll-top bath, freshly washed hair tied up in a towel turban, her toned body bathed in the spring sunshine shining through the Velux windows, and with Jo Malone candles flickering in recesses around the wall, she felt strangely liberated. How hard could it be? She'd pinched the box from Rachel's en-suite, and if her seventeen-year-old daughter was capable of a DIY leg wax, then *she* certainly was.

The pretty pink of the wax made Caroline think of the candy Wham! bars of her youth, and, pulling off the protective cover, she sniffed it compulsively. But it smelt of roses, not sweets, and she placed it gingerly on her legs. She pressed it down hard and rubbed it. There! Perfect. Only nineteen more to go . . .

As she applied the last strip to her leg, Caroline peered under her arm. Hmmm. There was a faint noticeable fuzz. In her how-to-wax quandary, she hadn't even considered *what* to wax. She hadn't picked out her outfit yet, but if she wore something sleeveless, that soft down would definitely be detectable. Decisively, she applied a strip to the contours of her armpit. Well, in for a penny . . .

Another thought occurred to her, and she blushed under her towel turban. Her eyes moved to her skimpy Rigby & Peller knickers, and she moved the elastic around her inner thigh a millimetre. Legs were a no-brainer. Armpits, considering their appearance, a must. But bikini line – surely not needed . . .?

She shook her head as if to banish bikini-line-related thoughts from it. What was she thinking? She was going on a first date, for goodness' sake – with a teenager! As if she'd get into any situation where the state of her bikini line would be the focus of attention.

But you're wearing matching black lace underwear, a little voice inside her head reminded her. *What's that all about?* Pinging the elastic of her briefs back into place, Caroline tried to convince herself that she often wore a flirty lace plunge bra rather than her comfortable and rather utilitarian nude T-shirt style.

She reached into a mirrored cabinet for another unopened box, and pulling out a tube, smeared a blob of cream across her top lip. No way was she going to attempt a DIY moustache wax – thank goodness she'd found the tube of bleach languishing at the back of her cupboard. Never mind that it was probably months (years?) out of date, it was better than any hint of dark hair. Again, she cursed the indecision that had not only led to her being in this predicament in the first place, but which meant that when she'd finally realised that she really had left it too late to pull out of the date – that she really was due to be at the pub with Adam in a matter of hours – she had also missed any hope of an appointment at her regular beauty salon.

Moving carefully so as not to catch her waxy legs, Caroline waddled barefoot through her bedroom. Holding her breath, she moved quickly past the walnut bed, the soft folds of the goosedown duvet in its crisply ironed Egyptian cotton cover. It was a little ritual she'd adopted since she'd asked Les to leave. For some reason, lingering in this room that had once been her retreat, her haven, her favourite place in the whole house made Les's absence worse. So she rushed through, not breathing until she was either safely under the duvet or safely in her walk-in wardrobe, her en-suite or on the landing outside. Breathing, Caroline had discovered, was tantamount to inhaling pain, and so she made sure she didn't indulge in the spaces where she'd once felt closest to Les.

In her walk-in wardrobe, she breathed in deeply, and looked at the rails of clothes helplessly. She didn't have a clue where to start. What did one wear to a night out in a *pub*? Walking down the centre of the tiny room, with her arms outstretched, she could touch the rail of clothes on each side and she wandered along it now, trailing her hands in the sleeves of tops, dresses, jackets and trousers as she passed. She reached the racks of shoes at the end, and stopped abruptly. Staring at the rows of Jimmy Choos, Manolos and Ginas, alongside her own Sapphires & Rubies designs, Caroline heard Babs give her age-old advice. '*Start with the shoes, darling.*' She grinned and surveyed her options. It was as good a place to start as any. Except ... glittery strappy sandals, soft ostrich leather courts, fierce patent platforms and leg-lengthening wedges – they were all here in abundance, but none seemed quite right for tonight. She sighed. To her right, several pairs of knee-length boots stood immaculately on their special shelf. She had a gut feeling even her faithful tan Marc Jacobs weren't going to cut it tonight.

She pulled out a black wrap DVF dress. It was one of her favourites; endlessly flattering, the soft jersey clinging to all the right curves, and creating the ones that her rail-thin body lacked. But tonight? A bit formal, austere even – it was dullsville play-safe and felt bookish when she mentally juxtaposed it to Adam's carefree youth. Her failsafe wear-anywhere Armani suit and a grey Burberry shift dress – the epitome of easy chic – were dismissed for the same reason. Even a ditsy Luella print shirt dress seemed blousy and *totally* uncool. She flicked through more hangers and pulled out a chiffon Sara Berman shirt in red leopard print. Worn with pearls and a pair of indigo bootleg Calvin Klein jeans, it had always looked quirkily cool, the pearls offsetting the sexiness of the blouse and adding an eclectic vintage feel to the jeans. But tonight, sexy meant mutton, and pearls would give it a granny-fashion feel. The last thing she wanted to do was accentuate her age . . .

Caroline sighed and, feeling a telltale trickle under her arm, remembered the fast-melting wax strips. She moved swiftly back to the bathroom. At least here she could make some progress.

Sitting on the edge of the bath, she lifted her arm tentatively. The strip attached to the wax had gone a little lumpy, and the wax gloopy. She pulled at the strip tentatively. It didn't want to come away. At least, *she* didn't want it to come away – it was going to hurt!

She pulled again, a little more forcefully, and dislodged the toe she was balancing on. With a loud crash, Caroline fell to the floor in a tangle of waxing, towels, bath products and a Jo

Malone candle, from which Pomegranate Noir wax trickled out to mix with the splodges of pink waxing strip.

'For crying out loud!' For want of any other outlet for her frustration, Caroline hit the marble floor with her clenched fist. It hurt. 'Ouch!'

'Mum?'

Caroline looked up sheepishly to see her daughter towering over her in the doorway, all long, gangly legs in black treggings, vintage tea dress and heavy black fringe over kohl-lined green eyes. She looked gorgeous. She looked like a rock chick. *She looked like Caroline wanted to look.*

With an unaccustomed pang, Caroline looked away shamefully. It was the first time she'd ever considered Rachel's youth, her poise, her opportunity, in comparison to herself. And she was shocked to find she felt something akin to – to what, exactly? Envy? Jealousy? She swallowed hard. She loved her daughter unconditionally. There was no way she should ever put herself in competition with her, surely?

Smiling brightly to cover up her consternation, Caroline lifted up her arm again. 'I'm in a bit of a pickle, darling. Fancy helping me out?'

Ten painful minutes later, Caroline padded back through to her wardrobe, touching her stinging armpits gingerly.

'You're sure it will go down, darling? Only I'm due to leave in forty minutes, and I'd like to be able to apply some deodorant before I go, at the very least.'

Rachel, striding purposefully in front of her, turned and gave her an amused look. It was the look, thought Caroline in passing, of a benevolent auntie indulging a small child.

'Mum, in a couple of minutes you won't even remember you've had anything done,' Rachel said, trying not to laugh. 'Anyhow, that'll teach you to read the instructions next time. Those strips are meant to be pulled off straight away, not twenty minutes later!'

'There won't be a next time. And the instructions didn't make that clear,' muttered Caroline. She smiled up at her daughter again, keen to change the subject and get on with the job in hand. 'Now, darling, what am I going to wear to this confounded drinks evening?'

'So, you want to look young and cool?' asked Rachel doubtfully.

And hot, added Caroline silently. Out loud: 'Yes, darling. I don't want to look like a doddery old maid. They're all a good ten years younger than me.'

And some. She was careful not to specify who 'they' were.

'And not too businesslike?' asked Rachel curiously.

'That's right,' said Caroline. Why the sudden inquisition? Rachel never showed any interest in the finer details of her social life. Why now, of all nights? 'It's just, you know, since your father . . .' *Strike me down*, she added silently, *for using my divorce to lie to my daughter*. She couldn't tell Rachel the real reason she was in a tizz, of course. But, heaven forbid, should this be the start of a downward spiral of deceit . . .

She brushed the unwelcome thought away. And anyway, this was just a one-off date that she'd been unable to get out of. She was definitely not going to do it again. Something to notch up to experience and move on from – a necessary part of her metamorphosis from the wreckage of her marriage. In a couple of months she'd come clean to Rachel about what she'd *really* been doing and they'd laugh together at her idiocy.

Her daughter turned to her, suddenly purposeful, and Caroline's heart nearly broke all over again when she saw the unadulterated love and concern in her eyes.

'Right, leave it with me,' said Rachel and disappeared back out of the room. Caroline stood gormlessly in the middle of her wardrobe, waiting for her to return. When she did, she was carrying a pair of her own faded grey Baxter jeans.

'The staple item for any night down the pub is a skinny jean,' Rachel explained animatedly. Caroline looked at her in surprise. Rachel was really enjoying this! 'So try these ones for size,' she continued, handing them to Caroline.

'Darling, I really don't think . . .'

'You'll get into them no problem,' insisted Rachel. 'You're pretty much my size normally, and you've been disappearing in front of my eyes over the past few weeks. Now, what shall we put with them . . . Here you go!'

She pulled out a petrol blue Prada blazer from the recesses of the wardrobe. Caroline let out a delighted cry. Of course! It was perfect. The shot silk material had a slight sheen to it and made Caroline's skin glow and eyes pop whenever she wore it.

'I think wear it with a white Calvin tee,' said Rachel over her shoulder as she rummaged around in the shoe rack. 'Classic cool. And these!' She pulled out a pair of dark grey suede Balenciaga shoe boots triumphantly.

Caroline took them from her gratefully. 'Darling, you're very good at this. You have a real talent for it!'

'No, Mum, I just spend a lot of time in pubs,' deadpanned

Rachel, embarrassed, and squirmed as Caroline tried to hug her. She turned on impulse and returned her mother's hug. 'I hope you have fun tonight, Mum,' she said earnestly into Caroline's shoulder. 'You deserve it.' She pulled away, finishing over her shoulder, 'I'd wear a leather cuff with that, though. It'll tough it up a bit.'

Caroline nodded, a lump in her throat preventing her from speaking. Suddenly, she wanted to gather her daughter to her, to tell her about her ridiculous plans for the evening, cancel Adam and snuggle down on the sofa with Rachel, eating popcorn and watching *Friends* reruns like they had when she was little.

But she didn't. Instead Caroline watched her daughter saunter off through her bedroom, off to Skype, Twitter and Facebook, leaving Caroline to finish getting ready.

Thirty-five minutes later, Caroline surveyed the results in the mirror. Her daughter certainly had a talent for putting a look together, she thought. To her surprise, the jeans fitted perfectly, accentuating her long legs and slim hips. Thanks to her unintentional heartbreak weight loss, the jacket was a little big on her, which lent it the 'boyfriend' feel of the moment. And the classic white T-shirt and chunkily expensive accessories gave the look an edge which she'd forgotten she could pull off. With her glossy black hair carefully blow-dried not to look too 'done', and minimal make-up, she could pass for a good ten years younger than she actually was.

Which was just as well, she thought wryly, as her date for the evening was a good ten years younger than that again … She walked carefully downstairs and collected her handbag from the hall table where she'd left it earlier that evening. Her keys were underneath it in a pile, and she picked them up, and then put them down again on impulse. Why hamper herself with the car?

'Byeee, Rachel! Bye, Mum! See you later.'

Feeling footloose and fancy free, Caroline didn't even wait for Babs to trill back to her, or for Rachel's muffled reply from deep in the recesses of the snug, and almost skipped through the front door and out on to the road, where the first vehicle to drive along was a vacant black cab.

'The Pembroke Castle, please.' The words sounded alien and she felt a shiver of the unknown mixed with – what? Excitement, yes, but also a sense of pride. This was her first spontaneous attempt at drawing a line between her past and the future and whatever lay ahead, she felt like fate was playing a part – as if it was a pivotal moment in her life.

The cab turned down another tree-lined street of well-kept Victorian houses, their whitewashed walls glowing luminously in the twilight, and she saw two girls in heels, leather jackets and skinny jeans walking along arm in arm, clearly also on a night out.

Oh, get a grip, Caroline, she told herself firmly. *You're doing what twenty-something women do on a Friday night – the only surprising thing is that it's taken you forty-two years to do it too.*

But she had never been very confident in bars and pubs, much preferring the predictable structure of a restaurant meal, or the comfortable safety of home. She felt a clutch of fear in her stomach as she imagined herself sitting opposite Adam for the whole evening. He was an up-and-coming model – a very pretty one, admittedly, but one barely out of school who'd probably only just started shaving. And she was an international businesswoman used to socialising with other high-flyers her own age or older. What on earth would he find to say to her? Or what, Caroline wondered with another rush of self-awareness, would *she* find to say to *him* . . .

'Here you go, love,' said the cabbie, pulling over outside a smart gastropub. A few hardy drinkers were sitting on the tables close to the pedestrian bridge, taking advantage of the mild spring evening. Caroline hoped Adam wouldn't want to sit outside – she hadn't factored evening chill into her outfit. But what if he was a smoker?

With everything in her body willing her to tell the cab driver to take her home again, Caroline wiped her clammy palms down her jeans, worked her lips together to distribute her lipstick, and opened the door.

'Here, let me get that.' The door swung open and Caroline, still hanging on to the inner door handle, looked up in surprise.

'Adam!'

He smiled. 'Yes, fancy seeing me here.' His husky voice was slightly more high pitched than she remembered, and he cleared his throat. He was nervous. The thought made Caroline feel better, and she smiled back.

'You look great,' he said.

'Thanks,' she said, self-conscious. She was still hanging on to the door, with one leg out of the cab and one leg in. She wobbled on her spiky heel as she realised how ridiculous she must look.

'I hate to ruin a beautiful moment, but some of us have got jobs to do,' grumbled the cab driver, leaning through the passenger window.

Adam smiled again, bashfully, and swept his arm out in front of her. 'Shall we?'

Caroline clambered the rest of the way out, paid the taxi driver, and took Adam's arm, giggling. Even in heels, the top of her head still only reached the bridge of his nose. He was really tall.

He bent down to kiss her briefly on the cheek, and Caroline nearly jumped out of her skin. As she pulled back, Adam went in to give her a second kiss on the other cheek, and they bumped noses painfully.

'Ouch,' she said.

He grinned sheepishly. 'Sorry. I always go for two. You're obviously into quality, not quantity.'

Caroline smiled and rubbed her nose, mortified. This wasn't quite the start she'd hoped for. But it was every bit the start she'd *imagined* . . .

He's nervous too, she reminded herself. 'Come on then. I could murder a drink!' she said, subconsciously adopting the bright 'motivational voice' she used at work when she needed to pep someone up.

Adam pushed open the door and indicated for her to walk under his arm as he held it for her. Trying not to linger at the sight of his tanned, toned forearm peeping out from under shirtsleeves rolled up over his jacket, she walked through the sage green doors into the warm hubbub of the bar beyond. Inside, the building was decorated in the ubiquitously smart rustic urban design of a mid-range gastropub. A faint smell of paint hinted that it was a fairly recently refurbished establishment, and as she approached Caroline smiled at the over-keen bar attendant wearing a pristine apron.

'I'd like a glass of Merlot, please,' she said. She didn't normally drink red wine on an empty stomach, but it seemed a bit more in keeping with the kind of persona she was projecting tonight. She was aware of Adam standing to her right, could just detect the faint smell of Aramis, but somehow couldn't bring herself to turn to him. She focused her attention brightly on the bar attendant.

'Large or small?'

'Ohhh, what the hell, I'll have a large. I'm not driving, after all,' she added to Adam unnecessarily. He grinned, a lopsided, shy grin that she found curiously endearing. He leaned on the bar to order a pint and Caroline took the chance to study his appearance. He was wearing a battered suede jacket over a stylishly crumpled cotton shirt and snugly fitted jeans show-casing a firmly honed bum. She averted her gaze quickly and leaned on the bar casually, determined to break the ice.

'So, do you live near here?'

'No – other side of London, actually,' he said. 'In Forest Hill.' He cleared his throat. 'It's in the south-east.'

Caroline laughed. 'I know it well,' she said. 'I grew up there. But it's not exactly the epicentre of cool, is it? Whatever made you choose to live there?' She was genuinely intrigued.

'I didn't,' he replied, looking her straight in the eye. 'My parents did. I still live with them.'

Caroline stared at him. She hadn't expected *that*. 'Oh,' she uttered lamely, unsure how else to respond.

They both looked around the bar awkwardly.

'So, erm, do you come here often, then?'

Adam shifted tentatively from one leg to another. 'No, not really. It's not what you'd call local.' Suddenly he raised his head, and fixed her with his gaze, his eyes dancing mischievously. 'I might ask you the same question. If you'd let me get a word in edgeways.' Caroline felt a frisson between them and shivered.

'That'll be ten ninety-five,' said the bartender, and Caroline automatically fished in her bag for her purse. Adam, hand in pocket, looked put out.

'I was going to get those.' Now his gaze was reproachful, and Caroline could have kicked herself. *Quit the parenting act, Walker!*

'Oh,' she said blushing. 'Well – maybe you can get the next one.'

Awkwardly they shuffled over to a cluster of tables. Adam made to sit down at the one closest to the bar, but Caroline headed for the most secluded corner spot. At the change of direction, Adam caught his foot on a table leg and half tripped, sloshing beer over the side of his glass.

He laughed self-consciously, and Caroline smiled politely. Oh dear. This wasn't exactly going smoothly.

They sat down in silence and looked at one another. Then they both looked down at their drinks. Then they both looked up at each other again.

'I –' they both started, and they laughed. 'You go first.' Again, in unison.

Caroline put out a hand and touched Adam's lightly. 'No, seriously, you go first.'

His grey-green eyes looked up at her from under long, dark lashes, and she felt herself shift uncomfortably under his gaze. There was something penetrating about the way he was looking at her, as if he could see into her soul. And lovely though those eyes were, she hadn't expected this level of intensity. She unlocked her eyes from his and fixed on an imaginary spot at the bar over his shoulder. Her heart stopped. In front of her, in the midst of a group of twenty-something girls standing around a bottle of rosé at the bar, was someone she recognised. She squinted exaggeratedly and, struggling to focus without her glasses, stretched her neck for a closer scrutiny. Yep, she was right. Her heart sank. Katrina Fothergill, the daughter of one of Sapphires & Rubies' most loyal clients. Caroline had known her since Katrina was at school. There was no way she wouldn't immediately recognise Caroline. Caroline felt the panic of certain exposure.

Wildly she looked left, and looked right. There was no way out. She looked back to the bar, and saw, as if in slow motion, Katrina turn her head in Caroline's direction. There was nothing else for it. In a flash, Caroline dived under the table and crouched there, heart pounding, between a polished table leg and a long-forgotten squashed chip.

'Caroline?' Adam's puzzled voice was muffled by the table. She made a noncommittal noise and waved a hand at him to try and stop him drawing attention to them.

Then his head appeared next to hers, upside down. 'Caroline, is everything OK?'

She smiled brightly and sat up, bashing her head on the underside of the tabletop.

'Yes! Yes, everything's fine!' she trilled. 'I just lost my earring, that's all!'

Adam studied the matching diamond studs in both her ears. 'Right . . .'

'But I found it! And, erm, I've put it back. So now, I can sit up again!'

Still upside down, Adam frowned in confusion. There was a pause. 'Right. So why don't you?'

'I'm coming!' sang Caroline, still desperately trying to buy time and feeling ever so slightly like she'd gone mad. 'Ready or not!' Tentatively, she peered around the table leg and over at the bar. To her relief, Katrina was now at the door, waving farewell to her friends. Caroline pulled herself up and sat back down, heart still racing, trying to act as if nothing untoward had occurred. She blinked at Adam, racking her brains for where they'd left off.

'So, erm, you were saying?' she asked hopefully.

Adam, still looking slightly perplexed, smiled shyly. 'I was just going to say – but you've probably already noticed – I'm not the world's best pub drinker.'

Caroline looked at him searchingly, interest piqued. 'What do you mean?' she said incredulously. Weren't all his generation hardened partygoers, brought up on the hedonistic combination of high disposable income and untold independence?

'Well, I know it's totally uncool, but I don't spend a hell of a lot of time in bars,' he said hesitantly. 'I find them a bit claustrophobic.'

'Then why ask me out to one?' said Caroline, even more intrigued now. That was how *she* felt about them!

Adam shrugged. 'It's just what you do, isn't it? Seemed as good a place as any. And besides, you're always in the papers out and about somewhere – I figured you'd be into it.'

Caroline baulked. Was that really how she came across, as some superficial socialite? She leaned forward interestedly. 'So where would you have ideally taken me, Adam?'

He gave a short, self-conscious laugh and looked away. 'Oh, I don't know. A romantic picnic somewhere, maybe.'

'A picnic?' Caroline tried to ignore the way the word 'romantic' was reawakening the butterflies in her stomach, and attempted to focus instead on what Adam was saying. She loved picnics – even if she hadn't been on one for years! Since Rachel was little, come to think of it. Caroline suddenly had an urge to run barefoot and feel grass beneath her toes, to lie on a blanket gazing up at the sky, and to drink warm white wine out of a plastic cup.

'Yes,' replied Adam defensively, looking at her searchingly to see whether she was mocking him.

She smiled teasingly. 'And where would we go on our romantic picnic?'

'We'd go to Greenwich Park,' he said without missing a beat.

He gazed unblinkingly into her eyes. Now, it seemed that her heart stopped for a millisecond. Greenwich Park. Her favourite place in the whole world. Where she'd spent hours and days of her girlhood. Where Les had proposed. Which was, she suddenly realised with a jolt, probably the last time she'd been there. 'Greenwich Park?'

'Yep. You never been there before?'

'Yes, of course I have,' said Caroline defensively. 'I spent hours there as a girl. '

'Well, you'll know why it's my favourite place in the world then,' said Adam passionately. 'There's a bench on top of the hill by the Observatory. It's like reading the pulse of the city. In the early evening you can watch London hurry home, come back out again, and then go to sleep. You can see the sky turn from blue, to twilight grey, to midnight blue and watch the stars race the street lamps to light up London.'

Caroline gazed at him, mesmerised, glass hovering halfway up to her mouth. Adam had picked the very spot she loved the most. Exactly the spot where Les had asked for her hand in marriage all those years ago. The one spot she thought she could have described better than anyone. Yet here was Adam describing it in words akin to poetry. She felt an unfamiliar feeling deep inside her. Was this coincidence, or fate ... or something more?

As she stared into his eyes, she saw a change in his, too. No longer simply admiring, there was something else – something ...

'Sorry, I just need to ...' he started, and leaned over, brushing her lips with his. Caroline felt a rush of white heat run through her, and instinctively looked around to see if anyone had seen. When she turned back to him, Adam's eyes were dancing again. She felt her legs tremble, and nearly dropped her glass of wine.

'Sorry. But you're beautiful. And I'm nervous. I just had to redress the balance,' he murmured. His breath was warm and touched her face like a soft breeze. Caroline felt like she was melting inside.

He leaned back and locked her with his eyes again. 'So, where would your picnic be?'

'Time at the bar, ladies and gentlemen,' called the bartender.

'Time at the bar?' repeated Caroline. 'Isn't that a bit archaic? I thought pubs were open all night these days.'

Adam chuckled and shook his head. 'No, only if they want

to be. Most stick to the old rules unless there's a pretty good reason. And I reckon tonight –' he looked around him at the handful of people left '– is not a good enough reason.'

'How systematic of them,' said Caroline wonderingly. She smiled and started to hum. 'System Aaa-dict! I never can get enough ... doo doo doo doo. Reminds me of my Five Star days. System Aaaaa-dict!'

Adam looked at her in bemusement. Caroline laughed hysterically, then, seeing that he hadn't found it quite as funny as she had, stopped abruptly.

'Don't you remember that one? It was one of their biggest hits back in ... Oh,' she trailed off as she realised he probably hadn't even been born then, 'no, of course you don't.' There was a momentary awkwardness as she looked around her at the emptying pub. 'So, if this is throwing out time ...'

'... then it must be time to go home,' finished Adam for her with a wink.

Caroline stared at him. Go home? Where to? Together? To his house? Surely not to her house? She gazed across at that mouth, those lips, and thought longingly of kissing him again.

She stood up slightly shakily. She'd had too much to drink. In fact, she'd broken the three-glass ceiling – that unwritten rule of drinking-before-eating for the over-thirties. Two glasses of wine, and she didn't know where she was. Three glasses, and she didn't know *who* she was. It was so unlike her – it must have been the nerves. And the whole thrill of the unexpected. He was so ... different to how she'd imagined. Adam put his hand on her arm, and she felt that spark again. She withdrew it quickly, and rubbed it absently.

'Caroline? I said, are you planning to get a cab?' Adam was

standing up now, buff muscles rippling under his shirt as he pulled on his jacket.

'Oh, yes – yes, of course.' She fumbled around for her bag. As she moved away, Adam gently placed his hand in the small of her back and then let it drop, his fingertips lightly moving across her bottom.

Caroline's heart beat a little faster, and her mouth felt dry, her hands clammy. Suddenly, the rules had changed. Something had happened between her and Adam, and he was no longer a gangly youth taking his chances with an older woman. They were equals. He was – she cringed to herself – special.

Caroline drew a deep breath, willing herself sober. She could feel the beginnings of panic. How much of this was real, and how much the result of her speed wine drinking through-out the evening? OK, so she and Adam had shared a 'moment' or two. But she'd turned from puritanical abstainer to sex-hungry predator in a matter of hours. What happened now? What was date etiquette these days? She'd spent years teaching Rachel how to deal with unwanted advances, how to equip herself psychologically for The First Time and all those times afterwards, but suddenly she felt miserably ill informed and totally unprepared herself. What were the *real life* rules about sex? Was she even sure that's what she wanted?

Outside, the evening chill had set in. Caroline, glad of its sobering effect on the red wine, pulled her jacket closer around her as Adam stood at the edge of the pavement hailing a cab. After a couple of moments, one pulled over, and Adam opened the door for her.

'Your chariot awaits, madam.'

Caroline smiled and curtsied. 'Why thank you.' He might

only be nineteen, but Adam had an endearing turn of phrase – almost, at times, old fashioned. It gave him the air of an old soul, and an element of maturity.

She skipped past him. What the hell. She was just going to take his lead on this and run with it. She was hardly ever irresponsible, after all. No time like the present to start!

She flopped back into the seat and waited for Adam to join her – but he made no move to get in the cab. Instead, he stood grinning at her from the doorway.

'I had fun tonight, Mrs Walker,' he said.

Caroline stared at him. So he wasn't planning on seducing her after all?

'So did I,' she admitted lamely.

Quickly, he swung into the cab and kissed her, softly and sweetly on the lips. Like the one in the pub, the kiss was lingering and filled with promise – until he pulled away and hopped out of the car again.

'Let's do it again soon,' he said, pushing closed the door. 'I'll call you?'

'Yes, do,' said Caroline weakly. She felt alive with desire, and stung with perceived rejection. He hadn't even tried to do more than kiss her! Did he not fancy her? Nineteen-year-olds were meant to be at their sexual peak. Adam was meant to be *desperate* for more . . .

She leaned forward. 'Primrose Hill,' she said to the driver and then turned and looked at Adam, as he stood watching the cab pull off. Even bathed in the orange glow of the street lamp, he looked gorgeous, his dark curly hair boyishly mussed, the light casting shadows across his chiselled features. He gave her a relaxed wave and then started walking along the pavement after the taxi, a slow, casual lope with all the confidence and leisure of his youth. As the taxi increased the physical distance between them, Caroline felt the metaphysical closeness ebb away. Adam's teenage stroll seemed to her to underline the gulf – in both age and status – between them.

He waved again at the disappearing car, and Caroline felt her stomach lurch again. She didn't just fancy him. She *liked* him.

But enough was enough. It could never work. Time to get real. She was never doing that again. Ever.

Chapter 6

IF I WAS TWENTY YEARS YOUNGER ...

For the first time that she could ever remember, Caroline felt a flutter of nerves as she climbed the staircase to her office. The slightly nauseous, gut-twisting feeling of Sunday nights when you hadn't finished your homework. The churning anticipation of childhood, when you'd done something naughty and were about to be found out.

Not that she'd done anything wrong, of course. But she'd spent her weekend swinging between shame at her date with Adam on Friday, and secret glee at how much fun she'd had. Not that she admitted it even to herself, of course. But as the weekend had progressed it had become tinged with disappointment at the lack of contact from Adam – alongside the confirmation that she'd been right all along. She should never have gone, and she should certainly never go there again.

So after last night's stern talking to – from herself, to herself – she'd thought that was the last of it. But today, there were nerves. She was convinced that someone, somehow, would know what she'd been up to.

'Morning Caroline.'

She smiled at Julie, her comely receptionist. 'Morning, Julie.'

Julie, like Trudi and like Molly, her finance director and several other key members of the team, had been with her since the word go, and Caroline had never regretted the choice of any of them, especially steady, loyal, funny Julie, instead of what would have doubtless been a steady stream of fly-by-night prettier front of house 'faces'. Julie's ever-increasing brood of grandchildren and soap opera of a life had kept Caroline entertained for years, just as the glamorous goings-on at Sapphires & Rubies had transfixed Julie, and Caroline knew Julie looked upon her as an extended – if rather sophisticated – member of her clan.

'So, how did it go?'

Caroline jumped and stared at her in horror. How on earth did Julie *know*? She hadn't mentioned her date to anyone. Unless . . . unless she'd been seen, out with Adam? Hurriedly, she racked her brain for anyone at the pub who could possibly have known who she was – other than Katrina. She definitely hadn't seen her and Caroline was certain there hadn't been anyone else there.

'What do you mean?' she responded, more sharply than she intended.

'How did it go?' repeated Julie with a wink, drawing out the 'go' musically.

'I don't know what you're talking about,' said Caroline crossly, blushing furiously, and bustled hurriedly past Julie's desk.

'The shoot day, of course! I had a day off on Friday,

remember? I never had the chance to find out how it all went.'

Of course. The shoot day. Julie looked on any kind of photo shoot as a Major Event, involved as she was in organising castings, greeting photographers, and ordering couriers to and from studios, and although she'd always refused the opportunity to go along to one, still insisted on knowing everything about every shoot before *and* after.

Caroline visibly relaxed, and shook her head in embarrassment. 'I'm sorry, Julie, I'm a little distracted today. It went fantastically well, thank you – the pictures were wonderful. We should get the low res edit in today – I'll be sure to show you. It should be our best campaign yet!' she added with an over-bright smile.

'I'm not surprised, with that young hottie heading it up,' said Julie, leaning across reception and tapping the side of her nose with a long scarlet fingernail. 'I saw his picture – very good choice, if I may say.' She dipped her voice to a stage whisper. 'Shame we couldn't have had him come into the office for his casting, though.' She gave a deep, gravelly laugh and winked at Caroline, who hurried away. Really! Of all the people for Julie to develop some kind of virtual crush on. Anyone would think she really did suspect something.

'I tell, you, Caroline, if I was twenty years younger . . .'

. . . *then you'd still be old enough to be his mother*, finished Caroline to herself as she scuttled across the production floor to the safe haven of her office. Once inside, she closed the door softly and leaned up against it, inwardly chiding herself. That was not only mean: she could almost apply it to herself.

Is that what everyone who'd seen her and Adam out together on Friday night would have thought?

She sat back in her chair and swung it gently. It was all academic, really. She'd got away with going out with Adam once, without calamity, and that was enough. And whether she wanted to risk it again or not, he hadn't called anyway, so there was nothing else to do but chalk it up to experience and move on. Find someone her own age, for a start.

A soft knock at the door brought her back to real time, and she smiled as Trudi looked around the door holding a mug of steaming coffee.

'Oh thank you, Trudi,' said Caroline, grateful for the distraction. 'How are you, and how was your weekend?'

'Oh, you know – good, thanks,' said Trudi. Caroline frowned. Her PA seemed edgy. Nervous, even. 'How was yours?'

'It was – erm – lovely, thank you,' said Caroline, feeling unaccountably guilty. 'Quiet.'

Trudi nodded in understanding, and opened her mouth as if she was going to say something, then thought better of it and closed it again.

Caroline leaned forward. 'Trudi, is everything OK?'

Her PA turned to her with a smile. 'Yes, of course. Why wouldn't it be?'

Caroline looked at her inquisitively. It was exactly the same theatrical smile she'd used herself earlier on Julie. Now she *knew* something was up. She smiled patiently. 'Because you're acting strangely,' she said.

Trudi shook her head efficiently. 'No, no, not at all. I've just got a lot on this morning. You know, after the shoot and all ...' She held her breath and looked anywhere but at

Caroline. 'So, erm, I never really checked with you on Friday that everything went OK with the shoot. No problems, or anything?'

Caroline's guard was now well and truly up. 'No, Trudi, no problems or – *anything*,' she said, emphasising the final word. 'Why?'

'Oh, no reason,' said Trudi, backing out of the room. 'No reason – I'll get on with sorting everything now. Oh, and Caroline?'

'Yes, Trudi?'

'Your mother called again. She says she's not sure whether to think you're purposely ignoring her or that I've turned into the most inefficient PA in the world.'

Caroline stifled a smile. 'Trudi, she's practically moved in with me. She knows more about my whereabouts and my state of mind than I do. There is no need for her to maintain permanent radio contact with me.' They shared a complicit smile.

'Door closed again?' Trudi started to pull the door shut after her.

'Open,' said Caroline firmly, brushing the thought of Babs aside. There were more important things to deal with this morning. Her radar was sensing trouble. Something was up. Someone must have found out about her and Adam. And so the last thing she wanted was to be shut away from her team.

The next hour and a half confirmed her suspicions. It seemed that everyone was acting strangely. Molly lingered uncertainly at the door to Caroline's office when she came with her customary good morning greeting. Leroy, her creative director, simply nodded through the office window and then hurried past rather than coming in for his usual chat, and even Eddie the postman gave her a wide berth, whistling edgily and waving rather than stopping to speak to her.

Try as she might, Caroline couldn't concentrate on the day's papers, her emails or priorities for her mid-morning production meeting. There was only one conclusion: they had all found out about her sordid date and didn't know how to approach her about it. Not that her private life was any of their business, she reasoned, but instinctively she knew that this was one scandal that would cross the boundaries of even the most loyal team. Their newly separated – not even divorced! – boss, dating a nineteen-year-old model that she'd met on a work shoot only days previously. Who was about to star in the biggest advertising campaign she'd ever run. She cringed. It sounded pretty sordid even to her ears.

Dated, Caroline reminded herself. Past tense. Not happening now. Not happening in the future.

She leaned forward over her desk. 'Trudi!' Her PA wheeled her chair backward from her desk so she could see Caroline. 'I've had none of the trade press today. Has *Bespoke* come in yet?'

A look of guilt flashed across Trudi's face at the mention of the fashion retail trade's monthly magazine. 'Oh, have you not seen that yet?' she said innocently. 'It's knocking around somewhere . . . I'm sure I saw it earlier.'

'Well, it shouldn't be "knocking around" anywhere until I've seen it,' said Caroline sternly, her conspiracy radar on red alert now. 'Please track it down and kindly ask whoever has it not to borrow it until I've seen it next time.'

'Yes, of course Caroline,' Trudi murmured, and wheeled herself back to her desk. Caroline waited for a couple of moments, guessing what was coming next.

She wasn't wrong. She heard a shuffling from Trudi's desk. 'Oh!' said Trudi in mock surprise. 'Look, it's here – it must have got caught up in this pile of papers.' She reappeared at the door, this time standing, and handed Caroline the magazine.

'Humph,' said Caroline, then groaned as she saw the lead feature. 'Oh God, what's he doing plastered all over the front page?' Don MacCaskill's picture was beaming at her out of the pages, all wolfish grin, Grecian 2000 hair and Hollywood white smile, from the middle of an in-depth interview detailing his plans for Morton for the next financial year. She looked up at Trudi. 'Is this what all the secrecy this morning was about?' she asked kindly. 'You should know better than that, Trudi. This kind of splash isn't going to upset me – he'll have given them something in return for this kind of coverage. A year's worth of display ad pages, for example, or – I don't know. Something more underhand, knowing him.' Trudi opened her mouth and then, seeming to think better of it, shut it again.

Idly, Caroline turned the pages, uninterested in Don's rhetoric. She'd heard enough of that, and his opinion of her and Sapphires & Rubies over the years in the form of dirty gossip and sarcastic asides at industry parties and the like – she certainly didn't need to read it in black and white. Trudi cleared her throat uncomfortably. 'Ummmmm.'

Caroline lifted her head. 'Yes, Trudi? Was there anything else?'

She went back to the magazine, still turning the pages.

'It wasn't so much the feature with Don MacCaskill that I was worried about you seeing,' Trudi said slowly.

'Oh?' said Caroline, still turning the pages. 'Then what was it?' Trudi opened her mouth to answer, but again, no sound came out. This time, there was no need. There, in print, was the answer for Caroline to see herself. Right across the diary page spread. SHOOT TO THRILL: WALKER REBOUNDS FROM MARRIAGE SPLIT

Her mouth went dry. So this was why everyone had been acting so weird. This was why everyone had been avoiding her. A grubby insider splash on the shoot — on *her*.

She forced herself to read on. It was your typical dime-a-dozen muckraking story on how the end of her marriage was 'clearly' taking its toll on her — how she'd turned up at the shoot dressed far too young for her age (*since when did Caroline Herrera and biker boots equal mutton?* thought Caroline absently). But worse was to come. According to the report she'd been 'all over' the photographer and young assistants — not to mention her very special focus on one Adam Geray, seventeen-year-old male model star of the shoot.

Trudi cleared her throat again. 'According to Molly, that model is actually nineteen, not seventeen,' she said timidly. 'So you can see the kind of quality writer they've used for it — they can't even get their basic facts right.'

Caroline put her head in her hands in despair. The fact that she'd been worried about some of her nearest and dearest discovering she'd been for a drink with Adam now seemed completely inconsequential. Things were much worse than she could ever have imagined. She'd been portrayed to the whole industry as some sex-crazed marriage cast-off intent on male attention from any quarter. And even though Caroline knew she hadn't behaved with any impropriety, how was anyone reading it to know?

But there was worse. This would cast her in the eyes of potential clients as the kind of woman who put her emotions before business, who let the lines between business and pleasure blur for the sake of a quick flirt and a superficial ego boost. All the years of carefully constructing her steely, confident business persona would crumble in an instant.

What's more, it wasn't going to do her position in her forthcoming divorce any favours. When it got nasty, Les was sure to gather up any ammunition he could in his bid to deflect attention from himself as the villain of the piece – and what else was this but handing him a virtual shotgun?

Most troubling of all was where the story had come from. It had to be a MacCaskill tip-off. This was undoubtedly what he'd given the paper in return for the cover splash. This was a sign to her that he meant business. This was luxury warfare. The question was, where was he getting his intelligence?

Caroline looked at her watch: 5.30 p.m., and she was exhausted. The phone hadn't stopped ringing all day, with thinly disguised calls from national diary magazines, investigative reporters and even worse, a tabloid hack – not to mention 'concerned' enquiries from clients and competitors alike. She had to hand it to MacCaskill – he'd played an ace card this time around.

Of course, as Trudi had drily pointed out, all this was better than no calls at all – which is the way some businesses would have been treated by their associates in similar circumstances.

At least, it seemed, her team were still fully behind her – and just as well, considering that each of them had been targeted in one way or another by journalists looking for an international slur or off-guard comment. Not only did her team know Caroline well, not only had several of them been present at the shoot, but they knew what MacCaskill was capable of, and were angry at his attempts to discredit their boss.

Caroline sighed and picked up her bag. She'd had enough. Rachel had a 'reading week' from school, and Babs had finally taken the hint and left, whisking her granddaughter off to her house in the country for some 'fresh air' and a change of scene. 'A change is as good as a rest,' she'd said firmly, when Caroline had half-heartedly opened her mouth to protest about uprooting Rachel, even if it was only for a break. She guessed her mother was right – it *would* do Rachel some good – but after the recent upheavals, Caroline felt that she should be keeping her daughter close by. She had intended working late tonight to catch up on her ever-expanding email inbox, but the idea of spending any more time in her office – filled as it was with elaborate bouquets sent by sympathetic acquaintances (Giles, one of the targets of the story, included) – had lost its appeal. The prospect of an evening all to herself at home was increasingly attractive: a chance to hunker down and hide away from the world and its nastiness.

Running the gauntlet of commiserating farewell smiles from her employees, Caroline escaped from the office and into the fresh air. She breathed in deeply, then looked around suspiciously. She'd had on–off experience of the paparazzi, and realised that right now she was a prime target for them. Today's *Bespoke* story wouldn't justify a national newspaper splash, but it had put her back on the tabloids' radar, and there was nothing to stop them muckraking around for more divorce dirt. Dipping her head, she hurried off to find her car.

Against her hip, she felt her phone vibrate through the leather of her handbag. More fallout to deal with, no doubt. Arriving at the car, she fished around for her keys and pulled out her BlackBerry. She climbed into the front seat, and nearly fell out when she read the text.

Evening gorgeous. How about round two sometime this week? Adam x

Caroline was hardly aware of her journey home as she drove, heart racing. Clearly there *was* one person in the world who hadn't read the *Bespoke* story. And why would he? It was, after all, a small story aimed at a very niche readership. She felt exhilarated, excited – and slightly ridiculous. But she'd convinced herself that she was never going to see Adam again. So why this kind of reaction? She needed to stop acting like a teenager and start thinking about how she could let him down gently.

Parked outside her house, Caroline contemplated her phone. She felt breathlessly out of her depth, but was determined to do this properly. A text just felt wrong. On impulse, she dialled his number. He picked up almost instantly.

'Adam?'

'That's me. Caroline?' His voice rose as if incredulous that she'd called.

'Yes, yes it's me. Listen, about your text. I just think – I'm not sure . . .' She hesitated. What the hell. After the day she'd had, the very last thing she should be doing was accepting an offer of a second date with Adam. But, against all odds, it was exactly what she felt like doing.

'Yee-ees?'

'I'm not sure I can do any time this week – I'm crazily busy every night with business commitments,' Caroline said finally, the words falling over each other to get out of her mouth. There was a disappointed silence at the other end of the line. 'But I'm – how about – I could do *tonight*?'

There was another momentary silence.

'Well, I'm sure I could move a few things around,' he said slowly.

'Oh, look, if you're busy . . .' said Caroline hurriedly, already regretting her over-keen response.

'You know what? All I've got on tonight is a Pot Noodle and a regular fixture with my PS3,' laughed Adam good-naturedly. 'There's a pretty good diner near you. Fancy a burger and a Coke? My treat.'

A hiccup of laughter burst from Caroline. On their first date, she'd insisted on paying for at least three-quarters of the night, and she restrained herself from doing the same tonight. 'Well, in that case, how can I refuse?'

'I'll text you the details,' said Adam. 'See you there at eight.'

Caroline put the phone down, still laughing, and pulled down the visor mirror. She took in her face, the first time she'd seen it smiling today, and wondered exactly who it was staring back at her. The old Caroline wouldn't have done this – flown in the face of trouble and invited even more. The weird thing was, although she knew it was wrong, it felt so *right* . . .

'So why go into modelling if you hate it?' probed Caroline. A couple of beers and a surprisingly tasty burger had lifted her spirits. It was now 10.30 pm, and they were strolling back along Green Street. It was early, even by her conservative standards. Adam, however, had a job at the crack of dawn and he had learnt his lesson from the Sapphires & Rubies shoot and was planning an early night.

He sighed. 'I don't *hate* it. I mean, the point of it is, if I play my cards right I'm going to make a stack of money in a short time which will mean I can then do what I want to do. But modelling's not exactly going to change the world, is it? Not to mention the fact that being pimped out on a daily basis by my agency isn't the greatest feeling in the world.'

'But your agency is one of the best,' said Caroline encouragingly, surprised by his intensity. 'And look at it this way. If you persuade a woman to buy the scent of her dreams when she see the Sapphires & Rubies ad, you'll have changed her life for the better – for she'll feel pampered, spoilt, and wearing it will make her smell great *and* boost her self-esteem. And you'll certainly have boosted my bank account! But you know, there's more to it than that,' she added hurriedly, as she saw his face fall at her flippancy. This obviously meant a lot to him. 'I mean, the whole industry is based on fantasy, and that's what we sell. If your picture can help someone escape their own particular brand of reality every once in a while, making their life a better place to be, isn't that making the world a better place? Albeit indirectly . . .'

'Humph,' grunted Adam. 'Let's just say it's not the kind of escapism I'd anticipated creating.'

'And what exactly *had* you anticipated doing?' said Caroline, intrigued.

'Making films,' said Adam shyly. 'I'd rather be behind the camera than in front of it. I've got ideas for how to combine digital photography with graphic design in film. I've got a place at the New York Film Academy starting in January next year. That's if I can afford it. If not, it's a UK university for me. Or continue what I'm doing, as the monkey, not the organ grinder.' He scuffed his shoe along the pavement, kicking an imaginary ball. 'But really, the most important job I'll ever have is a lifelong relationship. Like, it's all about working together on life every day, isn't it? And surely that's the biggest job that any-body could ever have.' Suddenly, he broke into a loping run and, grabbing at a low hanging branch, swung from it.

Caroline smiled at the fickleness of his youth. One minute philosophising, the next leaping around like a kid. Caught up in her and Les's very grown-up world of work and bringing up a daughter, she'd forgotten how uncomplicated young men could be. And she liked it. She was finding it liberating: exhil-arating, even. She felt something twang inside her – and it was anything but maternal.

She laughed as Adam slipped off the branch and struggled to keep his balance on the path. Running over, she grabbed his arm and helped him steady himself.

Giggling, they wobbled before gaining their balance. Caroline dropped her arms, but Adam kept his around her.

'This feels good,' he said, his grey-green eyes sparkling as they looked straight into hers, and he leaned in to kiss her.

It was the softest, sweetest kiss, and Caroline was momentarily lost. But before she could stop herself, her eyes darted to the left and then the right. She'd been comfortable in the diner, feeling sure that no one she knew was likely to walk in, but even though it was dark, here she was in the next street to her home. What if someone saw them? What if there were paparazzi lurking around?

At the thought, she stiffened and felt Adam pull away. He let his arms drop to his side, and he shuffled uncomfortably.

Caroline stretched her arm out to him. 'I'm sorry, Adam, I—'

'No, it's cool,' he said, shrugging, and started to walk slowly down the road again, head down.

Caroline hurried to catch him up, aghast that she had upset him, but eyes still searching out every dark garden for a hidden camera – or neighbour. 'No, really, I'm sorry. It's just ... look, stop a minute, will you?' They were about to turn into her street, and she couldn't have this conversation with him there. He turned to her sulkily. She had to reach up to touch his shoulders, and she grabbed hold of both of them. 'Something happened at work today ... a business rival is out to discredit me, and he's using my marriage breakdown as a way to get at me. All day I've been paranoid about the paps, and I suddenly remembered about it. If they had caught us kissing – well. It would be kind of disastrous for me.'

Adam looked up at her, eyes bright again. 'Only kind of?'

Caroline stared back at him mischievously. 'All right then, totally, horribly, outrageously disastrous.'

'Well, then, we'd better hurry back to your house, hadn't we?'

Caroline's heart lifted. He'd understood. And with her mother and Rachel staying at Babs's house in Hertfordshire, Caroline could maybe invite Adam in – and they could maybe revisit that kiss behind closed doors . . .

They strolled along in companionable silence. Caroline could tell Adam was being careful not to put his arm around her, or to let his hand brush hers. Funny that he hadn't questioned her more about exactly *what* had happened in the office. Instead, he'd just accepted it.

As they turned into her road, Adam stopped and caught her hand briefly with his. 'I'll say goodnight here then,' he said. 'We wouldn't want any of your neighbours grassing you up to the press, now, would we?'

Caroline smiled, feeling rather foolish. In the half-light it was hard to tell if Adam was gently teasing her or genuinely mocking her.

'Well, you're welcome to come in for a coffee,' she managed weakly.

'Oh, I don't think that's a good idea,' said Adam. This time his tone was *definitely* teasing. 'There might be a horrid paparazzo hiding in a hedge to take our pictures. It's fine – I can walk to the tube from here.'

They stood awkwardly for a moment. Then Adam touched his forehead in a casual salute.

'Well, Mrs Walker, I've had a very fine time tonight,' he said, his voice deep and husky. 'So I'll bid you goodnight.' He touched his fingers to his lips in farewell and then loped off into the darkness.

Caroline stood rather forlornly by the street sign watching the night swallow him up, feeling irrationally abandoned and let down.

Well, Caro, she thought helplessly. *You played a blinder there, didn't you?*

Chapter 7

THE FINEST STUFFED PIG'S EAR IN NEW YORK

'The only thing that would improve this place,' said Esther, wiggling her pert bottom into her seat, 'is a booking policy.'

Caroline tutted as she took the seat next to her. 'Aah, but then you'd complain that it had sold out and lost what made it famous in the first place.'

'I'm right there with Esther, honey,' put in Maryanne, bagging the next seat along. It was an age since the three of them had been together – and the first time since Caroline's marriage break-up and her now obsolete row with Maryanne – and there was no point letting a husband get caught in the crossfire of catch-up conversation. 'I was hungry *before* my hour-and-a-half-long aperitif.'

'Maybe that's the secret of its success,' said her husband Anthony with a nod to Maryanne's fourth dirty martini and a wry smile. 'Everyone is so completely sozzled by the time they take their seats, they could be served up with any old rot and think it was haute cuisine.'

He reached around the table and slapped Maryanne's bottom playfully. She smiled up at him adoringly. Caroline gazed at them. To anyone — even their best friends — they looked like the closest of close couples. Yet Maryanne was *cheating* on him. It beggared belief. She banished the thought from her mind. During the phone call she'd made to Maryanne to patch up their friendship, she'd promised not to judge her friend's behaviour again.

'Uh-huh,' disagreed Seth, Esther's diminutive cosmetic surgeon husband with a knowing shake of his head. 'This place does the finest stuffed pig's ear in New York.'

'Possibly the *only* pig's ear in New York,' observed Esther drily. Even sitting down, Esther towered over her husband, her new shoulder-length blonde bob accentuating her long, elegant neck. They made an incongruous couple — but then, thought Caroline ruefully, she knew first hand how appearances could be deceptive.

'Coming from the woman who bemoans the loss of Tavern on the Green to the New York restaurant scene!' retorted Seth. 'You'd have been lucky to get a lukewarm pork chop there.'

'Hey, Seth, the Tavern was my favourite too,' reminded Caroline mock-warningly. 'You diss Esther, you diss me too.'

'A prehistoric fairground with Eisenhower-era menu,' Seth continued regardless. 'No wonder it went bust.'

'Or, as I prefer to remember it, a fairytale venue with old-fashioned magic charms,' responded Caroline. 'For me, New York lost part of its heart when it lost the Tavern.' She thought fondly of the unashamed old-world-charm-meets-showbiz-glitz of the Tavern — its outdoor spaces lit by thousands of twinkling fairylights strung in the trees, the interior decorated in Gilded Age décor, its stunning crystal room home to vast, elaborate chandeliers – and the whole lot served by a live band, playing to a usually heaving dance floor. They'd all enjoyed many dinners there – but, like her marriage to Les, the restaurant hadn't lasted the distance, and she was going to have to relegate it to her past along with her estranged husband.

However, although it was the Tavern's polar opposite in every way, the Spotted Pig came a close second to it in entertainment value, she conceded as she looked around at her fellow diners, a conglomerate of Manhattan's trendiest and most successful residents packed into the pair of wood-plank rooms decorated with mismatched vintage fabrics, pig and mackerel mementoes, and window-box herbs. The wonder of this place, she thought, was that these people were the types who usually wouldn't stand for a five-minute wait in most other establishments – yet they were clearly so taken by its folksy-chic unpretentiousness that they were prepared to go along with the restaurant's 'drop-in only' policy, which allegedly made no concession to frequency of visit, fame nor . fortune: would-be diners could face a wait of up to two hours for a table. And, judging by some of the well-known faces dotted around the restaurant tonight, attacking their plates and wine glasses with an abandon forgotten in many of the city's diet-obsessed eateries, they weren't bluffing. Even rail-thin starlets cheated on their regimes with Roquefort-laden chargrilled burgers surrounded by thick tangles of shoestring fries.

'Jennifer Aniston was in here the other night,' said Esther to Caroline in a stage whisper, picking up her menu and speaking behind it theatrically. 'With her latest beau.' She drew out the 'eau' for emphasis and nodded authoritatively.

Caroline smiled. No one could so much as sneeze on the New York social scene without Esther knowing about it. The third cog in the wheel from Caroline's university days, funny, vivacious, beautiful Esther had shrugged off mediocre grades at Oxford and moved to New York, where she had used her wealthy background, her mother's contacts and her own not imperceptible charms to 'land' (her words) up-and-coming surgeon Seth Goldberg. Since then, she had become a leading light of the city's charity circuit and its ladies who lunch – carving out a full-time occupation as – again, in her own words – a 'committee careerist'. Despite her many commitments, with no children demanding her time, Esther's main occupation was still herself and she had the high-maintenance, perfectly groomed appearance to prove it – not to mention her husband's skills with the knife to maintain it. Seth had famously given Esther's body a top-to-toe overhaul when she turned forty. The results had been astonishing: 'natural' rather than pneumatic, giving her the body of a twenty-year-old – and her face the high cheekbones, flawless complexion and smooth brow of a model some ten years younger. With her lively hazel eyes and cheekily arched eyebrows, it was hard to tell she'd had anything done at all, especially with the annual 'tweaks' Seth gave her to keep up the look. This signature has-she-hasn't-she style of work had earned him worldwide fame, and fees that vastly outstripped those surgeons with more obvious trademarks – not to mention, in his wife, a walking advert for his work.

But inside the immaculate Upper East Side exterior, Esther was a loyal, kind, funny friend who had, over the years, become the glue that kept the three friends together. While

Maryanne was winning over Hollywood and Caroline was knee deep in nappies, neither had the time nor, often, the inclination to keep in frequent contact, but Esther had always been there, despatching advice on life and love from her throne-like easy chair in her ostentatious penthouse apartment. Esther was the breathing embodiment of 'if you've got it flaunt it', from her choice of interior décor to her lavish jewellery, to her currently carefully tanned, eye-popping (but silicone perfect) décolletage.

Caroline self-consciously fingered her own black chiffon blouse, carefully undone to the button just above her bra. Esther's rather brash beauty always had the effect of making her feel uncommonly dowdy, however glamorous she had felt on dressing. Tonight, her friend was wearing a digital print silk-jersey Pucci dress with plunging neckline, vertiginous S&M style Giuseppe Zanotti shoes, and the ubiquitous diamonds dripping from everywhere possible. Esther's perfect Manhattan highlights were, as usual, showing not the slightest hint of her mousey brown natural colour, and were expensively straightened into a smooth, shiny 'do'.

'Good hair,' observed Caroline.

'Thanks, sweetie,' said Esther, patting it carefully. 'Glossier than normal, huh? I've found an adorable new guy at Michaeljohn. I heard he was a wonder with a Jewfro and look! He is. I'm thinking of taking Seth there.'

Caroline and Maryanne giggled as they looked across the table at Seth, oblivious in animated discussion of the wine list with Anthony and sporting a fast receding hairline. His days of wanting help controlling his hair were long gone – it was assistance in keeping any of it on his head that he was in need of.

111

Esther's lifelong hunt for a treatment to tame her unruly head of frizzy hair, however, was legendary.

Esther's eyes narrowed. 'But I've got to say it, darling, you're not looking too hot. So tired! You can't get away with that kind of neglect when you're as thin as you are.' She patted Caroline's hand sympathetically. 'I know you've been through it, but there's no need to let everyone know about it! Why don't you book in with Seth while you're over here for a couple of little boosters? Just a little minitox maybe. He'll have you looking thirty again in no time.' She raised one eyebrow into her boiled-egg-smooth forehead for emphasis.

Maryanne shot Caroline a sympathetic look. Esther had been waging war on their adversity to Botox for at least a decade, and took every chance she had to make her point.

Caroline laughed. 'You never give up, do you, Esther? And thank you, but I'm hoping that beauty sleep will afford me something close to the same results while I'm over here.'

'Sleep?' said Esther wonderingly. 'In New York City? Good luck with that . . .'

There was a momentary lull as the waiter arrived to take their orders. Amongst her closest friends, in the womb-like ambience of the restaurant, Caroline felt herself properly relax for the first time as thoughts of Les, Adam and Don MacCaskill melted into the Atlantic that separated them from her.

'So, Esther, Seth tells me he'd only had his iPad for two days before you snaffled it from under his eyes?' interrupted Anthony, leaning across the table.

Esther looked horrified. 'Snaffled? Wash your mouth out with soap, honey. He was only using it to watch DVDs and play around with iTunes. I need it for much more important things – my wardrobe, for a start.'

'Your wardrobe?' repeated Anthony stupidly. The rest of the table looked at Esther in confusion. Seth, who, like his wife, wore his wealth on his sleeve and was as dripping in gold signet and bracelets as she was in diamonds, snorted. 'Esther has her entire closet photographed and itemised on it.'

Esther frowned at him. 'Darling, I told you, it just wasn't working on my iPhone. I couldn't see the items clearly enough.'

Seth leaned forward to the rest of the group. 'Even though she's the one who bought them in the first place.'

Esther kicked him under the table. 'It's not about remembering what I've got. It's about styling them up, darling.'

'I call it iStyle,' interjected Seth.

Esther turned to the others. 'And it's so my people can then pull them out for me. And, not unimportantly, it's also so I can make a log of what I wore and when so I never repeat myself.'

'Which would be logical if you ever wore anything more than once,' grinned Seth, sitting back in triumph as if that comment had made him victor of the exchange.

'OK, you two, enough is enough,' Maryanne said laughingly, her wavy red hair catching the light as she shook her head in mock disbelief. They were all used to the quick-fire exchanges of the Seth-and-Esther double act. 'Esther, you kill me, honey. If I had one iota of your dedication to glam, the words "character actress" would never have come within a hundred metres of me. But priorities, please. I can see the food arriving. Let's eat!'

★

113

Caroline sat back in her lounge chair shaking her head help-lessly. 'Noooo! I was meant to be having an early night!'

'Oh come on darling, don't talk rot,' said Anthony, pouring her more champagne. Somehow an after-hours coffee back at the Soho Grand, where Maryanne and Anthony had taken a suite, had turned into two bottles of Veuve Clicquot. 'Anyhow, how often do the six of us get together? Ooops, sorry darling, I meant five . . .' he trailed off, fingering his cravat and then running his hands through his foppish dark blond hair in embarrassment. There was an uncomfortable silence.

'Oh, Anthony, you idiot. Your penalty is to order us another bottle,' said Esther crisply. Caroline opened her mouth to protest, but Esther shushed her immediately. 'Come on – it's only another glass each. And we can't leave on that note – so actually Anthony, we should be thanking you for prolonging the evening.' She uncrossed her legs elegantly and stood up. 'Now, Caro, come with me to the bathroom, will you. My eyesight's not getting any better – Seth hasn't found a cure for that one yet, have you, darling? – and I can't bear to think *somebody* might be here and go unnoticed.'

Caroline could detect a cover-up when she heard one, but grateful for the chance to compose herself after Anthony's faux pas, she stood up dutifully and followed Esther through the subtly lit lounge bar. Esther knew she was useless when it came to spotting famous faces – she wouldn't be able to see them without her glasses anyway – but she'd thrown her a life-line, and Caroline loved her for it.

As the two women – one willowy and dark, the other cur-vaceous and bottle blonde – crossed the bar floor, more heads turned at the sight of them than vice versa, either through recognising them from society pages of magazines, or because of their glamorous aura.

They reached the loos and parted company at the cubicles. Caroline sank on to the loo seat and rested her head against the cool of the cubicle partition. Tonight was fun – but it was so *weird* being with the gang on her own, without Les. Was she ever going to get used to this singleton business?

As Esther reapplied her lipstick, she watched Caroline in the mirror. 'So come on, darling, tell all. Exactly what happened between you and Maryanne?'

Caroline jumped. Of all the reasons for Esther to pull her to one side, she hadn't been expecting that!

'What do you mean?' she said carefully. 'We're fine.'

'Oh, I know you're fine now, stupid,' said Esther in exasperation. 'But you weren't. I couldn't get hold of either of you for a good week. In the middle of a first divorce? Something's got to be up. So come on, what happened?'

Caroline sighed and sank down into a chair, rubbing her temples. She couldn't break Maryanne's confidence. But at the same time – she needed to get someone else's take on the whole thing. And who better than Esther, their closest friend in the whole world.

'I don't know where to start,' she said.

'Well, darling, I'd start at the beginning, and pretty quick if I were you. Because there's only so long we can claim to have been stuck in a toilet queue – and so I need you to offload this whole story in five minutes flat. Starting right now . . .'

Why had no one ever signed Esther up as a closer? Caroline wondered wildly. Salespeople who could sum up deals and 'close' them were like gold dust, and Les would kill to have someone with her powers of persuasion on his team at the bank.

'It's Maryanne,' she started.

Esther snorted. 'Darling, I could have told *you* that. No one ever opened an explanation of a fallout with "it's me".'

Caroline frowned. 'No, really Esther, it *is* Maryanne. You see, I've seen a side of her I never even knew existed. And I didn't – don't – know how I feel about it.'

Esther's face softened and, putting her lipstick in her clutch, she plopped down on the seat next to Caroline. 'I think there's probably a whole lot to Maryanne that none of us know about, darling,' she said gently. 'As with all of us. Don't tell me there's not elements of your personality we've never seen? Skeletons in your closet we don't know about?'

Guiltily, Caroline thought back to her dates with Adam. The playful side of her that he brought out had certainly not seen the light of day for years. An image of her bookish, studious university self popped into her mind. If ever. Certainly not since she'd been friends with the girls, anyhow.

And the cut-throat way she was trying to second-guess Les and play him at his own game. That was pretty far from the subservient wife she'd been for much of their marriage. Esther did have a point: there had to be a side to everyone that they kept to themselves. But—

'But not one that compromises all your principles!' she burst out passionately. 'Not one that practically mirrors the hell your best friend's husband has just put her through, not one that—' she stopped, flummoxed. She couldn't even explain herself why it had upset her so much. 'She's been having sex with other men behind Anthony's back,' she said mulishly. '*Younger* men,' she added accusingly. 'She even claims it's what keeps them together!'

Esther put her hand on Caroline's knee comfortingly.

'So is this about the fact that Maryanne is cheating on Anthony with young men, or that she's cheating at all?' she said, more kindly now. 'How would you have felt about this a year ago – before Les cheated on you, huh? Would you have been quite so quick to get on your high horse? Or would you have accepted it as part of what makes Maryanne and Anthony work? It sounds like she's not doing it to hurt him, you know. She's doing it to make them work better. Hah – for all we know, Anthony could know all about it and be fine with it.'

'I doubt it,' said Caroline darkly.

'Well, we'll probably never know,' said Esther shortly. 'But one thing I can tell you, is that if Seth ever found out about my little indiscretions, I'm sure he'd turn a blind eye if it meant maintaining the status quo. Not that I'm about to throw them in his face of course! That would not be cool. But you know, Caroline, Maryanne's not the only one with a rota of young lovers.' She nodded as Caroline's jaw dropped. 'Yep, I may not have as many as Maz, but I've certainly got the calibre! I have two or three little regular indiscretions and I make time to meet one of them most afternoons. You think I got this toned derrière in the gym?' She wagged a finger at Caroline. 'Uh-huh. It's from the workouts my boys give me. And darling, they are *hot*!'

Caroline shook her head sadly. Not Esther as well. Surely not.

Esther squeezed her knee and withdrew her hand, folding her arms authoritatively.

'Seth and I – well. He's a cute, round, hairy little man and most of the time I love him to death. The rest of the time I love hating him to death.' At the thought of Esther and Seth's quick-fire banter, Caroline laughed in spite of herself.

'But can you imagine what it's like sleeping with someone who's not only seen you naked, but seen you in *surgery*? Caroline, he *literally* knows me inside out!' Esther grabbed her Pucci-clad boobs. 'He chose these tits, darling! When he sees my smooth, pert bottom, he's not looking at it as a thing of wonder and planning what he's going to do to me when he gets me on my own, he's looking at every minor imperfection and planning when to get me in for my next lipo appointment. And whereas I love him down to his hairy little pot belly, he hasn't done it for me in the sack for years.' She stopped for breath and smiled dreamily. 'But those hot little homies with their smooth, taut six packs and 24/7 stamina? Well, now you're talking. And they feel the same about me. They can't keep their hands off me!' She looked at Caroline sternly. 'And so I think I can understand where Maryanne is coming from. And I also think, that if you don't want this to get in the way of our friendship, you've got to get over it, darling. Get over it, and get on with it.'

Esther's motto. Get on with it. But though she'd heard it a hundred times before, in this context Caroline was gobsmacked. Was monogamy so out of vogue that simply no one stayed faithful any more? She bit her thumb nervously. But there was something else. *Admit it, Caro*, she told herself sternly. *It's not the infidelity that's really bothering you. It's the fact that you think you're missing out.* It was the fact that her own 'hot little homie' didn't seem to have any kind of problem with keeping his hands off her. And the effect – combined with a little old-fashioned peer pressure – was startling. It had turned her from sex-regressed to sex-obsessed in a matter of weeks.

And in turn, it wasn't so much what it said about Adam that was worrying her. It was what it said about her. And what all this thinking said about how she really felt about him ...

Chapter 8

A WEEKEND IN THE COUNTRY

There was a wispy mist still hanging over the downs as Caroline drove the few miles across the Cotswold countryside to Daylesford Farm Shop. The sun would soon burn that away, she thought, turning it into a gloriously sunny June day. In other circumstances, she would pick up a coffee and a chocolate croissant along with her organic groceries and head back for a lazy day in the garden – a spot of gardening, maybe, a book and a late afternoon glass of chilled Sancerre. But not today. Nope, next stop after Daylesford was Kingham station, where a certain Adam Geray would be waiting for her, straight off a train from London. Not for the first time, she wondered what kind of madness had overtaken her now – had inspired her to contact Adam and invite him to her house in the country. Her *family* house in the country, she reminded herself crossly. This was her haven, her retreat – and here she was inviting a man she barely knew for an overnight stay?

After parking the car, she wandered through the pretty terrace, where a few couples and families were lingering over a late breakfast, and into the store. The atmosphere was one of relaxed calm, as the handful of casually but expensively dressed customers pottered around picking up delicacies. Caroline breathed deeply as she wandered around the cool stone interior. She loved this place – packed to the rafters with fresh, local, organic goods, full of the smells and colours of newly picked produce and the promise of good things to come from them. She always felt as though a gentle blanket of well-being was being wrapped around her, and today was no exception. Save, that is, for an unfamiliar feeling of slight unrest. The prospect of cooking for someone – anyone – usually filled her with excitement, but today all she felt was apprehension. She approached the butchers' counter tentatively, still unsure what to buy.

What *would* he like? He was a boy, he'd love a steak, she decided: keep it simple. The whole situation was going to be weird enough, and she didn't need to add complicated recipes into the mix. She'd half considered just taking him to the local pub for dinner, but the thought of facing all the regulars with him – most of whom probably didn't even know she and Les had separated – was too much to bear.

'Morning, Caroline – you're looking well!'

Caroline smiled self-consciously at Dave, the regular and permanently jovial assistant. She'd dressed carefully this morning, trying hard to create some kind of no-effort chic – but her casually tousled hair, 'au naturel' make-up and subtle jewellery worn with white Capri pants, striped Breton tee and Dior wedges were still a far cry from the jeans, T-shirt and ponytail she normally wore to shop here. And clearly, it hadn't gone unnoticed.

This had long been her weekend routine – buying the freshest of locally grown ingredients to take home and use to conjure up a delicious dinner for Rachel and Les. Before she could stop them, memories of hearty winter dinners together in their cosy dining room, and of sun-drenched summer barbecues on the deck that surrounded their pretty three-bedroom cottage flooded her mind.

She shook her head to banish the demons. Les wasn't there any more, Rachel was at her grandmother's, and there was no one else to cook for. What else would Caroline be doing if it wasn't entertaining her toy boy?

She laughed at the thought, and suddenly feeling cheered, chose a couple of juicy-looking steaks and sped around the rest of the store. She picked up a punnet of cherries from the huge wicker baskets arranged across the floor of the green-grocery section and selected a slab of creamy, salty mature Cheddar from the deli counter.

Back in the car, she realised she was now late, and had to resist the urge to put her foot down. It just didn't do to go hurtling around these windy roads.

When she pulled into Kingham station, Adam was there already, leaning nonchalantly against the wall of the station. Caroline's heart skipped a beat as she looked at him, bathed in a stream of mid-morning sunshine. He was, quite simply, gorgeous. And he was here to meet her! Casting aside any remaining second thoughts, she waved enthusiastically. Spotting her, Adam grinned his sexy lopsided smile and gave a half-wave back. She pulled up, impulsively got out and ran towards him, enveloping him in a hug.

Gently, he kissed her hello. Caroline breathed in as she kissed him back. He smelt of subtle musky aftershave, coffee and soap.

'So, you got here OK!' she said brightly. Adam looked at her in amusement. 'Yep, I guess ... It's the earliest I've been up on a Saturday for a while, though.'

'But it's eleven o'clock!' said Caroline, puzzled.

Adam continued to give her that amused look. 'Yes, and I had to leave home at nine to get the train here. If I'm not working, I'm normally still in bed at this time on a Saturday, let alone having already travelled over a hundred miles!'

Caroline pictured Rachel, who also rarely rose before noon at the weekend, and laughed. 'Oh right. Sorry! You'll get used to this. I'm an early riser.' She blushed at her unintended intimation that there might be another time. Adam, however, seemed unabashed.

'So, what's the plan? I don't spend many weekends in the country.' He slung his bag over his shoulder and fell into step beside her as they walked to the car.

'Well, I thought we could head back to the house, and – well – hang out?' said Caroline. Her vague response belied the military reality. Panicking about having a moment left unfilled, she had planned the entire day full of 'spontaneous' activities. Adam nodded at his bag. 'I was warned to come prepared. So whatever you want to do – tennis, horse riding, whatever – I'm up for it.'

Caroline stared at him in horror. She couldn't take him to the tennis club! Imagine what gossip *that* would generate. Nor, come to that, could she take him to the stables. The livery yard where Rachel kept her thoroughbred gelding was a hotbed of gossip as it was, and her daughter had become friends with several of the other clients.

'Erm – well – I rather thought we might take it easy today,' said Caroline. 'It's going to be hot, after all. I mean, we could go for a walk later maybe?' She thought of the picturesque (isolated) route she had planned for after lunch.

Adam shrugged. 'Like I said, whatever.' His face broke into an infectious grin. 'C'mon, I'm teasing you! Do I really look like I'm cut out for tennis? And the closest I've ever got to a horse was at a casting for a Mexican salsa commercial. One look at it rolling its eyes and pawing the ground and they didn't see me for dust!'

Caroline laughed disbelievingly.

'It's true!' swore Adam. 'And the worst of it is . . . I was really skint! I really could have done with that job. But, hey. Sometimes you've got to let your principles get in the way of life.'

Caroline was really laughing now – in fact her temples ached at the unaccustomed mirth.

'Well, don't worry, Adam. I promise, there'll be no tennis and no horse riding. Not this afternoon, anyway.'

The drive to the cottage was short, silent and relaxed. Adam, Caroline was relieved to discover, didn't seem the type that had to fill every silence with chatter. Instead he was content to take in the gently rolling countryside, the palette of fresh summer greens punctuated by the black and white of grazing cows, and the soft yellow Cotswold stone of walls and farm-houses.

But as they pulled into the gravel drive up to the lodge, Adam gave a low whistle. Caroline looked at him in surprise. Yes, the cottage was uncommonly cute. It was a former gate-keeper's cottage, and sat within three acres of garden that led prettily down to the river at the bottom. But its three bed-rooms were cosy rather than expansive and she'd never thought of it as having a particular 'wow' factor.

'And this is your *weekend* home?' asked Adam incredu-lously.

'Yes, we've had it for years,' said Caroline, suddenly defen-sive of her right to own not one, but three beautiful homes. 'We bought it before the housing market became inflated. The first time around,' she added, feeling 150 years old. Had she become so spoiled she didn't even notice luxury when it was staring her in the face? She thought guiltily of the state-of-the-art New York apartment that she also co-owned with Les.

'Well, I think it's very beautiful,' said Adam appreciatively. Caroline melted inside. That old-fashioned turn of phrase again.

'Then come in and see some more!' she said, impulsively grabbing his hand and pulling him through the front door into the hallway, desperate to show it off. Over the years more love and hard work had gone into making the cottage the luxury retreat that it now was than she cared to remember – but now seeing it through a stranger's eyes made her love it even more. Every old timber and exposed wall had been lov-ingly restored and set off with a subtle lighting scheme and careful choice of soft furnishings. The modern furniture lent it a contemporary feel that set off the history of the place to optimum effect.

Caroline had left the French windows at the end of the living room open, and the sunshine bathing the sun deck, the garden and the orchard beyond spilt into the room and over the pale beige seagrass flooring.

'It's not huge – but we never felt the need for anything outlandish,' murmured Caroline. 'Upstairs we have three
bedrooms, a master bathroom and an en-suite. It's always
seemed enough for us.'

Adam turned to her front, smiling. 'Seems enough to me,
too! So, where am I sleeping?' he said. Caroline felt herself
tense. In the past few days, her attraction to Adam, combined
with the irrational fear that there might be something wrong
with her for not inspiring Adam to make a move on her, had
morphed into a full-blown mission to prove a point and to
move their relationship on to the next level. This was where
she should make some casual aside: 'I've put you in my room.
There are fresh towels on your side of the bed.' Something
suggestive: 'Wherever I am, gorgeous.' Or even outrageously
provocative: 'Sleep? You won't be doing much of that tonight,
hot rod. Grrr!' Anything to break the ice and make it clear she
was happy for them to be more intimate.

'Well, I've made up the spare room. It's got a beautiful view,
and it's next door to the bathroom. I've got the en-suite,' she
added unnecessarily.

'OK, cool,' said Adam easily.

Caroline felt herself burn with irritation – at herself, for
being so ineffectual, and at Adam, for being so darned accepting. Didn't he think this whole thing was a bit weird, for
goodness sake?

'Can I take a look at the garden?'

'Of course!' They wandered through the French windows
and out to where the scent of the cedar decking warming in
the sun mingled with the smell of the rose bush climbing over
the arbour. Caroline instinctively moved over to twist some

new shoots around the fretwork, as Adam explored the grounds: the kitchen garden down the left-hand side, where Caroline would pick their salad for lunch, the second sun deck at the end of the garden, the weeping willow trailing its branches into the river with Rachel's childhood swing still hanging from it. Adam turned to her with shining eyes.

'Naomi would love this. We'd have to hold her up in it, of course.'

Caroline looked at him quizzically. 'Naomi?'

Adam's face softened. 'My little sister, Naomi. She's twelve, and she's got Rett's syndrome. She can't talk or walk and has to be fed through a tube. But she can still appreciate sensations like being on a swing.'

Caroline stared at him, full of compassion. She'd been so lucky – other than her father walking out on her and Babs, her life had never really been touched by true tragedy. And here was Adam, still little more than a boy, who'd spent much of his life helping a severely disabled sister grow up.

'Is she still at home?' she asked.

Adam's face clouded. 'No, she's in a care home. She needs too much round-the-clock specialist care for my parents to look after her themselves. They didn't give her up without a fight, though,' he added defensively. 'I try to get along to see her every couple of days at least. She loves it, and I help out with the fundraising a bit too. I mean, everyone's got to give a little something back, haven't they?'

Caroline nodded in agreement, feeling like a fraud. She gave money each month to a handful of charities, but the truth was, she could count on one hand the number of times she'd actively raised funds for charity. Suddenly, she felt shallow and ashamed. It had taken a nineteen-year-old boy to expose her lack of philanthropic activity even to herself. She had a sudden urge to do something about it. What, though, she hadn't a clue.

'Man, this shed is as big as my mate's flat!' called Adam from further down the garden. Caroline shaded her eyes to see him, and smiled indulgently as she saw him peering through the windows of the old summerhouse. Well, that was a typical man for you. Magnetically attracted to the toolshed.

He came back up the garden at a relaxed jog. 'Looks like you've got a couple of mountain bikes in there. Fancy taking those out later?'

Caroline shook her head, laughing. 'You've got to be joking,' she said. 'Those belong to L— my, um, ex-husband, and my daughter. You won't catch me on one in a million years.'

Adam grabbed her hands and swung them excitedly. 'Oh, c'mon Caroline! I've got twenty-four hours to see the Cotswolds and we'll cover three times as much ground on bikes as we will on foot.'

'That's what I'm worried about,' said Caroline. 'Myself, covering a lot of ground, after I've fallen off for the umpteenth time.'

He laughed. 'You won't come off. And if you do, I promise to throw myself under you to break your fall. It's a perfect day for it. Pub lunch, the lot. What do you say?'

Looking at his eyes, shining brightly and eagerly, Caroline felt herself relent. What the hell? You only live once, after all. And if they went in the right direction, they could definitely find a pub where she wouldn't know anyone . . .

Three hours later, the sun shining down on her face, her limbs pleasantly aching from the unaccustomed exertion, Caroline had to concede that Adam Geray had been right. Her confidence had built quickly on the bike and, using one of the crumpled maps they found on a shelf, they'd made their way across country to a tiny pub on the outskirts of a ramshackle hamlet. Now she had a half-pint of Magners in front of her. Cider! She hadn't drunk that since university. A ploughman's was about to arrive, and she felt – well – happy!

Adam, sitting across the picnic table from her, waved his hand in front of her face.

'Hello-o! Earth to Caroline. You look miles away.'

'I was just thinking—'

'Caroline! Yoo-hoo! What a coincidence – how are you? Look, Malcolm, it's Caroline Walker!'

Caroline's heart sank as she recognised the shrill tones of Martha, one of her village neighbours. Martha was a leading light of the local Parish Council and was constantly on at Caroline to 'get more involved'. Over the years Caroline had managed to find an excuse in every life stage she found herself in: she was too busy with Rachel, too busy with work, needed a rest after a hectic week. Today was no exception. Not only was Martha the last person she generally felt like seeing, she was *exactly* the last person she wanted to see her with Adam. Caroline gave Adam an apologetic look, pasted a smile on her face and turned, already resigned to a social mauling.

Martha, a sturdy, big-bosomed woman of a certain age with a smaller, thinner bespectacled man in tow approached eagerly, eyeing Adam with interest. 'Oh, and you've got Rachel with you too! How wonderful. We were only saying

129

the other day how we haven't seen Rachel for a long time. Well, probably since you and Les ...'

Caroline cut her off abruptly. 'Rachel's not here this weekend, Martha.'

Martha's eyes narrowed. 'Oh! Really?' Light seemed to dawn on her face and she looked Adam up and down again, this time more disdainfully.

'Table five?' The barman emerged from the pub carrying two ploughman's, blinking in the sunshine and looking around the garden questioningly. Caroline looked at him, eyes dancing. Other than Martha, they were the only people here.

'Um – I guess that must be us?' said Adam, winking at Caroline. At the absurdity of the situation, Caroline felt the urge to laugh hysterically well up inside her, the kind of laughter she hadn't experienced since school and she was doing something she shouldn't.

'Well, we should leave you to your ... lunch.' Martha stood aside to allow the barman to place the food on the table, gazing at it as if she had a particularly bad taste in her mouth.

'Lovely to see you, Martha,' said Caroline, waving determinedly. As Martha retreated, she looked at Adam and they shook with silent laughter.

'I never thought I'd be so glad to see a plate of cheese and pickle,' murmured Adam, and Caroline laughed harder than she could ever remember laughing.

It was quiet in a way it never was in London. A soft breeze from the open window moved the heavy drapes intermittently, and a roe deer barked in the distance – but other than that it was quiet. *Properly* quiet.

Caroline lay as she had been lying for at least the past hour – wide-eyed, staring into the dark. Contemplating. Contemplating life, love, and a whole lot of other random thoughts that she would never allow to plague her day-dreams – but most of all, she was contemplating what on earth was going on with her and Adam.

She just couldn't work it out. Their near-perfect day had ended, in her opinion, in a near-perfect way. A relaxed meal with a bottle of wine – well, two, to be precise – soaking up the last rays of the sunshine, and then a movie. And yes, there had been a bit of cuddling on the sofa. And a delicious, soft, lingering kiss goodnight. But that was it.

What did you expect? You were the one who put him in the spare room, the voices inside her head taunted. *Yes, but I was only trying to be polite!* she responded furiously. *He could have made the first move, after all.*

Caroline tossed and turned for a few more moments. She couldn't fathom it. Was she too old? Too wrinkly? Too *boring*? Even worse, was she some kind of meal ticket? An ego boost? A *friend*?

One thing was for sure. She had enough friends. She certainly didn't need any more. Let alone a nineteen-year-old boy. Even if he did make her laugh. Even if he did kiss better than anyone she'd ever met.

At the thought, she sat up in bed abruptly and scrabbled around underneath the bed for her BlackBerry. The LED was showing 12.45 a.m. Maryanne was a night owl – she'd still be up.

Caroline's fingers moved urgently over the keys. *R U awake? Urgently need to talk.*

She lay back, hand on her BlackBerry expectantly. After what seemed like an age, she checked it. 12.48 a.m. – and no response.

Idly, she flicked through her contacts book. Esther would know what to do. But . . . Esther refused to text on principle, and a phone call to her generally averaged at half an hour. Caroline wasn't sure she wanted to engage in that kind of conversation – not at this time, and not with Adam just in the next room.

The thought of Adam made something stir inside her. She flicked back to her texts. 12.51 a.m. Still nothing.

Caroline's heart sank as she flicked through the rest of her contacts. M, N, O, P . . . There was no one she could think of who (a) would appreciate a call from her at this hour, or (b) she would feel comfortable to confide in.

R. RACHEL! Caroline's heart leapt. Sod Maryanne! Rachel was Adam's age. She'd know what the protocol was. She'd know what to do. Caroline bit her lip ruefully. What had her life come to when the person best placed to advise her on her love life was her teenage daughter? She would never dream of asking Rachel about it directly. Still, there was no one close to Caroline who understood Adam's age group quite so well as Rachel. Maybe she could approach the subject *in*directly . . .

It was a solution – of sorts. With a sigh, Caroline turned over and tried to go to sleep. She'd worry about how she was actually going to broach it with her daughter tomorrow . . .

'Hi Mum. Good weekend?'

Caroline threw her arms around her daughter and

embraced her tightly. Rachel smelt of Miss Dior, the great outdoors and her grandmother's house. 'Yes, darling, thank you. How about you?'

Rachel pulled away and held one arm across her torso protectively, dark mussed hair falling over her face. 'It was all right.'

Caroline frowned. She'd noticed this recently. Since the split Rachel was occasionally defensive – sulky – both totally at odds with her naturally easy-going nature. She smiled indulgently.

'So what did you get up to, you and your grandma?'

'Oh, you know,' said Rachel. 'This and that.'

She wandered over to the fridge and looked in it uninterestedly.

'What's for dinner?'

Caroline pointed her thumb over her shoulder to the table behind her laden with a selection of deli meze. 'I brought you back some bits and pieces from Daylesford, darling. I thought if you couldn't come to the country, I'd bring the country to you.'

'Oh yum.' Rachel sat at the table, leaned over for a plate and started heaping it full of olives, hummus, sun blush tomatoes and pitta. This had been her favourite Sunday supper since she was a little girl. Caroline took a sip of wine. Dutch courage . . .

'So, did you see Robbie over the weekend?'

Rachel raised her eyes skywards at the mention of her new boyfriend. 'Mum, just because you weren't there, doesn't mean you have to interrogate me about it.'

'I'm not, darling! I'm just interested.'

'Well, yes – he came over on Saturday.' Rachel bit into a vine leaf, signalling the conversation was over.

Caroline, however, was determined that it wasn't. 'And – did he stay over?'

Rachel fixed her with her piercing emerald eyes. 'No. Grandma would make him sleep in another room, so what's the point?'

'Well, I think we both know the answer to that,' said Caroline, with a mischievous look. 'So you and Robbie – have you . . .?'

Rachel stared at her in horror. 'Mum! That's gross. I can't talk to you about that.'

'I just wondered, darling – you know – boys of that age – it's all they think about, isn't it?' Caroline bumbled on. 'I mean, all that testosterone and—'

'Mu-um!'

Caroline took a deep breath. 'I mean, darling, we've talked a lot about sex over the years and what happens and how to say no when you don't want it – but you're getting to that age now where you also need to be able to have an adult sexual relationship. Where you can make sure your needs are being met as well as his, and I thought maybe we should discuss in the context of Robbie and—'

Rachel held her hand up, palm facing her mother. 'Mum, you're freaking me out now. Enough already.'

'Oh, darling, I'm sorry, I—'

Rachel got up, taking her plate with her and turning her back on Caroline. 'I'm going to the snug. I Sky-plussed a load of telly yesterday.' The words were casual but the tone was unmistakable – *and don't try to follow me.*

Caroline sighed in defeat and popped an olive in her mouth, chewing mechanically. *You'll go to hell, Caro, for unashamedly using your daughter for your own gain. Not that it's got you anywhere with her but in the doghouse.* Time to find a Plan B. And fast.

Chapter 9

IT MUST BE A DELIVERY

'Oh, honey, what's with all the coyness? You're both, adults, right? You'll be on what – your third date?' Maryanne tutted, and Caroline could imagine the resigned look that was passing between her two best friends, sitting in the garden on luxury sun loungers at Esther's sprawling estate in the Hamptons, where Maryanne was due to present an award at one of Esther's charity functions.

'Fourth,' said Caroline miserably. 'Maybe he just doesn't find me attractive.'

From her corner of the transatlantic conference call, Esther snorted. 'What guy in his right mind is *not* going to find you attractive? Come *on*, Caroline. You're hot, darling! Looking on the bright side, this will cease to be an issue pretty darn soon. On the downside, it sounds like you might have to make the first move. The *right* move,' she replied sternly.

Caroline moved her phone to the opposite ear and sighed. 'I've already tried that. It didn't work.'

'Correction, honey,' retorted Maryanne. 'What you've

done is set up the situations for it to happen. But making a move? Uh-huh. Sounds to me like the only move you made was to moan to me when he didn't take the bait. Men are simple creatures, Caroline. He may have picked up on your timidity and interpreted it as lack of interest. You've got to make it plain, honey. Be more obvious. Make it so damn clear he can't possibly misunderstand you. You want a bit of bump and grind – and fast!'

Caroline laughed nervously. 'Well, that's all easier said than done.'

'Honey, just relax a little. Put on a little music. Have a couple of glasses of wine. You know why those are clichés? Because they work, honey. Loosen up! You'll enjoy it.'

'Hmm,' murmured Caroline, unconvinced. It was all right for Maryanne, with her fiery red hair, big eyes, pint-size body, pneumatic boobs and easy way with people. She was body-built for seduction. What man would be able to resist her? Or Esther for that matter, with her direct, ball-breaking approach and cosmetically perfect curves. But Caroline, with her long, gangly limbs and self-consciousness – that was another matter entirely.

'Anyway, Caroline, you deserve it,' said Esther in honey tones. 'God knows it must be long enough since you had you some decent sex, huh?'

'Les and I had a very satisfactory love life, thank you very much,' retorted Caroline defensively. So she'd never exactly felt the earth move. So what? She and Les had remained intimate on pretty much a weekly basis – until he had decided to extend those privileges to his work colleague, of course.

'Well, if you were trying to convince me otherwise, you

just failed,' laughed Esther. 'No amazing sex I had ever got called "satisfactory".'

Caroline tried not to feel riled at her friends as they cackled down the line together. They were only teasing, but sometimes their American bullishness – Maryanne's inbred, Esther's adopted after years living in the States – was too much for Caroline's natural English reserve.

Promising them a progress report after her next date with Adam, Caroline replaced the receiver with relief. Sometimes, asking her friends for advice was less like getting help, and more like Japanese water torture.

The only problem with their advice was that they weren't giving her counsel on the full facts. Whether it was because of their fall out, or Caroline's open criticism of Maryanne when she'd discovered she dated younger men, she wasn't sure – but for whatever reason, Caroline had found herself reluctant to divulge Adam's age. Or occupation. So far, all she'd revealed was that Adam was someone she'd 'met through work'.

But she was right on one count. This apparent lack of passion on Adam's part was becoming An Issue. And although they were getting on better and better every time they met, Caroline knew that without some kind of reassurance that Adam was physically attracted to her – and soon – this wasn't enough to sustain their fledgling relationship.

Fling, she corrected herself. All she could expect or want from a nineteen-year-old was a *fling* – a rebound affair designed to restore her pre-divorce self-esteem and give them both a bit of fun.

She scrolled down to the text from Adam that had sparked her call to Maryanne:

So Mrs Walker, fancy a rematch . . . How about dinner sometime this week? x

Feeling as if she was doing something really naughty, Caroline flicked back to her calendar to double-check her schedule for the week. Thursday was good. This time Rachel had reluctantly agreed to an overnight stay at Les's.

Would love to. I'll cook. See you at my house Thursday at 7?

Almost instantly, Adam replied.

Sounds good. I'll look forward to it, gorgeous. xx

Caroline's tummy did a somersault as she thought of Adam – his smouldering looks, grey-green eyes and finely honed physique. And he thought *she* was gorgeous? She put her BlackBerry down and headed for the kitchen. Cooking had always been her salvation. And finding the right recipes was the first step on the seduction scene of her life. Adam wasn't going to know what had hit him.

The doorbell sounded and Caroline's heart beat perceptibly faster. She looked at herself in the mirror: hair carelessly tousled; soft, dewy make-up; silken robe artfully arranged to display just a little too much flesh than was strictly platonic. She took a deep breath, and padded down the stairs with her freshly pedicured bare feet.

As she descended the lower half of the stairs, she slowed down. She could see the shadow of his silhouette through the stained glass of her front door. The glass frosting had distorted the image so he seemed smaller than normal, but with the enormity of the task in hand, in Caroline's mind he had grown to a hulking great ten feet tall. Nervously she stalled, one foot poised above the next step, willing herself to be more confident. There was nothing sexy about a gibbering wreck, after all.

She caught a glimpse of herself, reflected in one of the pictures in the staircase, and felt buoyed by the image she saw. Maryanne was right. She was *hot*.

At the front door, she readjusted her robe again, pulling it further off her shoulder. She opened the door a fraction, giving a tantalising glimpse of her silkily moisturised shoulder and clavicle.

'Hello, you,' she said teasingly. 'I've been waiting for you.'

'Caroline?' said a well-spoken, Middle England voice. A *woman*'s voice.

Caroline yanked the door fully open in horror, pulling her robe around her in shame. Standing resplendent in bouclé Jesire suit, blown-out hair and her trademark low, square heels, was her mother.

'Mother!' exclaimed Caroline in shock. 'What on earth are you doing here?'

'I could ask you the same question,' said Babs tartly, pushing past her daughter into the house. 'Dripping about the house in next to nothing. Honestly, it's the middle of the day!'

'I – erm – I've just had a bath,' said Caroline. 'And anyway, it's evening – I was, erm ...'

'Expecting someone?' finished Babs for her from the pretty garden room, where Caroline had laid a small circular table ready for a candlelit dinner.

Caroline's heart raced even faster. She wasn't ready to discuss dating – or Adam – with her mother. Not tonight, of all nights.

'Yes!' she cried, following her mother into the garden room. She surveyed the scene dismally. It was undeniably an intimate set-up, clearly created for romance. Or . . .

'I'm expecting Maryanne!' she said impetuously. 'She's a bit down in the dumps, so I promised her a special meal. I haven't cooked much since – well, you know – and so it seemed like the perfect opportunity to kill two birds with one stone.' She laughed shrilly. *Shut up, Caro, you're gabbling and over-compensating. She'll suss you out if you're not careful.*

'Right,' said Babs, unconvinced. 'I thought Maryanne was still in New York?'

'Yes!' said Caroline quickly. 'You're right! At least – she *was* in New York. Now, she's in London again. For an audition!'

Babs turned and fixed Caroline with her brown eyes. 'Well, how lovely. I haven't caught up with Maryanne for a long time. Have you got room for a little one?'

Caroline laughed manically again.

'Of course there's room, Mother, I'm just not sure I have enough food . . .' She looked Babs in the eyes and saw they were dancing with amusement.

'Caroline, relax, I'm not going to gatecrash your evening. I just popped in to say hello – I've been in town all day. The Women's Institute lunch at Claridge's I was organising. Remember I mentioned it?'

'Ummm . . .' said Caroline doubtfully, trying not to give away her palpable relief. But despite scouring the recesses of her mind, she was unable to recollect her mother ever mentioning it. It was unsurprising given the level of non-stop chatter that Babs had provided during her weeks in residence. 'I think I remember . . .' She tried another tack, attempting to redeem herself with some teasing. 'How did the blue rinse brigade take to Claridge's, then?'

Babs tutted fondly. 'I'll have you know it was an extremely glamorous event full of very dynamic, well-to-do women,' she said pointedly. 'It's not all jam and Jerusalem these days, you know.'

Caroline hid a smile. Her mother had long been a leading light of the WI and felt she was personally responsible for changing the image of her local branch from fusty village hall to stylish lunches.

The doorbell rang, preventing her from responding. Her heart started hammering again. Adam!

She pointed frantically in the direction of the front door. 'Erm . . . I'll just go and get that . . .'

Babs picked up her leather handbag from where she'd placed it on a rattan chair. 'Well that will no doubt be your guest. I should be off,' she said. She looked pointedly at Caroline's robe. 'And you should get dressed. I can let Maryanne in.'

'No!' Caroline almost yelled in panic. Babs looked at her, startled.

'I mean, you've only just got here! And it can't be Maryanne because she's . . . she's . . .'

Babs looked at her questioningly.

'She's always late!' said Caroline, backing out of the room. 'It must be a delivery or something!'

She ran to the door. This time it was definitely Adam's silhouette behind the glass. What the hell was she going to say to him?

She opened the door a crack, and he smiled nervously through it. 'Hi.'

Caroline felt her heart flip at his lopsided grin. 'Hi.'

There was a silence. Adam cleared his throat. 'So ... can I come in?'

Caroline stared at him. 'No. Sorry.'

There was another awkward silence. Adam shuffled on the spot. 'Oh, right. Well, erm ...'

'You're early!' said Caroline.

He looked at his watch. 'But you said 7 p.m.? It's ten past. I thought I was late.'

Caroline laughed shrilly. 'Nope! Early. I definitely said 7.30. And the thing is, I'm not ready.' She indicated her robe through the crack in the door and shrugged apologetically.

'Right,' said Adam uncertainly. 'So you're saying – I should come back at 7.30?'

'Yes please!' said Caroline brightly. 'Perfect!' Without waiting for his reply, she shut the door thankfully.

She waited until she saw his figure disappear down the drive, and then ran back in to see her mother, who was staring out at the garden.

'No Maryanne?' she said suspiciously.

'Nope. Told you!' said Caroline breathlessly.

'So who was it?' persisted Babs.

Caroline looked at her blankly for a split second. 'Gas man! Honestly, of all the times to call. Got rid of him immediately. Straight away! Anyhow – I really need to get ready, and ...'

'And it's time I was off,' said Babs. Caroline sighed gratefully. At last!

After seeing her mother out – and making sure she'd seen her actually, physically drive away – Caroline ran upstairs to her room, slammed the door shut and leaned against it, still breathless with nervous adrenalin. The shame of the near-miss now flooded over her. It could have been anyone at the door, not just her mother! What if it *had* been the gas man? She discarded her robe and pulled a shapeless pair of jeans and a blouse from her wardrobe, wanting to purge herself of the memory of having inadvertently tried to seduce someone at the front door – like some bored, sex-starved housewife cliché, she thought disgustedly, pulling a brush through her hair angrily.

The doorbell rang again, and for the second time that night Caroline took a deep breath before descending the staircase. For the second time, it was definitely Adam's silhouette she could see through the glass panels. And when she opened the door, it was his sexy, smiling face behind it.

'Hi!' she said cheerfully, leaning forward and giving him a chaste peck on the lips.

'Hi!' he returned, looking at her quizzically. 'Am I on time now?'

'Yes!' she said, wanting to explain but deciding against it. She didn't want to appear even madder. 'Come in, come in!' she said, feeling awkward. She looked behind him as if worried that her mother was going to pop out from behind the rhododendron bush.

'Thanks, I will,' said Adam, the hint of a bemused smile playing around his lips.

Caroline ushered him into the drawing room then fixed drinks and offered nibbles, unable to relax after her mother's invasion. Adam's presence – his eyes, his body, just the smell of him, dammit – had unsettled her again, reminding her of the goal of the evening. In her mind, it was as if Adam had been there to witness the whole thing, to see her running around like an embarrassed teenager, leaving her feeling unaccountably self-conscious. Adam, for his part, seemed to find the whole situation mildly amusing, if baffling.

'So, you must be starving – I'll just go and check on dinner.' Escaping to the sanctuary of the kitchen, Caroline rested her forehead against the cool of the fridge door. Here she went again, blowing things way out of proportion. Normally her self-esteem was hardly so lacking that she'd let something like that affect her. Quite the opposite, in fact. She should be finding the whole situation funny, sharing it with Adam even, not letting it spoil the rest of the evening with him. Bloody sex. Put that into the equation – any equation – and it changed all the rules without warning.

Once the starter was ready, she had recovered her composure. Time for a Plan B. The seductive menu she had planned would surely work its magic on Adam.

'Dinner is served,' she called. Adam raised an eyebrow as he loped through the doorway.

'Wow – you've made a lot of effort, Caroline,' he said appreciatively. 'Looks great.'

'Well, you're worth it,' said Caroline a little awkwardly, and smiled at him shyly. The look he gave her in return sent a white heat coursing through her veins, and despite her drab clothes she felt like the sexiest woman on the planet.

'I hope you like asparagus,' she said. 'It's the first of the season.'

Adam laughed, cutlery poised over his plate. 'I love it – I can just never work out how to eat it politely!'

Caroline fixed her eyes on his and licked her lips slowly and lavishly. 'It's not just about etiquette with food,' she said in a low voice. 'It's about the touch, the smell, the *feel* of it. I mean, who would have thought a simple vegetable could be *sensuous*?'

She picked up a piece of the asparagus and bit the tip off purposefully, still holding Adam's gaze. She'd seen it in a film years ago, and the suggestive subtext had been both sophisticatedly sexy, and devastatingly irresistible.

But as she chewed slowly, her eyes still full of promise for the evening ahead, she saw his expression change from admiration to amusement. Hang on, this wasn't how it was meant to be . . .

But then, he leaned over the table and she swallowed and closed her eyes. Her breath caught in anticipation as she felt him reach over to her and run his finger gently down her cheek.

'You've got butter running all down your chin, Caroline,' he said softly.

Caroline carried the dessert plates through to the kitchen and willed her head to stop spinning. After the second aborted seduction attempt, she'd got stuck into the Châteauneuf by way of compensation, and she was now regretting the fourth glass. Drunk sex, in her experience, was never great sex, and if she was determined that's how the night was going to end, she was going to need to pace herself a little better.

She turned on the Nespresso machine and lined up a tiny coffee cup. A quick ristretto shot should sort her out.

'Are you sure you don't want coffee?' she called through to Adam.

'No thanks – I'm fine with the wine,' she heard him call back, en route through to the lounge.

Caroline knocked back the coffee. Immediately feeling buoyed by the hot strong liquid, she picked up her own, still unfinished glass of wine.

She wandered through and stopped short as she caught sight of Adam lounging back on her sofa. Caught in a halo of lamplight, his hair seemed darker, even thicker, his features finer, his eyes more brooding. He looked like the hero of a romantic fiction novel. A young Darcy, even.

That moment decided it for Caroline. This was it. She made her way over to him, and he looked up expectantly. She sashayed across, slowly unbuttoning her blouse, and she saw his eyes at first light up and then become filled with desire as she slowly exposed more of her body.

She kicked off her shoes, and then suddenly she was standing over him, his sexy eyes looking up at her with unbridled lust. She leaned over, took his hand and placed at the base of her throat, moving it down between her breasts and over her taut stomach.

She gasped at the feel of his big, soft hand on her skin, and she leaned forward, hearing him groan as she straddled his legs and tried to climb on top of him.

There was a tinkle as she kicked over the wine glass Adam had placed by the side of the sofa.

'Oh, fuckit!' Caroline swore, as wine spilled over her feet and on the expensive Axminster rug. She clambered off, Adam half protesting.

'I'm sorry, Adam, that carpet cost a fortune – I can't let a full glass of red wine just sink in,' she called, as she hurried through to the utility room, blouse still flapping open.

She grabbed the spray-on carpet shampoo and some kitchen roll and hurried back into the living room, feeling – not for the first time that evening – ever so slightly ridiculous.

Adam was half-heartedly patting at the stain with a tissue, and she sank to her knees next to him and started to rub in the foam.

'Oh well, you win some, you lose some,' said Caroline, trying to cover the crucifying embarrassment she was feeling. She turned to Adam, still kneeling beside her, and the smile froze on her face as she caught his gaze, a mix of tenderness and passion. Instinctively her eyes moved to his lips, those perfect, Cupidon lips.

'I can't imagine you've ever lost at anything,' he growled, and grabbed her softly around the neck, pulling her to him gently.

He kissed her sweetly, then harder, more passionately. 'I've been wanting to do this since the first moment I laid eyes on you,' he murmured into her hair.

Then why didn't you? Caroline wondered to herself. It was all academic now, though.

Stroking her hair back from her face, Adam found his way down her neck with his lips, kissing, nipping, softly licking until Caroline thought she would die from breathless excitement.

And then his lips were caressing her body – her softly rounded breasts, her taut, flat stomach, her inner thighs. Caroline lay back on the floor, giving herself up to the waves of ecstasy she was feeling. And then, just when she felt she couldn't take any more, he was inside her, and she was feeling pleasure like never before, growing and growing, rising and rising until—

'OMIGOD! OMIGOD! OH. MY. GOD!'

As the ecstasy that had overtaken her abated, Caroline lay back, strands of hair stuck to her head with sweat, Adam lying on top of her in post-coital collapse. She was sated – and stunned.

Her first ever orgasm. So that's what all the fuss was about. That's what she'd been missing all these years. And was that what they really meant by 'having it all'? Because if that was the case, she had a hell of a lot of catching up to do.

Caroline snuggled further down into the duvet contentedly, and continued her secret observation of Adam sleeping peacefully beside her. He was lying on his side facing her, one tanned, toned arm over the top of the duvet, his face set in the deep, untroubled sleep of the young.

She had been there for several minutes now, snugly encased in the duvet, propped up on her downy pillows, just taking in his sleeping form – the rise and the fall of the duvet as he breathed in and out. She'd studied every contour of his face; every single long, black eyelash sweeping down over his cheeks, his straight, aquiline nose, the tiny mole by his earlobe, his strong, broad shoulders, and his lips – his lips! Caroline blushed as she remembered the things those lips had done, the places they'd been and the throes of passion they had sent her into the previous night.

What a night.

Her first orgasm had been quickly followed by her second, third, and – yes, even her fourth. Adam was not only a selfless lover, he was tireless too, and Caroline's whole body ached with satisfied desire. It was alien to her – this feeling of being so completely alive – from head to toe and encompassing every nerve ending in between.

Caroline stretched languorously, like the cat who'd got the cream – cougar who'd got the cream, she thought with a smile. She glanced at the alarm clock. 0715. She slipped out of bed, not wanting to wake Adam.

Pulling on her robe over her naked body, she padded downstairs and into the kitchen to make coffee. Humming as she switched on the machine, Caroline reached for the two tiny coffee capsules, lined up the mugs and pressed the button. She breathed in deeply, inhaling as much of the rich roasted smell as she could fit in her lungs. It was a beautiful day, she thought, peering out of the blinds. A gorgeous June day. She thought of Adam, lying upstairs in bed. Her bed. Maybe – just maybe – it was too good a day to waste on work. She had back-to-back meetings followed by the launch of a new art exhibition. The thought of the alternative was deliciously naughty. This was a week of firsts, after all – maybe it was time to start with an impromptu day off. Or even, a sickie ...

Coffee prepared, Caroline arranged the mugs on a tray with milk and sugar, and padded back upstairs. But instead of finding Adam's curly hair poking out of the duvet, there was only a crumpled sheet where his body had been moments earlier.

'Morning, gorgeous.' She turned and smiled as he appeared

out of the en-suite door, hair wet and mussed from the shower. Just as quickly her face fell as, crestfallen, she noticed his jeans on and belt half done up.

'Oh. You're going?' she stated flatly.

He walked over and kissed her softly on the neck, and she felt herself melt all over again.

'Mmm! Coffee,' he said picking up a mug eagerly and taking a huge glug, without waiting for milk or sugar. 'Wow, I needed that.' He smiled at her, the coffee froth making a moustache on his upper lip. Suddenly, his expression also changed. 'What's the matter?'

Caroline shook her head carelessly, pulling her robe tighter around her and trying desperately to cover up her disappointment. 'I just said, you're going.'

Adam grinned sheepishly. 'Yeah – I am. I've got a casting. Do you remember? I mentioned it last night. I've got to be in Acton by nine.'

Caroline nodded, although she had no such recollection. 'Oh, right. No problem.'

Adam moved in and grabbed her round the waist, trying to establish eye contact. 'Heyyy! I'm not ducking out on you. I promise!'

'I know that,' said Caroline crossly, removing his arms and wandering over to the bathroom herself. 'Anyway, I've got a lot on at work myself today. I'd better get a move on.' She brushed aside her half-baked plans for calling in sick and spending the rest of the morning in bed with him. Stupid her. Why hadn't she seen this coming? Now he'd had his wicked way, she wouldn't see him for dust. Silly cow. Silly OLD cow. She should have known better.

Suddenly, she felt Adam's arms around her, pulling her to him. She looked up at him, and the look in his eyes made her heart sing again.

'Caroline, I am categorically not doing the off – I'm going to a casting!' His tone was a mixture of fond amusement and devotion. He kissed her gently. 'And although I'm trying not to be offended that you might think I could walk out on someone like you, I'm sorry to disappoint you, but I'm not. In fact, I'm thanking my lucky stars you didn't boot me out once you'd had your wicked way with me.'

'What!' shrieked Caroline. '*My* wicked way?'

Adam ducked as she picked up a pillow and hit him with it. 'You made the first move, as I remember!' he said, laughing. Caroline blushed and laughed too.

'Anyway, I've got to go,' said Adam. 'I'll call you.'

'I'll see you out,' said Caroline, following him out of the bedroom and down the stairs.

She unlocked the door and opened it, raising her face for a kiss. He pulled her in to him and kissed her passionately. She gave herself up to the moment, relishing the mix of coffee and toothpaste – and the very taste of him. It felt right. And she felt happy. More, she felt fulfilled – for the first time in a long time.

'Morning, Caroline!'

Caroline pulled away in shock. Across the road, the morning sunlight glinting off his glasses as he peered over with undisguised interest, was Christian. Mentally, she pictured what he was seeing. Caroline, clearly just out of bed, passionately kissing a straight-from-the-shower teenager. And all before 8 a.m. Her heart sank. Christian, of all people.

So much for Adam, her little secret. She might as well have

taken out an ad in the *Daily Mail*. Or had 'cougar' tattooed on her forehead.

Either way, as of right now, her little secret was anything but.

Chapter 10

IT'S MEANT TO BE LIKE THAT

'Well, hello stranger,' said Babs in frosty tones. 'I was beginning to think I was *persona non grata*.'

What made me pick up her call, now of all times? wondered Caroline. She'd managed to avoid two earlier calls from her mother. But something had made her pick up this time. Because she'd got the wind up her tail and was feeling reckless, or because she felt the need to pay penance for the previous evening?

'Oh, hi Mother,' she said, her tone light and noncommittal. She felt a rush of mischievousness, and added innocently: 'I'm sorry, I didn't recognise your number.'

Caroline twirled around on her office chair, smiling and waving at Julie as she waddled her way around the office, making her customary early morning tour. 'Her rounds', she called it; 'reconnaissance' was the term Trudi had fondly given it, in a thinly veiled reference to Julie's inherent nosiness. It was a good job they all trusted her implicitly, as some of the information this gave Julie access to would no doubt make their competitors very happy, thought Caroline as she wound her hair around a pencil aimlessly. As the conversation with Babs took the same well-trodden path as always, she found her thoughts moving to Adam – to his lips, to the soft nape of his neck where he'd turned out to be so sensitive, to . . .

'Well, I've no doubt that mine would be the very last number you'd think of inputting into a new phone,' Babs retorted, referring to Caroline's new iPhone, which she had yet to completely master. I even had to call Les to make sure nothing had happened to you.'

'You did *what*?' The effect was of a needle scratching across a record, and suddenly Caroline's attention was fully on her mother again. 'Why would you call Les?'

'Well, you weren't answering, and I knew there was no point calling Rachel before noon,' said Babs pointedly. 'And after your behaviour last night, I was concerned. You were acting very out of character. Agitated, even.'

There was a silence, and Caroline mentally started to count to ten. It was none of her mother's business. She didn't need to explain every single move she made to her. She wasn't going to let Babs burst today's bubble. Babs cleared her throat delicately. 'You know he's got that floozy living with him, I suppose?'

'How do you know that?' snapped Caroline, surprised at how the force of the revelation had shocked her. She dug her nails into the palm of her hand and willed herself to hold it together.

'She answered the phone. Imagine that!' said Babs.

'It could have been the cleaner,' offered Caroline optimistically. 'Or maybe he's got himself a housekeeper?'

'Well, if he has she's the only one I've ever met who calls her employer "sugar",' said Babs tartly. 'I'm sorry, darling, this is all very insensitive of me. It must be desperately painful for you.'

Caroline's patience snapped, and she had a compulsive urge to get off the phone. An incoming call gave her the excuse she needed.

'Mother, honestly, I'm fine,' she insisted. 'But right now I've got a conference call, and I really need to go. I'll call you tonight for a proper chat, OK?'

'Just make sure you do—' began Babs, but Caroline cut her off before she could finish.

She answered the other call automatically, without even glancing at the caller ID.

'Hell-oooooo! You got something to tell me, honey?'

Caroline looked at her watch in astonishment. It was 9.30 a.m. here – which made it around 4.30 a.m. in the Hamptons, New York State. 'Maryanne, have you got up ridiculously early, or stayed up stupidly late?'

'Oh, c'mon, Caroline – since when did a different time zone come between friends? Anyhow, I'm flying to Tanzania this afternoon to go film that blessed coffee advert. And before I go to the middle of the frickin' desert, I just wanna know how you got on with your Adam.'

Caroline felt a smile twitch at the corners of her mouth and, remembering the previous night, felt instantly cheered. She'd got on OK, thank you very much, Maryanne. OK enough to make her feel more light-hearted than she could ever remember feeling. Almost skittish, now she thought about it. And that was even after a call from her mother and the spectre of Christian-the-big-mouthed neighbour spreading her news all over the neighbourhood hanging over her. Nonetheless, it was hardly the time or the place to open up to her best friend.

'Maryanne, I can't talk right now, I'm in the office.'

'OMIGOD!! You did, didn't you. You got him in the sack! How was it? You *totally* got laid!'

'Maryanne!' Caroline protested, screwing her nose up as the romance of her night was ripped apart by her friend's crude terms.

There was a gasp at the other end of the phone. 'Did you even go home? Caroline Walker! You dirty stopout.'

'Maz!' hissed Caroline warningly. 'We were at my house, OK? Rachel was out.'

'So you *did* screw him!' cackled Maryanne. 'Gotcha!'

Caroline sighed in defeat. 'Whatever happened, I'm still in the office. I'll call you later.'

She turned back to the *FT*, smiling to herself and shaking her head at her irrepressible friend. Unable to concentrate on any of the business stories for the first time in her career, Caroline pushed the paper away in boredom.

'Trudi, have you got one of the weeklies there – *Gloss* or something?'

Trudi popped her head around the door in surprise. '*Gloss?*'

Caroline nodded, smiling. 'Yes. I'm a bit over the *FT* today. I need something a bit more . . . entertaining.'

'*Entertaining,*' repeated Trudi suspiciously, looking at her boss as if trying to ascertain her state of mind. 'I'm sure there's a copy knocking around somewhere. I'll fetch it for you.

'Oh', she said, turning abruptly, 'and Caroline – if you

haven't read the *FT* you may not have seen that Morton have released their annual results. 'They're claiming a 10 per cent growth year on year and a million-pound rise in profits.'

Caroline raised an eyebrow. 'Are they, indeed. Well, I wonder where they've cooked those up from. They certainly don't reflect our estimates.'

'No, but Molly says they seem suspiciously close to our own results – just that bit better,' said Trudi sagely.

'Well, maybe we'll have to play them at their own game,' replied Caroline grimly, wondering how she could spin Sapphires & Rubies' annual report in order to blow MacCaskill's attempted coup out of the water.

Trudi tapped her pen against her teeth. 'Should I make you a copy of the feature, then?' There was no reply as Caroline turned back to her screen, frowning. What was it about men that meant they had to ruin any good mood just by simply existing? First Christian, now MacCaskill – before she knew it, Les would be making an appearance. The moment the thought crossed her mind, an email popped up into her inbox from Adrian Green entitled 'Proposed Access Agreement'. She sighed and marked it for attention later that day. No point making it a hat trick.

'I'll make you a copy,' Trudi repeated, as a statement this time. 'Oh, and Caroline,' she ventured nervously.

Caroline looked up at her patiently. 'Yes, Trudi?'

'Your button's undone.'

Caroline looked down at the silky Chloé blouse she'd matched with a flirty pleated above-the-knee skirt and own-brand pumps. Although cute not sexy, it revealed more flesh than she could ever remember showing at work, but what the hell? It was summer, she was in shape, and she felt like it. She'd left one more button undone than she normally would, showing the merest hint of chemise underneath – but the effect was girly and relaxed, rather than tarty.

'Yes, thank you, Trudi, I know. It's meant to be like that.'

Trudi smiled and shrugged. 'Oh, right. Sorry.'

She disappeared, and was almost immediately replaced by Molly, who was wearing her glasses on the end of her nose, pince-nez style.

'Is everything OK, Molly?'

'I was about to ask you the same thing, boss.' She looked quizzically at Caroline, who gazed blankly back. Molly nodded at the delicate bunch of tea roses in the vase on Caroline's desk. 'The flowers. I don't think I've ever seen your office with anything other than lilies in it.'

'Oh, those,' said Caroline, picking up the vase and sniffing deeply. She'd picked them up on a whim that morning – they had reminded her of her garden in Kingham, and the weekend she'd spent with Adam. 'I just fancied a change.'

'Hmmm,' said Molly, clearly unconvinced. 'Well, I suppose you've seen the figures Morton has posted? It's another aggressive move, Caroline, designed to grab all the headlines before we post our figures next week, and to make us look like we're lagging behind them. We're in good health, of course, but nothing quite like the growth MacCaskill is claiming, and—'

'Well, I really wouldn't worry about it,' said Caroline, as the thought of Adam's smooth, taut body popped into her head. 'Once he's sunk several mill into Kidster, MacCaskill will be laughing on the other side of his face – you wait and see.'

Just then, Trudi returned with a copy of *Gloss*.

'As requested.'

'Thanks, Trudi,' said Caroline, studying the magazine, and dismissing Molly by proxy. As her finance director huffed off, Caroline turned the pages interestedly. Copies of the celebrity gossip-driven high street fashion mag had littered Rachel's room for years, but Caroline had barely ever given it more than a cursory glance. She skimmed through the celebrity soap opera pages but found herself being drawn into the dynamic fashion features. There were stories about the latest mid-season 'drop' to hit the readers' favourite high street stores, about a new designer/chain store collaboration, and an affordable new diffusion line by a top end retail brand. She'd always assumed mass market meant cheap, but the clothes featured here were individual and, she had to assume, good quality – otherwise why would established brands risk their reputations by putting their names to them? But more than anything, it was fast-paced, exciting, and *fun*.

Caroline sat back as she reached the features section and a story about a reader whose younger sister had nearly died before a kidney transplant at Great Ormond Street Hospital, and who had since raised thousands of pounds for the charity. The moment Rachel had been born, Caroline had become so sensitised to the horror of 'what if' that she'd been unable to so much as read a traumatic headline. Now, she was drawn into the piece and the lives of the people it profiled – and she was moved to tears. Caroline turned back to her computer. She googled 'high street fashion'. A slew of magazine sites and online chain stores popped up. Accessing the sites, she felt her excitement rising as she took in the vibrant layouts; the range of designs; the 360-degree catwalk shots; the quick, easy way to shop. Why had she never thought of it before? Instead of expecting young people to make the pilgrimage to the Sapphires & Rubies store, or seek out its classy but frankly rather pedestrian website, she should be doing exactly what other, more canny peers had already done: linking up with a major retailer with the existing infrastructure, reach and funding she'd need to hit a wider audience. She felt exhilarated. This wasn't just going to be good business. This was going to be *fun*.

Before she could call Trudi in to share her excitement, her BlackBerry rang. Adam. Her heart skipped a beat.

'Hello?' She castigated herself for playing hard to get. Especially when he'd know his name had already shown up on the LED screen.

'Well, hello Mrs Walker,' he said in that sexy, gravelly voice. Caroline bit her lip as she had yet another flashback of last night's passion.

'Oh, Adam!' She feigned surprise, and again kicked herself for being phoney. 'How was it?'

'Well, I thought it was pretty bloody fantastic,' he murmured. '*You* were pretty amazing. How was it for you?'

'I meant the casting,' laughed Caroline, looking around her guiltily.

'Oh, who knows,' he replied casually. 'To be honest, my mind was elsewhere.'

'Adam! Your career is really important,' she said, and then reprimanded herself for sounding like his mother.

'Oh come on, Mrs Walker – don't tell me your mind has been completely on the job this morning?'

'Actually, I've come up with an idea for a major business expansion,' she said primly. 'It's going to be a really exciting new fashion franchise for me.'

'I don't doubt it,' said Adam. 'Does it involve skimpy undies and bed linen? Because that's the only fashion I'm interested in seeing you in right now. What are you doing this afternoon?'

Caroline bit her lip, sorely tempted by the idea of seeing him. 'We've decided to post our annual results early for the first time,' she said regretfully. 'I'll be here till all hours tonight. If my finance director gets her way, anyhow.'

'No worries,' replied Adam. 'I've got an appointment with someone else close to my heart, anyhow.'

'Oh?' said Caroline, more sharply than she intended. 'And who's that?'

'Naomi.'

'Oh, right,' said Caroline awkwardly, unsure what else to say. She felt more than a twinge of guilt as she was struck by the depth of Adam's commitment to his sister and her cause. Over forty years old, and what had *she* ever given back? And yet here was Adam, with a career in modelling at his feet, and he was still spending time helping others. The urge to do something herself returned with full force, and she looked around her determinedly.

She noticed Simone, her part-time logistics manager gesticulating at the window, and looked at her watch. She'd been due to hold a production meeting over half an hour ago.

'Adam, I'm sorry but I've got to go. I'll call you later, OK?' She was surprised at how natural the words felt.

'Uh-huh. You'd better,' he replied easily, and hung up.

Caroline waved Simone into her office, and cleared her desk ready for the meeting. As she did, she noticed *Gloss* at the top of the pile of papers, and the feature on the girl who had the sister with kidney failure. After the conversation with Adam, her plight touched Caroline even more than the first time around, and something in the girl's face – desperation, need, and *pride* – made her stop in her tracks.

'*If it hadn't been for the nurses at Great Ormond Street Hospital, and the people who raised all the money to help my little sister, we might have lost her for ever,*' she read. Caroline felt a rush of inspiration, and looked up with shining eyes as her team filed in.

She leaned forward. 'Molly, Leroy, Simone, Trudi, come on in. We've got a major new project to discuss.' A sea of expectant faces watched her. Their expressions said it all. Their boss had been behaving weirdly all day, and it looked like right now would be no different.

'We're going mass market!' announced Caroline. 'And not only that, we're going philanthropic. Our new high street line will not only make thousands of pounds for Sapphires & Rubies, it's going to make thousands for charity, too!'

Chapter 11

BEHAVING ODDLY

'So, that's it. We're ready to go. Well, almost. I'm just waiting for Rachel to turn up – I thought she would be a good litmus test of whether we've got it right or not.' Caroline bit her thumb, as she often did when slightly on edge.

'I'm sure she'll love it,' said Adam on the other end of the line. He sounded full of conviction. Why was it only she who was so nervous about how her new collection was going to be received? Caroline wondered. It had taken up so much of her thoughts and creativity, consuming her totally, that she'd almost forgotten her impending fragrance launch.

'And if that big introduction to Rachel goes well, you could always think about another one,' continued Adam lightly.

'Hmmm,' said Caroline, suddenly feeling cornered. She had managed to engineer it so Adam and Rachel still hadn't met. Rachel, of course, was intrigued by the sea change in her mother's social life – from high-profile functions to low-key outings – but Caroline was careful to remain vague about

164

what she was up to – and with whom. Rachel, apparently happy that her mother was getting out at all, had – for the moment anyway – lost interest. But the more Caroline saw of Adam, the more he was starting to question why he'd never met the single most important person in her life.

'So, anyway, I thought we could celebrate this evening,' said Adam, moving the subject along quickly. Caroline's heart sank ever so slightly behind her smile. She'd spent so long sitting at her desk over the past three weeks, the last thing she felt like doing was sitting in a restaurant or bar.

'Oh, that sounds lovely,' she said.

'It's my treat,' he said. Caroline's heart sank another couple of fathoms. Bless Adam – he always insisted on treating her when he could, but on his meagre earnings that generally meant a diner or gastropub. Not that there was anything wrong with that, normally – but tonight, she really wasn't in the mood.

'So I thought we could go for a romantic picnic.'

'A picnic?' Caroline laughed, remembering their first date conversation. 'And where exactly did you have in mind, for our romantic picnic?

She could almost see him smiling. 'Why, Greenwich Park, of course,' he said. 'There's a bench on top of the hill by the Observatory. Meet you there at seven.'

Caroline put down the phone slowly with mixed feelings. Happiness that Adam knew how to push her buttons like that. But also apprehension. Silly, really. It was only a picnic. Yet it would be the first time she'd been back to that spot – the exact place where Les proposed – for years. And for it to happen now, just as their marriage was breaking up . . . Call it serendipity, but Adam's suggestion seemed like so much more than just a simple picnic.

There was a knock at the door. 'Caroline, Rachel's on her way up.'

Caroline smiled her thanks at Trudi and stood up. She found herself unaccountably nervous as she watched Rachel chatting to Julie in reception, and she waved as her daughter tried to drag herself away from the predictable Spanish Inquisition. Caroline made a mental note to have a chat with Julie. Sometimes she needed saving from her own enthusiasm – only that morning Molly had had to shoo her away from a computer screen displaying the P&L for the new lines.

Caroline sat back down nervously. The speed of turnaround on the high street collaboration meant that, against all Caroline's principles, they'd been unable to do any market research. There had been just one consultation with Rachel and a hastily assembled focus group of her friends at ideas stage, and the rest had been born of Caroline's imagination and the skill of her close-knit design team. They were adept at interpreting her thoughts – but this time they had surpassed themselves.

Caroline looked with pride at the designer sketches of roomy totes, cross-shoulder satchels and bejewelled clutches – and textile samples for each – taped to the wall. Creating the new line had unleashed something inside her that years of balance sheets and management meetings had diminished: the fire of the creative process, of creating a brand. Or, in this case, a sub-brand. She couldn't remember ever having enjoyed work quite so much as during the past few weeks – or having achieved so much. They had whittled down the major chain stores that had expressed interest in collaborating with Sapphires & Rubies to just one. They had fast-tracked the agreement process and signed contracts in record time. They had designed an entire collection of accessories – younger, more free spirited than Sapphires & Rubies, yet with the unmistakable timeless appeal of Caroline's signature style – and found suppliers to produce them to Caroline's exacting standards, at the chain store's demanding price points. And they were lined up ready to roll out in the second drop of the store's autumn/winter collection in early September – just in time for the focus on the city that the buzz of London Fashion Week always brought.

Caroline felt a surge of love as she watched her daughter self-consciously make her way across the production floor. In her cut-off denim hot pants, vintage lace top and gladiators, she was a walking advert for festival cool. But no amount of style, beauty or expensive education could overcome the gauch-eness of youth. Of course, Rachel feigned self-confidence and bravado like every one of her peer group, but Caroline knew her too well to be totally taken in by it, and right now she felt an overwhelming desire to run over to her, scoop her up like she had when she was a little girl and carry her to the safety of her office.

'All right, Mum,' said Rachel, sweeping her fringe out of her eyes as she leaned over to kiss Caroline. 'What's up?' She peered closer. 'Mum, are those tears in your eyes?'

Caroline laughed unconvincingly. 'No, darling, of course not. Now, can I get you something to drink?' She felt edgy, jittery. Rachel's approval had become the highest of hurdles to overcome. She felt as though she were about to have the most important interview of her life. What if Rachel didn't like the new products? Where would that leave her?

Rachel waved a half-full bottle of Evian under her nose. 'I'm fine, Mum.' She rummaged in her bag, pulled out a torn-out page from a magazine, and thrust it towards Caroline excitedly. 'I've found the dress!' Caroline frowned in confusion and peered at the screwed–up piece of paper. Rachel pointed at it ecstatically. 'THE dress! For my party.' Caroline smiled. Rachel's eighteenth birthday party was fast approaching, and while Caroline had been trying to get her new collection out in record time, she'd also been juggling arrangements for the Big Day. And it seemed these days, not only did an eighteenth birthday party have to be large scale, special and unique, it had to be *cool* – an event which any self-respecting diary editor would be happy to have gracing their pages, even if few of the guests were on society radar. And so Caroline had spent hours over the past few weeks with Rachel, assessing the merits of one big-name club DJ against another, earnestly discussing whether to opt for traditional country marquee style, or cutting edge inner city club, and comparing her daughter's daily discovery of THE latest dress she simply *had* to have for the evening with the previous day's choice. She saw that Rachel was looking at her with a by-now familiar expression of joy and wonder. 'It's beyond perfect, Mum, and you did say you'd buy me a dress for my present. A proper dress, I mean – designer not high street. I can't turn up in something someone else has got, can I? And this is just what I've been looking for the whole time, it's – ooooh – is that your new ad?' She leapt forward eagerly, and Caroline followed her gaze in surprise. Rachel had not only been 100 per cent distracted from the hot topic of her party dress but had totally bypassed the wall of sketches and was checking out the perfume campaign finals. Of Adam.

'Omigod, he is *hot*!' Rachel turned to Caroline, grinning cheekily. 'How did you manage to keep your hands off *him* during the shoot?'

Caroline stared at her, open-mouthed.

'I – er – I . . .'

Rachel turned back to the advert mock-up. 'Man, what am I doing planning to go to uni when I could be hanging out with you at work and meeting guys like that?'

'Is Robbie not around today?' said Caroline tightly, desperate to change the subject and regain her composure.

'Oh, yeah, he's going to pick me up when we've finished here,' said Rachel vaguely, wandering around the office. 'Oh, wow, so is this what you want me to look at?' She walked over to the wall, nose practically touching the board of designs. She studied them carefully, methodically examining each one, then fingering the swatches of leather, suede and canvas as she'd seen her mother do so many times over the years.

Caroline, still giddy with the adrenalin of shock, watched her every move, hardly daring to breathe.

After a few moments, Rachel turned to her mother, eyes shining. 'Mum, these are amazing! Seriously cool. And they're going to be available on the high street? For, like, high street prices?'

Caroline nodded proudly. 'From £15 and £30. All over the country. And online.'

Rachel turned back to the wall excitedly. 'I love that one best,' she said, pointing to a mock-croc retro-style handbag. 'Or maybe that one' – a faux leopardskin clutch. Her face

169

suddenly serious, she turned to Caroline again, her emerald eyes dancing amidst a sea of black hair and kohl pencil the only thing giving away her real mood.

'There's just one thing, Mum.'

'Oh, and what's that?' asked Caroline, her smile responding to her daughter's cheeky look, but nervous nonetheless.

'My consultation fee. Can I have the whole collection for free?'

Drip, drip, drip.

The summer shower outside cast a grey light over Caroline's usually sunny office interior, and the leaking gutter played like a metronome, punctuating the collective thoughts of the staff squeezed solemnly on to her leather sofa.

Caroline stared at the sketches on her wall, but whereas the same time yesterday her face had been full of keen anticipation, now it displayed the grimmest of grim expressions.

Drip, drip, drip.

All that work, excitement, pulling together – and yet still there had to be a fly in the ointment. And it seemed that Morton – or, more likely, MacCaskill – had found one.

She pushed aside the morning's papers defeatedly, and Simone, Molly and Leroy, sitting opposite her desk miserably, looked at each other, worried. They'd never seen their boss so dejected before. This had to be serious. 'So run this past me again. How did our research not uncover this one tiny flaw in the plan? How did we not only leave ourselves wide open to criticism but manage to break every rule of our moral code? We were meant to be helping vulnerable children, not *exploiting* them!'

As always when she felt worked up, Simone located a blonde dreadlock and twisted it furiously. 'Caroline, the allegations of child labour go back ten years or more. We worked closely with the UK Trade & Investment Manufacturer and Advisory service who've been running stringent checks over the past five years, which is how long the current owners have been running the business. We also contacted the trade attaché at the British Embassy in China. It's a really straight concern now: happy, well-paid workers, a comprehensive health and safety policy in place, and a transparent accounting system. They even have a little school for the workers' kids, for God's sake! It's the best bloody factory in the Far East.'

'Yes, but that doesn't mean anything to our competitors. You know as well as I do that mud sticks – and it obviously didn't take very long or very much effort to sling some at Sapphires & Rubies. As far as they are concerned we're about to go stratospheric on the efforts of child labour. At least, we were about to – before this story broke.' Caroline groaned and put her head in her hands. 'And now the charity element looks like a smokescreen for cheap and exploitative production methods rather than what it is – a genuine wish to give something back.'

In silence the team looked at each other hopefully, willing Caroline's rant to be over.

'Maybe it's not Morton,' suggested Leroy brightly. 'Maybe it's some left-leaning human rights campaigners who are looking for an easy target to start their drum-banging.'

'It's Morton all right,' raged Caroline, stabbing the paper with her forefinger. 'This isn't just a pop at the business – this is personal. Look, it's raking over my split with Les again, and how it's affecting my professional life.' She picked the paper up and started to read out loud. '"*Walker, who, say insiders, is finding it difficult to come to terms with her impending divorce, has been cited as 'behaving oddly' on frequent occasions in the last few months. 'It's as if, for the first time in her professional life, she's got things other than her business preying on her mind', said our source.*"' Caroline laughed hollowly. 'I'm the most dedicated person I know! And if the divorce has had any effect on my work life, it's that it's made me even *more* dedicated!' She stopped short, aware that her outburst could be construed as exactly the kind of odd behaviour she'd been accused of in the paper. 'I mean, who writes this stuff? Where do they get it from?'

This time, it was Molly who ventured forth. 'Well, Caroline, from what you've just read, it came from "an insider". That is, someone who works here. Or . . .' she cleared her throat nervously. 'Someone who knows you socially.'

Caroline looked at her, dumbstruck. 'But – no one here would leak anything to the papers, would they? To Morton? We've moved so fast on this – everyone's been so involved – why would anyone –? What would anyone have to gain?'

She looked around her desperately, head spinning with the thought that one of her treasured team could intentionally want to feed her to the lions.

Molly smiled reassuringly. 'Caroline, there is no one here that would do anything like that. You know we're all dedicated to Sapphires & Rubies – and to you.' She swallowed hard. 'What I was meaning was – well . . . maybe – is there anyone outside of work who might have had access to insider knowledge? I mean, we've kind of put two and two together and worked out that you must be seeing someone new, and by a process of elimination, if it's no one in the team, then it must be someone – in your inner circle . . .' She trailed off in embarrassment.

Caroline stared at her, face thunderous.

'Let me get this right, Molly. You're insinuating – without anything to base it on – that I am so silly, so flighty as to have become involved with someone who might be involved in corporate espionage? And that were I to prove myself to be such a bad judge of character, I would also then indulge in pillow talk that would threaten everything I've spent ten years building up? That's charming, thank you. Next thing, you'll be suggesting my ex-husband has it in for me.'

There was silence.

'I think we'd better adjourn this meeting. I'll speak to you later.'

As they filed out of her room, she pondered the accusation. The timing was spot on. The time she'd met Adam was indisputably the time things had started going wrong at work.

It couldn't be him. Could it?

Chapter 12

HOW ABOUT AN APRON?

Caroline sleepily watched Adam's pert white bottom as he padded across the bedroom, grabbing her satin bathrobe and pulling it around him.

'Does it suit me?' he said with a cheeky grin.

'You look better without it,' she said lazily, plumping the pillow up and turning over, luxuriating in the layers of Egyptian cotton and goosedown duvet. With Adam's side now vacant, Pusspaws jumped up on to the bed to occupy the warm spot he'd left behind.

Caroline heard Adam wander downstairs, turn the coffee machine on and start crashing about with mugs. What was it about men, she pondered, that made them think they were being so quiet when they regularly risked waking the living dead just by making a cup of coffee? Maybe Adam wasn't so different after all.

She rolled over again and thought gleefully about last night – every hot, heavy, X-rated moment of it. Nope, he was *definitely* different. Different to anyone she'd ever known, that is.

And, she had to admit, there were *some* benefits to having a younger boyfriend. She pulled a hand out of the duvet and started to count them on her fingers.

1. The not-inconsiderable self-esteem boost of being seen with a hot guy. When she first got together with Les, she'd stopped noticing the reams of sexy young girls out with rich older men – selective eyesight, she thought wryly. But now she was 'with' Adam, she couldn't help but notice the envious looks she got from those very women – and admiring looks from the men, too, no doubt wondering what it was about her that could attract someone like Adam.

2. Adam was great in bed – make that GREAT in bed. Caroline blushed as she recalled the levels of ecstasy he could bring her to – and how . . . Like, he went down on her! Over and over again, for what seemed like hours! The closest Les had ever got to that was when he'd accidentally fallen asleep on her lap on the sofa one time, with his face buried in her trouser crotch. In fact, Adam was like her own personal sexual revolution.

3. Adam was also open to trying more things than other men she'd met (i.e. Les) – cultural as well as sexual. He was more emotionally open than Les, and happy to talk about his feelings. He wore his heart on his sleeve, almost.

4. Adam was from the same place as she was: not just physically, but mentally. He might go on about garage music, gaming and graphic design – none of which she had the first idea about – but he was passionate about other issues that she was, too – like the environment, children's welfare, family. Despite the generation gap, he seemed to value the same

qualities; loyalty and good manners, for a start. Godammit, he even held dear the same places that she did! Now that was surely no coincidence – that was fate . . .

5. Adam claimed to like the fact that she was more emotionally secure, not worried about things such as eating or drinking too much like girls his own age. (Just as well, considering their red-wine-fuelled first date . . .) So, it seemed there *were* men left in the world who preferred maturity over litheness and youth.

6. With Adam there were no moobs, jowls, snores, hair dye on the pillow or Viagra to worry about. And best of all, Caroline didn't have to 'bimbify' herself: Adam didn't seem to be intimidated by her intellect like Les had been. He almost seemed impressed by it and – shock, horror – had also read lots of the same books.

7. Last, but not least, he could download music for her and sort out her new iPhone on the 101 times she couldn't.

Caroline turned over again, pleased with her list. She'd spent her life justifying to herself everything from an extra square of chocolate to a new handbag – why not justify her right to have an affair with a younger man?

Then, all of a sudden, she sat bolt upright. As a list, it wasn't so much justifying younger men, as *one* man in particular. In fact, six of the seven reasons on her list were specifically about Adam. Which meant . . .

She hugged her legs in to her chest, mulling over exactly what that *did* mean. It meant that there was more to her and Adam than a couple of dates. It wasn't serious, of course – heaven forbid – but it meant he was in her life for more than a couple of dates. Which in itself meant ... She took a deep breath. It meant she was going to have to introduce him to Rachel.

Caroline bit her thumb nervously. When it came to Adam and Rachel, so far was so good. Through a mixture of careful planning and sheer good fortune, she'd managed to engineer a one-in, one-out policy without either of them so much as glimpsing the other's retreating back. She'd even got away with Christian seeing her and Adam together that morning. God knows how (there must be an awful lot else going on in the neighbourhood this month for him to worry about). But – she wasn't going to be able to put it off for ever. The question was: how would she introduce the concept of another man to Rachel, let alone one practically the same age as her daughter?

Caroline tried to block out the thoughts of what Les would say. *Let him say what he likes*, she told herself crossly. *It's all about you now, not him. Well, you and Rachel . . .*

'Breakfast is served, Mrs Walker!'

The chink of crockery on a tray as Adam kicked open the door brought Caroline back to the present, and she laughed out loud as she saw him carrying a wooden tray crammed with coffee mugs and a plate of toast and jam. Somewhere along the line, he'd lost her robe and was now wearing one of her aprons – a white linen number with a goose on the front.

'Very chic.'

He placed the tray on the bed and gave a little bow, turning as he did to reveal a red rose placed in his bum crack.

'I meant stylish chic, not bum cheek,' giggled Caroline, then shrieked as he backed up towards her.

'Take it out then – with your teeth!' he laughed, then turned again and launched himself at her. She pulled out the rose delicately between thumb and forefinger and stuck it behind her ear, then gave herself up to the sweetest of kisses.

As Adam lay across her, she felt him grow hard and waves of desire wash over her. His mouth moved to her neck, nibbling behind her ear and down across her décolletage and under the duvet to her breast.

'But what about breakfast?' she half-heartedly protested.

'I've lost my appetite – for food,' he growled.

He slid under the duvet and his full, soft lips continued their delicious journey down her body. Caroline sighed softly and gave herself up to the growing feeling of intense pleasure.

Suddenly, there was a crash from downstairs.

'What was that?' Caroline lifted her head in concern.

'It's nothing,' mumbled Adam from just inside her inner thigh. 'Now come back here. I've only just started with you . . .'

Caroline moaned gently and pulled the duvet back. The sight of his toned body lying across her turned her on even more, and she lay back in ecstasy.

The door burst open.

'Oh, Mum, I've had such an awful time! Robbie's been so mean to me and – MUM?!'

Caroline sat up in shock, pulling the duvet around her to cover her nakedness, and found herself staring straight into the horror-struck eyes of her daughter. Her first thought was concern: Rachel was very upset. Her face was tearstained, her eyes wild; but not – thought Caroline, cringing inwardly as she pictured the crumpled bed linen, the untouched breakfast tray, last night's discarded clothes lying in pools around the room – as dishevelled as she was.

'Rachel, I—'

But she was too late. Rachel turned and exited as quickly as she had entered, running down the corridor with huge, rasping sobs.

'Oops,' said Adam. 'I'm guessing that was Rachel?' His tone was deadpan, but his brow was furrowed in concern.

'Yes, of course that was Rachel,' snapped Caroline, jumping out of bed and searching for her robe. She tutted in exasperation as she remembered: of course, it was downstairs, wherever Adam had left it.

'How about an apron?' suggested Adam, holding it out to her.

'This is not a laughing matter, Adam!' Caroline stormed through to her wardrobe and pulled out some leggings and a baggy top.

'I'm sorry, I'm just trying to make light of it,' he mumbled, searching around for his jeans.

'Yes, well, don't,' she retorted sharply.

Adam stood up and crossed and uncrossed his arms awkwardly as he watched Caroline spring into action. 'Is there anything I can do?' he said sheepishly.

'You've done quite enough already,' she replied, instantly kicking herself for taking it out on Adam. She felt like a cornered lion, desperate to protect her young – and there was no time to worry about his feelings.

Pulling her fingers through her hair, she dashed out of the

room and along the corridor to Rachel's room. The door was firmly closed, and she could hear sobbing inside.

Caroline knocked softly on the door. 'Rachel?' There was no reply, only more sobbing, and Caroline opened the door slowly. Not for the first time, she thanked whatever instinctive wisdom had refused all teenage requests from Rachel to be able to lock her bedroom from the inside.

'Rachel, darling, can I come in?' She peered around the door tentatively. Rachel was lying face down on the pink satin duvet, hugging her dog-eared old stuffed rabbit, crying into a pillow. Caroline felt as if her heart was breaking when she saw the pain she'd inflicted on her.

'No! Go away! I hate you!'

Caroline flinched, stung by her daughter's vehemence, at the same time desperate to hold her, to cuddle away her pain as she had when she was little.

'Please, darling. Let me come in.'

'GO AWAY!'

'Rachel, please. Let me explain . . .'

Abruptly, Rachel sat up, rivulets of mascara-streaked tears running down her cheeks, face puffy and blotchy.

'Explain what, exactly? Explain why you were shagging some random bloke in your bed just then? In *Dad's* bed?' That's *gross*, Mum.'

Caroline's jaw dropped and she stood, mouth gaping, as she stared at her daughter. Rachel was right. The evidence had been plain to see. There wasn't much explaining to be done, really.

'But darling, it's not what you think.' Caroline shook her head irritably at her own lack of finesse. It was turning into the clichéd exchange between cuckolded spouse and adulterer, not an adult conversation between mother and daughter about a new lover.

'Oh, so what was it, then? A quote for some gardening? A job interview? A *casting*?'

As Rachel spat the words out, Caroline flinched again at the venom in her voice. Needing to bridge the physical gap between herself and Rachel, she edged through the crack in the doorway and perched on the end of the bed. Immediately, Rachel pulled up her legs to retain as much distance between them as possible. Caroline reached out and placed her hand on the duvet, in an attempt to bridge the gap.

'Darling, you knew I was dating.'

'Yes, but only casually!' cried Rachel. For 'casual', read platonic, realised Caroline all too late, aghast that she'd inflicted such distress on her daughter. Why on earth hadn't she kept her liaisons with Adam to hotels until she felt comfortable introducing them?

Caroline cleared her throat delicately. 'Sweetheart, casual dates are always going to lead to something more serious at some point. And yes, this has happened a little quicker than I had expected. But . . . I guess life has little surprises in store for everyone.'

'So you and —' Rachel paused, her face contorting with disgust as she pictured Adam — '*him* — you're serious?'

Caroline stopped thoughtfully. Serious?

'Well . . .' It was a catch-22. She hadn't even admitted to herself what their status was, let alone to Rachel, and she was reluctant to put any kind of label on it. But brush Adam off as not serious, and she would break the very moral code she'd brought Rachel up to believe in: that sex was about love, and not to be carelessly bandied about. 'We've been seeing a bit of each other, yes.'

Rachel wailed and hit the pillow. 'But that means it's definitely over between you and Dad – for ever! I thought dating other men would make you realise what you'd lost with Dad, not mean you'd find someone else!'

Caroline stared at her daughter. So that's what this was about. Well, alongside the shock of seeing her own mother naked in bed with a total stranger, anyhow. Rachel was still harbouring hopes that she and Les were going to get back together.

'Darling, it's far too early to tell what's going to happen between Adam and me.' Rachel tutted at the mention of his name. Caroline chose to ignore it. 'But irrespective of what happens between us, your father and I *aren't* getting back together.'

'That's not what he says,' murmured Rachel sulkily.

Caroline felt anger well up in her as she thought of Les, still trying to control her even after everything that had happened. 'Yes, well, it's a different situation for your father. He's got no reason not to trust me. But for me, Rachel, the trust has gone – and without trust, a relationship has no future.'

She edged closer to her daughter and started to stroke her hair as she had done since she was little. Rachel hit her hand away irritably.

'And anyway, I've had a huge row with Robbie, and you weren't there for me.'

'I am there, darling. I'm always there for you.'

'Yes, but so was *he*. I don't want *him* there. I just need you!'

Caroline felt her heart crack as she heard the raw pain in Rachel's voice. She resumed stroking her hair.

'And you'll always have me. We'll work this out, darling, you'll see.'

She just wished she felt as confident as she sounded.

Chapter 13

TAXI FOR MRS WALKER!

Of course, going out with someone who barely counts as an adult had to have its downside, too, mused Caroline, as she pottered around the kitchen to the thumping strains of emo music seeping out from Rachel's bedroom. And her daughter's reaction to him was always going to be one of them. Once Rachel had got over the initial shock, teen mulishness had set in and she had been shut away in there all morning, refusing, as she always did after a tantrum, to come out or speak to her mother. Caroline frowned. She hadn't had a row with Adam yet. Was this how he'd react when they did?

Caroline had spent the morning feeling strangely on edge. Once Adam had been unceremoniously ushered out, she had been left with a strange feeling of needing to be busy, yet not able to concentrate fully on anything. So, she'd done what she always did at times of uncertainty and resorted to cooking. She reached into a cupboard for the vanilla essence. Cupcakes were Rachel's favourite. Caroline had always seen food as a way to people's hearts, and she knew that if anything was going to bring Rachel round it was the smell of baking on the air. Folding in the mixture, she allowed the rhythmic motion to lull her into a positive mental attitude. Rachel would come round. It wasn't just Adam – she would have been upset at any new man entering their lives – let alone one she first met in such an uncompromising situation . . .

Caroline set the mixing bowl to one side hopefully. Rachel had always insisted on having 'lickings' when she baked – maybe the sight of it would pull her out of her current gloom.

Outside, a car beeped its horn and Caroline looked out of the kitchen window with interest. Living here, she was unaccustomed to any kind of outside noise – Saturdays were always quiet on her road.

A silver Toyota Prius private hire vehicle had pulled up outside her drive and the driver waved at her through the open car window. She waved back, gesturing that he had the wrong address. He peered at the house number on the gatepost and then indicated back to her that he thought he had the right one.

Wiping her hands down the apron a naked Adam had been wearing only hours earlier, Caroline opened the heavy Victorian glass-fronted door and called out.

'I'm sorry, I think you've got the wrong address! I haven't ordered a car. You must be mistaken.'

'Nope, love, just double-checked with the office – car for Mrs Walker on the Sapphires & Rubies account for eleven o'clock.'

Caroline shook her head firmly but politely. 'Well, I'm Ms Walker, and that's my company account, but I definitely haven't ordered a car.'

The driver sighed. 'Ordered this morning, apparently.'

'Well, as it's a work account and it's a Saturday, I am a hundred per cent sure it's not me,' said Caroline patiently. Then she paused. 'Unless . . . wait here one second.'

'Don't worry love, I'm not going anywhere,' said the driver flatly, as if this was a common occurrence in his long-suffering work-life.

Caroline jogged back up the drive. 'Rachel,' she called through the door and up the stairs. 'Rachel!'

'Yes?' said Rachel sulkily from the hallway behind Caroline. Caroline jumped, not expecting to find her daughter downstairs.

'Rachel, there's a taxi outside who claims he got the order this morning and I wondered – what are you doing with those bags?' Her mouth gaped open as she saw the carry-on bag and a large holdall at Rachel's feet.

'I'm leaving, Mum. I'm going to Grandma's initially, and then who knows where? But I can't stay here, clearly.'

Caroline stared at her, speechless. Seeing her daughter was deadly serious, concern was replaced with horror.

'Darling, what on earth do you mean? This is your home – of course you can stay here! You can't just walk out, with nowhere to go . . .'

'I have got somewhere to go,' insisted Rachel. 'To Grandma's. That's my home too, you know.'

The words hit Caroline as though she'd been stung. She opened her mouth to protest, but no words came out.

'I've got my own room, my own key,' continued Rachel. 'So what's the difference between there and here? Apart from *he's* not there. So it's better there, right? At least I'll be Grandma's priority. Unlike here.'

Caroline felt the heat of injustice rise in her chest, and she willed herself to stay calm. 'But darling, I would never put someone else before you, you know that! You've always come first. You always *will* come first. And—'

Rachel shook her head irritably. 'That's bollocks, Mum. It's all about him now.' She paused, her face contorted as if she'd remembered something particularly unpleasant.

'I've looked him up on the Net. He's the one from your perfume shoot, isn't he? The one I was looking at in your office? The one who's the same age as me?'

'Darling, he's not, he's nineteen actually—'

Rachel laughed 'Nineteen??? Oh, well that's all right then. You think that's normal, do you? God, Mum, you seriously have got no idea. He's younger than Robbie. *Younger than my boyfriend!* Well, ex-boyfriend.' Rachel gave a shuddering sigh as she remembered the other earth-shattering event that had taken place in the past twenty-four hours. 'The SHAME, Mum. Does that mean nothing to you?'

Caroline opened her mouth to reply, but Rachel's rant was unstoppable. Her voice was becoming higher and her face turning red with anger.

'Wait till Grandma hears about this. What's she going to say? I mean, there were even rumours about you two on the day of the shoot, from what I can see on the Internet. Have you never heard the one about not crapping on your own doorstep? What's it going to mean for your business if people think you're just some sad old divorcee looking to prey on all the models you hire for advertising? No one's ever going to want to work for you again! And what's it going to mean for me, if I can't bring home a boyfriend in case you decide to come on to him behind my back? If *he* thinks you're going to come on to him behind my back? It's too hideous for words. I can't bear it!'

Rachel stopped for breath. Caroline, realising the front door was open, moved to pull it to. As she did, she saw the hedge move across the road. She frowned. Christian again. He didn't miss a trick.

'And that's another thing!' screamed Rachel, shoving her foot in the door. 'Even the bloody neighbours knew about it before me!' She jabbed a forefinger across the road in Christian's direction. 'He's been going on about you moving on and looking great and having a new spring in your step and I thought he meant you were starting to get back to being yourself again. I've been agreeing, saying how fantastic I think it is, how it's been really hard for us all but that we were finally getting there – no wonder he looked so bloody shocked! And then he told me it was great you and I had so much in common. I thought he meant clothes and TV and stuff – not men!'

Caroline's mouth opened and closed, but no sound came out. She felt completely exposed – and utterly defenceless.

'Well, darling, I – can't we talk about this?' She held out her hands imploringly, feeling helpless against the tide of wrath she'd unleashed in her own flesh and blood.

'No, Mum, we can't talk about it. What's done is done – you can't change that.' Rachel picked up the holdall, tossed her head and stalked past Caroline and out of the front door. She paused and looked back over her shoulder. 'And don't call me. OK?'

Caroline stood stock still, her heart pumping loudly, mouth dry. Rachel was leaving. Her baby was walking out. And she couldn't stop her.

And her mother . . . She shook her head in dismay. What the hell would Babs make of it all?

As they bobbed along the winding country lane in her Aston Martin DB9, Caroline suddenly pulled over into a leafy, rose-covered lay-by.

In the passenger seat Adam swung over to his door in an exaggerated fall. 'Whoa! What's going on?'

Caroline undid her seat belt and looked at him grimly. 'You're driving, is what's going on. Come on – swap over!'

She opened the car door and walked around to his side. He was still looking at her with an amused expression on his face.

Caroline looked at her watch irritably and opened his door in frustration. 'Come on, Adam, what are you waiting for? We're running late as it is. You've asked me to let you drive the car more than once – well, here's your chance.'

Adam looked at her suspiciously. 'We're running late to meet your monstrous mother and you suddenly decide to let me, with my brand new driving licence burning a hole in my just-passed pocket, drive your swanky sports car? Don't say I didn't warn you . . .'

'We're not "going to meet my mother",' corrected Caroline crossly. 'And nor is she "monstrous",' she added almost as an afterthought. 'We're just dropping off some samples for her on the way back from lunch. I always send her stuff from my latest collections.'

'So why didn't you send them this time?' teased Adam, eyes dancing.

'Because I'm not going to waste money on a bike when

189

I'm practically going to drive past her doorstep, am I? Look, do you want to drive the car or not?' snapped Caroline. 'I'm not going to ask you again.'

Unabashed, Adam uncurled his long legs from the footwell and climbed out of the car, taking the keys from Caroline with a quick kiss on her nose. He whistled delightedly as he strolled around to the driver's door, swinging the keys from his fingers.

Caroline took his place in the passenger seat, not admitting even to herself why she hadn't sent them on. The truth was that yes, of course she could have couriered the samples and the first bottle of her new scent to her mother as normal. Instead, she was using them as a smokescreen not just to check on Rachel, but for a low-key opportunity to introduce her to Adam. It felt too soon – far too soon – to be packaging the meeting as a formal introduction, and heaven forbid she should give Adam the impression that this was anything other than a casual pub lunch in the countryside that happened to include dropping in on her mother – but with Rachel on the warpath about Adam it would only be a matter of time before Babs heard about him. And forewarned was forearmed . . .

She'd given the matter a lot of thought yesterday. In fact, she'd thought about nothing else. After Rachel had stormed off in the taxi, and Caroline had called Babs to warn her of her granddaughter's imminent arrival (brushing the argument off as a 'minor fallout'), and she'd cried her heart out, wrung her hands and covered every single scenario to sort this sorry situation out, Caroline had decided on a 'business as usual' policy. Her first plan had been to call it off with Adam and have Rachel come running back to her with her tail between her legs, but instinct told her that wasn't the answer. It wasn't just about Adam. Rachel's reaction felt more fundamental than just a teenage tantrum. It had something more monumental about it — like a rite of passage — and much as it was tearing Caroline apart to leave her daughter to her own devices for now, she sensed that this time, it was absolutely the best policy.

So here she was, hurtling around the countryside with her newly legal teenage lover behind the wheel, on course either to crash or meet her mother. Caroline wasn't sure, given the choice, which scenario she preferred. But what she did know was that turning up with her lover in the passenger seat would send her mother's old-fashioned sense of chivalry spinning long before Adam's age did. There were certain things that, in Babs's eyes, were 'a man's job', and driving was most definitely one of them.

'Left here!' she squealed as they approached the turning at 50 miles an hour.

Adam screeched to a halt and swung the car into an even smaller country lane, straight into the path of an oncoming tractor.

'BRAKE!' screamed Caroline. She had a sudden urge for a stiff drink and a cigarette. As they avoided the tractor with inches to spare, she turned to Adam accusingly. 'Are you actually trying to kill us?'

'Sorry,' he grinned, totally unabashed. 'This is fun, though, isn't it?'

'Is that what you call it,' murmured Caroline as the road opened on to a gently undulating village green and a smattering of beautifully kept painted cottages, including her mother's own pretty thatched house. It was an idyllic spot, that made her think of bicycles and cricket teas, and she loved coming back here. Today, though, her pleasure was tinged with a sense of nervous anticipation.

'So remember, compliment her on her scones and don't whatever you do ask her about my dad,' muttered Caroline as they crunched along the gravel road to the cottage. 'And for God's sake, take it easy with Rachel. No kissing me, touching me, hugging me. Or her.'

Adam laughed. 'No problem on any count. And anyway, I'm starving.'

'You only finished lunch an hour ago!' said Caroline in disbelief, thinking back to the hearty three-course meal he'd polished off.

'Always room for more,' he grinned as he pulled up outside the house. 'Of everything.'

Caroline blushed. 'And that kind of talk is also off the menu for the next hour or so,' she said warningly.

'Doesn't stop me thinking it though, does it?' Adam winked at Caroline as her mother, in a bright pink kaftan and purple headscarf with a basket of freshly picked flowers, rounded the corner. 'So, let the dog see the rabbit . . .'

Caroline stifled a laugh as they approached her mother, a laugh that turned to a soft smile as Babs seemed to get smaller and smaller the closer they got. Caroline had towered above Babs since she'd been an adolescent, and this was more pronounced now that Babs was starting to stoop slightly. Too much time spent leaning over her garden tending the foxgloves, thought Caroline fondly. Her mother could be nosey, cranky and difficult, but seeing her in this familiar setting, Caroline remembered how she admired her more than almost anyone, and loved her dearly.

'Hello, Mother.'

'Hello, Caroline,' said Babs, accepting the proffered hug and pulling back to look at her critically as if it was months since they'd last met. 'I must admit I was a little shocked to get your call. You look like you've lost more weight. Have you been eating? I've made some scones.'

Caroline grimaced. 'Yes, Mother, of course I've been eating.' She looked beyond Babs expectantly.

'Rachel's not here,' said Babs, anticipating the next question. 'She got wind of your impending arrival and took the first train into town. Something about going to a gig. But don't worry, she's promised to get the last train back here, and I shall pick her up from the station.'

Caroline swallowed hard: her mother was relating her daughter's movements to her, as if Rachel were a distant family friend.

'Thanks, Mother.' She smiled bravely. She had no one else to blame if she was feeling estranged from Rachel. She was lucky that the sanctuary of her grandmother's house was so accessible – a place that both Caroline and Rachel felt she was safe. 'Anyhow, I've brought you some gifts.'

Babs's eyes lit up as she looked Adam up and down gleefully. 'Haven't you just,' she said, accepting the gift-wrapped box from the top of the pile and studying his face intently. 'Well, you'd better come in. My scones aren't going to eat themselves.'

★

193

Two hours later, sitting in easy chairs in the shade of the gnarled old oak in Babs's archetypal English country garden, her mother had still not stopped fawning over Adam. No, she wasn't fawning – she was *flirting*, Caroline corrected herself. As well as a table heaving with every form of sandwich, cake and sweet treat you could mention, her mother had provided him with a guided tour of the garden, a photographic potted history of her childhood (including, Caroline had noted, many pictures of her mother in her glamorous youth) and her unadulterated view of what made a real man (everything Adam was and nothing Caroline's father was). All delivered with cutesy little remarks and winning smiles. Why she'd ever been worried about her mother not liking him, she didn't know. In fact, if Babs wasn't her own mother, Caroline could swear she was after him herself.

And in the midst of it all was the beatific 'I could get used to this' smile of a spoilt man spread all over Adam's face. There was certainly no grinning and bearing it going on there, thought Caroline – Adam was enjoying every minute, and indulging his gift of the gab with the same flirtatious tone of voice as Babs, as she indulged him with everything she could think of.

Right now, Caroline could tell, Babs was gearing herself up to produce the steak and ale pie Caroline had spotted earlier when she'd gone to the fridge for some milk. Caroline had to get in there – and quick.

'You know, Adam, we really should be going,' she said, walking over to him and touching him lightly on the knee.

His face fell. 'Really? I think Babs – your mother – was planning to invite us to stay for dinner.'

'Uh-huh,' said Caroline laughing, but giving him 'the look' at the same time. 'The traffic will be piling up already. We need to head back now if we're going to avoid spending all night on the A1.'

'Oh, Caroline, you can't deprive this poor boy of a square meal on a Sunday!' said her mother in mock horror. 'Stay, the pair of you, and travel back later when the traffic's eased up again.'

Caroline thought her eyes were going to bore a hole in Adam's until he picked up the hint. Suddenly, she saw realisation dawn in his eyes.

'No, really Mrs T – Babs – Caroline's right. We can't stay any longer.' He gave her a winning smile. 'But I tell you what – I'll give you advance warning next time we're coming and we'll stay for lunch, tea *and* dinner.'

Babs took the tea towel that seemed to be permanently in her hand and flicked his bottom with it. 'Promises, promises! Next time, you'll stay for the whole weekend,' she said playfully. She turned to Caroline reproachfully. 'You so rarely stay for any length of time, Caroline. It's always up to me to come to you. Next time, make it longer. I'm sure Rachel will come around eventually. I'll bet she and Adam will have a lot in common, won't they?'

A classic Babs-style barb indicated to Caroline that it was definitely time to leave. After promises from her mother to persuade Rachel to return home, and more protestations from Babs about them leaving at all, Caroline finally managed to shepherd Adam into the car, carrying as many packages of tinfoil-wrapped goodies as Babs could press upon him. Caroline shook off the thought that she, with her own penchant for feeding people up, wasn't a million miles away from her mother's effusive brand of hospitality.

As she pushed Adam out of the door, she felt her mother tweak her elbow.

'I don't know where you found him, my girl, but if there's more like him I want to know. He's hot stuff!' Babs winked and then waved flamboyantly to Adam. 'Don't be a stranger!' she trilled.

Really, thought Caroline, the only stranger present that afternoon had been her mother.

'I still don't get why I can't stay. If Rachel's not around, she can't be upset about it, can she?' reasoned Adam, back in the passenger seat for the journey home.

'I'm sorry, but it's too soon. I think we need to cool things off for a bit, until everything's settled. Much as I'd love you to come back,' added Caroline.

At a tube station, Adam clambered out reluctantly.

'Sorry,' said Caroline. 'But if I get caught up in the Sunday night traffic it'll be tomorrow by the time I'm home.'

'No problem,' said Adam easily. 'Unless you want to lend me the car and you can get the tube?' She laughed as he stuck his head through the window for a goodbye kiss.

As she made for home, Caroline turned on the radio and hummed to herself. That had all gone remarkably well. If things with Rachel could just sort themselves out, she would feel almost happy. She turned up the volume and sang out loud.

But as she turned into the driveway, she had a shock. On

the doorstep, her bags piled up beside her, and stroking Pusspaws adoringly, was Rachel.

Caroline's heart leapt, and she had to will herself to park up slowly rather than leave the engine running and smother her daughter in kisses. Slowly does it. Thank *goodness* she didn't have Adam with her.

'Hi, darling.'

'Hi, Mum. I forgot my key.' No mention of the argument.

'No problem, darling,' replied Caroline hesitantly, unlocking the door and standing aside as Rachel dragged her bags back in. 'Have you, erm, had a nice weekend?'

'It was all right. Grandma was busy with the garden. I was going to go to a gig tonight, but it was sold out.' She paused and dropped her eyes. 'I went round Suki's today and hung out, which was kind of cool. We talked. You know. About stuff.' She slung her holdall to the foot of the stairs and looked up shyly at her mother. Caroline thought she saw the glimmer of warmth in her green eyes. An unspoken olive branch? Rachel scuffed her Converse along the floor. 'Oh, and Robbie wants me back.'

'Oh, that's wonderful, darling,' said Caroline, taking the initiative and giving her a hug. 'So how do you feel about that?'

'Not sure,' said Rachel shrugging her off. Caroline bit her lip. Too much too soon, clearly. Still, at least Rachel had come home.

'Well, darling, don't rush into anything. If you're not sure, maybe you need to give yourself time.'

'Mmm.' Rachel stepped over her bags and started to climb the stairs. Caroline resisted the urge to pull her up on her messiness. Time for tidiness later.

'Oh, and Mum?'

Caroline looked up as Rachel turned round. 'Yes, darling?'

'Suki wants to know, are Adam's mates all as fit as he is?'

Chapter 14

THE SHAME!

Caroline let out a gasp as she pulled back the bedroom curtains and saw London shimmering under the haze that even at this early hour signified a gorgeous sunny day to come. The sky was blue, the sun was on its way out – and her first ever publicly posted annual report would be hitting the inboxes of the world's financial media any time now. And so, she decided spontaneously, she was going to walk to work. It was the perfect summer day, after all.

Well, *almost* perfect. For although there were no dark clouds on her life's horizon – now, a few days after their Sunday visit, she was fully reinstated back in Babs's good books (although thankfully not receiving as many texts from her mother as Adam currently was . . .), the launches were all in place to roll out as planned, and she and Rachel were officially back on speaking terms – she couldn't exactly say Rachel had welcomed Adam with open arms. In fact, Caroline's only discussion about it with her daughter since Rachel had come home had been fairly short. And conclusive. ('Just because Suki thinks it's cool, Mum, doesn't mean *I* do . . . Let's just both do our own thing and not talk about it, OK?') But whilst she and Rachel could avoid talking about each other's love life, and with the welcome distraction of her eighteenth birthday party the following month to plan together, they seemed to be getting along fine. Adam had – after a trial run two nights ago – adjusted to low-key liaisons in boutique hotels around the city with aplomb (five star luxury and room service – although he claimed it didn't match up to her own home and cooking – had clearly helped). Which meant there were many more days, like today, when she was waking up on her own again. Which she didn't like one little bit.

But the sunshine had realised its restorative powers and Caroline threw on a cotton T-shirt, a pair of beige Capri pants and comfortable tan brogues, popped a silk blouse and pair of nude peeptoe heels in her bag for work, a lipgloss for the function she was going to that evening, and set off for the office.

As she reached Regent's Park, she gave a happy sigh. There was something special about London in the sunshine; it could lift her mood like nowhere else. Just then, her iPhone rang, showing an undisclosed number on the screen. Caroline looked at her watch and frowned. 7.05 a.m. Too early for a UK call, too late for New York. An emergency? Remembering the imminent press release, she smiled. Of course – a financial journalist wanting to be the first with exclusive quotes on the Sapphires & Rubies sales figures.

Humming happily, she answered.

'Hello?'

'Caroline Walker? It's the *Sun* here. We'd like to talk to you about your relationship with Adam Geray.' Stunned, Caroline stood stock still.

'Caroline?'

She gathered her wits about her. 'It's Mrs Walker to you,' she said pleasantly. 'And forgive me for my naivety, but of what interest are my relationships to you or anyone else?'

The journalist was unfazed. 'Well, I think you underestimate your own celebrity, Caroline.'

Caroline winced. 'Celebrities' were people who were famous for doing not very much. If she *was* indeed well known, she would hope it was for her business prowess rather than simply notoriety. All that, of course, could be about to change . . .

The journalist's next words confirmed her worst thoughts. 'And when a famous businesswoman, a role model for young women the world over, leaves her husband for a younger man – a *much* younger man – particularly one starring in her forthcoming advertising launch, then I think you'll find your relationships do become extremely interesting to everyone.' He paused. 'So tell me about it – let's get your side of the story out there before the world makes up its own mind about what's happened – and judges you with their wallets.'

Caroline caught her breath. This wasn't a trade rumour. It wasn't even a 'News in Brief' in the *FT*. This was full-blown tabloid scoop. A national scandal. This was *major*.

'I'm sorry, but my only comment has to be no comment.'

Caroline sat with her head in her left hand, an unfinished latte congealing in a takeaway cup next to her. Her right hand sat limply on her computer mouse, with which she'd been at first frantically, and then, seeing the blanket coverage, more hesitantly, scouring websites since she'd arrived at the office an hour ago.

Forget the *Sun* scoop: her relationship with Adam was all over London. Scrap that. It was all over the UK. The world, even, for those that cared.

Outside her office, the mood was sombre. The team, having expected a manic day with media call after media call about the results, were well primed to deal with the weight of calls, if not the nature of them. But their tone was subdued, and their body language defensive. Even Julie was uncharacteristically on edge – the brash blonde of her hair seemed to have lost some of its peroxide shine, and her scarlet nails seemed duller than usual. Caroline bitterly regretted having put them all in this situation. Years of loyalty, and this was how she had repaid them. At least, having it foisted upon them by the world's papers without warning. Loyal to the end, their immediate reaction was to protect their boss, and Sapphires & Rubies, but they quite rightly felt let down by her for keeping this significant development in her private life from them.

Caroline shook her head at the irony. Some private life. As a happily married wife and mother, her home life had indeed, for the most part, been just that. She had been fêted at parties and functions, but the paps had more or less left her alone in her own time – except for the odd style stalker shot on the school run. But now, as a single woman, the rules had changed. It appeared that everyone now had an opinion on – and almost a stake in – where she decided to go, what she chose to wear, and who she chose to date.

Of course, she wasn't high profile enough to warrant this

kind of attention on her own. The *Sun* wouldn't have just stumbled across her and Adam. They had been tipped off. And there were no prizes for guessing who by.

The method was tried and tested. The information too exact. It was an industry job – and it had MacCaskill's fingerprints all over it. But there was more to it than that. Her team were convinced there was a mole in her life. Hell, *she* was now convinced that there was a mole in her life. And now, she sensed, her closest colleagues were putting the guilt at Adam's door. He was, after all, an outsider to their close-knit team. He had arrived on the scene at around the time MacCaskill started his most recent onslaught. And yet ... and yet Caroline's gut instinct told her it wasn't him. The problem was, if it wasn't him, who was it?

Her iPhone buzzed with a text from Adam and she frowned. She still hadn't entirely worked out how to use it. Not only that, she hadn't entirely worked out what to say to Adam about the situation. About anything.

The Sun keep calling. What am I meant to say???

Her heart sank. Adam, like her, was way out of his depth and, like her, must be panicking. But she couldn't face speaking to him about it. It would make the situation seem more real, and it would make her feel even more ridiculous. Not only that: it would warrant some kind of discussion of their status – and she wasn't ready for that.

Just keep saying no comment!!! she typed back urgently, and pressed send. At least, she hoped she'd pressed send.

Almost as soon as it had gone, the phone rang again. Caroline's heart skipped a beat as she saw the caller ID. Rachel. When Caroline had tried to reach her earlier, she'd just got voicemail. With the summer holiday well under way, she'd no doubt still been in bed.

'Hi, darling.'

'Hi, Mum,' came her daughter's voice, thick with sleep. 'Whassup?'

Caroline didn't even flinch at the street slang that was more and more part of Rachel's vocabulary, and which normally tested her patience to the very limit.

'Erm – I just wanted to flag something up for you, darling.' Mentally she kicked herself. This was her daughter, not a business associate.

'Oh, right?' said Rachel, her mother's tone making her fully alert.

'Well, we've had a bit of a nasty surprise today,' said Caroline slowly. Something that might affect you. You see—'

'OH MY GOD!' shrieked Rachel on the other end of the line. 'Mum, there's a whole load of photographers outside the house. And I've just pulled the curtains back practically naked!'

Caroline cringed as she imagined her daughter in her nightclothes – generally a skimpy vest and even skimpier briefs.

'Well, darling, that's what I'm phoning to talk to you about. But first, close the curtains and try to calm down.' She waited for a moment to let Rachel's outburst of expletives to recede.

'Who are they, Mum? And why are they outside our house?'

Caroline took a deep breath. 'Well, darling, unfortunately the papers have found out about my – erm – relationship with

Adam. And for some reason, it seems to have caused a bit of a stir.'

'They want to know about your *relationship*? With *him*? OMIGOD, you're so going to be all over the papers for having a toy boy. Mu-um! That's GROSS! Omigod, I'm sooooo never going to live this down. The SHAME! Mu-um? How could you do this to me?'

'Rachel, darling, this was never intended to—' Caroline stopped her protests abruptly as the line went dead. Well, at least she knew where Rachel was for the time being. From the sounds of it, her daughter wouldn't be putting a foot outside the door for a while yet. She sighed and flicked through her contacts, finding Les's number. Oh well, in for a penny . . .

She wasn't sure why she felt the need to call her estranged husband, but nevertheless she felt duty bound to let him find out from her. It didn't take a rocket scientist to work out that he would be next on the tabloids' list to call for a comment, and Caroline could only hope that if she got in there early enough, he'd feel duty bound to play it fair.

Her stomach churned as the phone rang. She didn't relish having any conversation with Les at any time, particularly this one. But the phone rang out, and with something akin to relief she left a brief message on his voicemail.

On a whim, she scrolled back through her contacts and frowned. She still hadn't copied over all her numbers. She scrabbled in her bag for her BlackBerry, and called Esther in New York. It was early there, but her friend was an early riser. The phone only had the chance to ring a couple of times before Esther picked up the call.

'Darling, there had better be a very good reason for ringing me at this time. And I mean *good* reason . . .'

Caroline cracked her first smile since the whole debacle had started, and relaxed a little. She needed her friend's advice. She needed her friend's support. But most of all, she suddenly found she needed her friend's ear. At least, now she could talk about it properly.

'Well, I hope you're sitting comfortably, because the reason is *more* than good . . .'

Ten minutes later, with Esther more than fully briefed on her relationship with Adam – and his age and the explosive effect he'd had on her sex life – Caroline finally stopped for breath. There was a momentary silence, then Esther burst into cackles of laughter.

'So what exactly is the problem, darling? So you got yourself a younger man. Good on you, I think. I'd have been shouting it from the rooftops long before the papers found out. I love it. And, I'll hazard a guess, so will all your kick-ass clients and a whole bunch of new ones, too. What are you waiting for? Use this as the biggest PR opportunity you've ever had. Milk it, darling!'

Caroline straightened up, head spinning with the rush of unexpected opportunity. The obvious choice at this point would be to dump Adam. But something was stopping her. And anyhow, Esther was right. Why hadn't she thought of that? In other circumstances, if she'd been the one handing out advice, she'd have said exactly the same thing.

She picked up the intercom and called through to her assistant.

'Trudi? Call the Ivy for me, will you. I want their best table, tonight at seven.'

She scanned her inbox and answered a few urgent emails. When she turned back to her iPhone to try Les again, she noticed another text in her inbox. Caroline smiled and clicked to read it. Now she had a plan, she was happy to talk to Adam again.

But it wasn't from Adam. It was from Les.

If you were calling to share your happy news with me, no need. Not only have I had every UK tabloid call me this morning, but you've just regaled me with the whole debacle – gory details included. Maybe hang up before making your next call in future . . . My regards to Esther.

Horrorstruck, Caroline replayed the conversation with Esther in her head – every girlishly embellished romanticism and intimate detail – and a wave of embarrassed nausea flooded over her. When she thought she'd hung up on Les, he must actually have picked up, and he'd been able to listen to her entire conversation with Esther in stereo. She threw the phone set across the room. Bloody iPhone. What else was going to go wrong today?

Caroline brushed an imaginary speck of lint from her pink halterneck Halston dress and looked out of the window tentatively. Next to her, Adam touched her knee and smiled gently at her.

'You OK?'

She nodded tightly. 'Yes, of course I am – why wouldn't I be?'

Adam shrugged and smiled again, and Caroline felt an irrational twinge of irritation. It was all right for Adam. What had he got at stake apart from instant fame and notoriety? That was hardly going to do an aspiring model and director any harm, was it?

She tried to swallow the huge lump in her throat and felt a flash of anger at Les. She shouldn't be doing this at her age – being expected to justify her love life, and in public too. Her hackles rose still further as she pictured the letter she'd received that very morning from his solicitors – no doubt following his discovery of her affair with Adam – contesting Les's unreasonable behaviour as grounds for divorce. Suddenly remembering Esther's words of advice, Caroline stole another look at Adam, his perfect profile silhouetted against the car window by the low, late summer sunshine and her heart softened. He'd scrubbed up pretty well for tonight, in a smart pair of Miu Miu trousers and a mod-style collared T-shirt with some sharp black Jeffery West shoes. From the evidence in front of her, justifying the love affair wasn't going to be difficult. It was everything else that went with it: the raking over every detail of her life, past and present, upsetting her family and friends, and feeling like public property.

The car pulled up on West Street and Caroline, safe for the moment behind its tinted windows, looked at Adam and smiled bravely. Why did it feel more momentous than simply stepping out of a private hire car and into a restaurant?

The answer was in the blinding assault of flashbulbs as, smiling determinedly, she let Adam lead her the few short steps past the photographers, under the outstretched arm of the uniformed doorman and into the safe confines of the Ivy. A few discreet calls by Trudi had ensured there were enough paps there to fill all the diary pages in the following day's papers and more. Caroline had decided to work this scandal to her own advantage – and work it she most definitely would.

The evening sun glinted through the stained-glass windows of the restaurant, giving the interior an almost ecclesiastical feel – and, despite the number of heads turning with interest and whispering ostentatiously as the maître d'hôtel led Caroline and Adam to their table, it certainly felt like a sanctuary compared to the maelstrom outside.

Caroline tried to concentrate on putting one foot in front of the other, and felt conscious of every move, every swallow, every blink. It felt like she was being forced to walk in slow motion, with no fast forward button, and she breathed a sigh of relief as she saw their table – the best in the house, from which to see and be seen – with Maryanne and Anthony already sitting waiting for them.

Anthony gave a low, appreciative whistle. 'Wow,' he said deadpan. 'Anyone would think the eyes of the world were on you tonight, darling.'

Caroline brushed the compliment away with a flick of her wrist. 'I've been looking for an occasion to wear this. Make a positive out of a negative, eh? Anyhow, I'd like to introduce you to Adam Geray.'

Now it was Maryanne's turn to whistle. 'So, you're what all the fuss is about,' she said, batting her eyelids coquettishly and adjusting her figure-hugging black Lanvin to enhance her curves. 'Well, it's great to meet a celebrity in the making. Come on – don't stand on ceremony, honey – sit down!' She patted the seat next to her welcomingly, and Caroline felt a wave of relief for her friend's natural warmth mix with an instinctive territorial pang of fear. Maryanne wouldn't make a *move* on Adam – would she?

'Hello, sweetie,' said Anthony, embracing her warmly. As he kissed her cheek, he murmured discreetly in her ear, 'Don't look around now, but a long-standing friend of yours has put in an appearance right behind us.' Caroline looked over his shoulder to a group two or three tables away. There, surrounded by be-suited cronies and giving her a wolfish grin, yellow teeth glinting in an unkempt-looking five o'clock shadow, was Don MacCaskill. Catching her eye, he raised a full glass of red wine to her.

'Well, I guess that's par for the course,' muttered Caroline, making a mental note to check up on who at the office had known about her soirée, and who could have tipped him off.

'Honey, I'm starving. Will you quit with the wounded starlet act and sit down so we can get on with dinner?'

Caroline smiled at her friend and sat down gratefully. Maryanne, she knew, was only half joking. It must be hard for her to have to relinquish the limelight to Caroline for once – especially when she had once coveted it so much, and knew that Caroline detested it. But now, Caroline decided as she looked around the table at two of her dearest friends and her lover – now, it was time to put other people to one side and concentrate on having a wonderful evening.

Which, Caroline decided two hours later, was easier said than done. Although she'd tried hard to concentrate on Adam's feverish questioning of Maryanne, and the way he'd devoured any titbits of information about the film industry (once he'd recovered from being more than a little starstruck in her presence, Caroline had noted with amusement), and though she'd tried hard to follow Anthony's colourful anecdotes about his latest business ventures and the characters which peppered them, the truth was she'd found it hard to forget the bank of photographers outside waiting for her to leave, to ignore the whispers and intrusive stares of their fellow diners or – mostly – MacCaskill's self-congratulatory smile across the room. She'd hardly touched her artichoke starter, and the restaurant's signature shepherd's pie – usually her guilty pleasure – had tasted of cardboard; she'd set it aside after only a few forkfuls.

A voice in her ear made her physically jump. 'Well well well. Fancy seeing you here, Mrs Walker. I hear it's been a busy couple of days for you?' Caroline's stomach churned as she turned towards the wide smile of Don MacCaskill, on his way to the loo. He nodded his hellos at the rest of the table. Maryanne pursed her lips, staring unwelcomingly at him. He was unmoved.

'Well, I'm sure you know better than anyone,' said Caroline, smiling coldly.

'Swings and roundabouts, my dear, swings and roundabouts,' said MacCaskill in self-satisfaction. 'Matter of fact, I'm having a round of golf with someone you know well at the weekend – your ex-husband.' He winked lewdly at Adam. 'Any message you'd like to pass on to him? About the business, of course. I imagine he's always been an unofficial kind of silent partner – but I guess with your current domestic circumstances he's quieter than ever, eh?' The implication was as good as spoken: Caroline was not only going off the boil, but she was foundering without Les's guidance and input. She seethed. So that was MacCaskill's latest tack. How long would it take for it to appear in a business diary page, then?

'Les and I have maintained an extremely cordial relationship during our current circumstances,' she said crisply. 'And I don't think our first ever *voluntary* public annual report was anything to be ashamed of. Quite the opposite in fact.'

MacCaskill held up his hands as if in self-defence. 'You misunderstand me, Caroline. Just a social enquiry between friends and business associates. I wish you a good evening, one and all.' He bowed his head theatrically and backed off, leaving Caroline speechless with fury.

Looking up, she saw a sea of inquisitive faces dotted around the restaurant, and she pasted her public smile over her face again. This was not the time to let her real feelings about MacCaskill be known. There was an awkward silence at her own table, and she cleared her throat to break it.

'I – er – I think I'll just go to the toilet,' said Adam, uncoiling all six feet of his body awkwardly and striding off in the direction of the men's loos, head down as if to duck the public interest.

Caroline sighed defeatedly. 'Well, I guess I'd better get the bill, then. No!' she put up a cautionary hand as Anthony made to insist on paying. 'This was my treat. You've helped me out no end tonight. Even if parts of it were painful.'

'Oh, well I've had a simply gorgeous time, honey,' slurred Maryanne, polishing off her white Burgundy.

Anthony smiled fondly at his wife and turned back to Caroline. 'Are you sure I can't get this?' he offered.

Caroline smiled at him. He was such a wonderful man. 'Anthony, I know it offends your aristocratic sense of chivalry, but please – you and Maryanne are my guests. And I can hardly ask poor Adam!'

Anthony looked at her searchingly.

'No, I suppose not,' he said slowly, and not unsympathetically. 'Oh well, enjoy asserting your independence, Caroline.' He looked meaningfully over at Adam reappearing from the direction of the Gents. 'I think you're going to have to get used to it.'

Chapter 15

GORGEOUS, WELL-BRED AND PEDIGREE

The world looked different from underneath a wide-brimmed hat, Caroline concluded, as she glanced over her copy of *Paris Match* to take in the gradual awakening of yacht life. More ... exclusive. And infinitely more glamorous. With each scene framed by the straw brim, the floating world around her and tinted sepia by her oversized vintage Linda Farrow sunglasses, it was almost like watching an old Hollywood film.

Well, an old film set on the most outlandish of modern superyachts, that is. You had to hand it to the Euro-rich, she acknowledged – they knew how to spend their billions. Italian coffee mogul Giovanni di Marco had *Serenity* completely refitted two years earlier by Blohm + Voss to include a new forward helipad (so his own helicopter didn't have to be moved when his guests arrived the same way), luxury accommodation for twenty-five guests and forty staff, and a 'News Direct' service so international papers could be printed on demand. (Which was most useful, he'd told them on their initial tour yesterday morning, for checking how many times one's holiday had been namechecked in the previous day's tabloids.) The contemporary interior introduced by Terence Disdale had done away with the blinging penthouse chic favoured by the previous owner and introduced a new 'beach house' look. The gold taps and lurid peach marble had now been replaced with natural materials such as rattan leather and stone – all top spec, naturally. Which made for, decided Caroline from her secluded vantage point at the top of the sun deck, a view that was a cross between a scene from *South Pacific* and a page from a luxury hotel catalogue. Not usually her scene, of course, and although she received invitations such as this on her own merit, she had never before accepted one. The prospect of spending a precious weekend with a few carefully chosen 'friends', acquaintances and business contacts, an itinerary of glamorous lunches and soirées, and the ubiquitous handful of carefully placed (and very well tipped off) paparazzi was usually enough to fill her with dread. But, all things considered, this invitation to accompany Maryanne on a long weekend as a personal guest of Giovanni's hadn't seemed too onerous.

Giovanni wanted to launch the star of his new coffee commercials in style: he had designs on them being the new Gold Blend, positioning it as the international coffee *de choix* for the well-heeled middle youth, and catapulting his Intenso coffee brand into the common vernacular – and the star being seen with all the right people at all the right places was a necessary part of the roll-out plan. Maryanne craved the limelight, saw this as her second bite of the cherry and would do anything to make the adverts a success. Caroline needed a break – at the very least, a change of scene – and in her current position a high-profile glamorous one that would be hitting the world's media made more sense than hiding herself away in the Cotswolds. Factor in a transatlantic appearance from Esther, who wouldn't let hell and high water get in the way of her attending a glamorous get-together, and the super-luxe glorified girls' weekend had come at just the right time. Besides, Caroline thought with a smile, this first-hand insight into the world of the super-rich was actually turning out to be *fun*.

Below her, a new St-Tropez day was gradually getting into gear, the on-board action gaining pace as the shadows cast by the blazing sun shortened. Suntanned deck hands in pale blue collared tees and white chino shorts served mid-morning refreshments from tiny silver platters to the handful of guests already up and about, and the barefoot pool boy was lazily hosing down the prow of the already gleaming boat.

Esther, replete on a striped sunbed, her immaculate blonde hair topping off a wet-look bronze one-piece, looked like a gorgeous ice cream cone – and was somehow managing to bask her face in direct sunshine without causing her make-up to slide off.

To her left, Maryanne was leaning on the railings in a cheeky knee-length Westwood sundress, looking out to shore expectantly, sunglasses on top of her head as the ocean breeze blew through her long red hair. With her hip cocked sexily to one side, she was every bit a kitsch 1940s sex bomb, thought Caroline proudly. And no doubt enhancing the view for Giovanni and his assorted business associates, from their shady spot on the lower deck, where they were ensconced with multiple espressos and the first of the day's many card games.

The yacht was slowing in preparation to be moored, and

feeling a prickle of perspiration under the rim of her sunnies, Caroline fanned herself with her magazine. Across the deck, she noticed Esther uncurl herself from her sunbed elegantly and douse herself liberally with the fine spray of her Evian water aerosol. Not for the first time, Caroline marvelled at the effort her friend must make to be that immaculately turned out at all times. How much preparation did it take to remember all those accessories? And how did you ever know which suitcase you'd packed everything in, let alone where? It had taken the on-board hair stylist a good couple of hours to get Esther's hair and make-up looking this wind-blown and natural. Caroline smiled to herself, thinking back nostalgically to her lacquered teens in the eighties. There was a lot to be said for having *va va voom* in vogue – it was so much easier to look like you'd actually *made* an effort.

'Hey gents, don't get too caught up in your Yacht Trumps, will you?' quipped Maryanne, spotting Giovanni dealing another hand to the four other millionaire moguls gathered around the lower deck's long, shady table. 'You promised us the high life – and by my reckoning we're due at Nikki Beach any time now.'

'No problem!' replied Giovanni, not missing a beat in his dealing. Cigar in the corner of his mouth, the white, wiry chest hair shining like spun silver on his mahogany-tanned chest, he was every bit the minted entrepreneur on holiday. 'Which just about gives you time to get ready for all the photographers I've got lined up ready to snap us arriving. We wouldn't want to look just like any old tourists, would we?' He looked around the group knowingly and winked ostentatiously.

Maryanne smiled good-naturedly at the reminder of her starring role. 'Well, at least you're under no illusions about who's going to be the focus of their attention,' she said crisply, pulling her sunglasses back over her eyes, turning back to the shore and striking a pose. 'And don't underestimate me,' she called over her shoulder. 'A real pro is always ready for her close-up, let alone a long lens photographer.'

'Ooooh, goody!' exclaimed Maryanne as she gazed at the beach scene. They lay on their sunbeds, lined up alongside one another in prime position on the exclusive turf of Nikki Beach's Club 55. 'This sure as hell beats Regent's Park on a sunny Sunday, eh honey?'

'That depends on what you want from your Sunday,' laughed Caroline, sipping her Laurent Perrier delicately.

Behind them, under an expanse of white parasols and muslin drapes, the dining area of Nikki Beach was teeming with Very Important People intent on doing Very Important Business – and more importantly, being seen to do it. Everything was happening with a slight delay, as if a camera was recording it all. A tanned, good-looking DJ in wrap-around shades pumped dance music through supersized speakers, glamorous poppets in strappy dresses shimmied slim brown shoulders to the beat and kissed the balding heads of their fat, self-satisfied executive boyfriends, who in turn were intent on proving how rich they were. It was the epitome of controlled hedonism – the kind of off-the-shelf partying that bought the squarest of people an instant cool, as long as they had the funds to sustain it.

To the untrained eye, the scene before them was like that

replicated on any stretch of the over-populated sands from Nice to St-Tropez. Sunbeds were systematically lined up to maximise every inch of sand, and all faced the sea. (In the South of France, tan lines came a poor second to seeing and being seen – and all the action happened along the shoreline.) Well-honed bodies in skimpy swimwear sauntered up and down the beach, and jet-skis sped back and forth along the shoreline. Except, on Nikki Beach the sunbeds were super-sunbeds created by international designers, the people weren't just moneyed but celebrities and the super-rich, and the beach taxi *de choix* was a launch from a superyacht.

The fine white sand, where it was still visible, provided a dazzling foil for the tall, willowy, Bergasol-tanned Russians being leered at by their squat, hirsute partners and the pneumatic Italian women with skin like hide, burnt mahogany brown by the sun, oiling themselves in Piz Buin Classic Brown. A couple of women covered head to toe in burkhas strolled past, giving sunbathers flashes of £400 bejewelled flip-flops from beneath their robes. Directly in front of the enclosure, a gormless looking German man with sunburnt shoulders and bright blue Speedos was perched on the end of a sunbed, earnestly chatting up a pair of lithe, sunkissed brunettes in their late teens.

'I mean, Giovanni's all very nice and everything, but his friends are just so *old*,' complained Esther, inspecting her freshly manicured nails. 'Couldn't he have invited some younger guests to join us for a bit of light relief?'

Caroline looked at her sympathetically. The cuisine served at last night's dinner had been wonderful, and Giovanni himself was a charismatic host, but she had to agree with her friend that his other guests could have been livelier. 'Esther, darling, I think *we* are meant to be the light relief,' she pointed out.

'Oh,' said Esther, for once stumped for a reply. 'You mean *we're* meant to be entertaining *them*? Oh God, then what are we going to do for after-dinner fun tonight?'

Her questions hung unanswered on the hot afternoon air as Maryanne elbowed Caroline sharply in the ribs and gave a delighted guffaw, unable to tear her eyes away from Speedo man, now standing up and showcasing a majestic erection through his tight swim pants. 'Oh honey, look – and to think at first sight I thought he had nothing going for him!'

Caroline stifled a laugh. 'Maryanne! He's a total lech.' She thought instantly of Rachel, still her baby girl but growing up fast, being put in a similar situation and felt a surge of anger towards the man. 'He's old enough to be their father.'

'GRANDfather,' put in Esther, looking appraisingly over the top of her sunglasses. 'Although compared to some of the age gaps on display around here, it's positively tasteful.'

'Still, it shouldn't be allowed,' said Caroline worriedly.

Maryanne tutted dismissively. 'And there speaks the woman dating a teenager herself. The world's changing, Caro! Age is just a number, honey.' She looked over at Speedo man, still unashamedly showcasing his crown jewels for all to see. 'Although I've gotta hand it to you, that guy is a class A ... prick!'

All three of them dissolved in hysterical laughter, trying to quell their giggles as the man stretched languorously and unselfconsciously.

'Now that's more like it,' purred Esther as a pair of lithe

young men walked past in denim cut-offs, their buff bodies a monument to their obvious gym addiction.

'Uh-huh,' concurred Maryanne, straw in mouth as she sipped her champagne cocktail. 'Where's your gaydar gone, honey? The only interest those two are likely to have in you would be in sharing your face cream. And your husband,' she added wickedly.

'Oh, I don't know, darling,' said Esther, patting her hair and rearranging the straps of her swimsuit to expose more perfect bust. 'I've turned a few in my time.'

'Yes, but which way, honey?' cackled Maryanne, and Caroline smiled in spite of Esther's withering look. The look froze on Esther's face as an emaciated woman in her late forties walked past in a bikini, her wrinkly skin hanging baggy on her bony frame, like popped balloon rubber.

'Good God!' Esther hissed with a slightly parted mouth, her lips not moving in a well-practised act of ventriloquism. 'What is she thinking?' She turned to Caroline and Maryanne in horror, her eyes wide behind her designer sunglasses. 'Now that, ladies, is a salutary beachwear lesson to us all. Your life in a one-piece starts at forty!'

'Don't be mean, Esther,' Caroline protested, laughing. 'She must be fifty if she's a day! And anyway,' she added pointedly, looking at Esther's latest change of outfit – a Versace cutaway leopard print costume. 'Yours is one piece in name only.'

'Yes, darling, in the same way my body is forty-two in number only,' retorted Esther matter-of-factly. For the umpteenth time in the years they'd known each other, Caroline marvelled at her friend's self-assurance. Esther was so kind, so funny, and so genuine, she could never be accused of arrogance – but she was rightly confident in the way she looked. As was Maryanne, continuing the 1940s screen siren theme in a scarlet Zimmermann halterneck that accentuated her ample bosom and tiny waist. Caroline ran her fingers through her hair, pushing it back from her face and twisting it up off her neck, and looked down at her own 3.1 Phillip Lim belted navy one-piece doubtfully – it was chic, sophisticated but maybe not quite *sexy* . . .

In between Caroline and Esther, Maryanne sighed. 'Why, oh why, are we talking about other women when there are all these lovely BOYS to be discussing?' she wailed, flinging her arms wide as if to embrace everyone on the beach. 'Talk about missed opportunities!'

'We haven't had any opportunities to miss,' observed Esther drily.

'That's because we haven't *made* them,' fired back Maryanne, sitting up on her sunbed and stretching her neck elegantly, looking around like a particularly glamorous meercat. '*S'il vous plaît!*'

She called over to a passing waiter – tanned, toned and twenty-something – and gave him a megawatt smile. Beside her, Esther groaned. 'Oh, Maryanne, of all the talent on display – did you have to . . .' The Nikki Beach uniform was all white, and the Fred Perry T-shirt and cotton micro shorts set off his floppy brown hair, blue eyes and muscly legs, toned no doubt by years of rugby and tennis. Recognising the predatory glint in her friend's eye, Caroline's instinctive shyness kicked in and she shrank back on to her sunbed and picked up a magazine, feigning interest in a feature.

'*Bonjour, mesdemoiselles,*' the waiter said, with the flash of a Hollywood smile.

Maryanne beamed at the implied youth and single status bestowed on the three of them by the greeting.

'Well, *bonjour*, gorgeous,' she said. 'Do you speak English?'

'Yes, a little,' the waiter replied fluently, in the accentless tones of an expensive European education.

'Ooh, and clever, too,' said Esther approvingly, suddenly taking more interest. 'Where are you from?'

'Lausanne,' he replied. 'I'm at hotel school there.' He smiled. 'My name is Freddy.'

'Well, Freddy, it's very nice to meet you,' said Maryanne coquettishly, drawing her knees up to her chest and hugging them to her. The effect was charming and almost childlike, thought Caroline admiringly – certainly enough to throw some poor innocent off balance, however cosmopolitan he thought he was. He didn't know it yet, but he was fair game. 'And what brings you to Nikki Beach, Freddy?'

'I'm here doing a *stage*,' he said with a smile, referring to the vocational training required by all privileged students at Switzerland's prestigious hotel and catering academies. 'Me and my best friend are here all summer. Not bad, is it!' He looked around the beach for emphasis, but Maryanne continued to look straight at him.

'Nope, not bad at all,' she drawled.

'So where's your friend, darling?' said Esther, taking off her sunglasses and fixing him with a sexy look.

Freddy, flushed at the attention, looked around him again, and gestured at another waiter – this one blond where Freddy was dark, but displaying the same sporty physique, St-Tropez tan and charming way.

'*Eh! Serge! Viens ici!*'

The other waiter nodded, gave a half-salute and ambled over, making a little bow to the three of them as he arrived.

Esther arched her back and stretched an arm out behind her, half lying back on the sunbed. With her legs arranged gracefully in front of her, she looked like the cat who'd got the cream, thought Caroline, fanning herself with her magazine and trying to stifle the giggle that threatened to emerge. Honestly, they were all acting as though they were teenagers again.

'Well, well, well, look what the tide just brought in,' said Esther, pleasure oozing out of her. She looked over at Caroline and Maryanne triumphantly. 'I think we just found our after-dinner entertainment, ladies.'

Maryanne produced her drinks card and handed it to Serge. 'Why don't you bring us over some drinks, and you —' she looked up at Freddy and patted her sunbed — 'sit right down here. And if your boss complains, tell him we insisted.'

Freddy laughed, with all the confidence of youth and a privileged background, and Serge gave another little bow.

'I would be delighted,' he replied. 'And I may also bring another friend?' He looked questioningly at Caroline, who shook her head hurriedly and buried her face back in her magazine, cheeks burning.

'So what would you like?' asked Serge politely.

'I'll have a Sex on the Beach,' purred Maryanne with an obvious wink. 'After all, when in Rome . . .'

Caroline spluttered from behind her magazine, torn between hilarity and horror. 'Maryanne!' she protested, but giggling as she saw Esther try to hide her own laughter behind a fan. 'You make us look like dirty old women.'

'Dirty old women?' scoffed Maryanne in a low voice. 'I don't think so, honey. Have you clocked how bloody fantastic we look, all lined up along here? And we're not just any sexy old women, either. We're cougars. Gorgeous, well-bred, *pedigree* cougars. Grrr . . .'

She leaned forward alluringly to Serge. 'In fact, *chéri*, make mine a dirty martini. But from now on, you can call it a *Cougartini*.'

Chapter 16

A (Contemporary) Vintage Performance

'No, no – drive round again please,' Caroline instructed her driver, leaning forward in her car seat. Thank the Lord for tinted windows, she thought: it wouldn't do for the paps to perceive her beating a hasty retreat at this stage of the evening.

But nor would it do for her to step out on the red carpet too early, she reasoned as she watched her guests' retreating backs make their flashlit way across the Duke of York Square into the minimalist space of the Saatchi Gallery. Not with all the questions they were bound to want to ask about both her love life and the state of her business. Nope, she was better off biding her time and, however out of character, making a fashionably late entrance that not only didn't allow time to stop and chat, but that made headlines for all the *right* reasons.

Not that she could really remember what the right reasons were any more. She gave Adam, sitting next to her in the back of the chauffeur-driven car, a sidelong glance. Imagine her, Caroline 'principles' Walker, shamelessly using her relationship for publicity. Although she and Les had been bona fide members of London's glitterati, she wasn't used to her personal life being the focus of attention. She had always guarded Rachel's identity carefully, and never allowed her on to the red carpet. Girls grew up so quickly these days – there was time enough for all that when she'd finished enjoying her childhood. But in outing her and Adam, Caroline was effectively offering her private life up as fair game for tabloid scrutiny for the first time ever – and at one of the most important launch parties of her life, too. Precious, her first fragrance – which was giving every indication of being an overnight hit.

'So is this MacCaskill character going to be there tonight?' asked Adam innocently. Caroline stared at him incredulously. For an old soul, he could be shockingly naive at times.

'Er, no, Adam,' she said, half wondering if he was serious. 'I think inviting your closest competitor and sworn enemy to your biggest ever product launch party, which will be populated by a large percentage of your family and friends, not to mention all your best clients, the world's most renowned beauty journalists *and* the UK press corps, might be tantamount to commercial suicide. Especially after said sworn enemy has attempted to sabotage the very same launch party by publicly accusing you of profiteering from your first ever charity venture via an articulately written letter in *The Times*.'

Caroline stopped for breath, blood boiling as she recalled MacCaskill's latest aggressive attack that morning. Riding on the coat-tails of the factory debacle to try and expose the fundraising element of her new high street collection was a cheap shot, but wrapped as it had been in middle-class niceties, it had come across as the concerns of a former public school boy made good, and she knew it would have done her damage in some quarters. What she had to hope was that it wasn't a quarter containing potential or existing clients.

Adam shrugged nonchalantly. 'I dunno,' he muttered. 'Sounds like a blinder of a move to me.'

Caroline stared at him, cursing the arrogance of youth and then immediately wished she had done exactly that. Inviting MacCaskill tonight would have been a stroke of PR genius. How better could she have shown the world at large that there were no deep, dark secrets in the Sapphires & Rubies closet?

Irritably, she stared out of the window again.

'Are we pulling up this time, ma'am, or should I go around again?' called the driver, looking at her in the rear-view mirror. Caroline glanced at her watch and then out of the window. They'd finished their circuit of King's Road and the pretty mews houses in the Chelsea streets behind, and were just pulling on to Sloane Square again. It was just gone half-past seven. She was officially late – but as the star of the show, she was allowed to be. As they slowly approached the Duke of York Square, tonight the focus of unprecedented crowds of onlookers and press photographers spilling out of their pen – a royal and her investment banker boyfriend were making their way up the carpet to frenzied paparazzi interest. If royalty had deemed it late enough to arrive, then it was time for Caroline to make her entrance.

'Now is fine,' replied Caroline, working her lips to redistribute her lipgloss, and straightened her skirt. The simple shift was crisply tailored and hugged Caroline's frame in a way that managed to be both sophisticated and sexy, the tulip skirt adding a modern touch to the classic style. The vivid scarlet silk dupion set off her pale skin, black hair and made her green eyes pop. She'd left her legs bare but for a pair of vertiginous black patent peeptoe Louboutins. Simple, sexy *and* cool – the perfect combo to enhance the dress. Her only accessory was a pair of antique gold and mother-of-pearl chandelier earrings she'd inherited from Babs, set off by the casual topknot she'd pulled her hair back into. The overall effect was a very 'now' take on the 1950s: stylish and businesslike, serious but young and fun too.

Adam leapt out first, and hurried round to open the door for her. Caroline smiled delightedly at this public show of chivalry, all irritation at his after-the-event stroke of brilliance gone, and immediately the cameras started to flash.

As she stepped out of the limo and on to the red carpet, the flashbulbs went wild. Adam held out his arm to link with hers and led her into the Gallery, the path lined with stainless steel planters containing hundreds of tea roses and lit by huge dressing-room-style lightbulbs along the carpet. The effect was exactly as she had hoped – contemporary vintage – and as she made her way along Caroline heard the crowd and the paps call her name. When she and Adam neared the entrance, they stopped by the press corps for posed photographs, and reporters stationed along the press cordon ran alongside it, holding out microphones to her in the hope of getting a quote.

'Caroline! Who's this then?'

'Caroline! Any plans to get engaged?'

'Caroline! What did Les say when he found out?'

'Adam – what's it like to have one of the world's most successful businesswomen as your first girlfriend?'

'Caroline! Have you moved in together yet?'

Caroline smiled through them all, but refused to comment. She squeezed Adam's hand in reassurance, but was surprised when his return squeeze had that exact effect on her. Just who was in charge here?

'Come on. We've given them enough – you've got a party to host,' said Adam, bending down to whisper in her ear. Caroline nodded, another flutter of butterflies appearing in her stomach. With everything else going on tonight, she had hardly given a thought to what was going on inside the venue. What if it didn't match up to her expectations? What if – horror of horrors – hardly anyone had turned up?

At the door, a woman with a clipboard was already self-importantly relaying Caroline's arrival down a walkie-talkie. She smiled efficiently.

'We've practically got a full house tonight, Mrs Walker,' she announced, waving her checklist proudly. 'Unheard of. Trudi's on her way.'

At the welcome sight of Trudi bustling along, mobile phone attached to her ear, Caroline relaxed slightly. If anything was really wrong, Trudi would have dealt with it. And if for any reason she couldn't, she would have called Caroline immediately. Her eyes widened as she saw Trudi's attire. A designer tunic and wedges? This had to be a record – she'd never so much as seen Trudi's legs before, let alone in heels. Bless her for making the effort.

Trudi gave Caroline a self-conscious smile as if she could read her mind. 'You look amazing, Caroline,' she said warmly. 'Got your speech ready?'

Caroline waved her bejewelled Judith Leiber clutch and

pulled a face. 'I've got some notes.' She felt herself tense up slightly again as the prospect of public speaking loomed ever closer and the enormity of the event ahead hit her. Focus, Caroline. The fuss about bringing Adam to her party had almost overshadowed the real point of the evening. This wasn't just a relationship showcase. This was business. Big business.

Trudi nodded approvingly. 'They'll all be hanging on your every word.'

I'll say, thought Caroline. *Trying to get an insight into what's going on with me and Adam, for a start.*

Caroline was the creative force behind tonight, but even she couldn't believe her eyes as she and Adam turned into the main gallery space and saw the overall effect. Adam gave a low whistle.

'Wow. You've really outdone yourself this time, Mrs Walker.'

The theme of the theatre dressing room lights continued along the corridor and into the modernist cubic space in front of them. They lined the walls, sending a gently atmospheric light into the soft rose pink drapes on the stark white walls and throwing half-shadows around the room. A square platform-like stage had been created in the centre of the room, surrounded by a moat of 5,000 tea roses and holding nothing but an old-fashioned shabby-chic dressing table with a large but simple posy of tea roses lying on it.

Caroline caught her breath. Before now, she'd only ever held parties in the Sapphires & Rubies store, but the expense of this huge production – starting with hiring the gallery space and ending with sourcing the thousands of tea roses – had been worth it. This space encapsulated her dreams of what the perfume itself would embody — the glamour of a vintage boudoir, the smell of her mother's powder compact, the comfort of something treasured, the excitement of the totally new and modern.

And as she looked around the packed interior, she realised it was already having its own effect on the gathered masses. A hubbub of anticipation was building in the crowd — and what a crowd. The latest big name DJ fresh from Ibiza spun ambient house at one corner of the room as crisply aproned waiters served trays of chilled Veuve Clicquot rosé, rose martinis and melt-in-your-mouth macaroons. The guest list read like a who's who gathering of the UK's yummiest mummies and London party set. Liz Hurley and Patsy Kensit were busy exchanging diet secrets and catching up on old times. Elle Macpherson was studiously ignoring Uma Thurman at the other side of the room. Princess Beatrice and Natalie Imbruglia were in a tight huddle, plotting something with Holly Branson, while Tracey Emin held court in the centre of a group of transfixed suits. Jaime Winstone and Daisy Lowe were messing about with Henry Holland and Agyness Deyn, while Yasmin Le Bon and husband Simon were in animated conversation with their two youngest daughters.

Suddenly a magnificent laser show swung into action, throwing the Precious logo all around the room and indicating the beginning of the presentation. Caroline swallowed hard, pasted on her brightest smile and took centre stage.

'Welcome, everyone, to your — and my — opportunity to revolutionise the fragrance world as we know it!'

The waiters started to circulate little strips of pale pink card which they sprayed with Precious. The crowd sniffed appreciatively and exchanged contented looks, as if confirming what they already knew. It was going to be a success. The guests, all of them Caroline's friends or clients past and present, knew her and obviously loved her, and as they edged closer to the stage and her infectious excitement, the atmosphere in the room was that of genuine goodwill. Caroline looked around at them, eyes shining, heart buoyed by the reception. As she scanned the room, she caught Adam's eyes by the side of the stage.

'This isn't just a new fragrance. It's the start of a new chapter. A new chapter for the brand it's been named after. And a new chapter for me!'

As the crowd applauded, Caroline found Adam's eyes again, and her heart sang. She meant that. She really did.

Chapter 17

IT'LL ALL COME OUT IN THE WASH

She must be insane. She'd lost her mind. What the bloody hell was she doing?

Caroline was officially in a spin. Which was a state of mind she increasingly found herself in these days, most often in front of her mirror. And she didn't like it. She didn't like it one little bit.

She shook her head, trying to rid herself of the taunt of a review of her perfume launch she'd read just this morning. Whilst in the main the reception had been positive, one snippy diary editor had written 'If Precious is the autobiographical scent Caroline Walker would have us believe, than she would have been better placed to name it Cougars and Cubs.'

Despite the plethora of glowing reports of her party in the society pages, and the rave reviews from beauty editors ('Precious may not yet be the scent of the year, but it is gearing up to be the fragrance of the decade,' wrote one influential blogger), it was *this* review that rankled, and that kept turning over and over in her head. Her cheeks burned with rage and humiliation as she thought of her creative talents and business acumen being reduced to a public joke over her love life.

That's what you get, Caro, for capitalising on your love life.

Ignore it. It was below the belt and below *her*, she told herself now, trying to pull her attention back to the ubiquitous sartorial dilemma as she embarked on yet another first.

Going out 'for a few beers' with Adam's friends at his local south-east London haunts may have been delivered as a casual invitation, but right now Caroline was feeling anything but relaxed about it.

'And Mum and Dad are away, so you can stay over at mine.'

Caroline's heart had sunk, but during their relationship they had spent most of their time together at her Primrose Hill home – especially now that Rachel was just pretending Adam didn't exist rather than actively campaigning against him – and she guessed she owed him at least one stopover. She sighed. It wasn't that she didn't want to go to Adam's house. It was just that staying over at his *parents'* place – in the bedroom where he'd spent his boyhood – felt so juvenile.

But he *was* practically a juvenile, and this was exactly what you got for cradle-snatching, Caroline reminded herself, as she turned her attention back to her wardrobe. She pulled out a white Nicole Farhi jersey tee, slashed asymmetrically across the neck and tied in a knot. Casual but cool, she thought, imagining it with a pair of figure-hugging black trousers and some ballet pumps. Rachel had worn something similar a few days previously and Caroline had thought how uncomplicated and unaffected the whole look had been. She held the top up against her body, swinging this way and that and looking at it critically from every angle.

Suddenly, she stopped and peered more closely at the mirror. Were those new wrinkles at the corner of her eyes? She pulled back and reinspected the overall effect. Yep, now she thought about it, her crow's feet were definitely more pronounced. Her skin seemed thinner, and less plump. I mean, the success of Rachel's look had been her plump-skinned, rosy innocence, not the brand of trousers. Caroline moved closer to the mirror again until her nose was practically touching it. And where had those nasolabial lines suddenly appeared from? She looked like something out of *Planet of the Apes*. She bit her thumb worriedly. Was she ageing faster than she'd thought? Maybe Esther had a point. Maybe there was a time in every woman's life when nature deserted her and she needed a little helping hand to look her best.

She sank down on to the chaise longue. What on earth was she doing, comparing herself to her daughter? That was no way to live. She'd never really been bothered about ageing – she was happy in her own skin, and she'd always seen any lines as proof of the life she lived, the baby she'd had, the work she'd put in. But since she had been with Adam, she was finding herself increasingly critical of her looks, more damning of her age, more competitive with other women. Other *younger* women.

It wasn't just that, though. Dating someone new for the first time at forty-two – let alone someone so much younger – meant Caroline felt herself permanently out of her depth. What to wear and when, waiting for Adam to call exactly when he said he would rather than a couple of hours (or, on one occasion, a day) later and getting texts she couldn't always understand (she really needed a dictionary for abbreviated text-speak, LOL!). Adam may have had none of the gravity-induced effects of middle age, but he also had no chest hair, expense accounts or chauffeur driven cars – or the ability to pay more than one in ten of their restaurant bills.

Not that she allowed his fiscal situation to bother her. There was more to life than a healthy bank account – and as well as fun, she found Adam's company far more stimulating than she could ever have expected.

In fact, *stimulation* was turning into a problem in itself. Caroline still enjoyed sex with Adam as much as ever, but now the novelty had worn off, to be honest she would be happy with it a couple of times a week. Or just the once every time they saw each other, at least. Whilst still happy to have redis-covered her carnal urges, she was now all about less frequency, more enthusiasm. However, there seemed no sign of Adam's libido waning. He still wanted sex all the time. *All* the time. Every night. Two or three times. It was exhausting.

She turned back to the mirror, feeling 105 years old.

Careful what you wish for, Caro.

'See ya!

'Byeeeee!'

'Hey, don't forget the gig. Next week. I can get you more VIPs if you need them!'

Caroline waved the tickets she was clutching. 'I won't forget, Danny, don't worry!' She laughed and grabbed Adam's arm as lanky Danny and swarthy Pete, his best mates in the entire world (and otherwise known as up-and-coming indie band Mogwat) stumbled off in the opposite direction.

'Brrrrr!' She shivered, cuddling in close to Adam. He pulled his arm away and wrapped it around her, sheltering her from the chill of the early September evening – a reminder that however much the afternoons might be bathed in late summer sunshine, the nip of autumn was only around the corner.

'They're nice,' she said, her voice muffled by his denim jacket.

'Yes, well, I've always thought so,' said Adam, giving her an affectionate squeeze. 'Who did you expect me to be friends with – a load of south-east London yobbos?'

'Of course not!' protested Caroline, when yes, she had to admit, that's exactly what she'd expected. Instead the pair had been charming company – not quite so mature as Adam, but well spoken, articulate and funny too. And, yes, she'd had a good time. Even if their cultural references and shared language meant she hadn't been totally sure what they were talking about most of the time.

And now, with a few G&Ts inside her, swinging an overnight bag from the hand clutching her VIP gig tickets, she felt a strange sense of release. She felt footloose and fancy free. She felt YOUNG again. In fact, younger than she had when she WAS young.

She giggled tipsily. Adam squeezed her again as he steered her down a leafy Greenwich street. 'What are you laughing at, pisshead?'

'I'm not drunk!' insisted Caroline. 'I'm just happy!' She pulled away from him and spun around, sending her bag swinging out. She turned her head up to the sky and watched the stars spin with her. She felt her arm wrench to one side

238

and pull her body with it, and she looked around in shock as she tumbled to the ground in a big tangle.

'You donut,' said Adam, laughing as he helped her to her feet. You got your bag caught up around the lamppost!'

Caroline laughed embarrassedly and stood up, her bubble of giddiness burst.

'Don't forget your tickets!' Adam winked at her, and she grabbed them from him sheepishly. 'Anyhow, we're nearly home. It's just up here.'

He nodded to a side street, and Caroline followed him through a gate and up the path to a smart Victorian semi. She relaxed as they walked through a neat, well-tended garden to a pillarbox red front door. This whole situation might have made her feel like a student, but Adam's parents' place was, of course, anything but student digs.

He opened the door and the hallway light spilled out across the path. Caroline was hit by the overwhelming smell of an unfamiliar house – a not-unpleasant concoction of years of family life. A faint mix of home-cooked meals, laundry, central heating and people. She breathed it in and took one step forward – and then stopped suddenly at the sight of it. Lying there, by her foot, on the mat. She put her hand to her mouth to stop the shriek that threatened to escape.

A Betterware catalogue.

The ultimate sign of cosy domesticity – but now, to Caroline, it had the ingrained evil of a terrible omen. Suddenly, all the feelings of imposing on someone else's family home, someone's life, someone's SON came rushing back.

She looked up at Adam, eyes wide with fear. 'I'm sorry, Adam, it's too weird. I just can't!'

239

His brow furrowed, but not with concern. In defence.

'Why? What on earth's wrong with you?'

Caroline shook her head. 'I'm sorry. It's just too weird,' she repeated.

'What's weird? My house? Or just you?'

He was upset now, and Caroline couldn't blame him. He was taking offence, thinking there was something wrong with his home. The home he'd grown up in.

'Me. This. Us. Here . . . I don't know. I feel like – it's your *mother's* house. The house she brought you up in. I shouldn't be here.'

'Why?' said Adam, hostility emanating from every pore. 'Because it's not good enough for you? Because we don't have an en-suite and there's no E-type Jaguar parked outside?'

Caroline gasped, shocked that he could think that. 'No! Adam, no! It feels wrong because – because – I don't know. I'm a mother too, you know. I own a family home, too, and – well, being here like this with you. It makes me feel like a mother, not a lover.'

Adam looked at her disbelievingly, and for a moment Caroline thought he was going to erupt in rage. But all of a sudden his eyes softened, and he shook his head at her.

'You are a soppy mare,' he said. 'Which is probably why I can never stay angry with you for long. So, it's a cab back to yours then, is it? Well, see if you can flag one down while I go grab a bag.'

Caroline stretched languorously and smiled as she opened her eyes. Home. There really was nowhere quite like it. It had been the right decision to come back – she was too old to start waking up in someone else's bed, and she knew she would have felt uncomfortable pottering about in someone else's house.

She rolled over and ran a hand over Adam's smooth, toned back. He grunted appreciatively and she kissed his shoulder lightly, then more insistently, then—

'Mu–um!'

Rachel's voice carried excitedly up the stairs. Caroline hadn't thought to leave a note last night warning her – she was meant to be at Les's all weekend.

Caroline jumped out of bed, ignoring Adam's groan of protestation, threw her robe on and padded downstairs.

'Morning, darling!' She put on her happiest voice, mindful of Adam's shoes by the door, in case his obvious presence had instigated an almighty sulk. But instead of a glowering frown, Rachel was smiling, eyes shining brightly.

'*Mum!* Whose tickets are these?'

Caroline glanced at the tickets in Rachel's hand. They were the ones that lanky Danny had pressed upon her last night.

'Um – they're mine?' The words sounded ridiculous even to her own ears. But Rachel was oblivious.

'But Mum! They're VIP tickets? To see Mogwat?' Rachel raised her voice at the end of every sentence – something she hadn't done since she was fifteen – during which time she'd sounded as if life was one permanent question. 'Like, what would you do with these?'

Caroline laughed. 'Well, actually darling, one of the band gave them to me. Danny, in fact.'

Rachel's eyes nearly popped out of her head. 'How do you

know Danny?' Her voice was now so high it was almost a squeak.

'Oh, I had a drink with him last night,' said Caroline casually, walking over and turning the Nespresso machine on. 'He's one of Adam's best friends. A very nice boy, as it turns out.'

Rachel was staring at her as if she was a stranger. 'You and Danny and Adam? In a pub? *Drinking?*'

'Yes,' confirmed Caroline. 'Oh, and Pete was there. He's in the band too, I gather?'

'That is soooooo cool,' breathed Rachel. Then, suspicious again, 'But you're not going to use these tickets, right? You brought them home for me?'

Caroline grabbed her daughter's face in her hands and kissed her forehead. 'Darling, you are welcome to those tickets. And I'm sure Danny will get you some more if you like.'

Rachel walked off, still staring at the tickets. 'That is *so* way cool. Wait till I tell Suki.'

She turned around suddenly. 'Mum?'

'Yes, darling?'

'We so have to get him round. Can you invite him to my eighteenth?'

Caroline smiled her assent and turned back to her coffee. *Well, would you credit it. Another brownie point for Adam.* He was racking them up, slowly but surely. You never know, Rachel might even get around to speaking to him one day . . .

As she wandered back into the bedroom, Caroline noticed the large dustbin bag Adam had brought with him last night tossed to one side. She hadn't paid it any attention in the dark of the taxi, but now she opened it. The stale smell of boys' bedrooms percolated out of it and she wrinkled her nose in disgust.

'Adam? Adam, this bag you brought with you last night. It's not your normal overnight bag?'

Adam's head peered out from under the duvet.

'I know, babe. Well, my mum's away, isn't she? It's my washing.'

Chapter 18

A LITTLE TEXT EDUCATION

It was just another average morning on Toucan Cay. The gently rippling turquoise waters of Coconut Bay lapped rhythmically at the untouched golden Caribbean sands, interrupted now and then by the flip of a tropical fish seeking some fresh island air, and the steady progress of a snorkel midway out to sea. Further out, the ocean turned a cornflower blue and was tipped with an occasional frothy crescent of white surf. A dragonfly hovered lazily above the water while the palms that fringed the half-moon inlet waved in the soft vanilla-scented breeze, providing shady spots of cool sand. The occasional wisp of cloud blowing across the sun was the only other respite from the relentless sunshine.

Suddenly, the idyll was rudely interrupted by an almighty splash. From the middle of the bay, the snorkel emerged, revealing at the other end of it Adam's half-submerged form.

'Whoa! Caroline! You've gotta come see this!' His words were all but lost on the soft Caribbean breeze, and from her shady hammock at the top of the beach Caroline smiled and waved excitedly, as if she could see but not hear him. Adam's enthusiasm for life was infectious, but she didn't share his newfound love of snorkelling. The very thought of putting a mask on made her recoil in claustrophobia, and the few times she had attempted it she'd breathed in normally the minute she'd put her head underwater, inhaling lungfuls of salt water and magnifying her panic. But yesterday, she and Adam had come up with the perfect solution – he would snorkel ahead, beckoning her over every now and again to dunk her head under and see what all the fuss was about. But, much as she found the frantic shoals of tiny yellow fish delightful, once was more than enough. And anyway, she had some work to do.

She sighed contentedly, taking in the panoramic view around her. Work – you could hardly call it that really, could you? Lying here in her sunshine yellow bikini and sparkly kaftan, hair still damp from her early morning dip in the crystal clear Caribbean Sea, sipping a deliciously chilled mango smoothie. No wonder Giovanni called this, his own exclusive private island, the most productive office in the world. Just in the last half-hour she'd finalised the plans for the rollout of the new range, come up with the idea for a line of Sapphires & Rubies cosmetics to complement the fragrance and booked the same hot DJ that she'd used for the launch party for Rachel's eighteenth.

She was keenly aware how lucky she was to be here – and at Giovanni's invitation, too. Most of Toucan Cay's visitors had to go through a stringent vetting procedure and *then* still had to cough up over fifty grand for a week's stay. But he'd insisted on sending her, along with Anthony, Maryanne and Adam, to the island for a recuperative break. They had been given the run of the hundred acre island paradise: Lococo, the huge Balinese style main house with its alfresco living, cushion-scattered couches, hammocks, and splendid super-king-size bedroom suite with wet room, outside stone bath, Jacuzzi and stargazing roof that in fine weather opened to reveal the romantic starry sky; the glamorous network of black volcanic rock fresh and salt water pools; the colourfully exotic flora that greeted you around every corner.

Elsewhere on the island, a purpose built creative space regularly attracted the crème de la crème of the international art and music industries. An expansive, temperature-controlled villa filled with art picked by the director of the Tate Modern gave on to a soundproof studio, edit suite, writing room and painting deck. A cinema wing held a library of films personally chosen by director Ridley Scott. This, too, was at their disposal. And even there, apparently, discreet staff were posted on every corner to attend to their every whim, at any time of the day or night.

As if on cue, Edwin, the groundsman employed solely to maintain the island's beaches' untouched appearance, strolled leisurely into view. He nodded deferentially to Caroline as he raked the sand. His regular 'Mornin, ma'am' greeting was delivered in a lilting West Indian accent, in a voice that was permanently smiling. 'Morning Edwin,' Caroline beamed back at him.

What a job, she thought. Spending all day working on one secluded island beach after another. No wonder he was so chilled.

She hugged her knees and watched Adam bob up and

down in the water. At least, what she could see of Adam. Currently that amounted to a tuft of hair sticking up at 90 degrees out of his mask, the snorkel, and his bum bobbing up and down in the water.

There was a shout, and some tinny cheers, and three or four of the staff children came running on to the beach and splashed out into the sea. 'A-dam! A-dam!'

Caroline giggled as they went running out to where he was snorkelling, all arms and legs and big eyes as they tried to keep their heads above water to get his attention. With a child's instinct for seeking out fun, they'd spotted him from almost the first morning they'd been here, and Adam's little fan club had been following him around the island ever since. It had become a standing joke amongst the four of them. Now, Adam feigned horror at their approach, and made as if to swim away in fear. Caroline laughed out loud as one by one they caught him, pulling him under by his feet and jumping on his head, trying to duck him. One by one they were caught out, and he picked them up as though they were light as feathers and threw them shrieking with mirth back into the sea.

He had the same easy way with children as he did with adults, a talent for treating everyone as equals, using the same laid-back charm to engage, interest and ultimately delight. It was a rare quality, thought Caroline, to be able to communicate so effectively regardless of race, class or generation.

As if he could read her thoughts, Adam looked up and blew her a kiss across the water. Caroline blew one back and waved, watching as Adam gathered the children into a line in the waist-deep water. She shielded her eyes from the sun as she looked closer. What were they up to?

She soon found out. One by one, they somersaulted into the water in a kind of acrobatic Mexican wave. She laughed and whooped as the kids high-fived Adam in delight.

He'd make a great dad, she thought absently. The thought was followed quickly by a pang. *Just not with me* ... She'd never given a second thought to what any future with Adam would look like. He'd always been a quick fling, a confidence boost, a bit of fun. But now ... Now that something more was within the reaches of her mind, it seemed there would be 101 practicalities that might get in the way. Kids being one, for a start. Of course, they'd never discussed it, but Adam came from a close-knit, caring family. He was bound to want the same thing for himself and his own family. But at her age, a family was the one thing it was unlikely Caroline could give him.

'Woo-hoo! That's quite a show!' cried Maryanne. Caroline turned to see her and Anthony, both in baggy chinos and linen shirts, fresh from their morning walk around the island.

'And quite a guy,' said Anthony, settling himself against the trunk of the tree and watching with a smile.

'Yes, he is, isn't he?' murmured Caroline almost to herself. Her body was doing funny things, and it had nothing to do with the heat, or the smoothie, or even the motion of the hammock.

It was to do with her heart. Somehow, somewhere, Adam had snuck his way in there. And somehow, somewhere, she'd fallen in love with him.

'Caroline, can I borrow your BlackBerry?' said Adam, frowning at his own phone. 'I've got no network, and I've been trying to send this bloody text all day.'

'Sure,' said Caroline, sliding her phone across the low wooden table to him. 'Sadly, I've been contactable all day!'

Sitting next to her in the deep cushions of the luxurious rattan swing chair, Anthony laughed. 'But you do such a good job of appearing to enjoy it, Caroline,' he said knowingly. Caroline smiled back at him. Anthony understood she was a workaholic and often teased her about it.

'Well, we can't all earn more interest from our trust fund than we do from our day jobs,' said Maryanne, only half joking. 'Some of us have to work for a living.'

Anthony dug her in the ribs playfully – but Caroline was sure she detected an edge to his body language. 'And some of us don't know the meaning of the word "work". Sitting in the desert all day drinking coffee, with a team of flunkies fussing around me doesn't sound much like hard graft to me.'

Maryanne eyed him archly. 'Just like swanning around London for a few hours catching up with old chums from school doesn't sound much like work to me. It sounds like fun!'

Anthony shrugged good-naturedly. 'Old chums are the best chums,' he said lightly. 'And it just so happens that my old chums like to do business with other old chums. It's kept you in Chanel for long enough, darling.'

'I know, honey, I know. And don't think I'm not grateful for that.' Maryanne leaned over and kissed her husband on the cheek, and Caroline breathed a sigh of relief that peace had been restored. She'd never known Maryanne and Anthony bicker so much as they had on this holiday, even if it was meant to be in jest. A soft breeze blew up from the shoreline, and she lifted her head to catch as much of it as possible. This was an idyllic spot, a decked area leading off from the hacienda's main sitting room looking out over a tiny cove – all white sand beach and gently breaking waves. The sun, now a flawless orange ball, had turned the sea every shade of orange and pink, throwing a pretty sepia light over the land. It was the perfect spot for a sundowner. Or two.

Adam laughed out loud, reading the LED screen of Caroline's BlackBerry.

'What's that?' she said, leaning forward with interest.

'Oh, nothing,' said Adam vaguely. 'Just got a reply to my text. Made me laugh.'

Caroline looked at him, feeling an unfamiliar prick of jealousy. 'Well, do you want to share it with us?' She kicked herself – she sounded like a nagging wife.

'Oh, no, don't worry – private joke,' said Adam, draining his rum punch. 'Anyone for another?'

'Oooh, yes – I'll get them,' said Maryanne, leaping up and turning towards the bar.

'There's really no need to get up, Maryanne – you only have to sneeze here and someone turns up to help you with it,' observed Anthony drily. Sure enough, the tall, wiry barman in collared T-shirt and chino shorts, with his head of well-kept, jaw-length dreadlocks, appeared from inside.

'Can I get you anything?' he asked politely.

'Now, there's a leading question,' said Maryanne coyly, adjusting her pretty vintage sundress with sweetheart neckline and flirty floral print. She squeezed the man's arm in admiration. 'Wow, feel that, Caroline. How often do you work out, honey? C'mon, I'll help you carry these drinks back.'

Instinctively, Caroline looked over to gauge Anthony's

reaction. His face was expressionless, but his brow was furrowed in irritation. No, worse than that – he was *angry*. Making a mental note to pull Maryanne up on her outrageous behaviour later, Caroline turned back to the sunset. It only took a moment to lose herself completely in its beauty, so that when her BlackBerry beeped to indicate a text, she physically jumped.

Not recognising the number, she frowned and clicked on the text button.

Can't wait 2 c u babe! Njoy the OLDS. Charlie xx

Caroline's heart stopped, and her mouth went dry. A myriad thoughts ran through her mind. Who was Charlie? Why was he calling Adam babe? And how dare he scoff at her and her friends?

She looked over at Adam, deep in conversation with Anthony about politics. As always, Adam was using the opportunity to soak up Anthony's superior knowledge, and challenge him on his views. It was a mature quality, Caroline thought – not just having the curiosity, but the capacity to listen and learn – that she was sure would take him far. Normally such a sight would reduce her to mush, but now, heart wavering with uncertainty, she was unmoved. Suddenly, she had an odd feeling of not really knowing him.

Casually she scrolled back through the text conversation with 'Charlie' to Adam's initial text to him.

Hey! Looking forward to hooking up again. Back in the real world on Friday. How bout Sat? Adz x

Bout time lover boy. Whose phone? Sat suits me. 7? x

Borrowed the phone. Back on mine as soon as. Text me Sat. xx

Caroline's heart was pounding so loudly she was surprised no one else heard it. She looked at Adam again, scrutinising him as never before. He was behaving so normally, surely nothing could be going on under the surface? But those texts … They were the texts of lovers, or wannabe lovers at least. And that wasn't even the half of it. Charlie? Illicit meetings? Was Adam not only seeing someone behind her back, but secretly *gay*? She looked around for Maryanne, but she'd returned to the bar as soon as she'd helped the barman deposit the drinks, and was now wrapped around a bar stool smiling coyly at him as he showed her how to make a rum punch. Caroline looked back to Adam, still chatting, oblivious to her consternation.

'Adam, you've had another text.' Caroline's voice was strange and tight, and she cleared her throat to try and sound more normal.

He dragged himself reluctantly away from his conversation and raised his eyebrows. 'OK, cool. I'll take a look in a bit.'

Turning back to Anthony, a new paranoia hit Caroline. Maybe Adam wasn't just interested in Anthony as a friend – maybe he *fancied* him!

Another thought occurred to Caroline. Saturday was Rachel's eighteenth birthday party. Surely Adam wasn't intending to miss that in favour of a bit on the side? 'Well, it must be important – I mean, to text you while you're on holiday,' persisted Caroline. 'Maybe you should take a look?'

Adam looked at her and sighed in mock frustration. He read it and nodded, then handed it back to her and resumed his conversation with Anthony. Caroline was gobsmacked. The bare face of it!

'So, who was it from?' she asked pointedly, heart in her mouth. She *had* to know.

Adam gave her a nonchalant look. 'Do you remember Charlene from the Precious shoot? The American girl? Well, she's going out with Wayne Steel, the fashion photographer, and she's moved to London for the time being. He's promised to do a test shoot with us. Could be great for my book. We're starting at the crack of dawn, though. Could be a killer if I've got jet lag – but I wanted to be finished in good time for Rachel's party.' He paused, as if reaching the end of a list. 'Anything else you want to know?'

'No, thank you,' said Caroline, stung, and she sat back feeling foolish. Charlene. A girl. And a very pretty girl at that. But one who was going out with someone else. What an idiot she was!

She watched Adam for a while longer, relief flooding her veins. A niggle of doubt remained, though, and refused to go away, no matter how hard she tried to banish it. He was innocent *this* time. But he hadn't defended her when Charlene had poked fun at her. What if – what if he decided she was too old for him? Became ashamed of her in the way you'd shrug off an embarrassing parent? Or simply decided he could have his cake and eat it, and look elsewhere?

At that moment, Adam looked up and caught her gaze, and his eyes softened in the half light as he gave her a secret wink. Caroline bit her thumb nervously as she felt herself melt again. Typical that this should happen just when she'd finally given herself up to him.

'I think I'll turn in,' said Anthony, standing up and patting his stomach. 'I'm still full from lunch, and I could do with a long bath and an early night.' He sent a wistful glance over to his wife. 'Say goodnight to Maryanne for me, will you?'

Caroline opened her mouth to protest, and then shut it almost immediately. She'd just got herself in a spin over a silly text: she had no idea how Anthony must feel about being made a public fool of by his wife.

Adam moved over on to the seat beside Caroline. 'Move over, baby – let me snuggle in,' he said in a low voice as he pulled her horizontal and spooned against her. He smelt of Cool Water and sea salt and rum punch. Caroline felt herself relax into him.

'Trouble in paradise?' he said questioningly, nodding after Anthony.

Nearly, Caroline thought, recalling the misunderstood text. Answering his question, she shrugged. 'Maz and Anthony don't have the most conventional of relationships,' she replied.

'That makes two of us then, doesn't it?' he murmured in her ear.

Caroline turned to face him as if she'd been shot. 'What do you mean?' she said sharply.

Adam laughed. 'Whoa! What did I say? I only meant, there aren't too many couples with twenty years between them, are there? Not this way around, anyhow.'

Caroline stared at him, trying to gauge his true meaning in the fading light. 'I guess not.'

Adam leaned over and kissed her softly. 'But that's a good thing, right? It makes us special. Even more special than we already are.'

'Really?' said Caroline doubtfully. Since when had the tables turned so that Adam was so completely and utterly in charge of this relationship?

'Really,' said Adam. 'I love you, Mrs Walker.'

Caroline lay there, stunned. It was what she'd wanted to hear since — well, since long before she'd decided she was in love herself. So why couldn't she tell him she loved him in return? And why, rather than setting her mind at rest, did those three little words fill her with even more doubts about their real meaning?

Chapter 19

SIMPLY A MATTER OF OPINION

As she walked through the subdued, uplit corridors of the party, Caroline took in glimpses of the rooms she passed, noting with approval the individual décor, the eclectic, quirky accessories and the cosy, chic designer furniture of the refurb. The library, the juice bar, the gym, the private cinema – all mini worlds within a world. She'd been here for a recce before booking it, of course – but it had still been unfinished then, with half-plastered walls and only the interior designer's mood board to give a taster of the final plans. But she'd taken her chances, knowing the developer's reputation and the fact that it was billed as the hottest new club to hit London. Nothing else would do for her baby's coming of age party, and the punt had been worth it. The finished product more than lived up to her expectations.

She tried to stop herself from wincing as the headache that had appeared as one of a series of rapidly advancing flu symptoms earlier that afternoon made its presence felt again. Thank God for 24 hour chemists, she thought – the NyQuil she'd picked up from around the corner just before the party started was bound to take effect soon. She'd taken a couple more a few moments ago to make sure. Caroline had spent months making sure nothing would get in the way of the best night of Rachel's life – and she sure as hell wasn't going to let a cold ruin it.

The hubbub Caroline had heard from the doorway grew louder as she turned a corner and entered the Marguerita Lounge, the most glamorous of the club's private hire rooms. A huge, bright space, its high ceilings gave it a summer airiness, whilst a dark, chocolaty wallpaper collage by cutting-edge designer Julie Verhoeven reached as far as the six-foot picture rails and lent a feeling of intimacy. The floor-to-ceiling sliding doors were tonight thrown open to allow the eighty or so guests to wander around the decked area surrounding the kidney-shaped slate rooftop pool. Ambient house music mellowed its way out of the surround sound speakers dotted subtly around the room, and a low-key laser light show played on the white screen behind the stage erected by the elegantly curved bar. It was a fitting backdrop for a gathering of London's next generation of cool, thought Caroline as she observed the collection of rock-chick-style girls, all kohl rimmed eyes, long, gangly legs and bed hair, and tall, lanky boys in tight jeans and T-shirts covering up their youthful awkwardness with swagger and bluster. She was still amazed Rachel could even know this many people. Wasn't it only five minutes ago that she'd been bouncing on Caroline's knee?

The thought made Caroline feel 105, and she pushed it to the back of her mind. Now was *not* the time for sentimentalism. It was the time to celebrate. She shook her head at the glass of champagne offered by a passing waiter and continued on her way through the party. As Caroline squeezed through the crowd, Rachel's guests juggled cocktail glasses and mouth-watering pastries baked by the in-house pâtisserie chef to clear a path for her, smiling in recognition. Caroline smiled back.

She caught sight of Adam, and as she watched him work the room, Caroline couldn't believe she'd ever suspected he was gay – even for the most fleeting of moments. The way he moved around women was too sensual, the way they responded to him too primal, for him to be anything but het-erosexual. He was a natural 'people' person, she thought, at ease with himself and others in a manner that was far beyond his years. Not to mention sexy, she thought, watching girl after girl pout at him coquettishly, give him a not-so-subtle flirtatious stare, or send a secret smile his way. So why was she still so reluctant to fully admit her feelings for him, not just to him, but to herself? Of course, he hadn't mentioned her reti-cence when faced with his own professions of love, but every now and then she caught him looking at her with big puppy dog eyes, waiting, hopeful that she would reciprocate. However, something was holding her back.

'Great party, Caro. You never lose it!' She jumped at his proximity as Les murmured in her ear. It was probably the closest they'd physically been since the split. She stepped back awkwardly in an attempt to reinstate some distance between them. Les was dressed in his ubiquitous Savile Row suit – his only concession to the informality of the evening an open collar and no tie – but looked different, somehow. Thinner. Smaller.

'Thanks, Les,' she said neutrally, and then pointedly: 'Is

there nothing going on downstairs, then?' The layout of the venue had the added advantage of keeping her and Les separate, and they had tacitly agreed that he would hold court in the elegant downstairs bar, meeting and greeting the guests as they arrived, leaving her free to celebrate her beautiful daughter's special night upstairs without any outside interference.

'Oh, it's heaving,' he said pleasantly. 'I just wanted to congratulate you.' He smiled at her and she turned away, not wanting to get pulled into a long and no doubt emotional exchange. 'And check out the competition,' he added, nodding across to Adam.

Caroline frowned at him and turned towards her boyfriend, just in time to catch another girl giving Adam one of THOSE smiles.

'Don't be ridiculous, Les,' she said flatly. 'No one sees it that way.'

'Except me,' he said under his breath, and then as she turned back to him sharply, smiled at her infuriatingly.

'Why don't you go and congratulate Rachel, instead?' said Caroline irritably. 'It's her night, after all.'

'No problem, Caro,' he said, the use of her pet name instantly grating on her nerves. 'I can tell I'm cramping your style.' He leaned over and brushed her cheek with his lips. 'Have a good night.'

Caroline tutted – lost on Les as he walked away from her – and surveyed the crowd. The spot where he'd kissed her seemed to burn, and she rubbed at it in annoyance.

She sought out her daughter – not difficult in her birthday present from Caroline, an asymmetric body-hugging Preen dress in chartreuse crêpe – and was overcome with a wave of pride. The colour set off her pale skin and dark, blunt-cut hair and, head and shoulders above most of her friends, Rachel made a striking figure laughing with some of her guests. The dress was a good choice for this coming-of-age evening, thought Caroline in approval – sophisticatedly cutting edge, but matched with an edgy pair of shoe boots and casual accessories, it also managed to emphasise Rachel's youth. Caroline's heart swelled as she thought of her daughter, an ingénue, setting out on life's great adventure. She tried to quash the recurrent feeling of envy. Being jealous of your daughter was *not* cool.

'There you are, gorgeous!' Adam grabbed her from behind and pulled her to him, kissing her on the neck. 'I've been looking for you. I've got some people I want you to meet!'

Caroline laughed delightedly and turned around, giving him a chaste kiss on the lips. 'There are eighty-odd people here that I need to meet,' she pointed out.

'Yes, but these are *important*,' laughed Adam. 'They're *my* friends.'

In a bid to max out the eye candy, Rachel had given Adam carte blanche to invite as many of his friends as he liked, so long as they fulfilled the criteria of good-looking, cool or interesting. And single, naturally. The ensuing discussions had created a fledgling bond between the pair, and Caroline had several times silently thanked her lucky stars that circumstances had given a reason for Rachel to finally accept Adam. In fact, she'd thought drily as she watched them chatter away about bands and DJs for the night on a couple of occasions, they almost had more in common than *she* and Adam did . . .

'So, this is Greg, and Wayne – and of course you've met Charlene?' Adam beamed proudly at her as he introduced them, their holiday discussion clearly long forgotten.

But Caroline hadn't forgotten, and suddenly it was as if someone had pulled a needle across her evening. Events screeched to an unwelcome halt when, as if in slow motion, Charlene – hand casually snaked around her boyfriend's waist, other hand proprietorially placed on Adam's shoulder – turned around, all baby blonde hair, peachy complexion and big blue eyes. Caroline didn't need to look too closely to see the pearly white perfect teeth, or the quizzically arched eyebrows, or even the knowingly intelligent look in her eyes. Her looks were the polar opposite of Caroline's dark hair and translucent skin, and she had all the qualities you'd look for in your ultimate desirable woman. Caroline knew this for certain, because she herself had picked them out as such during the casting for her Precious fragrance campaign.

In a flash, her own Stella McCartney jumpsuit felt pedestrian and try-hard, and her carefully blow-dried hair felt too big and 'done'. Her equally carefully applied make-up felt caked on in the face of Charlene's youth and vitality, and her accessories too twee.

'Yes, of course I remember Charlene,' she said, her voice shrill and forced. 'How lovely to see you again.'

'Well, hey Mrs Walker,' said Charlene easily. 'I guess you're sick of seeing my face, aren't you?' Caroline jumped as if she'd been shot and laughed manically.

'What on earth do you mean?' she said, looking around at the others in exaggerated confusion. 'Why would I be sick of your face, Charlene – we've only met once before!' Inside, she was dying. Was she so transparent that her thoughts were written all over her own face?

Charlene was still smiling but her eyes said it all. Caroline was some mad old British granny who needed to be tolerated because she had given her a major campaign, and because she was going out with Charlene's friend. 'Um – well, I'm on your latest campaign. I figured you'd have the creative all over your offices. I'm so proud of it, I've got magazine pages torn out and hung all over my apartment!'

Cute, thought Caroline as Wayne squeezed his girlfriend proudly and the others grinned at her fondly. Very cute. She tried to ignore the crushing embarrassment that was threatening to overwhelm her, and the nervous rash that was creeping up her neck where any normal person would have a pretty blush.

'Oh, right,' she said lamely. 'Of course.' A waiter walked past with a tray of Dom Perignon and this time, Caroline accepted one gratefully. She took a long, deep drink and snuck a sidelong glance at Charlene, busy refusing another flute from the same waiter. The model turned and looked earnestly at Caroline.

'I wanted to thank you – for the opportunity,' Charlene continued. The three boys stopped joshing and leaned in to hear. Caroline, uncertain what to say, felt more awkward by the second. Then, to her horror, Charlene's eyes filled with tears. 'My daddy only gave me a year to prove myself as a model before I had to go to law school,' she continued, genuine gratitude oozing out of every pore. 'But the Precious campaign, well, that proved to him I do have "something". Maybe not all it takes to make it really big, but—' A chorus of protests rose up from Adam, Greg and Wayne and drowned out whatever else Charlene was about to say as they assured her that of course she had a huge career in front of her, and she didn't know what she was talking about.

Caroline smiled maternally and turned to Adam, trying to get his attention. He caught her look and made an eyes-to-the-ceiling gesture and then nodded to Charlene, as if this happened all the time with models, and he as a fellow model was best placed to help reassure her. Caroline shook her head helplessly, and took another long sip of champagne. She glanced into the glass in surprise. She'd finished it already! This wasn't in her plan of taking it easy. She put her hand to her head and delicately massaged her temple. Yep, she was definitely feeling a bit squiffy. Unusually so. She would stop now.

Her eyes moved sideways – then nearly popped out of her head as she saw Adam's hand brush over Charlene's pert bottom. She stared in disbelief. It was a split-second move, but she was sure that's what she'd seen. She looked up at him for signs of guilt on his face – but there was nothing.

'Surely that's not the belle of the ball I see before me, with an empty glass?' said a voice behind her, and she turned to see Vernon, friend of Rachel's on–off squeeze Robbie. He held out a glass of bubbly to her with a little bow. She laughed in acceptance.

'Nice try, Vernon, but the belle of the ball is most definitely the *other* Ms Walker present tonight,' she said, nodding over to where a shrieking Rachel was being spun around by Robbie.

'Well, I guess that's simply a matter of opinion,' he said with a cheeky wink. 'Certainly not from where I'm standing.'

Caroline wagged her finger at him warningly, but laughed again and looked at him appraisingly. Vernon was an anomaly amongst Rachel's friends: he had the tall, broad and sporty frame of a keen rugby player instead of the thin and gangly rock look so prevalent amongst his peers. His hair was cropped short and his face ruddy from years of outdoor sports, and he wore Replay jeans and a Ralph Lauren polo shirt. He wasn't good-looking, but had a confident swagger that was appealing, if not endearing. She looked back over her shoulder at where Adam was still fawning over Charlene, and decided a few moments' banter with Vernon was exactly what she needed. After all, what harm could it do?

An hour later, Adam still hadn't reappeared and Caroline, quite frankly, couldn't have cared less. She peered over at Vernon's position opposite her on a pouffe in the corner of the drawing room with woozy eyes, and wiggled her bare toes at him.

'I warn you, I am a champion at toe wars,' she threatened. 'One false move and I will take your feet prisoner in an instant.' She swiped her big toe at him menacingly, and they both laughed. He took her foot in his hands – big, paw-like limbs that might almost have belonged to a wild bear – and resumed massaging it. At least, that's what he claimed he was doing – to Caroline it felt more as if he was kneading dough, but right now she wasn't complaining. After all attempts to flirt her way back to the top of Adam's consciousness had failed, she'd given herself up to the enjoyment of being fawned over. And Vernon did a very good line in fawning – in fact, he hadn't left her side since he'd brought her that first drink, showering her with compliments and, most importantly, making her laugh.

What would Adam say if he saw you now? a little voice persisted through the fog in her head. *He wouldn't see me now*, she answered crossly, trying to ignore her own conscience, *because he's too busy chatting up pretty girls his own age.*

'Has anyone seen Caroline?' At that very moment, she heard Adam at the door to the drawing room. Trying to hide, she shrank down in the leather armchair gesticulating wildly at Vernon not to respond. He slid off the chair on to the floor, pretending to hide, and she swallowed the childish giggle that threatened to emerge.

'Mate, have you seen Caroline – Rachel's mum – anywhere?' Adam didn't sound worried, she reflected – just annoyed. Well, two could play at that game . . .

'Caroline?' she heard another reveller reply. 'You mean Rachel's mum? Nope. Haven't seen her for ages, mate.'

'Oh.' Now Adam sounded exasperated, and Caroline felt a wave of indignation rise up in her. 'I've been looking all over for her.'

Caroline couldn't stop a look of outrage appearing on her face and pulled her foot away from Vernon. The liar! He'd probably only just stopped petting Charlene and was now looking for her out of some kind of mistaken sense of duty. Vernon looked up at her questioningly, and she put her finger to her lips to shush him.

Above the bass line from down the corridor, she heard Adam's footsteps retreat, and she felt a wave of relief, mixed with consternation. What did he mean by trying to ruin her night like this?

Vernon sat up and peered around her chair. 'He's gone,' he sniggered, and shuffled closer to Caroline, stroking her leg. 'Want to tell me what all that was about?'

'Oh, you know, just a domestic,' said Caroline uncomfortably. She wasn't used to discussing her private affairs with anyone, let alone someone she'd only properly met moments earlier.

Vernon gazed at her impassively for a moment. 'Well, there's only one thing for it,' he said urgently. He leapt up, grabbed her hand, and pulled her up off the chair. 'We need to hide somewhere else!'

'Vernon, don't be ridiculous,' giggled Caroline.

'He'll be back!' said Vernon warningly. 'Come on!' He pulled her through the room and she followed, stumbling slightly on her high heels and still giggling in spite of herself. Vernon led her through the semi-darkness, both of them giggling, until they reached the Ladies. 'In here!' said Vernon, and pushing her through, closed the door behind them.

It was a single toilet cubicle, plushly decorated with dark walls and low lighting. A velvet-upholstered chair stood in the corner.

'Oh dear. Bit cramped in here, isn't it?' said Vernon in low tones as he pulled Caroline in to him. She looked up at him, heart beating. She hadn't planned this . . .

He leaned in towards her and kissed her. It was a hard, wet, kiss and she recoiled slightly inside. It was nothing like Adam's soft caresses. At the thought of Adam, the knife turned in her heart again, and she gave herself up to Vernon's kiss. He sat down on the chair and pulled her on top of him, kissing her again. Caroline's heart was beating wildly. She shouldn't be doing this. She didn't want to be doing this. Did she?

She felt Vernon unbutton her jumpsuit, and felt his hand inside, reaching for her breast. She pulled back.

'Sorry, Vernon, I—'

Suddenly, the door crashed open and Caroline and Vernon turned in surprise. Her heart stopped. In the doorway stood Adam, hair ruffled, looking at them with a mixture of bewilderment, pain and anger.

'Caroline?'

'Adam!' Vernon dropped his hold on her, and she grabbed at her jumpsuit, trying ineffectively to do up the buttons again.

'What the hell do you think you're playing at?'

Caroline gaped at him, trying desperately to find the words. What the hell *had* she been playing at?'

'Mate – I was giving Caroline a massage, and—'

Both Caroline and Adam turned to Vernon incredulously, and he clamped his mouth shut mid-sentence. Then their eyes found one another again.

Adam stared at her for the longest minute she could ever remember, then turned on his heel and stormed out. Unsure what to do, Caroline let out a nervous giggle and watched him helplessly before the adrenalin of horrified shock kicked in and shot her up out of her seat.

'Adam! It's not what you think! Adam, wait!'

He was standing with his arm propping him up against the wall, his head on his forearm, as if trying to gather himself. Caroline's heart felt like it was going to burst. What the bloody hell had she been doing?

'Adam, I . . .'

He looked up, his face bereft.

'Honestly, Adam, nothing happened, I—'

'Nothing happened? NOTHING HAPPENED?' he thundered. 'You're in a toilet cubicle, half undressed sitting astride someone you've hardly met, and you tell me nothing happened? That's not what it looks like, Caroline!'

'Oh, and you're so the injured party, aren't you?' cried Caroline, outraged at the injustice of the whole situation. 'It's all right for you to spend all night flirting with someone else, but when you see me doing the same . . .'

'Flirting? Who the bloody hell have I been flirting with?'

Caroline stared at him, suddenly feeling ridiculous. 'Charlene,' she said in a small voice.

'Charlene?' he repeated. 'Charlene? You mean my friend who is totally in love with another good friend? You mean the friend who's only here in the first place because she diligently brought along a load of her male model friends to your daughter's party as requested by your daughter?'

'But it's not just tonight!' objected Caroline. 'The texts! On holiday! And she's so young, and beautiful, and . . .' The words sounded ridiculous even to her ears. But why couldn't he see what a mess she was in? How she'd got so muddled? And, she realised as she swayed slightly, so drunk?

Adam looked at her coldly. 'You know, Caroline, I used to think you couldn't see beyond appearances. And you know what? I was right. But it's not just you, is it? It's me. Because I used to think you were beautiful inside and out. But now I see that I was fooled, too. Goodbye, Caroline.'

And again, he turned and walked away. Caroline's legs seemed rooted to the spot, unable to follow him. Suddenly, she panicked. She'd been wrong, and now Adam was leaving.

Leaving the party, and leaving her life. She ran after him, through the door and along the corridor to the stairs. A group of revellers came out of the Marguerita Lounge and blocked her path, and she looked helplessly as Adam's back disappeared down the stairs to the exit.

As she watched, however, a blonde head appeared from one of the ground floor rooms. Charlene! Adam bent his head to her ear, obviously whispering something to her. She looked at him, holding his gaze for a long moment before nodding. Adam put his arm around her, then they disappeared out and into the night.

Caroline let out a little gasp and held her hand to her mouth. So she'd been right all along! There *was* more to Charlene and Adam than just friends. She swayed a little on the spot and frowned, moving her hand to her forehead. She felt disoriented. And deserted.

For the second time that year, she'd been abandoned by a man she loved.

Chapter 20

DESPERATELY SEEKING
A BRIGHT SIDE

The phone had still not rung. Unless – she'd missed it?
Caroline picked it up for the umpteenth time, checked for
missed calls and texts, and stared at it again. Her finger hovered over Adam's number before she put it down again. Filled
with remorse for what she'd done, with every bone in her
body she was aching to speak to Adam, to set things straight
between them – but something was stopping her contacting
him. She still couldn't quite get over the fact that it was
Adam's behaviour that had led her to spend so much of the
evening with Vernon, which in turn had led to . . .

She stood up restlessly and walked over to the window. She
could hardly bring herself to think about it. She'd never felt so
dirty, so low, so ashamed. Her stomach lurched again. Or so
ill.

This was like no hangover she'd ever had before. She felt
weirdly dizzy, displaced – as if everything was slightly surreal.

She turned her thoughts back to Adam. Of course, it wasn't

just what she'd done that was preventing her making contact. It was the mental picture she had of him leaving with Charlene, the persistent agony of where they were going – and what they were doing.

'Mum, we're making bacon sarnies – do you want one?' called Rachel from the kitchen. At the thought of food, Caroline felt bile rise in her throat. She took a deep breath and put her hand on the windowpane to steady herself. Another anomaly. Not that she had many hangovers, but after a night out she was always ravenous. In fact normally by now – she looked at her watch: 10 a.m. – make that *definitely* by now she'd have polished off a fry-up, or at least a couple of pieces of toast and Marmite.

'No darling, I'm fine thank you,' she called back. She didn't like to admit to herself that even if she'd been starving, she was unlikely to want to spend time with her daughter. Rachel was still full of the success of the night before, and Caroline was certain that her guilt was written all over her face, and that even if Rachel didn't see it, one of her overnight guests – Robbie, Rachel's best childhood friends Izzy and Olivia – would.

She picked up her phone again. Still nothing. It was no good, she *had* to talk to someone. Making her way delicately up the stairs, Caroline retreated to the perceived safety of her bedroom and sank back gratefully on to the bed. She pressed the speed dial button for Maz's number and waited as the heard the phone ring. Thank goodness Maryanne was back on British soil. It was at times like these you needed to offload on to a totally unbiased, non-judgemental party to gain a little perspective on things.

'Hi honey, so how was the big one-eight?' drawled Maryanne. 'Did your gorgeous daughter knock 'em dead like I've taught her to?'

Caroline felt a stab of guilt as she realised that once again, she was neglecting her role as Rachel's mother. Today, she should be making the bacon sandwiches, basking in her daughter's enjoyment of a successful party, and listening to the gossip – not *creating* it.

'Yes, she did,' she replied. 'She looked amazing, and had a fantastic time. She was disappointed you couldn't make it.' *And so am I*, she added silently. *Especially now.*

'I know, but the last thing she'd have wanted on her big night was me stealing the limelight,' joked Maryanne. 'Filming on this second blessed commercial didn't finish until the early hours – the party would have been over by the time I'd got into London. But enough about me – how was it for you, honey, relinquishing all the attention in favour of your beautiful little girl?' teased Maryanne.

'Oh, that bit was fine,' Caroline replied drily. 'It was relinquishing Adam's attention in favour of a twenty-something blonde model that I wasn't so keen on.'

Maryanne drew in a deep breath. 'So Mr Perfect isn't so perfect after all, huh? Well honey, it happens with them all, sooner or later.'

'Adam's a little different to *your* Mr Perfects, Maz,' said Caroline irritably. 'And I'm still not sure what the "it" that happened was. He was a little over-attentive with this girl, and then stormed off with her at the end of the night. So we're not speaking. But that's not the only thing.' She took a deep breath. 'I've – um – I've kind of messed up myself.'

There was a pause, 'You've cheated on Adam?' said Maryanne incredulously.

'No!' said Caroline, too quickly. 'At least, not all the way. Not how you think. It's just I—'

'Well, I never thought I'd see the day!' whooped Maryanne, laughing hysterically. 'You ARE a dark horse, Caroline Walker. Welcome to the club, honey. So, who was he?'

'He's a friend of Rachel's,' said Caroline miserably.

'Another cub!' laughed Maryanne. 'Good for you. Was he good? You gonna see him again?'

'It wasn't like that, Maryanne,' said Caroline, desperately wishing she'd never made this call. Maryanne was meant to be making her feel better, not worse. 'It was an absolute mistake.'

'They all are, honey, they all are. The key is, just don't let them become *your* mistake. Learn from my errors. Move on.'

Caroline felt panic rising in her chest. 'But – but what about Adam?'

'What about Adam?' scoffed Maryanne. 'Adam, this guy, the next one – they're all one and the same. I warned you, these cute little young guns are only good for one thing. A bit of fun. But you, being you, had to get all serious. Just be thankful Adam showed his true colours sooner rather than later. I mean, he could have moved in, you could have got married or anything! You've had a lucky escape. Look on the bright side, eh?'

Caroline sighed miserably. Try as she might, a bright side was proving pretty elusive this time around.

Half an hour later, Caroline lifted her pale face from the pillow. She'd never felt so wretched. This situation just seemed to get worse and worse. She knew Maryanne of old, and she should have known better than to turn to her for run-of-the-mill support. Maryanne always liked to have company in whatever she was going through, and she would have been overjoyed by the fact that in her eyes Caroline had become a fully fledged cougar – in the *Daily Mail* sense, that is. But their conversation only seemed to have compounded Caroline's misery.

At that moment, her phone buzzed, and she picked it up, suddenly full of hope that she'd see Adam's number showing. It wasn't. It was Esther. As usual, her friend was straight to the point.

'Caroline, I've just had to hang up on Maryanne and call you immediately. What on earth is going on over there? I've had some ghastly story from Maryanne about sex in toilet cubicles with complete strangers, and at Rachel's party, too. I mean, what in God's name has happened to you? Have you had a personality transplant? Are you totally mad? Or have you started on hormone replacement treatment?'

Caroline opened her mouth to defend herself, but nothing came out. Instead, she broke down in tears – huge great sobs that racked her entire body.

On the other end of the phone, Esther's voice softened. 'Oh, Caroline, I wish I was there with you. Take a deep breath and tell me all about it.'

At the end of a ten-minute monologue, Caroline had related the events of the whole evening in detail.

'And so now, I've never felt so low. So ashamed. So *dirty*.'

'But Caroline, darling, the one thing I simply don't understand is how you came to be so drunk in the first place?'

marvelled Esther. 'It's so out of character. Tiddly, yes. Giddy – well, sometimes. But out-of-your-head pissed, on the most important night of your daughter's life? What were you think-ing?'

'That's the thing, Esther,' said Caroline quietly. 'I did drink more than I should have, yes. But I'm sure I didn't have more than four glasses all night, even if I did drink a couple of them pretty quickly. They must just have affected me that way for some reason.'

'And how do you feel now?' persisted Esther in the manner of an FBI interrogator.

'Well, dog rough, to be honest!' said Caroline, trying to make light of it. Sharing the burden was making her feel slightly better. 'I'm more hungover than I can ever remember being. I feel dizzy and displaced. I'd almost describe it as an out-of-body experience.'

'And you can't remember anything about the end of the night?' continued Esther, in the same monotone.

'No!' said Caroline. 'Esther, you're freaking me out! This is like the Spanish Inquisition!'

'Well, darling, I'm about to freak you out even further. What you've described is all over the US networks at the moment. Your drink was spiked, Caroline. I don't think you were drunk. I think you were *drugged.*'

'Darling, it's not what you think. Esther even thinks I had my drink spiked. I'm sure that's not the case, but I certainly wasn't in control. I wasn't myself. I—'

'I'm surprised you even know what yourself is any more!' screamed Rachel, waving her phone around in anger. Only

275

moments earlier, the phone had delivered the unwelcome news that not only had Adam told Charlene exactly what he thought he'd seen in the toilets, but that she had decided to tell the world. 'I've got to admit, *I* don't. I mean, what is going on with you, Mum? You've gone from being a first-class businesswoman to being a first-class slapper!'

Caroline flinched at her daughter's anger. She was embarrassed, hurt and humiliated – and rightly so.

'Darling, please, I—'

'I mean, have you any idea what you've done?' continued Rachel, lost in her rant. 'Vernon might be a nice guy as a friend, but he's a total perv. He's the lech we've all been avoiding dating throughout school. The kind of guy who looks up your skirt at breaktime. The kind of guy who takes porn to school to read in the loos at lunchtime. The kind of guy who never manages to pull, but when he does, keeps their knickers as some kind of badge of honour!'

Caroline looked at her, horrified.

'In fact, we've even started to call him a knicker collector. That's the guy you had sex with last night, Mum! Thank God he's got no way of proving it. I mean, you're just going to have to totally deny everything. I'm going to have to totally deny everything.'

Something in Caroline's face made Rachel stop.

'Rachel, I can't believe you think all this,' said Caroline, reeling from the shock of her daughter's passionate outburst. 'The fact is, nothing happened. Yes, I got myself into a compromising position – but nothing happened, Rachel. NOTHING. HAPPENED.' She was shouting now, almost hysterical, and she bit her lip, trying to calm herself down.

'It doesn't matter what really happened, does it, Mum?' screamed back Rachel. 'No one else knows that, do they? Charlene's story comes from Adam – your boyfriend, for God's sake – and no one is going to buy your story now!'

Caroline looked at her miserably. She was right, of course.

At that moment, there was a text alert from Caroline's phone. Adam! Her heart leapt. Her hands were clammy and shaky as she clicked to read it.

So I see you and Vernon got along pretty well last night. Good luck, Caroline. With people like him in your life, you're going to need it.

In despair, Caroline turned back to her daughter, who was now slumped in a chair, leaning on the table with her head in her hands. After a long, painful pause, Rachel looked up and gave a strange hiccup. 'How could you do this to me, Mum? My eighteenth birthday is meant to be the start of the rest of my life.' She stared at Caroline, her eyes hard as flint and full of hatred. 'But as of today, my life is officially *over*. And it's all because of YOU.'

Chapter 21

The Autumn Of Discontent

Caroline handed over some change for her coffee. Putting off her return to the office for as long as possible, she numbly carried the corrugated cardboard cups over to a bench on the piazza and sat silently next to Babs. In front of them, a handful of late summer tourists were gathering to watch a silver-sprayed mime artist on his plinth; blankly, Caroline joined them and her mother in gazing at his careful robotics for a few moments. She found the precision of his movements, and the relaxed pace at which he made them, curiously settling and she felt herself relax.

A breeze scattered the first handfuls of crunchy brown leaves across the cobbles, and Caroline looked around in surprise. She loved the fact that even in the centre of the West End there were enough trees to create spring blossom, and then summer shade, and then finally piles of rustling leaves . . . She loved to be reminded of their existence. If the reappearance of Babs's faithful beige mac wasn't enough to indicate the change of season, this was confirmation. The air was cool rather than chilly, but the smoky scent of autumn was hanging on the air and instinctively she pulled her chunky knitted cardigan closer around her. She'd always enjoyed these first weeks of fall: the crisp, fresh air; the plumpness of the apples hanging low on the branches of the gnarled apple trees at the cottage; the storing of the summer's cotton and linen – once full of the promise of long, sunny days, but now looking so tired and crumpled – and the 'back to school' feeling of newness everywhere, from the latest fashion collections in store to the mellow contents of her larder and the comfort food that came from it. This year, however, autumn came with cold comfort. It was the definitive end of a landmark summer.

The summer of love. She chuckled out loud at the irony of her summer of sexual discovery – self-discovery, really – and the mess it had ended in. More hurt, more recriminations, more humiliation. Summer of love to autumn of discontent.

As if reading her thoughts, Babs placed a well-preserved, elegant hand on Caroline's knee. Caroline studied the familiar hands, the fingers long and elegant, the backs permanently tanned and dusted with age spots from a year-round garden addiction.

'You know, even though it's ages since you left, this time of year always reminds me of you going back to school,' said Babs nostalgically. Caroline smiled and squeezed the hand on her knee. Not for the first time this year, she'd been ridiculously glad to see Babs this morning. And not for the first time, Babs had surprised her with her open-minded, non-judgemental reaction.

Caroline took a sip of coffee and felt the hot, bitter liquid buoy her from the inside out. Popping into the office after a morning shopping in town, Babs had found Caroline absent and had called her mobile to find out where she was. Caroline bet if her mother had tried a thousand times to guess what she'd been doing, she'd never have got it right.

The words on the medical website rang around her mind for the umpteenth time since she'd decided to investigate what had happened on the night of Rachel's party. Remembering the NyQuil she'd taken, she'd googled to find out the potential results of mixing them with alcohol. The side effects of the pills were chiefly drowsiness and lack of alertness, but add into the mix the lack of food, and the champagne, she could well have been on a hiding to nowhere. *Had* been on a hiding to nowhere.

So, as she'd thought, she hadn't been simply drunk. And nor had she been drugged. The reality of her own stupidity was much worse than that. She'd done exactly what she'd always counselled Rachel against, and taken her eye off the ball to the detriment of her own personal safety. Effectively, she'd let herself get out of control and into a situation she'd never normally dream of getting into.

'Oh, Mother,' she sighed out loud. 'What a fool I've been.'

Babs leaned across the back of the bench and deposited her empty coffee cup in a bin. 'Well, we've all been there,' said Babs stoutly. 'Well, not quite *there*, but you know what I mean.'

Caroline allowed herself a smile and nodded sadly. She *so* should have known better.

'And there's only one thing worse than an old fool, darling,' Babs continued. 'And that's an old fool who doesn't learn from her mistakes.' She looked meaningfully at her daughter.

Caroline took another long sip of coffee, and tried to fathom the jumble of emotions she was feeling. There wasn't just shame. There was shock. So far in her life, this kind of thing had been something that happened to other people – a headline in the *Daily Mail* that indicated an unpleasant cultural development she needed to educate Rachel about. Which she had – over and over – with the inevitable pangs of panic and waking-in-the-night stabs of worry that were part and parcel of parenting. But never, ever, had she thought it would apply to *her*.

There was self-disgust, and guilt. But – and she hardly dared admit this even to herself – there was also relief. She hadn't had a personality transplant after all, lost her judgement so fundamentally that she had effectively broken all her own unwritten rules of moral behaviour. She could once again hold her head up in front of Rachel, and if not justify it all, at least find some kind of cause and effect to explain it. And – a little voice persisted – there was something to go to Adam with. Some kind of explanation. Some kind of reasoning. Some kind of hope.

The by now familiar contradictory mix of emotions that the thought of Adam inspired in her returned with full force, and she was overwhelmed with guilt and regret. It was over a week since Rachel's party, and he was still refusing to return her calls, and now she'd given up trying to contact him. As always, she imagined him, those grey-green eyes wide with shock, hurting like a little boy, and she was almost overcome by the physical urge to comfort him, to take back the pain she'd inflicted on him, to make it all better again.

Then, almost as quickly, the memory of him leaving with

Charlene hit her like a twelve-ton truck, and anger swept the guilt away. It wasn't all her, after all. Adam's behaviour had hardly been exemplary – and he had his own blame to shoulder in this whole sorry experience.

Caroline finished her coffee and stood up purposefully, kissing her mother goodbye and trying to ignore Babs's unspoken words, that she knew echoed the little voice inside her own mind. *You've now got a viable explanation for your part in the whole fiasco. What if Adam had, too?* As she marched back to the office, she inhaled the autumn air deeply and physically tried to steel herself against it. There was no point in brooding on it now. She'd spent enough long hours in her own time mulling over what had gone wrong and how to put it right. This was work time, and she had a busy day in front of her.

'Da da, da da, da da da da da daaaaaaaaa,' sang Julie to the *Blind Date* tune as Caroline opened the door to reception. She smiled uncertainly at Julie, who was smiling at her widely and expectantly.

'Hi, Julie.'

'Morning, Cilla!'

Caroline looked at her, bewildered. 'What on earth are you on about, Julie?'

'You!' trilled Julie excitedly. 'You're just Mrs Romance these days, aren't you?' She tapped her computer screen authoritatively with a long scarlet nail. 'It says here that our Charlene –' she broke off and looked at Caroline to make sure she was still with her – 'that's the girl in the Precious ads.'

'Yes, Julie, I'm well aware of who "our" Charlene is,' snapped Caroline. Why was the entire world intent on falling in love with bloody Charlene? At the very mention of her name, Caroline felt as if she'd aged twenty years. In comparison to the image of Charlene's Californian sunshine, Caroline's luxey fine-knit top and wide-legged navy Jaeger wool trousers felt frumpy and safe, and her pale complexion dull and sun-starved.

Caroline's irritation washed over Julie's head. Unabashed, she began to recite from the website on her computer screen. '"There must be something in the water at retail guru Caroline Walker's Covent Garden HQ. Not only has her current Precious perfume campaign spawned her own new romance with its male model star Adam Geray, some twenty years her junior, but now another of its stars has got engaged. Blonde bombshell Charlene Foulger has announced her engagement to fashion snapper of the moment Wayne Steel, who is thought to have proposed following Walker's daughter Rachel's swanky eighteenth birthday party last week. We don't know what Walker is doing right, but one thing's for sure – we'll have what she's having!"' Julie looked at her triumphantly. 'So there you go, Cilla – don't know what you'll have to buy first, a hat or your own wedding dress!'

'That's quite enough, Julie,' said Caroline firmly. 'I don't know where you find all this rubbish. But I might remind you that I'm not even divorced yet, let alone looking to get married again.'

Affronted, Julie turned back to her screen. 'It's not rubbish. We heard in the office yesterday, and so I looked it up to make sure. I just thought you'd like to know, that's all,' she said, busying herself by officiously straightening various piles of papers on her desk. 'You've never called my news sense into

283

question before. My general knowledge of current affairs is of huge value to this company. As you know, I keep everyone abreast of all the latest developments in the industry and further afield on a daily basis. I felt that this was of as much value as anything else.'

Despite her roller coaster of emotions, Caroline's lips twitched. Only Julie could repackage flagrant gossiping into a news service. Her detective skills would put Miss Marple to shame.

'Well, thank you,' she said, and then frowned as she saw a letter detailing marketing activity on Precious.

'But I'm not sure what that's doing here.' She leaned over and plucked the sheet from Julie's desk. 'God knows how that's found its way here.' Studying the sheet intently, she took the opportunity to escape and slipped through to the sanctity of her office. Desperate to process the feelings this latest revelation had unleashed, Caroline smiled briefly at her team as she shut her office door gratefully behind her. Leaning up against it, she made herself take long, deep, calming breaths.

So she'd been wrong again. If the website report was accurate – and she had no reason to doubt it – then wherever Adam and Charlene had been en route to after Rachel's party, it had resulted in Charlene getting engaged: to someone else. And even if the logistics of the website report were wrong, the headline seemed to be true. Charlene was engaged: to someone else. Which meant that she, Caroline, had got everything out of proportion. And sorely misjudged Adam.

Guilt washing over her, she picked up her phone, took another deep breath, and pulled his number up on her screen. It was time she sorted this out, once and for all.

Before she could hit dial, there was a hammering on her door. She jumped, and moved across to open it.

Behind the door, Molly stood holding several sheaves of paper. Her usually calm demeanour had gone, her glasses were pushed back on top of her head, and she looked extremely harassed.

'Molly – what on earth's the matter?' exclaimed Caroline.

'Sorry, boss, I hate disturbing you, but this is important.' She waved the papers in Caroline's face. Caroline was aware of an expectant hush in the office behind her, and she saw Julie appear in the doorway from reception.

'It's Beiber. They're approaching you and the board about a takeover bid. They plan to make an offer for Sapphires & Rubies. A huge offer. They want to buy the company!'

Caroline stared at her incredulously. This was big news. Whether the offer was welcome or not was almost immaterial. To have Sapphires & Rubies on radar with a world-leading holding company such as Beiber – owners and purveyors of some of the most successfully exclusive international brands of luxury goods – meant only one thing.

Sapphires & Rubies was moving up yet another gear. It – and, by association, *she* – was hot again.

Exhausted, Caroline blinked hard. Her eyes were red raw from staring at figures on the computer screen, and her brain ached from running through pros and cons and pros again of a possible takeover bid.

A hastily arranged board meeting – she and Molly present in her office, Elaine and Andrew virtually there on Skype – had been inconclusive. They were divided about the best way forward – as, to be honest, was she. She needed time to soak up the idea, not to mention the multimillion-pound offer. But right now, there was nothing more to be done. Except have a drink.

She brushed aside the desire to call Adam – she had neither the energy nor the inclination for any more soul searching tonight, and with the Sapphires & Rubies team under pain of death not to reveal the bid to anyone in case of a leak, she felt she should abide by her own rules, especially since she knew they all still half suspected Adam to be the source of the leak. Instead, she picked up the phone and called Maryanne. A few cocktails with her best girlfriend would do the trick – take her mind off everything that had been happening and clear it ready for another onslaught tomorrow. And, more importantly, it would be some light relief in a day when fun had been in very short supply.

Maryanne's number rang and rang. Unusually, no voicemail cut in. Confused, Caroline tried again. Again, it rang out. Suddenly full of irrational but instinctive concern, she dialled Maryanne's home number.

Again, it rang and rang, and Caroline was about to hang up when someone answered. There was a long, clumsy pause, and then Maryanne's muffled voice.

'Hello?'

'Maryanne!' said Caroline, feeling relief flood over her. 'I've been trying to get hold of you. For some reason I got all worried when you didn't answer your mobile.' There was another pause. 'Maryanne?'

There was a heavy sob at the other end of the line.

'Maryanne, whatever's the matter?'

'Anthony's left me,' came Maryanne's muffled reply.

'Anthony's left you?' Caroline repeated, stunned at the pure absurdity of the sentence. Anthony wouldn't leave Maryanne! That was the most preposterous thing she'd ever heard.

However, there were more sobs confirming what she'd just heard.

'But – Maryanne! Whatever for? *Why?*'

'I've been caught out,' said Maryanne, her voice tiny with misery and shame. 'Anthony paid someone to try it on with me.' She sobbed again. 'And I fell for it. I FELL FOR IT!' Her voice became hard and bitter as articulating the words out loud brought the truth home.

'He laid a honeytrap?' Caroline cursed the triteness of the tabloid soundbite.

'No, Caroline. Not any old honeytrap. He seems to know me better than that. He's always gone on instinct. So he paid a twenty-something chancer with the gift of the gab to try it on with me. A *cougar catcher*. And I was well and truly cougar caught out.'

Again, silence. Caroline was speechless. Finally, Maryanne spoke again.

'So that's it. He's gone. It's over.'

Chapter 22

THE GREAT UNKNOWN

'I don't understand, Mum. What were you doing in the toilet with him in the first place? It just doesn't make sense.'

Caroline sighed. Why had she decided that tonight of all nights was the time to discuss the Vernon Situation with her daughter? A couple of hours at Maryanne's house, counselling her through Anthony's departure, had left Caroline even more wrung out than before. She'd meant to call Adam – but arriving home to find Rachel not only sitting at the kitchen table, but in a softer, more conciliatory mood than she'd been in since the party, had inspired Caroline to make them both a cup of cocoa as she had done when Rachel was little, and try and put her misdemeanour in context. Typical that this wasn't quite going to plan.

'Rachel, darling, please – I wanted to talk the whole thing through with you thoroughly to make you see how you should always be careful when taking medication, and how you really shouldn't ever mix it with drink. I wasn't drinking heavily, but the effect was as though I'd taken some pretty full-on drugs – as though I'd almost had a personality transplant, if you like. I was being reckless, nonsensical. In a way, I'm glad Adam *did* burst in on us, before I ended up doing something even more out of character, and something even more serious. I know no one is going to believe me, and that's not going to help either of us save face, but there are more important things at stake here than public opinion. The reason I'm discussing this all with you again is because I want you to understand what happened and why, and to try and convince you that I'm still me – the same mother I've always been – if extremely sorry for the embarrassment I've caused you.'

Caroline's voice caught in her throat at the thought of what repercussions her actions might have had on her daughter, and she stopped. Bursting into tears wouldn't help anyone – there had been enough emotional outbursts in this house over the past few months. What Rachel needed now was a calm, steady influence; essentially, her mum.

'Oh, Mum!' Rachel got up from her chair and raced around the table to fling her arms around her mother. 'I thought you'd turned into a right old slapper! I don't care what anyone else thinks, at least I know you're not – and that's the main thing!'

Caroline hugged her daughter back tightly, sure that there was a positive in Rachel's backhanded compliment some-where. After a couple of moments, she stopped trying to extrapolate it and gave herself up to the hug. Who cared, indeed, what other people thought, if she and her baby were back on the best possible terms?

'It was an amaze party, Mum, and that's what everyone will remember in years to come,' came Rachel's muffled voice from the depths of Caroline's shoulder.

Again, Caroline tried to ignore the sinking feeling inside her at the thought of her current reputation amongst Rachel's crowd and what would happen if it came out publicly at this sensitive juncture in her career. But again, she pushed it away. In the grand scheme of things, it really didn't matter.

Rachel pulled away. She smiled, and Caroline recognised the look. It was the 'o-ver!' look that meant Rachel had dealt with the situation and moved on. She felt a simultaneous wave of relief and pang of bittersweet nostalgia for a moment that had already gone.

'Anyhow, you had this ve-ry important looking letter arrive today,' said Rachel, leaning across to the dresser. All her life, Rachel had been fascinated by the post and what was in the envelopes that fell through the letterbox every day for Mummy and Daddy. Caroline smiled at the familiar ritual. Rachel handed her an envelope stamped Recorded Delivery.

'Oh!' Caroline stared at it with a feeling of foreboding. She hadn't been expecting anything official. She opened it tentatively and pulled out an official looking letter, threatening in its simple formality. She stared at it wordlessly.

Her decree nisi. In a matter of months, if the conditions set out in these papers were met, she and Les would be formally divorced. Caroline didn't need to read over them to know what the conditions were. She'd been through them enough times with Adrian to know them off by heart. But after all the excitement of getting married, the ups and the downs of their lives together, and the misery of the past few months, this seemed a curiously unemotional way to end their relationship.

'What is it, Mum?'

Before she had the chance to answer, the home phone rang. Caroline automatically looked at the kitchen clock. Ten forty-five. Who would be calling them at that hour?

With a sense of needing to expect the unexpected, Caroline got up and retrieved the remote handset from its perch on the wall.

'Hello?'

'Caroline?'

'Les?'

'Yes. Yes, it's me.' *No, it's not you*, Caroline wanted to say. *It's your voice but – tired. Defeated. Broken.* But she didn't say it out loud.

'Is everything OK?' she asked. Needlessly. She already knew something was wrong. Something was very wrong.

'Mum?' She looked up across the kitchen at Rachel, who, with a child's ability to assess tone of voice, body language and broken sentences in a split second, was now panic-stricken and striding across the room towards her.

'Mum, what's going on?'

Caroline accelerated through the milky twilight and checked her satnav for what seemed the seventeenth time in as many minutes. It was very considerate of Les to check himself into a rehabilitation centre in Hertfordshire, just a half-hour drive from her mother's, but what Caroline hadn't bargained on once she'd dropped Rachel off with Babs for the night, was accidentally inputting the satnav to take her the most winding, convoluted way possible. She'd only realised once she was in the very heart of rural Hertfordshire, and so reprogramming it to take her a more direct route would still involve a lot of

291

faffing around on tiny roads to reach a major route – and would take time she didn't have.

She checked the time anxiously. It wouldn't do to be late for her first 'family support' session – the irony! – especially considering how low Les had sounded last night. She relaxed when she saw she still had half an hour to go, and the satnav was showing only a further ten minutes to her destination. Thank goodness for organisational OCD. Her innate need to leave at least an hour earlier than necessary for long journeys had meant that despite hitting the A1 slap bang at the start of tonight's rush hour, and despite Babs insisting she stop for 'just one' cup of tea, she still had time to spare.

Nervously Caroline thought of what lay ahead. Of all the horror scenarios that had run through her mind last night when she'd answered the phone, Les's apparent nervous break-down and ensuing depression had absolutely been the last thing she'd imagined.

And she still couldn't fathom it. She had very little experience of mental health – and so even less understanding of it – and, she was ashamed to discover, very little patience with it. Her first reaction to Les's admission on the phone had been irritation. *For God's sake!* she'd wanted to scream. *What do you have to be depressed about? You're the one who led the life of Riley for months, screwing around with your bit on the side, and then got to move out into a swanky new flat with her. And you're not the one who had most of the parental responsibilities to bear, nor the fear that your livelihood and main passion in life would be snatched from you by a vengeful ex, nor the stigma of being a woman over forty who'd been left for a younger woman.*

She'd wanted to shake him, to tell him to pull himself

together and get a grip. But she hadn't. She'd listened while he told her how he'd slowly felt unable to deal with life any more, how he'd quickly become disillusioned with his new girlfriend, with his new life, and how it had suddenly become too much for him.

Caroline's second reaction was one of disbelief. How had super-capable Les turned into a shadow of his former self, in such an apparently short time? Rachel, too, was shocked. She claimed she'd noticed none of the signs during her weekends at Les's. No, the other woman hadn't ever been there – so she wasn't aware of any friction (or even any kind of serious relationship, noted Caroline – trust Les to keep those blame-loaded cards close to his chest where his daughter was concerned). Yes, he'd lost weight – but then Caroline had to admit she herself had noticed this at Rachel's party and had put it down to him surviving on a bachelor diet. Yes, Rachel said, he'd seemed tired, yet he seemed to be up at the crack of dawn. But Les had always been an early riser, and it certainly hadn't given her any cause for alarm.

And why should it? Caroline had reasoned. Rachel was still looking for nurturing from her parents herself, not expecting to have to nurture them. And yet that's what had ended up happening over the past few weeks. Again, Caroline felt awash with guilt at their recent failings as responsible parents.

She pulled into a long gravel drive that cut through a man-icured lawn and led to an imposing red-brick Georgian building. Lights shone out from the lead shot windows, glowing welcomingly in the accelerating darkness. It looked, she thought approvingly, like a comfortable country house hotel.

Inside was no different. As Caroline was led through

plushly decorated corridors by a stout house matron, she was accosted by none of the sterile hospital smells she'd expected. Instead, there was the hushed atmosphere of a gentleman's drawing room, and the combined smells of beeswax polish and the faint aroma of a roast dinner on the air.

The matron stopped outside a mahogany door and rapped on it smartly with her knuckles. 'Mr Walker? I've got Mrs Walker for you.'

She smiled kindly at Caroline. The *ex*-Mrs Walker, Caroline had the urge to say. Or soon-to-be, anyway.

The door opened, and Caroline had to stop herself gasping out loud at the transformation in Les. It was just over a week since she'd last seen him, yet it could have been ten years. His eyes were dark, hollow and vacant, and sunken into sharply jutting cheekbones. Here, in his jeans, shirt and slippers, he looked smaller too, probably thanks to the huge amount of weight he'd lost, but partly in comparison to the Louboutin platforms Caroline had changed into before leaving the car. (Nothing like a psychological prop for a stressful meeting, after all.)

He smiled at her, but it reached no further than the corners of his mouth.

'Hi, Caro.'

'Hi, Les.'

They stood for what seemed like an eternity, unsure who should make the next move. Clearly the matron had been anticipating an embrace that never came: the smile slowly froze on her face, until she clapped her hands in a businesslike fashion. 'Well, I'm sure you both have lots to talk about,' she said. 'Call me if you need anything.'

'Thank you,' said Caroline and Les in unison, and smiled uncertainly at each other. That, at least, had broken the ice.

'Come in,' said Les, and shuffled off in front of her into his room. Caroline followed, letting the door swing softly shut behind her.

The room was square and of average size, decorated in warm tones of russets and burnt orange. The furniture was standard issue, polished in a mahogany colour. On a chest of drawers, Caroline noticed, Les had placed a photograph of the three of them. It could have carried the caption 'The Walkers in happier times'.

Les indicated a small, minibar-style fridge below the writing desk. 'Fancy a drink?'

'I could murder a G&T,' she said cheerfully. What was it about visiting hospitals — because that was what she considered this to be, after all — that made you act dementedly happy?

Les smiled apologetically. 'Soft drinks only, I'm afraid. Even the merest sniff of whisky could send an inmate over the edge.'

Caroline laughed in spite of herself at his use of the word 'inmate'.

'Les, surely you're a *patient*? Or a *client*, at the very least?'

He shrugged. 'I'm in here, that's enough for me.' He busied himself looking in the fridge. 'I think I might even struggle with the tonic, Caro. It's the quinine, you know.'

Caroline laughed again. 'Don't worry, Les, a mineral water will be fine.' She perched uncertainly on the chair and smiled in thanks as he poured her a Perrier. He pulled out the chair at the desk and sat astride it, leaning on the back.

'I hope you don't mind meeting me in my room,' he said awkwardly. 'I'm not quite ready for the communal areas yet.'

'No, this is fine,' murmured Caroline, sipping her water. There was a silence. 'Rachel will be here tomorrow. She was unsure about coming tonight. I think it all seems a bit weird for her. The Great Unknown, you know?'

Les nodded and bent his head to the floor. His hair seemed to have changed from steely grey to bright white, thought Caroline. Or was that just the light?

She gazed at him for a moment, uncertain what to say – or even where to start.

Suddenly, Les looked up at her, his piercing blue eyes taking her breath away as they had done the first time they'd met, all those years ago. A lifetime ago. What had happened to those two people who'd been so full of love and hope for their lives together?

One had reverted to type, she told herself sternly, thinking about the bachelor life Les had led before he'd met her. And ruined the other's life. And now, by the looks of it, he'd ruined his own, too.

She hardened her own stare as Les held her gaze steadily. 'It was the decree nisi, you know,' he said simply. 'That really did me in. This,' he gestured at his shrunken form, 'has been coming on a while, but when the paperwork arrived yesterday, I – I suddenly lost it.'

Caroline stared at him. 'What do you mean, "this" has been coming on a while?'

'The depression. The – the breakdown.'

Caroline shook her head irritably. She refused to believe

that Les could have had a breakdown. He'd got what he wanted, hadn't he? 'For how long exactly?' she snapped.

He looked at her sheepishly. 'How long have you got?'

'I don't think room service is round-the-clock here,' said Les as he went over to the tea and coffee station inside the cupboard. 'But I did spot a sachet of instant chocolate.'

'A coffee will be lovely, Les. Black, though – I can't stand that UHT milk,' she added, spotting some telltale cartons in a bowl.

It was later, much later, and Caroline was feeling infinitely more relaxed in his company. So relaxed, in fact, that the Louboutins lay discarded on the swirly carpet and her feet were tucked up under her on the chair. She was exhausted, of course – when wasn't she these days, on this emotional roller coaster she seemed to spend her life on? – but strangely exhilarated. They'd talked – really talked – and she felt she knew more about Les right now than she had done for years.

As he bumbled about making coffee, she thought back over what they'd talked about – his growing frustration with his life over the past few years, his boredom at work, and his increasing obsession with his own mortality. Self-dissatisfaction, he called it – but it sounded like a classic midlife crisis to Caroline. However, she was careful not to mock him: she had been guilty of not noticing it when they were still together, after all.

In turn, in the spirit of opening up and confessing all, she'd told him how she'd messed things up with Adam – and nearly with Rachel – at the party. And how all this came at the worst possible time for her career – when she and Sapphires &

Rubies stood to be higher profile than they ever had before. At this moment, however, the focus was on Les and his most recent significant other.

'But what I still don't understand, Les, is why you would leave one relationship' – she was surprised at how easy it was to talk about their marriage in the past tense with him – 'that wasn't making you happy for another one that wasn't,' she said. 'If your – your *affair* made you that miserable once you'd moved out, why didn't you just end it and concentrate on yourself?'

He turned to her and shrugged, and then sighed. 'I guess I saw you making such a success of your new life and felt the pressure to do the same with mine.'

Caroline snorted in disbelief. 'Success? Two broken relationships in a year and a regrettable, and very public, indiscretion in the toilet of a private members' club – at my own daughter's birthday party? How is that a successful new life?'

Les shook his head. 'I don't mean just in your private life. I mean at work, too. Sapphires & Rubies is going from strength to strength, and you look like you're really enjoying it.'

'I was,' Caroline said, then corrected herself: 'I *am*. But it hasn't been easy. I've had to learn to juggle more than ever, and I've also scored some own goals in trying to do too much too soon. I've handed MacCaskill a few pearls along the way, too.'

'Humph, MacCaskill,' spat Les. 'Scum of the earth.'

Caroline started at the depth of feeling he displayed. She'd forgotten how deep Les's hatred of her nemesis ran. In fact she'd turned Les into almost as big a threat as MacCaskill.

'I half thought you were in cahoots with him,' she admitted. As she saw the betrayal in his eyes, she hurried to explain herself. 'There's some kind of leak at work. And I thought you wanted to get at me, and would be able to do it through Sapphires & Rubies. He told me you two were meeting up . . .' she gulped, trying to remember the logic of the fantastical twists and turns of her own mind. She started again. 'Everyone at work is convinced Adam was spilling secrets to him, but I'd almost persuaded myself it was actually you.'

Les stared at her in disbelief.

'Why would I do that?'

Caroline suddenly felt very stupid. 'To get at me. To make sure, if you couldn't get me, you'd get your share of Sapphires & Rubies instead.' Even as she said the words, they sounded like some third-rate crime plot.

'I may have behaved badly, but don't let's forget I'm the one who wanted you back!' exclaimed Les.

Caroline tried not to hit out at the injustice of it all. *His* injustices that he'd foisted upon her. 'You have to try and remember, Les, that I was in pieces after your affair. I may not always have been thinking straight.'

Les shook his head. 'I would never try and ruin something that means that much to you. Exactly the opposite, in fact,' he added quietly.

Caroline was on him in a second. 'What do you mean?'

'Nothing.'

She stared at him. 'I don't believe you. What do you mean?'

Les gave her a sly look. 'I might know someone on the board of Beiber. I knew they were after UK acquisitions, and they had sounded me out about the wisdom of investing in Morton. I may just have mentioned to them that it was a questionable move, but that I knew of another, much more viable proposition.'

Caroline stared at him. She didn't know whether to kiss him for his intervention, or berate him for trying to control her life even after they'd split up.

'So why meet up with MacCaskill?'

'I wanted to keep him off the trail of Beiber while they looked into Sapphires & Rubies. There's not much that gets past MacCaskill, and I figured that a major American investor sniffing around Sapphires & Rubies would never escape his notice.' He took a sip of coffee and wrinkled his nose at the taste. 'Eugh. Instant coffee doesn't get any better, does it?' He gave Caroline a searching look. 'There's another reason. I'd seen MacCaskill out for dinner one night with Elaine Constantine.'

At the mention of the Sapphires & Rubies shareholder, Caroline stared at him incredulously. 'What was *Elaine* doing with MacCaskill?'

'Well, that's what I failed to find out,' said Les. 'It might have been completely innocent – they are both single, after all – but in my opinion it's a coincidence too far.'

He placed his coffee cup on the side gently.

'And all that considered, it still seems to me that MacCaskill isn't your main worry at the moment.'

Caroline raised her eyebrows. 'Oh?'

Les shook his head. 'Well, we know MacCaskill of old, don't we? We know how he operates. In my opinion, in business as in life, it's the Great Unknown that you really need to watch out for. And the biggest unknown in your life currently seems to be your mole.'

Caroline continued to stare, heart thumping. Les gave her a level gaze.

'We've got to find them, Caroline. And get them out, once and for all.'

Chapter 23

BISCUIT–GATE

It felt like D-Day, thought Caroline as she looked out through the glass of the boardroom windows at the Sapphires & Rubies team scurrying around beyond, hell bent on urgent business with the threat of annihilation hanging over them if they got it wrong. Was this how it felt to be under siege?

Well, she supposed, they *were* under siege. Of sorts. A hostile takeover bid from MacCaskill at close of play the previous evening had sent panic levels into orbit. Suddenly, the warm and fluffy offer from Beiber needed to be considered as a matter of urgency. A 24-hour matter of urgency, to be exact. And with MacCaskill's astronomical bid demanding her scalp as part of the deal, there was now a gun hanging over their heads as well as a price tag.

'Well, the overall opinion from Rothschild's is to sell – that much is clear,' said Molly crisply, gathering up her notes from their meeting with the banking giants.

Caroline sighed. 'I guess so.' The early sales of Precious and the high street line were astonishing, and their profile looked set to send Sapphires & Rubies into orbit. Factor in the company's existing profit margins, and it was one hell of a business proposition. Realising the extent of what she stood to gain – and lose – without the right direction, she'd called in Rothschild to help assess the company's value, put a price on its assets and direct her next move.

Molly gave her a compassionate look. 'Caroline, it's true what they said – that as the company has grown, you've increasingly been involved in the actual running of the business rather than in developing it. I mean, what are you going to do when the business goes stratospheric? Which it will. One person can only spread themselves so thinly. You already work tirelessly on the brand's behalf, you host countless events, make endless PR appearances. But as it goes up another level – especially on an international stage – you'll need to do much, much more. And knowing you, the bits you're going to love – the creative side, the face to face contacts, the personal connections you work to get those lucrative celebrity product placements, the personal fittings every year with Academy Award nominees and cult shows like *Mad Men* – are the bits that are going to give. You can't do all this and be a behind-the-scenes business mogul and have a life, besides. At least, not with a brand the size that Sapphires & Rubies promises to be.' She paused, clearly choosing her next words carefully. 'And there's another thing. There's no doubt you're good at the business side of things. But is that where your passion really lies? Because over the past few months, while you've been actively developing the brand, designing collections, moving the product lines along, I've seen much more of the old

Caroline. You've been more engaged, more enthusiastic – and definitely happier.'

Caroline let Molly's words sink in. Yes, she had. But even with the imminent threat hanging over her, she was finding it hard to reflect on her recent success without factoring in what had been going on in her personal life. Her break-up with Les had refocused her mind on her business, reigniting a drive and a passion for it that had lain dormant for months. Years, even. Yet, she had to hand some of the credit to what had happened in her personal life *after* the break-up. Because however dismissive she'd been of Adam at the beginning of their relationship, he had definitely had an effect on her creativity. He'd made her see things differently. He'd inspired her. He'd made her *happy*.

'So,' continued Molly, 'no matter what the board says, the best possible outcome for you – and, in my opinion, Sapphires & Rubies – in all this is to do what Rothschild's advise. Sell, but to a buyer who will allow you to stay on in a creative capacity. You make your millions but retain a stake in the company. Sapphires & Rubies gets the heavyweight investment it needs to move on to the next level. And we all get to keep our jobs!' Molly's cheeky pay-off made Caroline smile, and as she felt the tension in her face relax she suddenly realised how on edge she'd been throughout the morning's first meeting.

'That, my dear, is a given in any deal I'm party to,' said Caroline firmly. She sighed, tensing up again. 'But what if the board decide to go for MacCaskill's offer, and I'm booted out?' She looked worried. Molly shrugged dismissively, as if it was an unlikely outcome – but was unable to give her boss any real reassurance.

'Well, it won't be a unanimous vote if they do,' she said stubbornly. 'I'm sure as hell not going to go for it.'

Caroline smiled. They both knew that Molly's 10 per cent shareholding was unlikely to hold much sway with the rest of the board – and as Caroline's right hand at work, she would not have been party to any illicit pre-EGM discussions or hurried alliances that had taken place.

'The thing is, Molly, I've got no defence mechanisms in place. Like, a golden parachute or supermajority, or whatever they're called.' Caroline closed her eyes in regret at her naivety when she'd first invited investment. The thought of anyone wanting to buy Sapphires & Rubies at that stage had been preposterous anyway, but having a clause written into her new contract as CEO that she'd receive a large bonus in cash or stock if the company was acquired, to make the acquisition more expensive and less attractive, had seemed even crazier.

'I mean, I'm not the type of founder or CEO to do a terrible job of running a company, all the while making it very attractive for someone who wants to acquire it, and still receive a huge financial reward.'

Molly nodded in agreement.

Caroline sighed ruefully. She'd always wanted to run a democracy – not a dictatorship. But having safeguards in place to protect her against unwelcome acquisition offers suddenly made a lot of sense – albeit a little bit too late.

Trudi appeared apologetically at the door. 'Sorry to interrupt you, Caroline, but the board have arrived in reception. I wondered if we should show them in? Julie's starting to spin out there . . .'

Caroline allowed herself a smile at the thought of Julie, torn between her natural urge to gossip and her natural loyalty to the company. She seemed to have taken the news the hardest, and had been acting oddly all morning.

'Well, we'd better put her out of her misery,' said Caroline, sharing a complicit look with first Trudi and then Molly. 'Before "the board" put me out of mine.' The board. It always seemed like such a grand title for the four of them – but it had suddenly taken on ominous significance.

Trudi shook her head firmly. 'It won't come to that, I'm sure of it, Caroline.' She held out a piece of paper. 'And anyhow, if, as you always say, a business is only worth the people working for it, then this one won't be worth a dime if they try and get rid of you.'

Trudi pressed the paper on Caroline, who stared at it blankly.

'We're not going anywhere,' said Trudi passionately. 'We'll all resign if MacCaskill takes over. And that's not just a promise, it's a pledge – I've got our signatures here.'

Caroline's eyes filled with tears as she realised the depth of feeling her staff had for her – and for the business. Unable to speak, she squeezed Trudi's hand and then busied herself with tidying up her own paperwork.

'Well, you'd better send in the troops,' she said darkly. 'Let's see if they're ready to bail out or stay put!'

Taking her seat at the top of the table, Caroline watched as her receptionist led Andrew and Elaine across the office. Elaine, as always, was perfectly coiffed, dressed smartly and expensively in skirt suit, 15-denier tights and sensible mid-heels. To her surprise, Andrew had brought a suit out of retirement, which in itself underlined the severity of the occasion. Combined with a bright red tie, it had the effect of making him seem younger than his sixty-seven years, and taller than usual, and Caroline had a glimpse of the retail powerhouse he'd once been. The sight of Julie tugged at Caroline's heartstrings. Would this be the last time she watched her waddle across the office floor, blouse buttons straining under the pressure of her ample bosom, peroxide yellow hair scraped back from her face and piled elaborately on top of her head like a flourishing suburban pineapple?

As Julie opened the door, Caroline stood up to greet her investors and gave her an intimate smile, but to her surprise Julie refused to meet her gaze. Wow, she thought, this news really had rocked her to the core.

As she embraced them both, Caroline kept one concerned eye on Julie. Where she would normally be fussing around the guests, making them comfortable and taking orders for teas and coffees, she was hovering uncertainly, hand clutching the edge of the table and eyes shifting nervously from one shareholder to the next.

Caroline frowned worriedly and then tried to catch her eye. 'Julie, would you be so kind as to find out what everyone would like to drink?'

Julie nodded quickly, but still averted her eyes from Caroline's. 'Of course,' she said, in a strangely high pitched tone. 'Teas, coffees?' She looked around wide-eyed and tightened her grip on the table so that Caroline could see the whites of her knuckles. She seemed to freeze for a split second – then disappeared, without waiting for a reply.

Dismissing her weirdness as nerves, Caroline looked around

the table with a smile at the three familiar faces – Molly, Andrew, Elaine – then hesitated as her confidence deserted her. She thought back to her phone conversation with Les the previous evening. She'd always discussed major business decisions with him, and last night had been no different – she'd suddenly felt the need to share it with him, and she'd been glad she had. He'd agreed with her that she should fight MacCaskill's takeover attempt every step of the way – but the prospect of either Andrew or Elaine withdrawing their support filled Caroline with sudden dread. She looked down at the table, trying to gather herself, and caught sight of the petition from her team. Buoyed by the combination of Les's faith in her, and their support, she looked up.

'So, welcome to this most Extraordinary of Extraordinary General Meetings,' she said with a smile, and there was a ripple of muted laughter around the table. 'I think we'll start without waiting for the refreshments – after all, we may well need some light relief in not too many moments' time.'

She smiled, but both Andrew and Elaine gazed back at her impassively. They were giving nothing away, she thought. Was that a good sign, or a bad? She cleared her throat. Trudi, who sat to one side taking minutes, gave her an encouraging nod, and she nodded back, more confidently than she felt. 'So, let's start by recapping on our hostile takeover bid. MacCaskill has made a tender offer for Sapphires & Rubies that totals £150 million investment in the company. Actually, he's made the same offer for my shares, but I think it's a given that I'm not going to voluntarily sell to him. Particularly as the bid is made on the condition that you show a vote of no confidence in me and I'm replaced as

CEO. We have – we *had* – 24 hours to make a decision about this.'

There were more murmurs around the table acknowledging her succinct summary of their situation. But it wasn't news to anyone. They'd all been fully briefed the previous evening and all, no doubt, were coming to the table with their own thoughts on what they should do.

'There are two alternatives,' continued Caroline levelly. 'We opt for the still very generous – but much lower – offer made by Beiber, but still risk the very brand ethos of Sapphires & Rubies being diluted by, or even lost within a large US corporation.' She looked around the table, trying to engage Elaine and Andrew in eye contact in turn. 'Or, as we seem to be keen to sell – and indeed have been advised this is a prudent move – but not in agreement on the terms, we hold fire and look for a white knight to make a desirable bid on our terms.'

The boardroom door burst open and the five of them, as one, jumped. Julie entered, bearing a tray laden with coffee, tea, water and a large plate of biscuits. Still avoiding Caroline's gaze, she robotically distributed the refreshments, with none of her usual warmth or friendliness. Last to be deposited were the biscuits. Julie placed them purposefully in front of Caroline, and, with her tongue sticking out the side of her mouth in concentration, gave her boss a sidelong glance as she moved them closer to her. Caroline smiled encouragingly, and nodded towards the door.

'That will be all, thank you, Julie.'

Julie looked at her oddly, smiling brightly, her hand still resting on the edge of the plate. 'OK, Caroline! So I'll just – leave them, shall I?'

Caroline looked at her uncertainly and glanced around at the rest of the board. Was this some kind of joke? Her receptionist acting like a demented loon during one of the most important hours the business could arguably ever have? 'Yes, Julie, that sounds like a good idea – why don't you?'

Hoping that acquiescing would appease Julie, Caroline reached out for a custard cream. As she did so, the sleeve of her Celine jacket caught the glass Julie had filled moments before, and spilled the water over the plate.

Julie let out a strangled cry. Quickly righting the glass, Caroline put her hand to her mouth apologetically. Trudi rushed over with some tissues.

'Oh, Julie, I'm so sorry!'

But Julie didn't seem to hear her boss. She was staring at the sodden plate in horror.

'Julie?' Caroline repeated gently. Really, had she known Julie was going to be so traumatised by today's events, she would have given her the day off. 'Julie, maybe you could take these away and bring us some more.'

Julie continued staring. 'Some more,' she repeated quietly. 'Another plate!' Abruptly, she burst into action, picking up the platter so that crumby, murky water slid on to the table, and rushed out of the room.

Caroline looked around apologetically and picked up where she'd left off.

'So, I can refuse him personally. And if either of you are with me, then together we still have the majority share of Sapphires & Rubies.'

Andrew leaned forward keenly. His voice was calm and neutral, but his eyes shone intensely. 'Yes, but for how long?

It's a bold offer. Audacious, even. He means business, Caroline. And in business, the person who has the money has the control.'

Caroline shook her head, trying to hide her emotions behind an impassive face. 'No, Andrew – the person who has the *cunning* has the control. And I intend to have both.'

Elaine laughed, a tinkling noise devoid of humour or warmth. 'Well, Caroline, with all due respect that's fine for you. But MacCaskill is offering us a life-changing amount of money for our shares. As far as I'm concerned, this isn't just about what's best for Sapphires & Rubies. This may sound brutal, but it's also about what's best for us. How could Andrew and I justify turning down a fortune to our families, let alone to ourselves?'

Caroline closed her eyes to give herself a second's respite. If she didn't know better, she'd just think that Elaine was a money-grabbing old witch who wanted to cash in her chips to the highest bidder. But Elaine was already rich, and power had always meant as much to her as money. Les's words were still ringing in her mind. Maybe there was more to Elaine's standpoint than she was letting on. Maybe, just maybe, she was also hiding split loyalties.

The door opened once again, the noise bulldozing the tension like a knocking ball. Julie reappeared, with more biscuits.

Caroline tried to wave her away with a subtle shake of the head. The last thing they needed now was another distraction. But to her shock, from the corner of her eye she saw Julie look right through her, and continue doggedly on her path, arm outstretched to place the biscuits in the centre of the table.

Caroline glanced at the paperwork spread over the table and looked back at her meaningfully.

'Julie, I'm sorry – I don't think we've got room.'

Julie stood motionless, staring at the table. 'No room?' she repeated stupidly.

Caroline looked imploringly at Trudi to help. This was turning into a farce. Light refreshments were all she needed when her entire livelihood was on the line. Trudi got up and tried to usher Julie gently out of the room. Caroline turned back to the paperwork, but out of the corner of her eye she was vaguely aware that Julie had started quivering.

'You have to have biscuits!' she heard Julie moan. Elaine tutted in disgust and Andrew looked away, embarrassed as Trudi continued to coax Julie out of the room.

'But I've brought biscuits!' she insisted.

Her patience worn to the limits by the stress of the situation, Caroline snapped.

'Julie, please!'

But Julie's face was contorted, possessed even – the look of a woman totally unhinged.

She opened her mouth, and Caroline flinched instinctively. When Julie spoke, it was almost a howl.

'JUST TAKE THE FUCKING BISCUITS, WILL YOU!'

Julie lay, sobbing, on the floor while the board stood around helplessly and looked down on her in horror – as they had been doing for the past five minutes. Caroline was kneeling next to her, trying to coax her to stop crying and tell her what was wrong – but every time she tried, Julie would whimper and pound the floor with her fists.

'It's all gone wrong. It's all gone wrong,' was all she would say.

'Do you think we should call a doctor?' whispered Caroline. Trudi, crouching next to her, shrugged and stood up. 'I don't know,' she replied. 'She seemed all right to me. I mean, sure, she's been a bit stressed, but haven't we all?' She started to clear the debris of the broken biscuit plate that was scattered across the floor.

'Hang on, what's this?' Caroline looked up in surprise at the tone of Trudi's voice. Trudi was holding a piece of porcelain with something black attached. Caroline furrowed her brow as Trudi inspected it closely.

'Yes, what *is* that?'

Trudi's face set in a grim expression as she inspected it more closely. She looked up at Caroline, then around at the rest of the board's expectant faces. On the floor, Julie gave another, louder whimper.

'I'm not sure that we need to call a doctor,' she said hollowly. 'We need to call the police. We've been bugged.'

Caroline arrived home, dropped her bag on the dark of the hallway floor and trudged through to the kitchen. Although it must only be just after nine, the lights were all out save for one in the cooker hob – which she and Rachel habitually left on as a 'welcome home' for one another if they were due to be late – and there were a couple of stray glasses and a dirty plate by the side of the sink. Rachel's washing up never quite made it as far as the dishwasher, and the kitchen had the after-party feel of being almost-but-not-quite tidied up. But right now, Caroline was too tired to care. She sighed deeply and leaned

313

on the granite worktop, staring into space and feeling world weary. Her eyes were red and itchy, and she wasn't sure whether to laugh or cry. Today had been like something out of a TV soap opera – and a bad one, at that.

Julie's apparent breakdown had been the tip of the iceberg. After the discovery of the bug, the board meeting had broken down completely. Chaos reigned supreme, as Julie became inconsolable, and members of the board stalked out in shock.

Caroline and Trudi had managed to persuade everyone else that it was not in the interest of anyone present – nor would it help the value of Sapphires & Rubies – if they called the police. Instead they had moved Julie to the relative privacy of Caroline's office and interrogated her thoroughly. Caroline was still reeling from her answers.

It turned out that Julie, for the past few months – the exact date was unclear, but common sense held that it was around the time the first press leak emerged – had been drawing two salaries. One, from Sapphires & Rubies for her work as a receptionist. And the other from Morton, for her work as a corporate spy. Caroline, still numb from the shock of the betrayal by someone she thought was a close ally, still couldn't quite believe it. Julie – loyal, ever-present Julie – had been spying on her, trading not only her closest corporate secrets, but her personal ones too. She felt blindsided, stunned.

But she'd had to think, and act, quickly. Keeping Julie under guard in the office, she'd recalled the board to the EGM. Seated back around the table – this time with Pret A Manger sandwiches in place of the biscuits – they had resumed negotiations. Negotiations that now had a very different bent.

It transpired that Julie hadn't been MacCaskill's only attempt to break the ranks of the Sapphires & Rubies defence. He'd tested Andrew and Elaine individually, to see who was a potential weak link, and who could work on his behalf to persuade the board to act against Caroline. Both claimed to have resisted his attempts – even Elaine, noted Caroline with interest. It was Elaine, however, who had apparently called Andrew before the EGM the previous day, and who had been keen to sell to Morton.

Caroline turned to the window to pull down the blind, and absently stopped as she noticed Christian's front door open and her neighbour appear, looking up and down the street suspiciously like a meerkat on nightwatch. He looked as if he was after a scent, she thought with a giggle, no doubt sniffing out the street's latest scandal. What must he have been occupying his mind with since Caroline and Adam had broken up, leaving him bereft of gossip? Some other poor neighbour's domestic dramas, no doubt – imagined or otherwise. Every cloud had a silver lining, after all – and falling off Christian's radar must be hers. She tugged at the pull cord and then stopped, intrigued, as his front door opened again and someone followed him out. A woman. A blonde woman: very curvaceous, very showily glamorous – and very definitely *not* his ex-wife. Confident that she couldn't be seen in the dark of the kitchen, Caroline peered closer as the woman strolled towards his car. Christian was scurrying from shadow to shadow, trying to hide from the street lamps and the light spilling out from his front door and simultaneously urging the woman into the car. Caroline smiled at the comedy in the far-cical scene.

'Hi, Mum. I thought I heard you come in.'

Caroline jumped as Rachel emerged from the back of the room, wearing an oversized cardigan, sleeves pulled down low over her wrists, clutching a cup of tea.

'Darling girl! How long have you been there?'

Rachel shrugged. 'Not long. I was just hanging out in the conservatory. You know, thinking.' She looked at Caroline with concern. 'So what happened? Did you win?'

Caroline smiled. She'd called Rachel with a brief outline of what was happening several hours ago, and she knew her daughter would have been on tenterhooks about it. 'Darling, it's not a case of winning or losing.' Although, she thought privately, she had definitely lost a valuable asset and friend in Julie – albeit a long time ago. 'But I guess you could say I won a couple of moral battles, and I haven't come out of it a business loser – yet.'

'What do you mean?' asked Rachel neutrally, sliding into the chair opposite Caroline, still hugging her tea.

She smiled at the unspoken question in Rachel's eyes. Her daughter might be able to feign indifference with her friends, but not with her mother.

'Well, I guess the moral battle is that what comes around goes around. MacCaskill went to all that trouble and expense to try and make sure his offer on Sapphires & Rubies was accepted, when he would have been better off doing nothing,' said Caroline, the relief palpable in her voice. 'As it turns out, his offer was so inflated that Andrew and Elaine felt they couldn't do anything but consider it. It was a once in a life-time offer, after all.'

Rachel looked puzzled. 'So they're going to go for it? How does that work in your favour?'

Caroline shook her head. 'No, darling. They *were* considering it. But after his underhand behaviour this afternoon, no one in their right mind would consider doing business with him.'

Rachel stared at her, wide-eyed. 'So everything goes back to normal?'

Caroline smiled. 'Not quite, darling. I've seen things a bit differently over the past few days. The opportunities that selling could bring to the company. The opportunities it could give me – and us.' She held out her hand and squeezed Rachel's arm. 'And to be honest with you, I feel like I've lost faith in my board. It's time to move on, darling. Within the company, of course. But with different investors, and with a different outlook.

'We're going to reconvene next week and vote on it – but it looks like we're going to sell to Beiber. With some pretty stringent conditions, of course.'

Rachel placed her cup on the table. 'Cool.' Caroline could tell that mentally, she'd already moved on from their conversation. 'Erm, Mum – there's something else.'

'Oh?'

'Grandma's on her way over here.'

Caroline frowned. 'What, now?' Rachel was one thing – she was enjoying mulling things over with her daughter – but she wasn't sure she had the energy to face a Babs inquisition. 'Why's that?'

Rachel grimaced. 'She's coming over to look after me. You're needed in New York.'

Caroline looked at her, fear rising in her chest. What now?

'Esther's ill. Like, really ill. She called earlier. She wants you there.'

Chapter 24

RED EYES ALL ROUND

Strange how just one individual could transform an entire house in a matter of moments, thought Caroline absently as she threw her cosmetic bag into her overnight case and zipped it up. There was no need for anything other than hand luggage – she had all she needed at the apartment – but as she planned to go direct to Esther's home from the airport, who knew how long it would be before she managed to get to her own place.

Babs's arrival just moments after Rachel's announcement had turned the house from the snoozing calm of a household on the verge of sleep into a hive of activity. Lights blazed from every room as Babs arranged cars, organised packing, and cooked up a late night snack for Rachel. She was a whirlwind of productivity, thought Caroline gratefully, as she bounced her bag downstairs and prepared to leave for the flight to New York – and not just that, but a soothing, reassuring presence in a world that currently seemed to delight in throwing Caroline curveballs. She looked at her watch anxiously, and relaxed

when she saw the time. Thank heavens for fast track booking – it cost the earth, but it meant she could arrive at
Heathrow at 10.30 p.m. and still make the overnight flight.

'Make sure you've left all your contact numbers – and
Esther's,' said Babs from her position at the stove. 'It's bad
enough trying to get hold of you when you're two feet away
from Trudi, let alone across the Atlantic.'

'OK, Mother,' said Caroline, tearing a sheet out of her day
book and dutifully listing Esther and Seth's contact numbers.
Suddenly feeling a wave of despair engulf her, she sank on to
a kitchen chair and began to sob.

Babs put down her wooden spoon and turned to envelop
her daughter in a hug.

'Darling, you should know by now that it never rains, but
it pours. It'll all come good, darling, you'll see.'

Caroline sank into the hug and took comfort from the trite
Babs-isms. Clichés only became clichés from having a uni-
versal truth about them, she reminded herself. Maybe that
would be the case now. Maybe, just maybe, everything would
indeed come good . . .

There was one thing to be said about the red-eye flight,
Caroline thought as she got straight into a taxi and headed
into Manhattan – and that was the lack of queue for a car at
the other end. Caroline stretched her legs out and wriggled
her toes as she settled back on the faux leather seats of the
yellow cab. Her eyes were dry and her skin had the tight,
parched quality that a long haul flight always gave it, but she
felt surprisingly fresh. Despite the worry, the events of the
day had caught up with Caroline and after a stiff brandy,

she'd actually managed to sleep for most of the eight-hour flight.

Just as well, she thought, considering what would be waiting for her at the other end. She'd still had no contact with Esther, other than sending her a text last night to tell her she'd be there in the morning, and she had no idea how her friend was coping. In all the years they'd been friends, she'd never known Esther to have so much as a cold, and she could hardly imagine the knock this would have given her effervescent friend.

As the taxi drove over the bridge into Manhattan, Caroline allowed herself just a few moments of self-indulgent dismay at the way their lives were panning out. Right now, it seemed that any ill that had befallen her or Maryanne or Esther over the years paled into insignificance in light of this year's events.

Guiltily, she thought of Maryanne. What with everything that had been happening at work, and with Les, and with Vernon, she'd not given Maryanne the TLC she felt she should have since her split with Anthony. Maryanne, true to form in times of her own crisis, had gone to ground, and Caroline could imagine exactly what she had been doing. Maryanne's first response to anything going wrong in her own life was to act as if it wasn't happening. So she had stopped all contact with anyone immediately involved – and Caroline knew she would be included in that – and then continued with business as usual, but a hundred times more intense. Which meant, in all likelihood, shopping, champagne and shagging. Head in the sand, that was Maryanne. Caroline just wished she had more time to help her out of it.

As the taxi wound its way towards Park Avenue, the warm

yellow light of morning bathed everything in a warm autumnal glow, and Caroline drank in the Manhattan scenery. She loved New York in the fall; well, she loved New York at any time – but it was the perfect place for crunchy strolls through fallen leaves, cosy Sunday brunches and long lingering coffees watching the world go by. It was a place to be in love.

What would Adam make of the city? Caroline screwed her face up and tried to imagine him here. He'd love it, that was for sure – but she couldn't quite imagine him in her former mid- to uptown environs. He was more suited to the creative cool of downtown Manhattan than the uptight glamour of Park Avenue. And exactly what did that say about where she fitted in these days?

Caroline felt a pang of longing for Adam. She still hadn't called him. But he still hadn't called her . . . She tried to shake off the dull ache that had appeared inside her at the thought of him. Was he thinking about her? And if so, what was he thinking?

The taxi driver pulled up outside Esther's apartment block and Caroline hurried into the plush lobby. The uniformed doorman – all brocade and brass buttons – accompanied her in the elevator to the front door of Esther's duplex penthouse apartment. So far, so normal. But as they rose to the Manhattan skyline, Caroline was shocked to discover her hands were clammy and her mouth dry. Esther was one of her best friends, for goodness' sake – what was she expecting to find?

Esther's ferocious Filipina housekeeper, Maria, answered the door with a curt nod. 'Mrs Goldberg is in the sitting room,' she said in a high-pitched voice with a heavy accent.

Her curly, glossy black hair was pulled back tightly in its customary bun, and though her bright eyes hinted at a devilish sense of humour, they were set constantly to 'despairing' over her 'crazy' employees. In all the years she'd worked for Esther, Caroline had never seen her crack a smile – Esther joked that the weight of her hairy upper lip kept it downturned at all times – and so she followed meekly behind Maria through the sprawling apartment to Esther's expansive day room.

The magnificent, six-bedroom apartment with its 20-foot ceilings and roof access was one of New York's prime pieces of real estate, and it had been lavishly decorated to reflect its high-class status. The flocked silk wallpaper, elaborate Chinese carpets and ornate gold-plated furniture were too stately and elaborate for Caroline's taste, but they were undoubtedly impressive, and wandering through did make you feel like you were New York royalty. Which, Caroline supposed wryly, Esther kind of was.

As she entered, Caroline could see just the top of Esther's blonde highlights peeking above the velvet chaise longue, facing the windows framing midtown views on two sides of the oblong room. From here there were sweeping views of Central Park, resplendent in its red, gold and orange autumn finery. But even the park, thought Caroline, was not as resplendent as the view inside the apartment. Diagnosis had not interfered with Esther's innate grooming, nor her sense of the dramatic. And lying back on the crimson upholstery, with her bright blonde hair, fuchsia DVF wrap dress, knee-length leopard print trench coat and gold slingback Louboutins, Esther was the epitome of louche glamour.

'Oh, Caroline!' At the sight of her friend, Esther jumped

up – still steady in five-inch heels, even in her current predicament – and fell into her arms. 'Thank God you're here! Seth's a bag of nerves, I'm all over the place and – wow, did you hear about Maryanne?'

Caroline pasted a smile on her face, but inside she was shocked. Beneath her immaculate make-up, Esther looked gaunt and pale, and she had huge purple shadows under her eyes. Seeing Caroline's reaction, Esther clicked her tongue dismissively.

'Just think, darling, all that surgery over the years, and it only takes one little doctor's report to send me spinning!'

'It's hardly the same thing, Esther,' protested Caroline.

'No, I guess not,' said Esther. 'But it's still the same approach, when you think about it. Identify something that's wrong, work out what to do with it, then move it or get rid of it. Except this time, obviously, I'm really hoping they get rid of it.'

'Get rid of what, Esther?' asked Caroline gently.

Her friend looked at her, eyes shining with unshed tears. 'Breast cancer,' she stated flatly.

Caroline drew a sharp intake of breath, and gazed back at her friend compassionately.

'Oh, Esther. I'm sorry.' She moved as if to embrace her again.

Esther held up her hands and Caroline, sensing it might open the floodgates of despair, drew back.

'So what next?' asked Caroline.

'Oh, well, you know the drill – more tests, to establish just how riddled with it I am.' She squeezed her boobs fondly. 'To be honest with you, I'm surprised there's anything of me left in these babies, between the implants and the tumour. Then it'll be decisions, decisions, decisions – when to operate, whether I need chemo, radiotherapy, and all the rest. Thankfully, my obsessive moisturising of my little beauties means that I'm pretty much in daily contact with them, so they reckon I've caught it quite early. Literally, one day the lump wasn't there, next day it was. Just sitting there, calm as you like, under my bra strap. Of course, I haven't been able to wear one since. Can't bear to be reminded of it. All that designer lingerie, just sitting there unused. Just as well I've put a hold on all the action I was getting!'

Caroline tutted gently at her friend, but didn't remonstrate with her. She knew her well enough to recognise that this flippancy was part of Esther's defence mechanism. Esther wasn't used to feeling out of control, or scared, and to feel both at the same time had clearly rocked her to the core.

'Well then, one good thing has already come out of it – you've stopped playing around behind Seth's back,' said Caroline lightly.

Esther grabbed hold of both of Caroline's arms and looked her straight in the eye. Caroline flinched – Esther's hands were ice cold and felt bony and waxy to the touch.

'Don't judge me, Caro,' she said. 'I'm not messing around because I haven't got the energy, not because of some kind of slushy sentimentality about what makes a marriage work and what doesn't. Seth is my rock, but he's been crushed by this development, and I need all my strength to support him through it. I, in turn, need *you* to get *me* through it.' She loosened her grip on Caroline and gave her a cheeky smile. 'And look where playing by the rules got you, anyway, darling –

hardly love's young dream now, are you? Whatever did you do to scare off that young man of yours? Maryanne said he was *hot.*'

Caroline felt her hackles rise with irritation. 'I didn't do anything to scare him off. Well, not intentionally, anyhow.' Suddenly overwhelmed with a longing for Adam, she sighed and sat down on the stool opposite Esther. Despite the inappropriateness of her timing, she had an urge to offload all her confused mixture of emotions to her friend.

Esther looked at her watch theatrically and rang a bell.

'Martini time, darling! It's past noon after all. Well, nearly. And I am sick to death of talking about the C-word, and positively aching for a diversion. So tell me your news! Not the boring business stuff, darling – save that for Seth – but the *real* news . . .'

A couple of hours and more martinis later, Caroline had confided everything to Esther. How she'd met Adam, how he'd made her feel, how too late she'd come to realise what he meant to her, and how she'd messed it all up with Vernon. And how confused she'd been – still was – about the whole thing.

Maria entered the room. 'Mr Goldberg called – he wondered if you would like to meet him for a late lunch at the Carlyle,' she announced.

Esther clapped delightedly at the mention of the famous New York hotel bar where she and Seth had married all that time ago. 'Seth might be crushed, but he hasn't lost his touch,' she squealed. 'Come on, Caro, let's have a wash and brush up and go drink champagne. Forget all our woes!'

Caroline smiled. 'You're incorrigible,' she said, standing up and stretching. She'd allow Esther this one escape, but she was determined that over the next few days there would be no Maryanne-style ignoring the situation and hoping it would go away. She was here for a reason, and she was determined that she was going to encourage Esther to face her demons, and really come to terms with her illness, the way her friend had just enabled her to talk about her own issues, and reconcile herself to her own situation.

Esther stood up too, and grabbed Caroline's hands again to steady herself. But she didn't let go. Squeezing her fingers tightly, Esther gave her a searching look again. Its intensity almost took Caroline's breath away, and she drew back instinctively.

'Go get him, darling.' Esther was so close Caroline could smell the martini on her breath, mixed with her heavy signature Roja Dove Diaghilev scent. 'Life's too short to fanny around. Do what I always say.

'Get on with it.'

Chapter 25

OH, WHAT A NIGHT

'Maryanne, this must be the twenty-third message I've left you. I'm back in the same time zone as you now, and I'm worried, so will you please call me.'

Caroline shook her head in frustration at her obstinate friend, who as far as she was concerned was avoiding her on purpose. She hung up via the Bluetooth connection, and turned her attention back to her journey. What she should be doing right now was calling Adam as she'd promised herself, yet she felt unaccountably keyed up about going back to Les's rehab again. Caroline forced herself to relax and turned the volume on the radio back up. A song she loved came on, and she started to sing. It was the first time she'd done this since Les left – family sing-songs on long journeys were a Walker tradition, and anyway, she hadn't much felt like singing for a long while.

'Oh what a night!'

An oldie but a goodie. It was the kind of song you couldn't help but feel nostalgic about. The kind you immediately associated with the best times – in particular, it reminded Caroline of weddings. And now she came to think about it, she was sure that, despite their three very different unions, it had been played at all three weddings: by the Studio 54 DJ who'd spun vinyl in the early hours at Esther and Seth's society wedding at the Carlyle, by the sixties cover band at Maryanne and Anthony's English country wedding, and by the jazz band at her and Les's smart city wedding at Greenwich Observatory.

One song, so much hope. But look where it had got them all. Caroline felt a stab of regret as she played over the events of the summer and the effect they had wreaked on their lives.

She couldn't remember a more intense time of her life, when she felt she'd experienced so much – and when she'd learnt even more. So much had happened, even since her discovery of Les's affair back in March, now a full seven months ago, that she felt like a completely different person. In fact, given what she now knew about love, life and the people she shared both with, she *was*, in many ways, a completely different person. Who could even tell if the new Caroline would react in the same way to the discovery as the old one?

Because, it seemed, it wasn't just Les who had affairs. Other people had them too – her two best friends, for example. And what's more, it wasn't a clear-cut case of simple unbridled lust. They had their reasons – reasons, that against her better judgement, Caroline was beginning to understand. Maryanne's devastation at losing Anthony put her indiscretions in a different light: maybe, just maybe, she had known what was best for her marriage – until she'd gone too far. And the way Seth and Esther were an unstoppable force together in the face of

her cancer, and how her infidelities seemed almost inconsequential, to both of them. At the thought, Caroline's heart
jumped into her mouth, and she nearly made an emergency
stop. Maybe, then, Les had had *his* reasons? She bit her lip.
She'd never even thought to ask herself this, let alone *him*.
What might have happened if she'd asked and, what's more,
stopped to listen to his reasons? What had they thrown away
without even trying to salvage it?

Caroline hit the steering wheel. *Just stop it.* Some things
about her might have changed, but the fundamentals didn't.
Fine if it worked for other people, but infidelity *definitely*
didn't work for her. Les had abused her trust, broken their
marriage vows and ripped their lives apart – end of story. And
what's more, it was in the past now. Better keep it that way.

So why, then, had she still not called Adam?

'In fifty metres, turn left for your destination.'

The listen-to-me-now tones of the satnav woman broke
into Caroline's thoughts, and she turned up the drive to the
manor house.

To her surprise, Les was standing outside the imposing
main doors, spotlit by a security bulb glowing out of the half-
light. She stared intently at him on her approach, the
reflection from the car windscreen covering up her gaze. It
was a much-diminished Les from the swaggering banking
supremo, that much was clear, but he seemed to have regained
some of his signature sparkle. He looked taller, more upright,
and as she got closer, there was definitely the hint of a twinkle in his eyes.

Caroline's heart hardened against him with the memory of
the pain that twinkle had caused her. *Sometimes the very thing*

that you fall for is the thing that turns everything sour, she thought wryly. So what was it that had first made her fall for Adam?

Suddenly, Caroline caught her breath as she saw Rachel – who had travelled ahead by train to help her father pack – emerge carrying Les's battered leather holdall. As he spotted his daughter, Les ran lightly back up the low steps, took the bag from her, and ruffled her hair delightedly. Caroline slowed down, watching the pair act out a once familiar ritual. Sure enough, with Rachel giggling delightedly, Les picked her up and swung her around, running back down the stairs with her. It was something he'd done with her since she was little enough to fit under his arm, and even though she was now nearly as tall as him, Les seemed to have no problems carrying her weight. In fact, right now he and Rachel were clearly lost in the joy of being reunited, all issues apparently forgotten, for the moment at least. Placing his daughter carefully down on the drive, Les drew her in to him for a hug, and Caroline swallowed hard as she watched her daughter gladly enter his protective embrace: she felt a little like a thief stealing in on a private moment, but also wished with all her heart that she, too, could be part of that hug. Les the Protector. With a pang, Caroline suddenly realised how much she missed him.

The wheels crunched rhythmically on the gravel as Caroline pulled up alongside the house, and she wound down the passenger window and leaned across, smiling.

'Am I disturbing something?' she said, grinning as Les and Rachel drew apart, and Rachel rushed across to her.

'Mum!' She stopped by the door and leaned in, giving Caroline a guilty kiss. Caroline laughed.

'Darling, there's no need to look like that,' she said, looking over her daughter's shoulders at Les. 'I'm thrilled you and your father are getting along so well.'

Rachel turned and followed her eyes. 'We never *weren't* getting along,' she fibbed haltingly, and Les laughed, giving her a reassuring hug.

'Well, you're certainly looking more chipper than the last time I saw you,' Caroline remarked in surprise.

'There's nothing like having your family around you to perk you up,' said Les with a grin, bending to stick his head through the window and giving her a kiss on the cheek too. Caroline pulled away instinctively, and there was a momentary pause as they looked at each other awkwardly. Her family, she repeated mentally. Her family.

'And a bit of boardroom melodrama will always put me in a good mood.' Les grinned conspiratorially, moving smoothly over the pregnant pause. 'Especially when you come out on top.'

Caroline tutted. Les always did like to tempt fate, whereas she, more superstitious by nature, preferred to maintain a more open (if not pessimistic) point of view. 'I haven't exactly come out "on top", Les. Like I said in my email, we've got rid of the Morton threat. We still have some pretty major decisions to make, and some delicate negotiating to get through.'

'You survived a coup,' he said proudly. 'And for that, I'm taking you out for dinner tonight to celebrate.'

Caroline laughed uncertainly. Doing her ex-husband the courtesy of picking him up in his hour of need was one thing, but dinner? Hadn't she just signed papers swearing she hadn't spent that kind of time with him since their split? 'Dinner?' she repeated. 'I'm not sure . . .'

'Yay!' cried Rachel, jumping up and down and clapping excitedly before opening the back door and clambering in. 'You're going out on a date! How cool is that?'

'We're doing no such thing,' said Caroline crossly, leaning back into her seat and looking the opposite way out of the windscreen. 'That's typical of your father, throwing out inflammatory statements when he hasn't consulted the people involved first.' But at the thought of his irrepressible nature, a smile played around the corners of her mouth. She folded her lips over it, cross with herself for being unable to be genuinely annoyed with him, but also secretly enjoying the feeling of their familiar family dynamics.

'Oh, come on, Caro, why not?' Les opened the door, slung his holdall in the back and climbed into the passenger seat. 'I need to shake this place out of my system. I'm in the mood for some fun. Look on it as a rite of passage if you like – marking the end of our divorce. A thank-you for helping me out these past few weeks. There's a hundred and one reasons for sharing a restaurant table – take your pick.'

Caroline watched as Les confidently reached for his seat belt and fastened it, and had a sudden wave of nostalgia for their life together. She'd loved this man for so long and now, she realised with a jolt, she'd missed him. He was right. What harm could a simple meal do?

Les leaned across to the radio, his hand hovering over the dial with intent as he caught Rachel's eye in the back seat. 'What d'you reckon, darling? Has your mum finally found some taste in music in the past few months?'

Rachel giggled. 'Of course not, Dad. She still listens to Magic FM.'

'When you've both quite finished tearing me to pieces,' said

Caroline, pulling away and smiling in spite of herself, 'I might remind you who's in charge here. I don't notice either of you with a set of car keys – or a driving licence, for that matter.' She fixed Rachel with an amused stare in the rear view mirror, and then turned to Les. 'And actually, I'll have you know I've started listening to Smooth FM,' she countered.

Les whistled and turned back to Rachel with a wink. 'Wow – cutting edge stuff your mother's into these days.' He shook his head as if in awe. 'Well, let's have a listen, shall we?'

Caroline laughed as the strains of another oldie filled the car, and Les whooped and slapped his knee. 'I haven't heard this for years. Remember this?'

Caroline nodded. 'It's Sister Sledge, isn't it?'

Les rolled his eyes and turned back to Rachel. 'Well, some things don't change. Is it Sister Sledge ... honestly. You remember this, don't you, darling?'

Rachel laughed. 'I remember you and Mum and Auntie Esther dancing around the kitchen to it at a party, trying to pretend you weren't drunk whilst Uncle Seth was practically asleep in the leftover canapés,' she retorted. 'And Mum, it's the Pointer Sisters, not Sister Sledge.'

'Both of them have sung it!' protested Caroline.

'We are family!' sang along Les, squeezing Caroline's knee. 'Come on, girls, sing along!'

He turned round again and Caroline heard Rachel's voice join in, at first shyly, and then unselfconsciously, full throttle. Just like the old days. Caroline found herself humming along as she listened to them belt out the lyrics, and then was unable to resist joining in herself as the chorus started over.

'We are family!'

The three of them, out of tune with the music, yet still so in tune with each other. And it felt good. Really good.

Caroline looked at the sommelier doubtfully. 'Honestly, I really don't think. . .'

'Caro, we're meant to be celebrating. And *you're* meant to be relaxing,' Les insisted. He turned back to the sommelier and nodded confidently. 'We'll have another.'

Caroline shook her head disapprovingly, but relented. How easy it was to slip back into old habits. An old *life*. She'd forgotten how it was to be with Les – how he took control, how he nurtured her, how special he could make her feel. . .

'So, how well founded are your reservations about Beiber?' continued Les. 'Or would anyone with designs on your baby elicit the same suspicions?' There was a hint of a smile about his lips as he stabbed a spear of broccoli.

'Are you accusing me of letting my emotions get in the way of sound business sense?' Caroline said huffily.

Les grinned in triumph. 'Well, aren't they?'

Caroline opened her mouth to protest and then clamped it shut again. 'Well, maybe a little bit,' she admitted. 'It might be all about the money for many of Sapphires & Rubies' investors, but it means more than that to me. If I sell – as Rothschild's and everyone else in the world seem to think I should – then it has to be in the knowledge that everything I've built up – and I don't just mean balance sheets, I mean the brand, the work ethos, the team –' her voice caught as she thought of someone else having a say in how she developed her beloved company, which, as Les had quite rightly pointed out, was almost like another member of the family.

Les nodded. 'Yes, I agree. 'But,' he countered, 'don't forget that new ideas can also breathe new life into a company, not just destroy the old one. And if we're canny with the way we negotiate this deal, you can come out of it with all the assurances you want on the future of the company, and a major stake in it for yourself. What that role is, is something we need to decide.'

We. That word sent a feeling of warmth pulsing around Caroline's veins. She hadn't though of herself as part of a 'we' for seven long months. Well, unless she counted herself and Adam, of course. They had been a 'we' for a while, in the sense of making logistical plans for evenings, weekends and holidays, but not in the fundamental, life-affirming sense that Les had just used it. Was that because they'd never had the chance to become it, or because they simply never would?

'Hey. Earth to Caro.' Les waved a hand in front of her face, and Caroline looked up at him, startled.

'Sorry, I was miles away.'

Les gave her a sheepish smile. 'You often are. Were, I mean. Somewhere nicer?'

Caroline felt a wave of guilt as she realised she'd been thinking about Adam. 'No, don't be silly.' She shifted uncomfortably on her seat. Les took a long swig of wine.

'I'm sorry, Caro, this was selfish of me. Hijacking you, and your evening.'

Caroline frowned. 'Don't apologise. I'm having a lovely time. Which is actually what I was just thinking about, if you must know.'

'Really?' said Les, unconvinced. 'Sorry, it's just that I'd

come to know that look pretty well before we – I – we split. Took me back a bit, that's all.'

He nodded his thanks as the second bottle of Châteauneuf du Pape arrived, and sat back allowing the sommelier to pour.

Caroline stared at him. 'Took you back to what, Les?'

He shook his head as if to brush off her question, and then seemed to change his mind. 'To when we were together. To feelings I had quite often of being – well – a bit of a spare part, to be honest.'

'You felt like a spare part – where? In our marriage?'

Les nodded. 'I know. Stupid, isn't it? I look back now and wonder where it came from. But it seemed to me, at the time, that the more successful you became, the more I was sidelined out of my role as husband, father and – well – provider.'

Caroline stared at him, aghast. It was so long since she'd seen Les's softer side that she'd almost forgotten it existed. 'And how long did you feel like this for?'

Les shrugged and looked embarrassed. 'I don't know. Months, years? Who knows. It's all immaterial now, isn't it? The time for solving it has gone. It's one of the many issues we should have taken time to deal with before they became arguments, let alone before we stopped even caring about them.' He sighed. 'One of our strengths was that we never tried to change each other. But it was also a weakness. I never tried to change you, and I know you never tried to change me – but really we should have changed things within our relationship. But then – I don't know. Seeing that look in your eyes, I realised you've got more to be preoccupied with now, haven't you? Not just Sapphires & Rubies, not just Rachel, but . . . him, too.'

Caroline could hardly bear to look at Les, with all the hurt she could see in his eyes. But there were other emotions there too: insecurity, and something else – jealousy? She remembered how it hurt her to think of Les with someone else – not just another woman, but one who was younger, lither, prettier, maybe. How it still hurt.

'Les, you can't punish me for moving on with my life,' she said gently. 'What was I meant to do, hang around moping over you for ever more? You were the one who left me, remember – whatever the reasons for it, it was you who broke up our marriage.'

There was an awkward silence. 'I know, I know – and God knows I regret it,' said Les. He looked up at her shyly. 'There were reasons, you know, Caro. I mean, clinical reasons. There's more to four weeks in rehab than a few good nights' sleep, you know. My depression – apparently my affair,' he scoffed at the word as though it wasn't even worthy of the title. 'My affair was a symptom of my state of mind. I was actually really ill, but I was behaving like someone going through some superficial midlife crisis. Life, eh? Nothing like kicking you in the arse when the chips are really down.' He shook his head sadly, then looked up at her again, those blue eyes overflowing with an expression that Caroline felt would break her heart in two.

'And being with you here, now, makes it even worse. It's like you're the same Caroline, but different. And thinking of you with him – well, it underlines everything. What I've lost, and what another man stands to gain.'

There was another long silence – a more comfortable one this time, as they reflected on the cataclysmic events of the previous months. Finally, Les clapped his hands and raised his glass.

'But wasn't this meant to be a celebration? Cheers, Caro – here's to you, and that fabulous future I couldn't quite handle, and everything fate has in store for you. The good stuff, I mean.'

'To the good stuff,' repeated Caroline wistfully, clinking her glass against his.

The question was, which good stuff was it that she really wanted?

The same question reverberated around her mind hours later as she lay in bed, eyes wide open, sleep determinedly escaping her, with the familiar sound of Les snoring next to her. Once upon a time this noise would have sent her to the very edge of distraction, but right now it made her feel safe. Happy, even.

But confused. Oh so very confused. Just as life sorted out one big dilemma, it handed you another one right there, ready to replace it.

And tonight, not because of her reunion with Les – the wine-fuelled lovemaking that had followed their heart-to-heart over dinner more passionate, intense than it had been before, and, with the confidence that had come with her relationship with Adam, infinitely more satisfying – but almost in spite of it, she'd learnt one very important lesson. The lifelong quest that she, her friends and their generational peers had spent so long following: the drive and the desire to Have It All. Could they? Should they? Caroline had been determined that yes, she could – whether it was friends, family, career, or now Adam and Les – absolutely have it all. Well, now she knew for certain.

Of course you could have it all – just not all at the same time.

And now she'd got that sorted, she was more confused than ever.

What *did* she want now? Was it Les, or was it Adam?

And could she have either?

Chapter 26

REARRANGING THE SPICE RACK

'CAROLINE! Honestly, you're worse than me. Who'd have thought that of all of us, it would be your life that turned into the biggest soap opera of all?'

Caroline laughed. It was true. Her life – both at home and at work – was so farcical at the moment that mirth seemed the most appropriate reaction.

'Oh, I don't know, Maz – I think we've all had our moments this year.'

Their thoughts immediately turned to Esther, starting her chemotherapy that morning, and they fell silent. Caroline stared unseeingly into her martini. Surgery had revealed that she'd been lucky – the cancer hadn't spread to her lymphatic system – but she was undergoing a course of chemo as a precaution. Typical Esther, she'd spent the previous day at the hair salon. 'And then I'm not washing it. At all,' she'd announced determinedly. 'No point encouraging it to fall out. I'm hanging on to it as long as I possibly can!'

'So, anyway,' said Maryanne purposefully. 'I have a pressing appointment with my personal shopper, and we still haven't solved your dilemma. You can't possibly make a decision about any of this until you've seen Adam. You really have to phone him, Caroline.'

She gestured for the bill, and Caroline pulled a face. Maryanne had been dismissive of Caroline's reunion with Les – as well she might, considering her own situation – and despite having written him off previously, was infinitely more interested in the idea of a reunion with Adam. She looked at Maryanne fondly across the table of Bar Boulud, underneath the plush Mandarin Oriental hotel in London's Knightsbridge. The soft lighting of the plush hotel bar was designed to flatter everything that fell under its glamour, but Maryanne really did seem to be regaining something of her former sparkle. The past month had felt like an eternity, as Maryanne refused all contact, hiding away, licking her wounds and coming to terms with Anthony leaving her. But finally, yesterday – oh happy day! – she'd called Caroline out of the blue and demanded cocktails and catch-up. She was still a shell of her former self – thinner, hollow eyed, less exuberant – but her long red hair had some of its natural lustre again, there was a ghost of a half-smile across her lips, and Caroline had the instinctive feeling she was starting to bounce back. Very like she herself had done, in fact. Caroline smiled. She'd be fixing Maryanne up with Adam's friends before she even knew it. As Maryanne paid the bill, she entertained herself for a few moments by wondering which of Adam's friends she might set up with her friend.

Well, of course, she'd have to phone Adam first ... It was now a full six weeks since that late September evening she'd last seen Adam, and with everything that had happened since, it felt like a lifetime to her. As she was frequently reminded by Rachel's approach to things, time had a greater significance for the young. Who was to say similarly cataclysmic things hadn't happened to him during their time apart?

'So, do you fancy coming with me?' said Maryanne. She pointed across the road. Although only at the beginning of November, Knightsbridge was twinkling in the glow of Christmas lights and Harvey Nicks was aglow with the promise of seasonal sparkle.

Caroline shook her head. 'I'll give it a miss, Maz. I've got a stack of paperwork to do at home. Selling the company was meant to give me less to do, but it seems that until we've agreed a buyer, I'm right up to my eyes in it all.'

They strolled out into the biting cold of the winter evening.

'Well, that's fair enough, but I'm only letting you go if you promise to call Adam,' said Maryanne, kissing Caroline on the cheek as a black cab pulled up.

Caroline hugged her tightly. 'I'll think about it. Take care of yourself, OK?'

'Oh, don't worry about me. I'll be fine,' said Maryanne dismissively. Then, more urgently. 'Phone him!'

Caroline climbed into the cab and shut the door, pulling a face through the cab window.

'Phone him!' repeated Maryanne. The cab started to pull off.

'OK, darling – I will,' called Caroline, waving through the open window. 'I promise!'

★

There is no need to rearrange your spice rack, Caroline Walker, she told herself crossly as she looked for another task to do. *It's been that way for months, and can happily stay that way for another few months.*

She put down the cloth and antibacterial spray that she'd been cleaning the inside of the fridge with and looked over to the kitchen table, where the pile of paperwork she'd dumped there two hours previously remained untouched. Her iPhone sat forlornly – also untouched since she'd arrived home. Procrastinating was always easiest in the kitchen, where a plethora of unnecessary jobs awaited her. After all, if there was nothing left to clean, she could always cook something, and then clean up afterwards.

So, what next – paperwork or Adam? She sat down, perching on the chair, and picked up her phone thoughtfully. She guessed it should be Adam. The paperwork could wait – but she'd been putting off the Adam call for a full six weeks. There was only so long she could make excuses to herself, after all.

Maybe she'd have a glass of wine first. The effect of the martinis she'd had earlier with Maryanne had long worn off, and this was one call that she needed Dutch courage for. What the hell was she going to say?

Her stomach lurched with nerves as she pulled a half-full bottle of white burgundy from the fridge and poured a generous measure into a wine glass. She glanced over at her phone again, still sitting on the table but now taking on sinister significance, and poured out a little bit more. Who knew, it could be a long phone call.

Or, she thought with another lurch as she wandered back

to the chair, it could be a very *short* call. What if he was angry, abusive? She bit her lip. Or what if, even worse, he was unmoved?

She took a deep breath and searched for his number in her contacts. It glared back at her, so familiar and yet, unused for a matter of weeks, so alien. Her thumb hovered over the call button. *Come on, Caroline, what are you waiting for? Call him. CALL HIM.*

Her phone rang, springing into life and making her physically jump. Adam? She stared at it in shock, but Adam's number had disappeared from the screen and been replaced by another. Her mother's.

Heart sinking, Caroline hesitated. Half of her wanted to ignore it. She'd been so close – so close to calling Adam. A conversation with her mother was bound to take ages, and then what if she couldn't get up the nerve to call him afterwards?

But still, a little voice inside her said, *this is the perfect excuse to put it off a little longer. Go on, answer it . . .*

'Hi, Mother,' she said brightly.

'Hello, darling,' said her mother's voice. Except . . . it wasn't really her mother's voice. Tinnier than usual. A little forced? 'How are you?'

'I'm fine, Mum,' said Caroline, her voice dipping with concern. 'But how are you? You sound – weird.'

'Me? No no, darling, I'm fine,' said her mother. There was a silence. 'Except, I've had some news today that I thought you should know about.' She suddenly sounded weary – unbearably weary.

'What's the matter, Mum?' Caroline's voice was sharp with worry.

Again, silence. 'Oh darling, I'm not sure how to tell you this. But it's your father—'

'My father?' interrupted Caroline. She hadn't heard her mother volunteer that word for years – and even then it had been in reference to something negative. 'What about my father?'

Babs cleared her throat cautiously. Her voice was soft, uncertain. 'Oh darling – he's had a heart attack. It's serious. They're not sure he'll pull through.'

There was a long silence. Caroline felt like her world was spinning around her at helter-skelter speed. Her father – dying?

'Caroline?' said Babs, timidly. 'Caroline, are you still there? This must be an awful shock to you.'

Caroline opened her mouth to speak, but no words came out. She was in shock, certainly – but right now that shock was centred on the depth of her feelings. She hadn't seen him for thirty-six years – so how come she felt she'd been hit by a sledgehammer?

'Caroline, how do you feel, darling?'

She laughed, a hard brittle laugh that had no joy in it at all. 'How do I feel? Well, I wouldn't know, would I? I never knew my father, and now it seems as though I may never do. So how should I know how I feel about him dying?'

The log crackled and spat as the flames danced around it, the glowing coal embers coming back up into life and brightening up the grey of the Saturday afternoon gloom.

Caroline shivered and hugged her mug of hot chocolate, feeling no comfort from either its cosy hug or the roaring fire.

She looked through the French windows at the wintry garden. Usually, there was nothing like being holed up in the cottage on a cold afternoon to make her feel warm from the inside out, but today it was having no effect.

Her first instinct on hearing the news about her father on Thursday evening had been to escape, but of course there were matters to sort first. Work had been relatively simple – with the respective merits of three offers now being considered for Sapphires & Rubies, the next board meeting was not until the following week, and the office could easily do without her for one afternoon.

And with relations thawing between Rachel and her father, persuading her daughter to go to Les's for the weekend had been no trouble, especially when he'd dangled the carrot of a Christmas shopping trip in town.

And so Caroline had headed out to the cottage the previous lunchtime, turned her phone off and hunkered down, hiding away from the world until she'd come to terms with how she was feeling.

The problem was, she still didn't *know* how she was feeling. Had no idea how to judge how she *should* be feeling against what she actually *was* feeling. Except that it wasn't good.

Although he'd left when she was tiny, the news of her father's illness had sent her spiralling into a period of intense mourning. But what exactly was she mourning – the father she never knew, who hadn't even died yet? The little girl who had so missed him? Maybe her own vulnerability ... More than likely, a mixture of all three – but one thing was for sure. The sense of her own mortality had hit her like a physical blow. She felt as if she'd aged ten years overnight, and despite a full twelve hours' sleep, she had awoken this morning bone tired – permanently exhausted and overwhelmingly nauseous.

And there was regret, too. The years of estrangement, for so long so logical, now seemed unfathomable. Her new understanding of the complexities of divorce had suddenly thrown her father's defection into a new light. She had an overwhelming urge to hear his side of the story, to understand exactly what had happened that would have made him turn his back not just on Babs but on her, too. But something was holding her back.

Caroline was also lonely. For whom, she wasn't sure. Ghosts seemed to loiter in every room of the cottage. She craved the unadulterated joy of having Rachel around, but knew that would mean talking to her about a grandfather she'd never met, eliciting in itself a multitude of questions Caroline wasn't sure she was emotionally strong enough to consider nor informed enough to answer. She found herself coveting the comfort of Les, in so many ways a father figure himself. She needed Adam's light-heartedness and curiously wise way of looking at the world. And, despite the complex web of feelings her father's fraility had evoked in her about her mother, part of Caroline ached for Babs's comforting practicality – and unconditional love.

Despite being overwhelming en masse, however, none of these feelings was proving strong enough to persuade her to call anyone, and so here she was, alone, with nothing to base her feelings on and no way of finding anything, and trying to work her way through her emotions.

A robin redbreast, a long-term winter resident of the cottage garden, hopped up to the back door, and Caroline smiled in delight. Since she was a little girl, Rachel had looked forward to his first appearance of the year, his arrival heralding for her the run-up to Christmas. Caroline sipped her hot chocolate and watched him strutting around the sundeck. Christmas had been one of the few times of the year she'd allowed herself to think about her father in any depth, wondering as a girl what it would be like to have the traditional family Christmas with a father who dressed up as Santa Claus and who carved the turkey. After she'd married and had Rachel, it had been a time for wondering just how he could have turned his back on his family – or, at the very least, his daughter – and the chance to watch her grow up.

Suddenly, the robin flew up on to the fence and then up into the safety of the holly bush, and Caroline looked to see what had startled him. There were no other birds, cats or anything obvious. With nothing else to do, she got up to investigate.

She opened the French windows, peering out into the misty garden. A noise from the path up the side of the house caught her attention, and she tiptoed out on to the slippery cold wooden decking and wandered around to where the noise had come from.

There was a shriek, and a crash.

'Mother?'

'Caroline!'

Caroline found herself staring into the startled wide eyes of Babs. She was holding a large box file full of what appeared to be letters, and the contents of another were strewn around her over the path.

'Mum, what are you doing here?'

'Oh darling, I've been so worried about you and – well, I have some things to show you.'

Kneeling on the ground, trying desperately to gather up the papers, Babs looked so small, so helpless, that Caroline couldn't maintain any hard feelings towards her.

'Well, since you're here, you'd better come in,' she said. 'I'll put the kettle on.'

They'd been sitting in silence for a good ten minutes now. Babs had taken the seat next to Caroline on the sofa, and they were wordlessly sipping their coffees, staring in turn into the fire and out of the windows. There was so much to say, but since neither knew where to start, it seemed easier to stay quiet.

One of the boxes caught Caroline's eye. 'So, what did you bring to show me?' she said, interest suddenly piqued.

Babs looked away shiftily, refusing to catch her eye.

'It's, erm, some things of your father's,' she said haltingly.

Caroline stared at her incredulously. She had never realised Babs had anything of her father's. Certainly, all the times Caroline had asked as a child, Babs had told her he'd taken everything with him.

'What kind of things?'

Again, Babs avoided eye contact, and instead got up and busied herself with opening the first file and toying with the papers inside.

'Some, erm, letters and things.'

Caroline stared at her, feeling the weight of an impending revelation hanging in the air. She almost didn't want to know.

'*What kind* of letters and things?'

350

For the first time since she'd arrived, Babs held her gaze, her eyes a mixture of fear and conviction, shining defensively.

'Letters that your father wrote you. Cards that he sent you. Since he left us.' Babs stopped, her voice breaking. 'Since he left *me*.'

Caroline stared at her, hardly daring to breathe.

Babs clutched the file to her chest as if it was a cherished person she was loath to let go of. As if it were her father, thought Caroline, through the fog of her own pain.

Eventually, Babs relaxed her hold and held it out to Caroline. 'He didn't ever want to leave you, Caroline. He wanted to leave *me*. And I told him he couldn't have both. He couldn't leave me, and still see you. But he still left! He still left!'

A lone tear spilled out of her eye and trickled down her face. Caroline felt wretched at the sight of her mother's still-raw pain, hidden away for all these years. Yet at the same time she felt her heart hardening into flint at the things that pain had denied her.

'But he kept sending you things, Caroline. Birthday cards. Christmas cards. Letters. Even when you never replied. I kept meaning to give them to you, to show you, but it was – is – too painful. So I . . . I didn't. And I wanted you to see them, before it's too late.'

She gulped back the sobs, and looked at Caroline pleadingly. 'Don't do what I did, Caroline. Don't cut yourself off from people. Reconcile yourself with him. With your father. Before it's too late!'

Caroline stared at her mother in a blur. She'd known Babs longer than anyone else in her life. Knew her better than she knew herself. But suddenly, it was though her mother was a stranger.

'Too late for what, Mother? For me to forgive my father, or to forgive you?'

The room was stuffy and overheated, the still calm of its epi-centre juxtaposed with the quiet efficiency of the nurses bustling in and out, and the regular beeping of the various machines hooked up to her father.

Her father. Caroline hesitated again, unable to cross the threshold completely, as if to walk just one step into her father's hospital room was to traverse a dangerous unchartered ravine. The words sounded alien, for so long relegated to an inaccessible place that belonged to other people, but never to her. She'd never had a father. And now she did. Kind of.

The ward sister smiled kindly at her as she straightened his sheets. 'There isn't much of visiting time left,' she said in low tones. 'Do come in – and I'll leave you both in peace.' She took a final look around the room, and Caroline followed her gaze, taking in the unfamiliar surroundings. Her eyes hovered over a bunch of flowers on the bedside table. She looked down at her hands, empty save for her handbag. It hadn't even occurred to her to bring a gift. And if it had, what would she have brought – chocolates? Grapes? The thought was quite incongruous.

Left on her own in the room, Caroline walked slowly over to the bed and peered down at its inhabitant. Weird to think that was one of her closest blood relatives. Lying there, his eyes closed, his skin waxy and yellowed by ill health, he looked just like any of the nameless hospital patients she'd passed on the way here. There was no rush of recognition, no urge to wake him and remonstrate with him, no – well. No nothing, really. Why on earth had she come?

She cleared her throat awkwardly and looked around in shock as the sound seemed to reverberate around the room. She perched on the bedside chair, in a bid to make herself feel less obvious.

She stared at her father. What should she do now? What had she expected to find, to achieve here?

At a loss for anything else to do, she picked up his hand and held it between hers. It was thin, and elegant – a piano player's hand, just like her own – with the soft, warm, crêpey skin of the ageing. Absent-mindedly she stroked it, feeling the bones hard beneath her palm. As the rhythmic movement relaxed her, she gazed into his face, trying to make it fit with the face of her most distant childhood memories, with the face of her daydreams, and with the face of the nightmare of him leaving her.

Out of the blue, she felt the slightest pressure on her hand. She looked down in surprise, then up at her father. He remained motionless. Had she imagined it? Heart quickening, she looked up at the monitor. There seemed to be no change in his condition. Then, she was certain, she detected a flicker of his eyelids. She stood up, looking down into his face.

'Father?' Her voice cracked at the unfamiliar word. 'Daddy?'

Then, magically, his eyelids opened to reveal lively green eyes – bloodshot and blurred by age and debilitation, maybe – but they were unmistakable. She'd looked at them every day of her life, wondering what the rest of the man who'd given her them was like. Her eyes. *Her* daddy.

There was another squeeze – this time unquestionably tangible – and his dry, mottled lips opened as a tear formed in the corner of one of those familiar eyes.

'Caroline?'

Chapter 27

READY FOR YOUR CLOSE-UP?

'Mum, can I borrow your gold hoop earrings?' Rachel's face popped around the door of her dressing room, and Caroline laughed. Yet another eighties revival had reignited Rachel's interest in her old clothes and, more importantly, jewellery. These would be only the latest in a long line of loans – most of which, she noted in amusement, had not yet been returned and had obviously turned into 'gifts'.

'Yes, darling, of course.' Caroline patted the long stool she was sitting on in invitation and Rachel came and sat next to her as she pulled the earrings out of a jewellery box.

'Here you are.' She handed them over to her daughter and they looked at each other in the mirror – literally mirror images of each other, thought Caroline with a wave of love. She kissed her daughter's head. 'You look lovely, darling.'

Rachel was wearing a vintage maroon Alaia minidress – again courtesy of Caroline's wardrobe archive – and fierce grey Kurt Geiger shoe boots. The dress's giant shoulder pads accentuated Rachel's tiny frame, and the array of friendship bracelets and Claire's Accessories bangles emphasised her youth. In the mix of designer, vintage and high street, she was a true product of her generation, thought Caroline proudly. Just a particularly beautiful one.

'Thanks, Mum.' Rachel leapt up. 'I've just got to phone Scott and Suki and then I'm ready to go.'

Caroline opened her mouth to protest – the car was already outside waiting for them, after all – and then shut it again. Rachel was '*beyond* excited' about tonight's film première – the second release in the latest cult movie trilogy – and Caroline knew she'd want to share it with her new boyfriend and friends. She'd always been a soft touch where Rachel was concerned, and last week's revelations over her father had made her even more malleable. And, she was sure, it hadn't gone unnoticed with Rachel, either.

'OK, but no longer than ten minutes, darling, or they won't let us in!'

'No worries, Mum,' called Rachel from her room.

Caroline gave her hair a final brush and stood up, popping a purse-size spray in her gold clutch. She surveyed her appearance. Not bad for an old bird. She'd chosen a Malene Birger cocktail dress with plunging neckline and gold snakeskin Sapphires & Rubies shoes – just glam enough to hold her own but not to try and compete with Rachel's showstopping look. She was now the foil for her daughter's beauty – and was determined that she wasn't just going to get used to it – she was going to *enjoy* it.

She looked around for her phone and picked it up to put in her bag. On a whim, she scrolled through her contacts and stared at Adam's number. With Babs now *persona non grata*, she'd missed him more this week than at any other time since they split up, and had wanted to confide in him more than anyone else. Instead, she'd kept it to herself, limiting her discussions of her father's illness to a carefully scripted conversation with Rachel. She was bottling it up, she knew, but right now she didn't know how else to deal with it. The tumultuous emotions Babs's revelations had released into the mix would take time to sort through, and the prospect scared her.

But Rachel's infectious excitement and the prospect of a fun evening ahead of her had made Caroline feel unusually carefree – a feeling she'd not had for several weeks – and on a whim, she dialled Adam's number. Her heart was racing fast as she listened to the ring tone, and her hands were suddenly clammy, but she willed herself to stay on the line.

'Hi!'

'Hi!' Caroline responded, her heart in her mouth at the familiar sound of his voice.

'This is Adam. Leave a message and I'll get back to you.'

Caroline's heart sank like a plunging stone, and she hung up without leaving a message. Had he seen her call and rejected it? Or had he simply not seen her call? She willed herself to remember how many times it had rung out before she'd heard his message, before remonstrating with herself. *Leave it, Caro. He'll see you've called and get back to you if he wants to.*

'I'm ready, Mum!'

Caroline slipped her phone into her bag and took one last look in the mirror.

Show time.

★

'Caroline, where's Adam?'

'Is it true you've split?

'Caroline, over here!'

Caroline gave the bank of photographers a dazzling smile, her hand placed gently on Rachel's back as they faced the onslaught of flashbulbs. Despite years of pleading, she'd so far refused to take Rachel to such a high profile event as this, but she figured that Rachel was now old enough to attend without having her head turned or becoming tabloid diary fodder. Not to mention that anyone who was anyone had a ticket to tonight's event, and there was a host of A-listers who were guaranteed to provide far more interesting column inches than Caroline and her daughter. The *Hollyoaks* actress in front of them, eking out her own moment in the spotlight for as long as possible by wiggling her curvaceous figure slowly down the red carpet in a lime green body con Herve Leger tube dress and six-inch Rupert Sanderson stilettos was slightly scuppering Caroline's plans to get down the red carpet as quickly as possible, but she had one experienced eye on the A-list movie star behind them, manoeuvring her long, tanned, shapely legs out of her limo and into the limelight, and she knew it wouldn't be long before the press corps shifted their attentions.

She pressed her hand further into the small of Rachel's back. 'Let's move forward slowly, darling, and give the next guest her turn!'

Rachel, busy working the photographers like a pro, obediently turned and walked slowly towards the cinema, still smiling widely. They climbed the stairs into the cinema entrance, and joined the throng of designer dresses, fake tans and tuxedos in the foyer.

'Look, Mum! There's Marvin from JLS! And Robert Pattinson with Kristen – so they're back together!' Rachel squealed even louder. 'AND look – Simon Cowell!' Caroline smiled indulgently as she saw Rachel's excitement mount. She looked about fit to burst. Caroline herself looked around interestedly, drinking in the atmosphere. She nodded at a few acquaintances, and waved over at a glamorous newsreader who'd been a loyal Sapphires & Rubies client ever since launch.

All of a sudden Rachel dug her in the ribs and turned wide-eyed towards Caroline. 'Mum! Look, it's Adam!'

Caroline's own eyes widened in shock as she spotted Adam standing in the corner with a couple of gangly, grungy-looking girls his own age. He was laughing at something one of them had said, and looking just to the right of her. As she stared at him, he turned and caught her eye. Time seemed to stand still as they held each other's gaze. After what seemed like an age – but could only have been a nanosecond – Adam broke the spell by smiling and giving her a mock salute. Caroline relaxed as she saw unmistakable warmth in his eyes. She waved, mock sheepishly, and smiled back.

'Go and talk to him!' hissed Rachel. Dragging her eyes away, Caroline turned back to her daughter.

'Darling, it's neither the time nor the place,' she said *sotto voce*, her lips hardly moving. 'It's just about the most public place you could ever choose to have a first conversation with an ex.'

Rachel tutted. 'Not that you want him to be an ex, Mum,' she said. Caroline started. What did Rachel know about how she was feeling?

'Oh come on, Mum,' protested Rachel. 'I've never seen you as happy as you were when you were with Adam. Not even with Dad!' Caroline looked at her in surprise. 'I mean, Dad when you were together,' muttered Rachel. 'And anyway, I know I wanted you two to get back together, but I've changed my mind now. He treated you like dirt, but Adam never did.' Caroline, surprised at Rachel's about-turn, looked over at Adam again hopefully, but he was deep in conversation with one of the girls. So much for little boy lost, hurt and confused since their split. He looked gorgeous, grown-up – and *happy*.

'Well, that was then,' said Caroline dismissively. 'And anyhow, tonight's about you and me having fun. So – ready for your close-up?' She nodded at the second bank of photographers, ready to take portraits of all the guests against the sponsors boards.

Rachel giggled. 'I guess so.'

'I still don't know why you won't go and speak to him, Mum,' persisted Rachel, as they gathered in the foyer on their way to the after party.

Caroline turned to her with a glare. 'Rachel, darling, I've told you – now is not the time or the place. And if you must know, I did call Adam earlier – so if he wants to speak to me, he only has to call me back.'

'OK,' Rachel looked around her morosely. Suddenly, she seemed to perk up. 'Mum, have I got time to go to the loo?'

Caroline glanced at her watch. 'Yes darling, if you're quick.'

Rachel disappeared, and Caroline moved to one side of the foyer, pulling her iPhone out of her bag and checking through her emails.

'Anything urgent, Mrs Walker, or are you interruptable?'

At the sound of Adam's voice – low, intimate and so close she could feel his breath on her ear – Caroline jumped and looked up in shock.

'Well, don't look so surprised to see me!' he laughed. 'You did know I was here, after all! Surely you weren't going to sneak out without talking to me?' His tone was light-hearted, but Caroline detected uncertainty in his eyes.

'No, no of course not,' she said hurriedly, crossing her fingers behind her back at the fib.

He looked at her teasingly, more confident now.

'Are you sure?'

Well,' admitted Caroline. 'It's a bit public here, isn't it? I mean, there's been a bit of press speculation and . . .'

'. . . And you weren't sure how I'd react? Or you weren't sure if you wanted to talk to me at all?'

Caroline looked at him earnestly. 'Of course I wanted to talk to you. I've wanted to talk to you since Rachel's party. But I just didn't know how.'

There was a silence, and Adam looked around him shiftily. 'How about now? I mean, not here,' he added hurriedly. 'We could go somewhere else. Somewhere quieter.'

'I don't know . . .' said Caroline doubtfully, looking around for Rachel. 'I promised Rachel we'd go to the after party. It's the first time I've brought her to an event like this, and—'

'Mum! Look who I found!' said Rachel, dragging Adam's friend, lanky Danny behind her. 'Oh, and look who *you* found.' She smiled guiltily and Caroline looked from Adam to Rachel in shock. Was this some kind of set-up?

Adam shrugged innocently and then, seeing Caroline's

consternation, gave in. 'I bumped into Rachel on her way to the loo,' he explained.

'Oh did you, indeed,' said Caroline suspiciously, fixing Rachel with a glare. Her daughter grinned impishly back at her.

'Anyhow, I'm sure you have lots to talk about, Mum, so can I go to the after show with Danny?'

Caroline stared at her, open mouthed. 'But we're going together, Rachel – aren't we?' But instead of looking at her daughter, she found her eyes locked with Adam's, and the question seemed directed at him.

'Well, I thought you might like to go for a drink,' he murmured, shifting from one leg to another.

Caroline looked from her daughter's dancing eyes to the furtive invitation in her ex-lover's, and back again.

'Do I actually have any choice?' she asked no one in particular.

Deep in the belly of a dark Soho wine bar, Caroline tried to savour the delicious awkwardness of the moment rather than being swallowed up by nerves. This was the kind of moment you should be able to bottle, the frisson of a first date when your senses were so finely honed that even the merest whisper could send your pulse racing – combined with the comfortable familiarity of finally finding your way back to a cherished, long-lost lover.

'So, how've you been?' said Adam, returning from the bar with two large glasses of Merlot. Take it easy, Caro, she thought, remembering the effect the same wine had had on their first date together.

'Fine,' she said awkwardly. She took a deep breath and looked at him. God, she'd missed those eyes. 'Well, not fine at all really. I've been bloody awful. But most of all, I've been totally, miserably, 100 per cent sorry.' They locked eyes again and laughed, and the polite formalities disappeared at the unspoken admission that they were pleased to see one another, and suddenly both were overcome with a rush of words tumbling over each other in their hurry to get out.

'But as well as completely, bitterly angry, I feel full of remorse,' Caroline admitted. There it was. She'd said it. They'd covered Maryanne, Esther, the business – and now, as the bar staff were clearing up around them, she had broached the subject of her father, and the multitude of emotions she felt over his reappearance in her life. Exactly what was it about Adam that made her open up her very soul? 'Not just for the way I felt – still feel – but for the way he must have felt. Imagine always sending those cards and letters and never hearing anything back! And what's more, he's still in intensive care. I may never have the chance to properly say "thank you". For making me who I am, for setting me up in the business I'm in now – or for inspiring me to be the entrepreneur I am now.' She looked up at Adam, her eyes full of the vulnerability she felt when the helplessness of her past overcame her.

'Look, I appreciate it's not completely cut and dried, Caroline, but your father could have made more of an effort to see you,' said Adam awkwardly. He put his hand over hers and squeezed it gently. It was warm and strong – just as she remembered it. 'You might not have been the businesswoman you are if you hadn't felt you'd got something to prove. And don't blame it all on Babs. You can bet your life it's more complicated than even she's made out. Whatever happens with your father, you've still got her. I reckon, keep going to see him. See how things pan out if – and when – he gets better. But don't let him cause any more pain than he already has done.'

Caroline gazed at him. 'How did you get to be so wise?' she said wonderingly.

'Spending time with people like you, I guess,' he countered with a smile. They laughed companionably. A chair scraped behind them and jolted Caroline back into the present.

'Look, we'd better go. But Adam ...' He looked her directly in the eye. 'You know I'm sorry, don't you? That I never meant it – this – to happen. I'd go back and change everything if I could.'

He shrugged. 'I know. Shit happens. It's how you move on from it that counts, I guess.'

They stared at each other, neither willing to volunteer the next move.

'I'm sorry, but we're ready to close up ...' ventured the barman behind them.

They turned as one and wandered out of the bar, careful not to touch each other. As the bar door swung shut behind them, a taxi approached with its light on and Caroline waved to flag it down. As her arm swung back down by her side, Adam caught Caroline's fingers. It felt as though she'd had an electric shock, and she looked up at him in surprise. He bent down and gave her a lingering kiss on the lips.

Caroline gazed out of the taxi window, full of bittersweet longing. How apt. A wonderful evening that had finished on a delicious kiss – but no more. Everything said, but nothing resolved. Just as it was in the beginning . . . They'd come full circle.

She sighed and turned away from the window. So what now?

One thing needed doing, though. She delved in her bag for her phone, and ignoring the late hour, dialled.

After the longest pause, there was an answer.

'Mum? It's me. We need to talk.'

Chapter 28

GOSSIP FODDER FOR DENTIST OFFICE MAGAZINES

'This is like something out of *Sex and the City*,' laughed Caroline, as she clinked her martini with Maryanne's and Esther's.

'But without the sex,' deadpanned Maryanne with a grimace, referring to her own current drought.

'And with lots of City!' joked Esther, resplendent after a successful first course of chemotherapy in full make-up and a Hermès headscarf.

Caroline laughed excitedly. It felt good to have something to celebrate for a change. This year – in particular the past couple of months – seemed to have been one soul-destroying disaster after another. But finally, the deal with venture capitalist Eclipse Luxury Holdings had been signed and sealed the day before: Sapphires & Rubies had been sold to them for a record-breaking £500 million, ensuring the future of the existing team – bar Julie, of course – and retaining Caroline as creative director, overseeing brand and product development. She was not only set to reach the *Sunday Times* Rich List on her own terms, but she'd secured a strong future for the business and for Rachel. And the Ivy Club felt like the best place to be, with two of her favourite people in the world. Exclusive, exquisite and intimate.

'In fact, let me read from the *Evening Standard* profile,' continued Esther proudly, holding up that evening's newspaper.

'"It would be unfair to dismiss Walker as mere gossip fodder for dentist office magazines; an exotic figurehead for the NW1 set with £300 haircuts and a personal trainer on speed dial. In the past decade she has revealed a formidable layer of business nous that few could have predicted of this former yummy mummy.

'"Walker knows that she has to present herself in a certain way. She has cleverly realised that people look at her and that inspires the people who buy the range. Caroline is her own company's muse. But her image gained its own momentum once the business was a success; it was her eye for business and style that really got it started."'

Esther rustled the paper for impact and peered over the top of it imperiously. 'Well, Mrs Walker, I'm surprised you're not charging us for your company this evening. Or your style advice. I mean, can you give me some new ways to tie my headdress?'

'Or tell me what I can do with the ruins of my life?' put in Maryanne with a wink. Despite her buoyant exterior, Maryanne was still single and feeling bruised. Only a few days before, she'd discovered Anthony was having a passionate relationship – with an older woman. The irony of the situation had not escaped her, and dealing with the fact that Anthony had not only moved on from her, but had discovered his long-dormant sex drive, had knocked her for six. There was a new vulnerability about her that, whilst regrettable, actually, thought Caroline, quite suited her.

'Oh, because I'm really an advert for a successful personal life, aren't I?' Caroline admonished Maryanne with a playful swipe. She felt her stomach turn over and she frowned. 'I think I need a glass of water. I'm getting too old to be having too many pre-dinner cocktails.'

'Nonsense,' scolded Esther. 'The only cocktails worth having are the pre-dinner kind. And anyhow, they're the only thing I have an appetite for at the moment.'

'I didn't say no more cocktails,' giggled Caroline, gesturing for the waiter. 'Just some water to wash them down with.' Privately, she made a mental note not to have any more to drink – she was finding it difficult enough keeping up with her friends tonight, and the last thing she wanted to do was ruin the evening by making herself ill.

Maryanne leaned across the table and plucked the newspaper out of Esther's hand, surveying the profile. 'Great pic. Who did your make-up?' There was a silence as she read the rest of the piece and Esther finished her drink.

Maryanne looked up proudly, serious for a moment. 'You always said you would make it a truly global brand.'

Caroline laughed. 'Well, I didn't buy Sapphires & Rubies just to have an accessories shop in London, did I?'

Suddenly Maryanne squealed as her phone buzzed. She checked her new text. She looked up incredulously. 'I don't freakin' believe it!' Unable to contain her excitement, she stood up and did a little dance on the spot. Caroline and Esther laughed with her, looking bemused.

'Maryanne, you might want to sit down,' said Caroline through her giggles, pulling her back on to her seat as fellow club members looked around at her curiously. 'Or at least tell us what's going on so we can join in.'

Maryanne whooped irrepressibly, but sat down obediently. She looked at the text again and then up at her friend.

'Sex and the what? I've only gone and landed the lead role in a new TV drama about thirty-something women!'

Esther looked puzzled. 'Darling, do they know you're over forty?'

Caroline shushed her. 'That's amazing, Maz! What's the premise?'

Maryanne looked around at them mischievously. 'They're all having affairs! So I'm well freakin' qualified for the job! But get this . . .' She looked back at the text. '"The producers loved that I had the sass of a heartless bitch with the vulnerability of a woman spurned." Since when did I get *vulnerable*?'

She looked so disgusted that Caroline wanted to laugh out loud. Instead, there was a momentary silence as Caroline and Esther considered how best to respond. In the end, there was no need. 'So what are we waiting for?' whooped Maryanne. 'Forget the cocktails, I'm all about the Dom Perignon!'

'That's amazing,' said Caroline, genuinely pleased for her friend. 'But where are you going to get the inspiration now you've taken a vow of celibacy?'

Maryanne gave her a reproachful look, still intent on getting the waiter's attention. 'I've got years of inspiration to fall back on. And anyway, I never said *celibate*, I said *faithful*,' she insisted. 'I've just got to find me a man, and I'll be right back in the saddle.'

'Meanwhile, of course, you could always confer with me,' said Esther, adjusting her skirt carefully. Although the plunging necklines were, for now at least, a thing of the past, her Versace dress was as skin-tight and figure hugging as ever.

Caroline stared at her in undisguised amazement. 'Esther, you're not?'

Esther rolled her eyes. 'Of course I'm not. Yet. But that's not to say I've stopped being adored. As my energy has returned, so have my afternoon soirées – it's just that the, erm, nature of them may have shifted a little.'

Caroline shook her head. 'You're incorrigible, Esther.'

Maryanne was more direct. 'You're a fool, Esther. Have you learnt nothing from me?'

Esther leaned forward and placed a hand on Maryanne's. She winked at Caroline. 'Of course I've learnt from you. And from Caroline. And you know what the most important thing is that I've drawn from it all?'

She sat back smugly, with the knowing expression of a wise woman with an audience in thrall.

'The truth is, Maryanne, that you can have a great marriage, but whoever you are, there are still no guarantees.'

The waiter arrived with the champagne, and she raised a glass triumphantly.

'And so my new motto is my old one: Whoever you are, whatever you do – you just need to GET ON WITH IT!'

Chapter 29

TESTING TIMES

Get on with it. The phrase had been running around Caroline's head all morning, as she battled with the nausea that had threatened to wipe out the string of press interviews she'd had lined up yesterday, her celebratory dinner with Les last night (very little booze but still, another unplanned and very enjoyable indiscretion) and even (almost) spoiled her enjoyment of the huge bunch of flowers Adam had sent her this morning. But the thing was, try as she might, she really couldn't raise the energy to get on with 'it', or with anything else, for that matter.

She'd put it down to overindulgence during her dinner with the girls, but that didn't explain feeling so hugely under par today. Well, not just under par. Physically, horrendously sick, and with an overwhelming physical urge to curl up in bed that she really couldn't justify. And although the two-day hangovers that had blighted any major celebration during her thirties and forties were now part and parcel of seriously overdoing it, the fact of the matter was that it was ages since she *had* overdone it. Ages. In fact, now she came to think about it, she hadn't really fancied alcohol for weeks.

All of which had led her to this soulless Primrose Hill waiting room – a rare visit to a doctor. She was seldom ill, and even when she was, she would visit the private doctor she'd had since she married Les. Just how long was it since she'd been to see a GP? she wondered. Not long enough for the waiting room to have changed, that was for sure. She could have sworn that the dog-eared posters and NHS leaflets on giving up smoking and obesity that adorned the grubby cream walls were here last time she visited. The signature smell of disinfectant and airlessness certainly was. But it was long enough ago for her to have no idea who her GP was. Or even recognise any of the names of the practising doctors at her registered surgery. But the fact that she wasn't normally ill made her even more determined to get to the bottom of this little ailment as soon as possible – and for some reason, she'd been loath to consult her normal doctor. He'd seen her throughout her pregnancy with Rachel and her marriage to Les, and she didn't feel up to discussing the split and her current circumstances with him.

'Caroline Walker?'

The smiling receptionist leaned forward as she called Caroline's name, and she pointed to another door.

'Doctor White. Through the doors and second on your left.'

Caroline smiled her thanks and made her way through to the consulting room. She knocked on the door, which echoed hollowly.

'Come in!'

The smiling doctor, dressed in a no nonsense floral print wrap dress – Zara, if Caroline wasn't mistaken – with her hair pulled back into a ponytail couldn't have been much older than Rachel. Well, Caroline corrected herself, she *must* be older than Rachel – at least ten years, if you factored in her requisite training – but with her fresh-faced appearance, she could have passed for twenty-three.

Feeling riled already in spite of herself, Caroline took a seat and proceeded to describe her symptoms.

'So, I've been feeling really sick, which isn't like me. And lethargic – which also isn't like me. And, you know, I've just sold my business and am about to effectively have a boss for the first time in – well, ever! – so I want to be on form. And I've been having these mad mood swings . . .' As she continued, she watched the doctor's face carefully, which began to set into an expression of recognition – and complete lack of surprise.

Again, Caroline felt irritation rise. She knew her symptoms didn't sound earth shattering – but they were impacting on her life! She hadn't been to the doctor's for years, yet had been a higher-bracket taxpayer all that time. This upstart was going to listen to her, and treat her seriously, if it was the last thing she did!

Suddenly Caroline stopped talking, and checked herself. What was happening to her? This lack of patience was so unlike her.

The doctor took the opportunity to say something herself. 'Mrs Walker, when was your last period?'

Caroline stared at her, stumped. When *was* her last period? 'Erm – I'm not sure,' she stuttered. 'I mean, it's been a while.

I've been under a lot of pressure, I've been stressed – I thought . . .'

Feeling foolish, she racked her brains.. She couldn't actually remember. It was a while, that was for sure. She'd put it down to the stress of the takeover, the split from Adam, the loss of her father . . .

'And have you had sex in that time?'

'Yes!' said Caroline, affronted.

'With a regular partner?'

'Yes!' repeated Caroline automatically. This was beginning to feel like an interrogation. A very unwelcome one. And now she came to think about it . . .

'And did you use protection?'

'Yes.' Caroline squirmed. 'Erm, mostly.' The truth was, she *almost* always had with Adam. Of course, in the early days, but latterly there had been one – maybe two – occasions when they'd thought to hell with it. And – oh God, could this get any worse – she hadn't with Les, of course. Force of habit. Two men, two period-free months, one big problem . . .

'But I'm forty-two!' she blurted out. 'You can't possibly be insinuating that I'm PREGNANT? I'm ill! I need medication, not a pregnancy test!'

The doctor looked at her as if she was mad. Which, on reflection, might not be far from accurate.

'Mrs Walker, I'm sure you're feeling unwell. But I don't think you are physically ill. The symptoms you describe – they are closer to pregnancy than any bug. And it would be irresponsible for me to prescribe anything without you taking a test first.'

'This is preposterous!' said Caroline, picking up her bag and standing up to leave. 'I can't possibly be pregnant! I'm going to seek a second opinion!'

As the black cab bounced through the grey London streets, Caroline felt her blood stop boiling, and common sense prevail. The doctor had only been doing her job. And if she'd thought about it sensibly, she might have come to the same conclusion herself, without having not only wasted the doctor's time but made a show of herself into the bargain.

She sighed. However unsavoury her proposition was, the doctor had a point. As they drove past early Christmas shoppers, heads down against the biting wind, the grim realisation of what she could be facing set in.

'Just here, thank you.' Caroline motioned for the driver to pull over on Long Acre, and, stepping out of the cab, headed purposefully down James Street towards the piazza. But instead of turning right on to Floral Street, and towards the office, she carried straight on, towards Boots.

Time to find out once and for all. Time to buy a test.

Epilogue

Unaccustomed to the exertion, Caroline stopped for breath halfway up the hill, and took the opportunity to drink in the familiar view. Familiar, yet unfamiliar. She marvelled at what changes must have been wrought in each of the boroughs within eyesight during the years since she'd first climbed this hill. What lives had played out within this fantastically buzzing vista. Even today, a bank holiday, the city was humming despite the blanket of a New Year's Day hangover – chimneys were spouting plumes of smoke, trains were snaking around the Docklands Light Railway, and the London Eye was turning rhythmically, packed full of little ant-like tourists and holidaymakers. How had Adam described this scene? The pulse of the city, or something . . .

Caroline gulped lungfuls of crisp, clean air, savouring the way it brought her body alive. She loved the contrast of feeling the sun on her face but the chill of the winter air in her bones.

Otherwise, there was something quite hyperreal about today. Not just the bright January sunshine that was burning through the gloomy mists that had set in over Christmas week. But there was an edge to everything – the world seemed bathed in technicolour, sounds had an uber-clarity about them, and she was super-sensitised to the smells around her.

She checked her watch. She was early, of course. Pregnancy had finely honed her habits and enhanced her character traits – so she'd had to get used to arriving everywhere half an hour early, rather than her habitual five minutes.

Pulling her cape underneath her, she plopped down on a sunbaked area of grass where the sun had melted the frost and dried the grass underneath it too. The frozen ground was cold through the denim pockets of her jeans, and she pulled her cape further down underneath her bottom.

New Year's Day. A new start. New resolutions. And she couldn't remember a year that she was more relieved to see the back of. Or, come to that, a year she was more glad to welcome in.

She stroked her tummy thoughtfully. After the initial shock – and, yes, horror – who would have thought how happy she could be, in her circumstances, at her age, to be expecting a baby?

After taking the test – and then another one, to be sure – her first concern had not been herself, or her age, or even the father – but Rachel. And Rachel, as always, had surprised her. Delighted her. Clearly having now resigned her fully to the 'unorthodox mum' category, Rachel had been overjoyed at the prospect of having a younger sister or brother. Caroline thought happily of her daughter, who, having announced she was going to apply to study fashion at Central Saint Martins, first taking a gap year assisting session stylists, was currently spending her Christmas holidays doing work experience on the shop floor at Sapphires & Rubies, soaking up knowledge like a sponge and delighting customers with her eye for a flattering line, or an individual look.

Not for the first time, Caroline marvelled at the unpredictability of youth. And it – Rachel – had inspired her. With Eclipse Holdings' choice of general manager *in situ* at Sapphires & Rubies to run the business side of things, she was finding more time on her hands than ever before. She was moving things on, expanding the brand, adding new lines and – hopefully – attracting more consumers at every turn. She was also working on an ambitious expansion plan, facilitated by Eclipse Holdings' investment, that would see a hundred or more Sapphires & Rubies stores roll out in thirty-two countries around the world over the next five years. Once her morning sickness had (finally) stopped, she'd been more energised than ever before. She'd never felt so motivated, so inspired – and ideas bred ideas: now she was feeling the need to diversify even further – to spread not just her creative visions, but her work ethos. Being pregnant again had reminded her first hand of the difficulties of combining childcare with career development, and she had plans for launching an online advisory service for women wanting to either introduce flexible working to their business, or ask their boss to introduce it on their behalf. She already had several key investors interested – only this time she was going to be more canny about who she invited in than she had first time around.

Caroline felt a tiny flutter in her tummy and she smiled down at the little bump that was just starting to show.

'Hiya, Blob,' she said affectionately. 'How you doing?'

It was Esther who'd given her bump its nickname. Both the girls had been overjoyed at Caroline's news but, typically with a brand new shot at the limelight, Maryanne was far too pre-occupied with her own life to give much attention to the weekly progress of Caroline's pregnancy and was categorically not in the slightest bit interested in talk of baby showers and nurseries. ('I mean,' she'd said dismissively on the phone the previous day, 'it's not like it actually does anything at the moment, right? I'll come into my own when it's two. Or thereabouts . . .') And it wasn't just filming for the TV show that was taking up Maryanne's time. Her divorce from Anthony had uncovered huge debts. The trust fund he'd claimed earned so much interest was more or less depleted, and his business interests were bordering on bankruptcy. And although, thanks to the family pile, Anthony was theoretically land rich, the running costs made him, in practical terms, cash poor. All of which meant that, without a pre-nup, Maryanne's impending divorce could leave her penniless. But instead of wallowing in the loss of Anthony, her aristocratic privileges and, potentially, several million pounds, Maryanne was high on life, enjoying the notoriety of suddenly being the UK's favourite divorcee, with every latest twist and turn in her soap opera gracing the nation's newspapers, and she'd fallen back into the arms of the latest available cougar consorts (all in the name of research, of course, although as she frequently pointed out, without the bad karma of actually cheating on someone).

Esther, on the other hand, was fully embracing bad karma, and with signs that her treatment had been successful, was enjoying a renewed vigour in life – and lovers. 'Think of them like a gym membership,' she'd said with a wink, patting Caroline's knee fondly. 'They keep me in trim – and reach the parts of me Seth can't!'

Caroline shook her head wonderingly at the thought of her best friends – two of the most headstrong, opinionated, beautiful people she'd ever met. What chance had she had, growing up with them? Or with her mother, for that matter?

Caroline drew her knees to her chest and hugged her legs thoughtfully. It hadn't been an easy couple of months, reconciling herself to her mother's lifelong deception and re-establishing their relationship through the emotional fog of hurt and recriminations.

But her father, still weak, still bedbound but on the mend, had been philosophical about it. And, Caroline had reminded herself over and over, Adam's words reverberating around her head, he could have done more to contact her. It wasn't all her mother's fault. It was all part of life's rich, complicated tapestry: her job, now, was putting the past to bed and making sure her – and her family's – future was as pain-free as possible.

But not only had finding her father been an opportunity to put a lot of other ghosts to rest, she'd found her pregnancy had also helped, reminding her of the desperate feelings of inadequacy that new motherhood brought, of the primal desire to protect your baby from everything and anything. Babs had done what Babs had felt best, and, however wrong it might have been, Caroline had to focus on the positive. Babs was her mother, and Caroline owed her the unconditional love Babs had always lavished on her – albeit in her own, unorthodox way. Now, Caroline let out a snort of laughter as she pictured her mother uncomfortably announcing her latest hobby over Christmas dinner. She'd taken a lover, too. A younger lover. 'Well, darling, you can hardly expect me to sit on the sidelines while you girls have all the fun, can you?' she'd exclaimed. Caroline, too stunned to reply, could only observe as Rachel expressed her concern about the age gap. 'Oh Rachel,' Babs had joked, squeezing her hand reassuringly. 'Please don't worry about it, darling. It's serendipity. If he dies, he dies.'

Serendipity. Caroline had never really believed in fate, but after a year like this one, how could you not? She leapt to her feet with a sudden rush of joy, brushed her jeans down and continued with her climb. And thank goodness fate had this particular twist in store for her. Because there'd been another reconciliation during the previous month. And against all odds, she was finally – finally – back together with the man she wanted to spend the rest of her life with. As the Greenwich Observatory came into focus, Caroline screwed her eyes up at the figure standing on the brow of the hill. Her heart lifted. Even without her glasses, she could tell it was him. Standing there, waiting for her. Other people might have shared their history of this spot, other lives might have played out in the panoramic view that surrounded it, but this was *their* special place. Hers, and the father of her new baby . . .

Are you a COUGAR?

Take our exclusive quiz to see whether you might be following in the footsteps of Caroline Walker or Maryanne. Simply add up your points for each answer using the key at the end of the quiz to discover your true calling!

1. When you meet a man, you think:
    a) Is he marriage material?
    b) What would he be like in bed?
    c) Would he make a good friend?

2. You're on a date and the bill arrives. Who pays?
    a) He should pay the bill
    b) I pay. I like being in control
    c) We should split it in half

3. When it comes to children, you:
    a) Aim to be with someone who wants to start a family
    b) Want to be with someone who will love the children you already have
    c) I don't have or want children

4. You look, dress and feel:
    a) My age
    b) 10 years younger
    c) 10 years older

5. You like to have sex:
    a) Several times a day
    b) Several times a week
    c) Once a month will do

6. In a relationship, you like:
    a) To be in control, you call the shots
    b) An equal partnership
    c) The man to take the lead

7. Your ideal man is
    a) My age
    b) Younger
    c) Older

8. Financially, you like a man who:
    a) Earns more than me
    b) Makes much the same amount as I do
    c) Doesn't earn as much as I do but isn't intimidated
       by that

9. When you see actors like Ashton Kutcher, Robert Pattinson or Zac Efron, you think:
    a) I'm old enough to be their mother
    b) I'm old enough to be their mother but they're oddly attractive . . .
    c) Any time. Anywhere.

10. In your experience, who has proven the best in bed?
    a) Men under 20 – they have the most stamina and staying power
    b) Men in their twenties and early thirties – they have energy plus experience
    c) Men your age or older – they know exactly what they're doing

11. Can you see benefits of dating a younger man?:
    a) Yes – They make me feel more alive, attractive and adored
    b) No – I like my men to be wordly
    c) It doesn't matter, because you can't control who you fall in love with

Now turn the page to discover whether you're a traditional tabby cat or a kick-ass cougar . . .

Add up your points!

1. a) 0   b) 2   c) 1

2. a) 0   b) 2   c) 1

3. a) 0   b) 1   c) 2

4. a) 1   b) 2   c) 0

5. a) 2   b) 1   c) 0

6. a) 2   b) 1   c) 0

7. a) 1   b) 2   c) 0

8. a) 0   b) 1   c) 2

9. a) 0   b) 1   c) 2

10. a) 2   b) 1   c) 0

11. a) 2   b) 0   c) 1

The results!

Under 10 points
You're a traditionalist
More of a quiet kitten than an independent cougar, you're happy with a more traditional life. You're looking for an older man who will treat you right, pick up the bills and help you bring a happy family into the world. But don't get stuck in a rut — you never know when something in your life might change and the cougar lifestyle will suddenly become that little bit more appealing . . .

10-16 points
You have cougar tendencies
You're a woman who knows what she wants and you're open to new ideas, but you'd be equally happy settling into a stable relationship with a man your own age if he were to come along. You might nurture a crush on Robert, Ashton or one of their young Hollywood peers, but would you act on your desires?

17-22 points
You're a cougar
You're a confident, assertive woman who knows what she wants and goes after it. You don't need to be in a relationship to feel happy with yourself and your life. As you get older you are feeling sexier and more sensual and you're open to trying different things. Enjoy your cougar status by entering into relationships without guilt or expectations.